LIGHT

LIGHT

A Novel

Paul Dale Anderson

2 on 5 Publications

Rockford, Illinois USA

2AM Publications
3211 Broadway
Rockford, Illinois 61108-5941
www.2AMPublications.com

Publisher's Note: This is a work of fiction. Names, characters, places, and incidents are a product of the author's imagination. Locales and public names are sometimes used for atmospheric purposes. Any resemblance to actual people, living or dead, or to businesses, companies, events, institutions, or locales is completely coincidental.

Book Layout © 2014 BookDesignTemplates.com
Author photo on back cover by Timothy Hatch

Light/ Paul Dale Anderson -- 1st ed., September 2015
ISBN-10: 0-937491-15-2
ISBN-13: 978-0-937491-15-7 (pbk.)

For everyone who has ever served in the Armed Forces of the United States of America and for everyone who has made personal sacrifices for others in the name of God, Country, Duty. This story is dedicated to you.

"In the councils of government, we must guard against the acquisition of unwarranted influence, whether sought or unsought, by the military-industrial complex. The potential for the disastrous rise of misplaced power exists and will persist.

"We must never let the weight of this combination endanger our liberties or democratic processes. We should take nothing for granted. Only an alert and knowledgeable citizenry can compel the proper meshing of the huge industrial and military machinery of defense with our peaceful methods and goals, so that security and liberty may prosper together."

--President Dwight David Eisenhower, Farewell Speech to the Nation, January 17, 1961

"Up the hill, down the hill, over the hill, under the hill, around the hill, through the hill, take the hill."
--*Old Army marching song.*

"Today we take the hill," ordered the General.

"But isn't that the same hill we took last month?" grumbled a private to his sergeant when the order came down to the grunts who did the actual fighting.

"Yeah," said the sergeant. "Only we had to move on to take another hill. But the enemy came back last week, so now we gotta go take the same hill all over again and do it the hard way."

"Don't make no sense to me," grumbled the private.

"This is war," said the sergeant. "Since when is war supposed to make sense? Get your ass in gear, soldier. We got ourselves a hill to take."

---*words similar to those spoken by Greek soldiers at the hot gates of Thermopylae, Roman soldiers wintering in Gaul, Persian soldiers in Greece, British soldiers at the Khyber Pass, Israeli soldiers in Palestine, and American soldiers in Cuba, the Philippines, Guadalcanal, Korea, Vietnam, Afghanistan, and Iraq. I ought to know. I was there in spirit.*

Book I

And God said, Let there be light: and there was light.
And God saw the light, that it was good:
And God divided the light from the darkness.

Holy Bible, King James Version, Genesis 1:3-4.

CHAPTER ONE

Bill Ramsey wasn't dead yet.

Though Ramsey's left arm felt completely numb—entirely useless after a 5.56 millimeter bullet had splintered his shoulder bones and ripped his deltoid muscles to shreds and he bled so badly from where a second bullet penetrated the muscles of his lower back to lodge near his right hip that both his shirt and pants were completely soaked in blood—he continued his steady climb up the steep mountain, forcing one foot in front of the other. He knew it was merely a matter of time before he bled out or his pursuers found him and finished him. Time was on their side, not on his. Time could be a fierce enemy, as dangerous and deadly as the armed men following close behind.

Ramsey left behind a trail of blood that anyone could easily follow in broad daylight, but he didn't dare take time to bandage his wounds or hide the trail. He figured he wouldn't bleed out for at least an hour yet, and he had a lot to do in what little time he had left.

But his long legs still moved, and he climbed higher and higher up the mountain, certain his pursuers would follow him like odor on excrement. If only he could reach the summit—the peak at the very top of the mountain—he might have one chance in a thousand to get down the other side and reach his hidden radio. He needed to communicate what little information he had before he died. He didn't like those odds, but they were all he had.

If he could get the information out, he would have completed half his mission. Then, knowing he had done all he could humanly do, he might be able to die in peace.

He knew another way down from the top of the mountain, a way he presumed his pursuers wouldn't know existed. Bill Ramsey was a thorough man, and he had studied satellite surveillance shots of this entire sector before he began this mission. Bill had served as a U. S. Army Ranger for nearly twenty years. He had survived two tours in Iraq and four in Afghanistan because he studied the terrain before each mission as intently as a teenaged boy studied foldouts in *Playboy* or *Hustler*. He knew all the routes in and all the routes out before advancing into enemy territory, and he had never failed to complete a mission. He certainly couldn't afford to fail now.

They were coming fast behind him now. There were fifteen or twenty of them climbing the steep path up the mountain, but they didn't have his stamina or determination. Even with a hole in his shoulder and a bullet in his back, Bill Ramsey could run faster than they could. He made it to the top of the mountain and looked around for the other way down.

Ramsey felt light-headed, partly from the altitude and partly from loss of blood. His vision blurred, and his eyes refused to focus. He couldn't see the trail even though he knew it lay directly in front of him.

"Goddamn it all to hell!" he wanted to yell but he couldn't yell, he couldn't say anything at all, because he found his tongue wouldn't work and his lips wouldn't move and his lungs were already filling up with blood from the hail of bullets that suddenly slammed through his chest from behind and ripped ragged holes the size of quarters as they exited out the front. He had underestimated his pursuers, and they were much closer than he had imagined. He experienced a moment or two of rather intense pain, then he fell face down in the dirt and debris and felt the very last of his life blood leak out.

Bill Ramsey looked down at his inert body from up above, maybe ten or twenty feet above, seeing the whole of the mountaintop as if from a great distance and with a new perspective and clearer vision. Four men, dressed as he had been in camouflage battledress and heavy field jackets with no insignia, scrambled up from the same path Bill had just traversed and aimed guns at his body splayed on the ground. Bill watched as all four fired dozens of rounds into his remains as if to add insult to injury. Just how dead did they want him to be?

"Deader than a doornail," said one of the men after kicking the corpse several times and turning the body over.

Another man radioed for a body bag, and a third man rummaged through Bill's pockets. "No weapons, no ID," the third man said.

"Camera? Radio?"

"Nothing."

Other men arrived, and they all stood around looking at the body until two more men came up the trail carrying a heavy plastic body bag and unzipped the black bag completely, laid it on the ground, rolled the corpse onto the plastic, forced the head and legs to bend at nearly impossible angles so the six-foot frame would fit neatly inside the bag, and zipped it up.

"Can we call for a cart?" one of the two asked the man with the hand-held radio.

"Forget it. Pick him up and carry him."

"All the way down? That's a long way."

"You getting old or something?"

The two men bent down and picked up the body bag, but it slipped almost immediately out of the hands of the man who had asked for a cart. He got a better grip on the plastic, and picked up his end again. Then the two men trudged slowly back down the path, their legs bowed from carrying dead weight, and Bill watched them get smaller and smaller until they disappeared around a bend in the trail and his mortal remains disappeared with them.

Bill felt himself pulled in two separate directions at once. One part of him wanted desperately to follow his bullet-ridden body, while another part of him wanted to remain right here where it was to overhear whatever conversation his killers might have. He remained on the mountain and listened in.

"Who was he?" asked one of the men scrubbing blood from the ground with bleach while another man used a whisk broom to sweep dirt over the spot where Bill's body had fallen.

"We'll find out for certain when we run his prints," said the man with the radio. He was a big man, six-two or three, maybe two hundred pounds, with close-cropped brown hair and brown eyes. He had a scar over his left eye that ran all the way across his forehead and made him look like Doctor Frankenstein had stitched him together and badly botched the job. "Could be active military, could be CIA. Could be lots of things."

"How much did he learn?"

"Enough. He found us, didn't he?"

"You sure he was alone?"

"The only thing I'm sure of is he's dead. And dead men tell no tales."

"He could have telephoned or radioed someone."

"No, he couldn't. There's an electronic blackout in place that blankets this entire area with static. Cell phones and radios don't work worth shit. Our own radios barely get through the blackout, but only on one set frequency which we constantly monitor. And if he used our frequency we would have picked up his transmission."

"And we found no radio or phone on him," added the man with the whisk broom. "And we were right behind him all the way. I didn't see him try to dump anything or stash equipment. Did you?"

"Anyone else see anything?" asked the scarred man with the radio. When they all shook their heads, the man with the radio said, "Me, neither."

"Then we're clear?" asked the man with the broom.

"As soon as you finish cleaning up the mess," said the man with the radio.

"How did you find out he wasn't one of us?" asked the man with the broom. "We're getting so big, growing so fast, I don't know half of the people I have to work with. Anyone could be a spy. How could you tell?"

"Carl Rossiter recognized him," said the man with the radio. "Carl said the guy's name was Ramsey and they had been in the same Ranger battalion in Afghanistan."

"So what? Most of us were Rangers or Special Forces or Seals or Marines. All of us were in Afghanistan. What's that prove?"

"Yeah. But Ramsey was gung-ho. A straight arrow line officer. Rossiter said Ramsey wouldn't sell out in a million years. Now finish up, and let's get out of here."

Bill watched the men start down the mountain, but when he tried to follow them he found he couldn't move more than a few yards past the spot where he had died. It was almost as if his legs were bound with heavy iron chains, invisible chains, holding him here on the mountaintop. He could move a little ways up and down, and he could move a few feet this way or that. But he couldn't get off the top of the mountain no matter how hard he tried.

Bill Ramsey had never wondered what happened to the human spirit when the human body died because it had never seemed important before. Despite almost twenty years in the military where he had killed many men and expected someday he might be killed himself, he had been far too busy living and concentrating on staying alive to think about what might happen after dying. Like most people, he had believed a kind and beneficent God would sort that out for him when the time came and he had absolutely no say in the matter so it never concerned him. But now that he was dead, he had plenty of time to think about it. All the time in the world. Perhaps even an eternity.

How was it possible that he could see and hear as if he were still alive? How was it that none of those men could see him while he hovered only a few feet above their heads? How was it that he felt no more pain, not even a little? How was it that he was stuck here, neither fully dead nor fully alive? How was it that he still felt a driving need to move, to go someplace, to tell someone about what he now knew, to complete his mission even though he were dead?

Those were questions Bill Ramsey couldn't answer. Not yet, anyway.

*   *   *

Anyone who said he saw his entire life flash before his eyes just before he died was a liar. No one remembered what happened when last they died. Sometimes people were so busy with the very act of dying that they didn't pay any attention to the details, the fine points, the sequence of events, and sometimes pain got in the way of remembering and confused things. If any of them had thought much about it, though, they might have asked: What good could it possibly do to review one's life while that life was in the process of ending? What purpose could it serve?

No, the man who had once called himself the Lone Ranger, and who now called himself Vajrapani, knew from personal experience it wasn't before or during your impending death that you examined all the details of the life about to end, but only *after* death occurred. It was then and only then—during the afterlife, the life between lives—the laws of karma demanded you relive all the times of your life, the good times as well as the bad, so you might choose to live better next time around. And there would always be a next time. And a time after that. And a time after that.

Any misery you caused others during your lifetime, intentional or unintentional, was then visited on you ten-fold during the afterlife. Whatever suffering others had endured because of you, you felt as if you were them. There were important lessons to be learned from each life you lived. And if you didn't learn those lessons in one life, you would be doomed to repeat your mistakes until you did.

The Ranger had much to atone for before he died again. And he would have to answer for all of it after he was dead. Each man he had killed had a right to seek retribution, and the Ranger had killed hundreds of men in this lifetime alone.

These truths became self-evident to the Lone Ranger as he received initial instruction in the Pho-wa—the Vajrayana practice of conscious dying that transferred consciousness at the time of death—from the Venerable Lama Lokesvara Sailendravarman, Abbot of the Lamasery at Angkor Wat. As part of the training, the Ranger had to recall all of his previous lives and recognize the patterns recurring in each of them. And there were indeed recurring patterns.

In most of his previous lives, he had been a warrior, a soldier, and he had usually died fighting for causes he believed in or to protect people he loved.

He had begun his current life 48 years ago in Oak Park, Illinois, a suburb of Chicago, the eldest of three children, born to a father who sold life insurance for MetLife and a mother who was a librarian at Loyola University on the far north side. Neither of his parents, nor either of his two siblings, ever understood his fascination with all things military. They thought it was only because he had grown up watching reruns of The Lone Ranger on Channel 9 and John Wayne westerns and war movies on VHS tapes borrowed from the public library that he wanted to grow up to be like his boyhood heroes. That was part of it, of course; but it had been something more, much more. He could see that now, though he didn't know it then.

Shortly after he turned eighteen, and two months before graduation from high school, he had enlisted in the U. S. Army with a guarantee that after graduation from high school and successful completion of basic training, advanced infantry training, Ranger Assessment and Selection Program (RASP), and airborne training, he would go to the U. S. Army Ranger School at Fort Benning, Georgia. He kept his part of the bargain, and the Army kept theirs. He graduated top of his class and earned a promotion to Private First Class. He continued to excel in the military, and he was promoted ahead of his contemporaries. He went to Kosovo in 2000, and by September 11, 2001, when the first plane crashed the Twin Towers, he was already a combat-experienced buck sergeant.

He went to Afghanistan for the first time in October of 2001, then to Iraq in March of 2003. He did two more tours in Iraq and two more in Afghanistan. Then the shit hit the fan when his special recon team was ambushed by Taliban in the hills outside Kabul. Seven of his men were killed instantly, and the

Ranger was mortally wounded and left for dead. He lay on the field of battle for three days before he was medevac'd to an Army field hospital where they pieced him together and patched him up. He spent a long sixteen weeks rehabilitating at a medical facility in Germany before heading back to Afghanistan.

But his experience had drastically changed him, and he saw enemy everywhere, even among men he served with. True, some of the Afghan troops he had helped train were Taliban sympathizers and they continued to leak information about Allied troop strengths and troop movements to Al Qaeda. True, Taliban soldiers continued to ambush American patrols and Afghan suicide bombers continued to take the lives of Americans and Afghans alike at military bases and in large cities. But not everyone in Afghanistan was an enemy. Some Afghans were innocent civilians just trying to live their lives any way they could.

The Ranger couldn't see that then. He was so filled with hatred and the need for revenge that he began killing Afghans indiscriminately. He crawled out of camp at night and killed every Afghan he could find.

During the day, he was the fiercest of soldiers in battle, taking no prisoners. He would still be killing Afghans to this day if a Ranger captain hadn't put two and two together to come up with an unrealistic body count that spelled PTSD, Post-Traumatic Stress Disorder. Captain Ramsey ordered the Lone Ranger to go to a shrink for extensive medical and psychological evaluations. The Ranger failed four of the ten primary scales on the Minnesota

Multiphasic Personality Inventory (MMPI)—number 4, dealing with conflict, struggle, anger, and a lack of respect for rules; number 6, dealing with trust and suspicion; number 8, dealing with odd thinking and social alienation; and number 9, indicating he constantly displayed a high level of excitability—and the shrink yanked his top secret security clearance immediately. Within a week, the Ranger was back at Fort Benning being unceremoniously drummed out of the service, declared unfit for further military duty, and medically discharged from the beloved Army that had been his whole life.

That's when he really went crazy. He thought up all kinds of ways to get back at the politicians who made the policy that led to the Army being ordered to coddle the Afghans instead of killing them all, and he even considered planting a bomb in the U. S. Capitol building and blowing the damn place up, taking out everyone inside and himself with it.

Or maybe just shooting some of the key policy makers at their homes or at some fancy political event. He could have done it, too. He had the knowledge and skills. And it would be easy enough to buy a sniper rifle on the black market.

It was while looking for a sniper rifle for sale in the classified ads of a magazine that catered to ex-military and mercenaries that he saw the help-wanted ad for "former military personnel who had served in the Special Forces, SEALS, Rangers, or Marines."

He applied for a job as a "security consultant." He was given a gun—a Beretta nine millimeter not much different from the Army-issued M-9—and assigned to a partner for training. After a few weeks, he was given a new identity—complete with Social Security card, driver's license, and passport—and a new partner, an unsavory fella who was mustered out of the Marines for the same reason the Ranger had been mustered out of the Army.

When his employers asked him to beat up someone, he did, taking out some of the anger and frustration he felt on helpless victims. When his bosses asked him to kidnap and torture someone, he did. When they asked him to kill someone, he did. And they paid him well for his services. He set up bank accounts in Switzerland and the Cayman Islands and watched his money grow.

And when his employers were absolutely certain of his abilities, they sub-contracted him to do wet work for a Chinese firm that ran a factory in Illinois as a front for computer espionage operations. He didn't know that at the time, of course, but after the factory ordered him killed for failing to complete their orders in a timely fashion and after he learned what they were really up to, he killed the man sent to kill him. Then he aided the FBI in fighting the factory and discovered the factory was more than just a front for the Chinese military.

That's when he met Lokesvara Sailendravarman. The old monk had come to America to assemble a team of men and women who were also more than they appeared at first glance, and the Ranger just happened to be one of those men and so was Lokesvara. Lokesvara was said to be the reincarnation of the Bodhisattva Manjusri, the embodiment of enlightenment and the conqueror of death. Lokesvara taught the Ranger how to meditate, how to recall each of his past lives, and introduced him to Vajrapani, the protector of all Buddhas. Now the Ranger and Vajrapani were one being, two spirits occupying the same human body. Though Vajrapani only manifested when the Ranger called on him to act, Vajrapani possessed powers and abilities beyond the human capacity to imagine. He could control the weather with but a single gesture, calling down rain and lightning from perfectly clear skies. It was said Vajrapani possessed the might of ten-thousand men, and his diamond resolve was tempered only by his great compassion.

Lokesvara had taught the Ranger lots of other things, too, and now the Ranger knew how to raise the sleeping Kundalini within his very core, how to fan the flames of internal fire with Tummo breathing, how to release his spirit to travel on the astral plane, and how to physically teleport anywhere in the world.

After defeating the Chinese general who was the manifestation of Yama—death itself— and whose actions had threatened to destroy the world, the Ranger hung up his guns for good and sought initiation as a Buddhist monk. He gave away to the poor all of his worldly possessions, including millions of dollars in Swiss and Cayman bank accounts, and he became just another one of the many students at Lokesvara's lamasery near the ancient temples of Angkor Wat in northern Cambodia.

One of the Ranger's sacred vows was never to take the life of another sentient being. He had since broken those vows out of necessity, and someday he would have to pay the price of his actions. Such was the law of karma.

"In Tibet," instructed Lama Lokesvara in a voice so soft and gentle that the Ranger had to strain his ears to hear him, "everyone practices Pho-wa as a way of life. All who live, even incarnate *Tulkus* like me, face death every day of our many lives. Death is inevitable, for without death we are unable to be reborn. But through Pho-wa, we can learn to overcome our fear of death and that is the first step to overcoming death itself."

"I don't understand," said the Ranger.

"Conquering the fear of death is to conquer death itself," continued the Lama. "Do you fear death, my son?"

"Not anymore," replied the Ranger in a voice that had become as soft, though not as gentle, as that of his mentor. "But I still have a healthy respect for death."

"Just so," said Lokesvara. "Now pay attention. There are nine ordinary gates, or pairs of gates, called *buga*, through which the spirit may enter or leave the human body. They are the same gates you must close to protect yourself when your spirit travels outside the body: two eyes, two ears, two nostrils, one mouth, two nipples, one navel, one genital, one urethra, and one anus. But there is another aperture, called *mahamundra*, at the crest or crown of the head. It is through this aperture in the *sahasrara* that we may release the spirit in full consciousness to travel where we will, to ascend to the spirit realm or descend into the underworlds, to enter another body human or otherwise, to prepare for rebirth when we are ready to be reborn, or to reach nirvana when we are truly enlightened. The spirit is immortal and never perishes, though the physical body dies and decomposes and is no more, for the human spirit—like the spirits of all sentient beings—endures forever. All things change, but spirit continues in spite of death. Life must go on. And it does."

"But we do die. I have seen enough dead bodies to know. Death is real."

"When we do die physically, our spirits desert the body at the precise moment of death. If we are prepared for death, our spirits move on to the spiritual realms to prepare for eventual rebirth. Moving on to another realm normally happens, but not always, within seventy-two hours or three days after the moment of dying. As we find ourselves pulled into one of the spiritual realms—the world above where enlightened spirit guides greet us and teach us to relive the events of our past lives, or the nine underworlds where emissaries of the demon rulers torture us the way we may have tortured others when we were alive—we see clearly the rewards or pitfalls of our choices in life. Then, after an appropriate period, we are reborn.

"But if we are not prepared for death—if death comes suddenly and takes us unawares—our spirits can remain chained to thoughts of the physical world and we are unable to go on to the spirit worlds because we have unfinished business here on the physical plane we must complete before moving on. The Pho-wa helps us to prepare for death so we are never caught unaware. Pho-wa practice enables us to enter the spirit realms and facilitates rebirth. We can come back with full consciousness intact, that we may continue our journey from the place we left off, but in a new body and with greater understanding. Thus we may progress toward enlightenment and someday, when we are ready, achieve nirvana."

"What is nirvana and why would I want to achieve it?"

"Nirvana is a Sanskrit word that means to blow out the flames of desire and never again suffer pain nor death nor delusion. Nir means out, va means to blow breath, na means never. It is the end of the journey when you have completed your mission and earned your rest. You become liberated from *samsara*, the continuing cycles of birth, desire, suffering, death, and inevitable rebirth which allows again the unabated karmic cycle of desire, suffering, and death to occur. When you achieve nirvana, your spirit lives forever in a pure land, a land of pure spirit and total awareness and full enlightenment, free of ignorance and delusion, free of pain and suffering. When you achieve nirvana, you stop becoming and can just be, content that your job here is done."

"It is said, Master, that you are the embodiment of a bodhisattva, that you achieved enlightenment and yet rejected nirvana. Why is that?"

"As are you, my son, a bodhisattva. You embody the enlightened spirit of the Bodhisattva Vajrapani, yet both you and Vajrapani continue to live and act in the physical world because your job here is not yet done. You and I have taken an oath not to achieve nirvana until all sentient beings are enlightened and liberated. So we endure the cycles of samsara that we might continue to act in the world."

"Sometimes I feel the Lone Ranger's job will never be done."

"That may be true, my son. As long as evil exists in the world—as long as there is desire without compassion, as long as the greedy acts of unscrupulous men cause needless suffering, as long as death and destruction drive men mad with the need for power over other people and natural processes—your job is not done. Nor is mine."

"I am done with killing. I have killed enough. I will not kill again."

"You cannot escape your destiny."

"Are you saying I'm a born killer?"

"You are a born warrior, my son. You are a protector of the Buddha, the Dharma, and the Sangha, as am I. You have skills that are useful. And sometimes necessary."

"I will never kill again. I have taken a vow."

"We shall see," said the old man. "We shall see. Never is a long time. Things may happen that will change your mind."

“I will not kill,” said the Ranger, sounding certain. “I am done with killing.”

“We shall see,” said the old man again. “We shall see.”

* * *

“We lost Bill Ramsey,” said Colonel Robert McMichaels, Deb’s new section chief at INSCOM, the U. S. Army Intelligence and Security Command operations center at Fort Belvoir, Virginia. Bob McMichaels was a full-bird colonel, tall, broad-shouldered, and good looking with a commanding voice. “Bill’s one of ours, and we want him back. At the very least, we need to know what happened to him.”

“And you want me to find him?” asked Deb. CW4 Debra Johnson was a recently assigned senior intelligence analyst at INSCOM, transferred from the Defense Intelligence Agency auxiliary shop in Arlington. Deb was a petite blonde in her late-thirties, her long blond hair rolled into a bun when she was in uniform, and she had worn the uniform with pride for nearly nineteen years. She had seen combat in both Iraq and Afghanistan, and she was one of the best intelligence analysts in the U. S. Army.

“Yes,” said the Colonel. “We have a need to know. Is Ramsey alive or dead? If he’s dead, how did he die? And what did he learn before he died?”

"Where was he when you lost him, Colonel? How long ago did you lose contact?"

"Mountains of northwestern Pakistan," said CW5 Edward Morsay. Eddie was also a big guy, six-one, two-ten. Eddie had been Deb's mentor since 2004 when she was appointed a junior warrant officer in the 82nd Airborne Division Headquarters in Iraq. "Ramsey's somewhere northwest of Islamabad. He hasn't reported anything in two days, and that has us worried. We know the general vicinity where he disappeared, but we have no idea where he is."

"What was he doing there?"

"Following a lead."

"What kind of lead?"

"American mercenaries recruited from our troops in Afghanistan," said the Colonel. "They're being trained at a secret base somewhere in those mountains in Pakistan near the Afghan border. Bill went in to find their base and infiltrate their operations."

"Do we know for certain Bill Ramsey's dead?"

"Bill hasn't reported in," said Eddie. "He's meticulous about reporting. If we don't hear from him by tomorrow, we can be sure he's dead. He won't allow himself to be captured alive. But if he is still alive, he'll find some way to contact us."

Chief Warrant Officer Debra Johnson looked at the situation map where Ramsey had marked, before he left INSCOM HQ to begin his mission, the likely location of the mercenary base in northwest Pakistan, just east of the Pakistani border with Afghanistan. There were no visible roads in or out, and the entire valley was surrounded by rugged mountainous terrain. A river, fed by melting snows from mountains to the north, wound all the way through the valley to connect with other waterways in the region. It looked like the only way to get there was by helicopter.

Or by boat.

"How did Bill go in?"

"He built a raft. Floated downstream from the drop zone."

"How was he getting out?"

"Over the mountains."

"Jesus. He builds rafts. He climbs mountains. What kind of guy is this Bill Ramsey?"

"Major, Infantry," said the Colonel. "75th Ranger Regiment. Trained in recon and intel. On short list for light colonel. One of our best and brightest."

"And he went in all alone? Why?"

"Bad vibes," said Eddie. "They're recruiting our boys leaving Afghanistan, paying combat vets big bucks to work for them after their enlistment with Uncle Sam's over. Some of our guys are already on their payroll before official separation. Bill didn't trust anybody to cover his back. He went in alone."

"So who has enough money to finance a private army? And why would they spend that kind of money to recruit and train former American soldiers? What do they think they can accomplish? What's their objective?"

"Some Saudis have more than enough money," said Eddie Morsay. "Someone supporting Al Qaeda, possibly, but not the Saudi government itself. Or maybe someone in Iran, or even the Iranian government. The front for recruiting our guys is a private security consulting firm in Richmond, Virginia. They do a lot of work that's legitimate, supplying bodyguards and escorting shipments for industry and large corporations all over the world. Some of their men protect oil tankers from Somali pirates. But the men they're sending to that training camp in Pakistan are being groomed for something else."

"Any idea what?"

"No," said Colonel McMichaels. "That's why we sent Ramsey in there. We thought a man on the ground might learn something satellite surveillance couldn't tell us. Without Bill's reports, we're back to square one. That's where you come in."

"We want you to drop everything else and focus on this," added Eddie. "Put together the pieces of the puzzle from SIGINT, satellite feeds, bank transactions, visa applications, anything even remotely connected to their operations in Pakistan. You're good at seeing connections others miss. Report directly to me, and I'll report to Colonel McMichaels. As of today, you have access to the full resources of INSCOM's computers. But be discrete, Deb. We don't know who works for them, and we don't want to give away what we know or don't know."

"What about Bill Ramsey? Will you send someone in to get him out?"

"No," said the Colonel. "Bill knew he was on his own when he went in. If he doesn't get out, we'll have to write him off as MIA."

"There's more at stake here than just one life," said Eddie. "Remember that, Deb. These guys are playing hardball, and so are we. But in this ballgame there are no rules, and it's winner take all. Winners live and get to keep on playing. Losers are out of the game for good."

"I don't like to play games," said Deb.

"Then you're in the wrong business," said the Colonel.

CHAPTER TWO

Randy Edwards knew it was a mistake to keep a loaded handgun in the drawer of the nightstand next to his bed. At one time he had slept with the gun beneath his pillow, but it made the pillow lumpy and hurt his head. So he had moved the gun from beneath his pillow to the single drawer in the nearby nightstand.

From time to time Randy Edwards found women to sleep with him on the Tempurpedic foam mattress of his king-sized bed, and they distracted him from thoughts about the gun. But tonight Randy was all alone, and he thought about the gun a lot.

Randy knew all about guns. He had served four years in the U. S. Marine Corps, and he had been to Afghanistan twice during those four years. He was proficient with the M16A2 rifle, the M4 carbine, the M9A1 Beretta, the M249 machine gun, and the M40A5 sniper rifle. He had medals to prove it.

About a week before Randy left Afghanistan for the last time, he had been approached by two men he knew were employees of a civilian security firm the U. S. Government contracted to provide logistical support and training to U. S. and Afghan troops. As the military prepared to wind down operations, more and more private contractors had appeared in-country. Some days it seemed like there were more contractors carrying weapons in Afghanistan than armed soldiers. Randy had seen these guys around for a while now, wearing bulletproof vests and carrying M4s. They were always talking to one of the soldiers, or one of the Marines or airmen, and Randy had wondered what their job was that they had nothing better to do than to stand around shooting the shit all day.

"Hey, short-timer," said the taller of the two, a man in his mid-thirties. The other guy was shorter and ten-years younger. Both were in civilian clothes and had no name tags. "We hear you're going back to the real world like yesterday. Not going to re-up?"

"You think I'm crazy?"

"Got a good job lined up back in the states?"

"I'll find one."

"I hate to tell you this, Marine, but there's a recession on in the states. Jobs aren't easy to find these days. Especially, good-paying jobs. Companies are laying off, not hiring. You got any marketable skills? The Corps teach you anything useful? Anything besides how to shoot and how to follow orders?"

"Not really."

"You're single, right?"

"Goddamn right."

"The company I work for is hiring ex-military to do special jobs. They're especially interested in single guys. You interested in making some decent money doing what you've been trained to do?"

"What kind of money?"

"Twice what the Corps pays. But that's just to start. If you work out, five times that. Maybe more."

"What will I have to do?"

"Same as you're doing now. Carry a weapon. Follow orders."

"Where?"

"Wherever the company sends you. Could be back here. Could be anywhere."

"How long?"

"You sign up for two years. After that you take it a year at a time. If you like the money, you stay in. You want out, you're out. Simple as that."

"Let me think about it."

"You do that. Here," he handed Randy a business card. "Call the home office when you decide. Don't take too long. This is a limited-time offer, only good for six months after you get discharged. If you get too soft in civilian life, we can't use you. So stay in shape, Marine."

Randy took the card. He had shoved it in the bottom of his duffel bag and forgotten all about it until he got home. But when he'd unpacked his duffel bag, he'd found the card and stuck it in his wallet.

After he'd rented this half-furnished apartment over a storefront for cheap near the University of Minnesota in Minneapolis, he'd found the card in his wallet and thrown it in the drawer of the nightstand next to his bed. It had laid there for months and he'd put the gun in there right on top of the card.

Randy had looked for work on and off for six months after he got out, but the only jobs he could find were minimum wage or fast-food restaurant work and he was much too proud to dish up French fries all day. It hadn't bothered him much, as long as his money held out and the weather was nice. But Minnesota winters were dark, and the cold got under his skin, and he'd blown his wad by buying a fancy new car for cash.

Now the world was white with snow, his car was plowed in where he'd left it parked on the street two days ago, and Randy Edwards felt trapped in a world that made no sense to him anymore. He had no future to look forward to, no past worth remembering. The girls he had slept with meant nothing more to him than a quick lay, and he sure as hell didn't want to get married, but he didn't like living alone either. The friends he had known in high school had all moved on to bigger and better things. Most were married now, and the ones who weren't married had good paying nine-to-five jobs that kept them from staying out all night cruising the bars and clubs and drinking themselves into oblivion.

And his parents were getting old right in front of his eyes and he couldn't talk to them about what he'd seen and what he'd done because they wouldn't understand any of it even if he told them, and they still wanted to treat him like a kid instead of a grown-up and he couldn't stand that any more now than he could when he was eighteen. His brothers and his sister had started families while Randy was gone, and they had kids of their own to occupy their time and he didn't relate well with kids. He didn't want to see his family any more than they wanted to see him. He had declined their invitations to get together for dinner on Christmas after the boring, almost torturous, dinner he'd shared with all of them at his parents' house on Thanksgiving.

He missed the camaraderie of the Corps. The guys he'd left behind in Afghanistan were more like family to him than his own family had ever been, and he began to miss them terribly.

He missed them more and more each day.

And he missed the warm weather he remembered in Afghanistan. Even up in the mountains, it didn't seem as cold as it was here. He had grown up with the cold, and he hated it.

When he decided life wasn't worth living anymore, he thought about the handgun he had stashed in the drawer next to the bed. It was a .22 caliber revolver he'd purchased at a pawn shop for a few hundred bucks right after he'd gotten back to town. He could stick the barrel in his mouth and pull the trigger and it would all be over in a flash.

He took one last swig of Jack Daniel's from the bottle that was still half full, and he reached in the drawer for the gun.

And his fingers touched the card.

He had forgotten all about the card. He had barely glanced at it before shoving it in his duffle, but now he read it for the first time. "WLSCTC, Inc. Worldwide Logistical Security Consultants and Transportation Corporation, Inc." Beneath the name was an address in Richmond, Virginia. And a phone number with an 804 area code.

Instead of putting the gun in his mouth, he dialed the number on the card.

"WLSCTC," answered a sweet-sounding female voice after two rings and couple of clicking noises. "My name is Laura. How may I assist you today?"

"Are you still hiring?" Randy asked.

"Are you former military?"

"Four years in the Marine Corps."

"Name, rank, and service number?"

Randy gave them to her.

"Randall Edwards?" she asked. "Service in Afghanistan?"

"Two tours," said Randy.

She read him the dates he was in-country. "Is that correct?" she asked.

"Close enough for government work," he said.

"Are you willing to make a two-year commitment?"

"Why not?" he said.

"Are you still in Minneapolis?"

"Yes," he said. "How did you know?"

"Caller ID," she said. "And Minneapolis was your home of record when you entered and left the service."

"You have access to my service record?"

"I have a copy of your DD 214 up on my computer screen."

"What else do you know about me?"

"Only as much as I need to know. Can you come in tomorrow for an interview?"

"To Virginia?"

"We'll reimburse you for plane fare. And meals. Or, if you prefer, we'll make travel arrangements for you."

"Do that."

"I have you booked on a United flight," she said almost immediately, "tomorrow morning at 11:05. You change planes in Chicago at 12:30, and you arrive in Richmond at 4:06 PM, Eastern Time. Someone will meet you at the airport when you pick up your luggage. Is that satisfactory, Mr. Edwards?"

"Yes."

"Please pack for a three day stay. If you pass the initial interview, you'll undergo a thorough physical examination and then you'll take some aptitude and psychological tests. In the evenings, we'll treat you to southern hospitality. I've booked a return flight for you to Minneapolis/Saint Paul on Sunday. Any questions?"

"Yeah," he said. "What's the weather like in Richmond this time of the year?"

"53 degrees. Chance of rain."

"Any snow?"

She laughed. "Richmond gets flurries sometimes in January and February, but snow doesn't last long around Richmond. Nothing on the ground to speak of. Why?"

"Just asking."

"Pick up your ticket at the airport two hours before flight time. We'll see you tomorrow afternoon."

"You'll be there?" he asked. "Will I see you, Laura?"

She laughed again. "No," she said. "I don't work in Richmond."

"Oh?" he said, sounding disappointed. "Where do you work?"

"That's classified," she said, and then Laura hung up and the line went dead.

* * *

It was snowing in the mountains of Pakistan. Bill Ramsey didn't feel the cold, nor did he feel any of the snowflakes pepper his face with wetness. As snow continued to fall from the dark clouds passing low overhead, the white stuff—both the snow and the clouds themselves—passed through his spirit body as if his body wasn't even there. Which, he concluded, it wasn't.

If he thought he saw his hands and feet, it was simply because he expected to see hands and feet. He was used to seeing hands and feet when he looked down, and his hands and feet looked like they moved when he willed them to move. Except for feeling neither hot nor cold, he felt no different than he had felt when he had been alive.

But he knew he wasn't alive. He had died on this mountaintop three days ago, and there was no place else he could go. He was stuck here. His legs moved, but they wouldn't move off the mountain.

His mission had been to locate the mercenary base camp, infiltrate their ranks, learn their plans, and report back. He had accomplished half of his mission. He had yet to accomplish the other half.

He had seen enough to know the camp posed a real threat to national security. There were more than a thousand men going through training right now, and who knew how many more had already completed training? They all had sophisticated weapons and body armor, better than anything the U. S. Army had in its inventory, and they were all experienced combat soldiers. And they had effective command and control, an established chain of command with competent leaders at each level to direct operations. Some of the non-coms were British, recruited out of the SAS. Some were former U. S. non-coms, Army Rangers, Navy Seals, Marine Recon. A few were German, Australian, or South African Special Forces. Everyone spoke English, though some spoke with slight accents.

There were no officers to be seen anywhere in the camp. Everything was run by noncoms, and there was no saluting, no parade formations, no insignia of rank, no time wasted on traditions and courtesies. Non-coms carried radios, and everyone else was considered a trainee. Training consisted of intense hand-to-hand combat and advanced martial arts workouts, running confidence courses and live-fire assault courses, daily practice on rifle ranges and machine gun ranges, sniper training, demolitions and explosives, small unit tactics, urban deployment and house-to-house searches, plus night recon and infiltration. If Bill had been asked to design the ideal advanced training program for already-experienced combat troops, he would have created something similar.

But everything was too well-organized to be a stand-alone operation. The guys with the radios took orders from someone, and that someone took orders from someone else higher up. Ramsey wanted to know who was at the top of the food chain, and who was financing the whole shebang.

And he wanted to know how many other training camps and forward operating bases there were in existence. Where did these men go after they completed training? And what exactly were they training for? WLSCTC did do legitimate security work, but none of their contracts with the government or private industry utilized even a tenth of the men they were training just at this one camp. Something big was brewing, and Worldwide Logistical Security Consultants and Transportation Corporation was at the heart of it.

But he was stuck here with no way to move, shoot, or communicate. His new body was totally insubstantial, and it moved up and down, back and forth, only about ten meters from where he had landed face-down in the dirt when he died.

Surely, there must be some way to get the word out. It was imperative that the people back at INSCOM know what was happening. The worst-case scenario was that INSCOM would send a team in to find him. They wouldn't stand the chance of a snowball in hell.

Now that the people running the training camp knew their camp had been discovered, they would be watching for others to come. Any one of their highly-trained snipers could take out a helicopter with a single well-placed round to the rotors, and their machine gunners could take out a whole formation of flying machines before even one could touch down close to the camp.

And if but a single American chopper got shot down in Pakistan, it was sure to create an international incident. Pakistan didn't take kindly to military incursions into her sovereign territory, especially after the execution and extraction of Osama bin Laden. American requests for Pakistan itself to investigate the camps would fall on deaf ears, as similar requests to shut down Taliban and Al Qaeda strongholds near the border with Afghanistan had been routinely ignored.

Ramsey had no doubt the Pakistani government, or at least some of the more influential Pakistani generals, allowed this camp and others like it to exist in exchange for appropriate bribes.

It was in their best interests to ensure the camps remained operational. They would stand in the way of any armed intervention by the United States military. In order to shut the camp down, INSCOM would need to cut off the money supply at the source. That meant finding who was funding the entire operation, not just funding training operations in Pakistan but running the entire operation, and putting them out of business permanently.

Things got really complicated whenever large sums of money were involved, and whoever was behind this had already sunk billions of dollars into it without blinking an eye. They had a large investment to protect, and they had already proved they were willing to kill to protect their investment. How much more were they willing to invest, and how many more people were they willing to kill, to accomplish their goals?

And what was it they planned to do with the private army they were building?

Ramsey wished he knew the answers to those questions, but he didn't. Bill Ramsey had no way now to learn the answers, and for the first time in his military career he had failed to complete a mission. Someone who was still alive would have to finish his mission for him.

He had no idea who that someone might be.

*   *   *

Deb Johnson searched what few financial records of the Worldwide Logistical Security Consultants and Transportation Corporation, Inc., she could find. Tracking down important information from obscure sources, finding links between data bits that others overlooked, was what Deb loved best about her job and she was really good at doing her job. Deb had three earned master's degrees: a Master of Science in Accounting from Kogod School of Business at The American University in Washington, D. C., where she had also completed courses in international finance and global management; a Master of Science degree in Cybersecurity and Computer Science from George Washington University's Foggy Bottom campus; and a Master of Science degree in Strategic Intelligence from the National Intelligence University in Washington, D. C. She had earned all three after entering the service with only a Bachelor's degree in accounting.

Deb concentrated on following the money trail because international business was supposedly predicated on making money. Deb called up the banking records and IRS returns of WLSCTC first, going over every detail. WLSCTC had lucrative contracts with the U. S. Defense and State Departments, and they provided security services to corporations in Great Britain, Germany, South Africa, Australia, and the United Arab Emirates. Their declared annual gross income exceeded several billion dollars, and they had paid taxes on a net income of less than two hundred thousand.

Their major expenses included salaries, bonuses, insurance, taxes and licensing fees, legal fees, lobbying fees, transportation and travel, equipment, and real estate investments. Their income to expenses ratio was untenable, and they often spent twice as much as they took in. They had declared losses two out of every five years they had been in business.

WLSCTC had made sizeable real estate investments in property all over the world, including the large corporate complex outside Richmond, Virginia, and offices and some kind of training facilities in western New Mexico. They owned all kinds of aircraft, and they leased space and landing rights at major airports all over the world.

Worldwide's corporate structure included a retired three-star general as Chairman of the Board, and a dozen former U. S. Senators and Representatives as Directors. The Chief Executive and Operating Officer was John Brakken, a retired Army colonel. Though there was a double-dipping law that prevented retired government employees from working for the government again without losing part of their retirement pay, there was nothing that prevented them from working for government contractors and keeping their full retirement.

Brakken had been a Quartermaster officer after graduation from a Reserve Officer Training Corps program, and he had worked his way up the ranks to a senior position in the procurement and development office of the Pentagon. He had an earned MBA from a highly respected university, and he had close ties and valuable connections to people high-up in the military-industrial complex that made him indispensable to a company like WLSCTC.

But John Brakken was merely a figurehead, and WLSCTC was little more than a legitimate front for something much bigger. Somewhere there must also exist a secret shadow organization that pulled the strings of the Brakken puppet and made him prance around on stage. Brakken had connections and basic knowledge of how to run an organization, but Deb knew he didn't have the balls to pull off something like this on his own. She had met John Brakken twice in her career, once in Iraq where he had been a deputy G-4, and once when he came to Afghanistan on an inspection tour of facilities. He was a competent staff officer who knew who to bribe or who to butter up to get what he wanted. People like Brakken were necessary during wartime.

Brakken was someone who was too used to following orders from his superiors to be the big brains behind the whole shooting match. He was good at relaying orders to his troops and making certain his orders were properly implemented, but he was no strategic planner.

Neither was the Chairman of the Board, Roger Kieffer. Though the Chairman had received a promotion to Lieutenant General before he retired, he had never been much more than a political lackey. His military career had been less than distinguished, and he never would have made it to one star, much less three, if it hadn't been for competent subordinates who carried their own weight plus his. Deb had known lots of officers like that during her career. The Army had been top heavy with tarnished brass since 9/11.

Because WLSCTC was a privately-owned close corporation and not traded on any stock exchange, someone must have made a sizeable initial investment to finance start-up without looking to return an immediate profit on that investment. Privately-owned corporations weren't required to report details of their finances to the federal government. But they were required to report the names of major shareholders to the state in which they were incorporated.

All of WLSCTC's stock was held by another privately-owned company. And all of the stock in that company was held by yet another privately-owned company, and that company was wholly-owned by a private trust that was controlled by a Swiss investment bank.

Deb had requested Signal Intelligence (SIGINT) support from the National Security Agency, but NSA had been unable to monitor radio communications in and out of the Pakistan camp. If they were communicating with anyone by radio, the signals weren't going beyond the mountains where NSA could pick them up by satellite. WLSCTC had established some kind of electronic blackout over the area that masked their transmissions from outside scrutiny.

Why would anyone need such elaborate security measures to protect a training facility? What were they hiding that they didn't want Uncle Sam to know about?

Deb was frustrated that she was dead-ended on two fronts. She couldn't follow the money, and she couldn't follow a communications trail. What did that leave?

Telephone taps on WLSCTC offices in the United States, obtained under Foreign Intelligence Surveillance Act (FISA) guidelines, had revealed nothing of interest. But e-mail and internet communications were also being monitored, and one or two of the e-mails sent by someone named Charlie@WLSCTC.com from an IP in Dubai were cryptic. "Go 1," read the earlier e-mail. "Go 2," read the second.

What Istanbul was to World War II, Dubai was rapidly becoming to modern-day world politics. Strategically located at the mouth of the Persian Gulf, Dubai was part of the United Arab Emirates and bordered Saudi Arabia on the west and Oman on the south. It had one of the largest and busiest shipping ports in the world, and Dubai was an ultra-modern city that was home to many large international corporations and also served as a regional center for international banking and finance. Dubai's International Financial Centre was a tax-free zone that charged no corporate taxes, had laws written entirely in English, allowed 100 percent foreign ownership of businesses, and it provided transaction secrecy that rivaled or surpassed the Swiss banking industry.

And Dubai was only a stone's throw across the Persian Gulf from Iran.

Dubai was connected to the rest of the world through an undersea fiber-optic cable laid on the ocean floor, allowing internet transmissions that were extremely difficult, if not impossible, to intercept. If WLSCTC was using Dubai to link with its parent companies, NSA couldn't hack them at the source. E-mails could only be intercepted and read after they had reached their destination.

Deb added Dubai as a location of interest to the situation map, then she drew a red line connecting Dubai with Richmond and another line connecting Dubai with the training camp in Pakistan. She already had a line running from Richmond to Pakistan. As she gathered more data, she would add other points of interest and more lines. Every point and every line brought Deb one step closer to seeing the big picture.

The line between Dubai and the training camp ran straight through Iran and Afghanistan. Was that significant?

Intelligence work was like fitting together the pieces of a huge jigsaw puzzle. Each piece added color and shape to the overall picture. So far, nothing made much sense. But that could change overnight. Deb decided to sleep on it. Maybe things would make more sense in the morning.

Deb had worked ceaselessly connecting dots and ferreting out data since before seven this morning, and she felt tired. It was already nearly nine PM, and she hadn't eaten since noon. It was definitely time to go home, fix a small dinner, take a nice long hot bath, and get some much-needed sleep. She had to be back at work at seven tomorrow, and tomorrow, as Scarlett O'Hara liked to say in *Gone with the Wind*, was another day.

Deb drove out the main gate of Fort Belvoir, turned right, and took U. S. 1 north the fifteen miles to Alexandria where she rented a small apartment she shared with Bill Porter, an electrical engineer. Bill was off doing work on a computer installation somewhere in upper New York State, and he wouldn't be back for at least a week. Deb had the whole apartment to herself.

After dinner, she called Bill's cell phone and they talked for half an hour, more to hear each other's voices than to say anything important. After she clicked off with Bill, Deb filled the bathtub, climbed in, and soaked the tension out of her shoulders. Because she had sat with her shoulders hunched over computer screens most of the day, she felt more tired than she would have had she hiked twenty miles uphill with a full pack strapped to her back. All that work, and so little progress frustrated her. She still had too many questions and too few answers. She needed answers, and she needed them now.

Eddie had done an admirable job laying the initial groundwork, uncovering the connection between WLSCTC and the single training camp they knew about that led to Bill Ramsey's mission into Pakistan. But there had to be more secret camps around somewhere. WLSCTC had been recruiting men for nearly a decade, and only a handful of recruits were employed in legitimate security work. WLSCTC already had more than seventeen thousand men on their payroll, and there were probably a thousand new men going through training at any one time. Where did those men go after training? And how many other privately-held companies had as many or more armed men on their payrolls? We were talking big numbers here. A highly-trained private army of well-armed combat-tested troops ready for immediate action. Why? Who needed a private army at their beck and call trained to kill? And who was willing and able to pay for it?

And why weren't any of those men coming home when their contracts were up? Were the pay and benefits that good that none of them ever opted out? Why hadn't anyone blown the whistle on what was going on?

The logistics to support an army of that size was mind-boggling. Not only did the men need food and clothing, but they needed weapons and housing and recreational facilities. And that meant booze and women. Lots of booze and lots of women.

Fighting men were notoriously horny, and they would do almost anything for a chance to have sex with a woman they could completely control and force to do whatever they wanted, things they would never think or dare to do with wives or girlfriends back home. In the old days, mercenaries pillaged and plundered in order to rape helpless women in conquered territories, women that were considered spoils of war and fair game for men with guns or swords. Military leaders had traditionally turned a blind eye to the sexual perversions of their men, or they provided "comfort women" in facilities where troops partied with attractive girls who wouldn't and couldn't say no. It was considered part of a soldier's compensation and served in lieu of higher wages. Imperial Japan had provided such comfort places for their troops during World War II, and so had Germany. America and England had allowed houses of ill repute to flourish in red-light districts around military bases the way General "Fighting Joe" Hooker had allegedly done during the Civil War. It was considered far better to control the sexual urges of fighting men than to let the men act on their own, and unscrupulous leaders used sex to keep control of their men and prevent desertion. Sex was a powerful motivator for men who carried guns. If your side didn't provide it, the other side would. More than one man had abandoned his post or switched sides for a good piece of ass, and young men were notorious for thinking more with their little heads than their big ones.

Deb had heard about some of the facilities contractors had supposedly supplied to mercenaries in Bosnia, Iraq, and Afghanistan. Rumor had it that there had been similar places in Thailand for contract soldiers working during the Viet Nam Conflict. If rumor were true, why wasn't there hard evidence to confirm the existence of those places? How could such things go on and nobody talked about the sordid details? And what happened to those women when the men were through with them?

Deb got out of the tub and toweled herself dry. As she ran a brush through her long blonde hair, she looked at her own body in the mirror above the sink. Was this the kind of body men would kill for?

At thirty-eight, her breasts were still firm and round. Her abs were tight, her waist narrow. Thank goodness she had never been pregnant. There were no stretch marks to mar her lily-white tummy.

But she was no longer the young woman who had turned men's heads in college. Despite daily runs that kept her in shape, her hips were beginning to show signs of middle-age spread and her buttocks weren't as tight as they once were. She wasn't twenty anymore, and it showed.

What twenty-year-old men wanted were young girls and plenty of them, the kind of girls they might have known in high school but were afraid to approach for fear of rejection. But give those men guns and permission to do anything they wanted with a young girl, and you had them hooked. They would do anything you asked just to get another go with the girls. It was like an addiction to drugs.

As an intelligence operative, Deb had seen countless cases of men—some very powerful world leaders—compromised by lust. Even Prime Ministers and Presidents were vulnerable. Bill Clinton and General David Petraeus, the former CIA director, were good examples. There were countless others. Some of the best spies were women like Mata Hari, an alleged German agent in France during the First World War. Powerful men became putty in the hands of a beautiful woman, things that could be molded into tools that could be used and abused.

In fact, a woman didn't even have to be beautiful to turn a man into putty. Beauty was in the eyes of the beholder, and if a woman had enough sex appeal, the man would make her beautiful in his own eyes. Natural beauty wasn't necessary. Any woman with breasts and a vagina could turn the trick if she were trained.

Deb crawled into bed and turned off the light. In the morning she would begin to look for women, young women, who had disappeared recently anywhere in the world. If the mercenary army was being controlled with promises of sex, there had to be women involved. Find the women, and you would find the men.

* * *

Randy Edwards passed the physical exam with flying colors, as he was certain he would. Though he wasn't in the same shape he had been in the Marine Corps, he still did daily sit-ups and pushups and he could run a mile in under eight minutes without feeling winded. But the psych tests had worried him. He certainly wasn't the same man he had been when he enlisted in the U. S. Marine Corps at eighteen. He had seen things in Afghanistan that no man should ever see: death and destruction, mutilation and mayhem. And he had killed other human beings. At least a dozen or more times that he knew about.

He wasn't real certain if he had fired the bullets that killed at least ten of the enemy, or if someone else in his unit had fired the actual rounds, but those ten men were dead just the same and it had certainly been his intention to kill them if he could. Two of the other men he had killed he was absolutely sure of killing because he had fired those bullets up close and personal. He had seen heads split open, guts rip out. Taking human life always changed two people profoundly: the target and the shooter. The target was dead and the shooter was still alive, but the shooter was changed by the very fact that he was alive and the other guy wasn't. Sometimes it just didn't hit you as fast as the bullet hit the dead guy, but it still had an enduring impact.

Proven killers must have been what WLSCTC wanted, because a guy by the name of Earl Wright called Randy into his big office, pumped Randy's hand vigorously, told Randy he had successfully passed the grueling exams and background checks, and offered Randy a contract of employment.

"You don't have to sign right now," Wright said with a smile. Wright was a guy of average height, slim and trim, with a fresh high and tight haircut, and he looked and acted like some captains or majors Randy had known in the Corps. "I want you to have a chance to read it over real good first, and tomorrow I'll be happy to answer any questions you have. But tonight we go out on the town and celebrate. You do drink, don't you?"

"I was a Marine," Randy answered. "All Marines drink like fish."

"Good. I'll have someone drive you back to your hotel. Get some sleep. Eat in one of the hotel dining rooms and put it on the bill. We'll pick you up at twenty hundred and make the rounds. Dress casually."

Wright showed up promptly at 8:00 PM, and he escorted Randy through the hotel lobby to a waiting limousine, a shiny new black Lincoln with an older African-American driver dressed in a suit that matched the color of the car.

And then they took him to a special place, somewhere way out in the country with a stone fence all around the property and an iron gate that swung open when the driver pressed a button on the Lincoln's dash.

From outside, the house looked like one of those big, old-fashioned mansions built sometime after the Civil War by rich carpetbaggers who needed someplace to spend their newfound wealth. Randy learned there were sixteen bedrooms, two drawing rooms, a huge dining room converted into a well-stocked cocktail lounge, and more beautiful women than Randy had seen in any one place in his entire life.

"This is Edie's place," said Wright. "C'mon, let me introduce you."

Edie was a woman in her early sixties, a bottle blonde, and elegantly attired in a tailored navy-blue evening dress and matching high-heeled shoes. She wore a string of dazzling pearls around her neck and matching pearl earrings, and Randy thought they looked genuine and probably were worth a small fortune.

"Edie," said Wright, "allow me to introduce our newest employee, Mr. Randy Edwards. Randy, this is Edie McCullough."

"Hi, Randy," said Edie, offering her gloved hand and a warm smile. "Welcome to the Club."

"The Club?"

"That's what I call it. What I run here is a private club just for men, special men like you, Randy. Most of my clients are veterans. What would you like to drink, hon?"

"How did you know I was a veteran?"

"You're going to start working for Earl, aren't you? Everyone he brings here is a veteran. Or a politician. And you don't look old enough or pompous enough to be a politician. Now what can I bring you to drink?"

"Anything?"

"Anything."

"I'll have a Jack Daniel's with a beer chaser."

"Sounds like a real man's drink."

She was back in a few moments with a tray. "Follow me, gentlemen," she said, and she took them into one of the drawing rooms and closed the door. "Now we can have some privacy."

She set the tray down on a coffee table and took a seat on a velvet-covered couch, patting the cushion next to her for Randy to join her on the sofa. Earl Wright walked to a wooden desk in a far corner of the room and turned away from them as if he were more interested in reading titles of leather-bound books in a built-in mahogany bookcase than in what Edie had to say.

"So, tell me, Randy, what kind of girl do you want to-night?"

"Huh?" Randy wasn't sure he heard her correctly.

"I assumed Earl had told you and I wouldn't have to explain," she said softly. "You get to choose the kind of girl you want to spend the night with. She'll do anything you ask. So, tell me. What kind of girl do you like?"

"All kinds," said Randy, feeling uncomfortable. Did she think he was queer? "I like all kinds of girls."

"That's kind of broad, don't you think? Surely, you want a girl who is good looking. Do you prefer mature or immature? Heavy or slim? Chocolate or vanilla?"

"I never thought about it much."

"Then we'll ask a few of our girls to come in and you can choose which one you like best. The next time you come, you can pick another. Try them all. The company is paying for it."

"The company pays them? They're prostitutes? This is a whore house?"

"No, hon. They're escorts, not prostitutes. They're employed by the same company you work for. They get a regular salary, health benefits, social security, and if they make you real happy, they'll get a good-sized bonus. They would be insulted if you tried to pay them. They're just ordinary working gals. I'll call them in, and you can see for yourself."

She picked up a tiny silver bell from a coffee table and shook it three times to ring in the girls. A door at the back of the room opened, and a dozen young women, dressed in pastel-colored blouses and skirts or slacks, paraded in on high heels. None of them looked ordinary.

"Look them over real good. Ask them questions, if you like. You can have any one of them tonight. She'll take you upstairs and make your dreams come true."

Most of the girls looked to be between eighteen and twenty-five, but one was obviously almost thirty. Two were slightly on the chubby side, and one looked downright fat. The others were slim, trim, and athletic. One was African-American, one was oriental, and the others were white.

Randy picked a petite redhead with freckles that looked like a first-year college girl. She said her name was Doreen.

"Doreen is yours for the night," said Edie. "She will do anything you ask. Anything your little heart desires. Doreen will show you the fantasy rooms upstairs, and you can use one or all of them for the entire night. Have fun."

"And I'll pick you up in the morning," said Earl Wright, as if he had heard every word of the conversation. "After lunch, we'll talk about the contract. If you sign, I'll bring you back here again tomorrow night. Then someone will drive you to the airport so you can go home and put your affairs in order before deployment. Sound like an okay plan?"

"Roger that," said Randy. He didn't know whether to salute Wright or not. He didn't know where Earl Wright ranked in the corporate structure, but he suspected somewhere in middle management. Like maybe a captain or a major at battalion level. Maybe tomorrow, after he signed the contract, he would learn more about Mister Earl Wright.

Before heading upstairs, Doreen insisted on refilling Randy's drink. She even got a drink for herself, a glass of bubbling pink champagne.

Doreen showed him into all of the rooms and explained their purpose. There was a dark room lit with candles that contained wooden racks, whips, and chains, blindfolds and handcuffs. That was called the Play Room. There was a room with needles and knives and operating tables Doreen called the Surgery, and a brightly-lit room with stethoscopes and speculums and looked like a doctor's office which Doreen called the Examination Room. There was a room with a Jacuzzi and hot tub and sauna. There was a room filled with dildoes and penis pumps and all kinds of toys. Doreen looked relieved when Randy chose a conventional room with a king-sized bed.

Doreen took the lead and undressed Randy, kissing his body all over as she removed each article of clothing. Then she shoved him back on the bed and did a sexy dance around the room as she peeled blouse, skirt, shoes, pantyhose, bra, and panties from her pale flesh.

She looked almost anemic in the faint light from the bedside lamp. Her red hair stood out in stark contrast to her pale skin.

She had shaved all of her body hair, and she was as smooth and round all over as a baby's bottom.

Though Doreen looked young, it was obvious she was more experienced than Randy.

Where he was shy and hesitant, she was bold and assertive.

Randy didn't last long the first time. They took a time-out to finish their drinks and order another round. The second time lasted longer.

Sometime during the night they talked. Randy learned that Doreen was indeed a college freshman, attending classes during the day and working for the company at night. She said the company paid her tuition and the money she earned paid her rent and bought books. She was bright, articulate, and attentive. And she was relatively new, beginning last summer right after she turned eighteen. Someone at the financial aid office of the university had provided a list of employers who paid college tuition. WLSCTC was on the list.

When Randy opened up and told her about some of his experiences in Afghanistan, Doreen had listened sympathetically, nuzzling his neck with her lips and lightly caressing his lower abdomen with her nimble fingers. Then they made love one more time and they fell asleep in each other's arms.

When Randy awoke on Saturday morning, Doreen was still there. It hadn't been a dream. Randy woke her up, rolled on top of her, and began again. This time Randy fucked her, really fucked her, pounding her until she screamed in ecstasy and bit his ear. Maybe she was more experienced than he was, but he bet nobody had ever fucked her like Randy Edwards did that morning.

Afterwards, they showered together and called downstairs for breakfast. Fifteen minutes, later, a girl dressed like a maid arrived with a huge tray filled with their breakfast order and a large fruit bowl filled with apples and oranges and pineapples and melons.

Randy had barely managed to get dressed in time to meet Earl Wright at noon. They had lunch at a fancy restaurant where everyone seemed to know Wright by name, and then they went back to the office to go over the contract.

"Each time you sign a new contract, you get a night like last night," Wright said. "Since the first contract is for two years, you get two nights. Did you have a good time?"

"Yeah," Randy said.

"You could have done anything you wanted with her, you know," Wright said. "She gets a bonus for every bruise, every broken bone."

"You got to be shittin' me," said Randy.

"No," said Wright. "I'm not. We provide excellent medical services for all our employees."

"You think I'm some kind of sicko?" asked Randy. "You think I would hurt that girl?"

"I'm just saying that you could hurt her if you felt like it. What you do with the girls is between you and them and none of my business. We want you to be satisfied, that's all. Some guys get off being a little more aggressive. So, Randy, here's the deal in a nutshell in case you were too busy last night to read the contract." Wright smiled, laid a copy of the contract on the desk, and pointed to each paragraph as he recited from memory what sounded like a speech.

"Forget about the parties of the first part and the second part. That's all legalese mumbo-jumbo that means you and the company. In return for an exclusive two year commitment of all your time and good and faithful service during those two years—that means 24/7 like it did in the Corps—WLSCTC will deposit monthly in the bank account of your choosing the following amounts: five thousand dollars base salary; additional amounts to be determined as a bonus for superior performance; and other compensation mutually agreed upon for hazardous duty. WLSCTC will provide you with pre-paid travel, housing, meals, work uniforms, entertainment, and business tools. Tools means weapons and armament. You, in turn, agree to keep your mouth shut about anything you hear or learn or do. If you breathe one word to anybody outside the company about anything, this contract will immediately terminate and you will be prosecuted for breach of contract. Do you understand what I'm saying here, Randy?"

"Yeah, I think so," said Randy. "Like those security clearance papers I signed in the Corps."

"Yes, exactly like that." Wright's friendly smile had disappeared. "If you breach security in the military, what happens to you?"

"You're branded a traitor. You get sent to Leavenworth or shot."

"Exactly. What did you do in the Corps when you found out someone was leaking classified information to the enemy and you branded him as a traitor?"

"We took him out with friendly fire."

"We operate the same way. Think about it as a carrot and a stick. The carrot is the big money you can earn, plus extras like last night. The stick is the promise of what will happen if you say anything to anybody about what we do. Is that clear?"

"Yes, Sir."

"Last chance, Randy. Are you in or out?"

"I'm in. Where do I sign?"

Wright smiled again as he handed Randy a pen. "Sign here and here. Initial next to the amounts, here, here, and here."

Randy signed his name and initialed the dates and dollar amounts.

"Now one more time," Wright said, producing another copy of the contract. "We keep one and you'll get one after the CEO signs it and gets it notarized. Any questions?"

"What do I tell my parents?"

"You can tell them you took an overseas job with a government contractor, nothing more. Hell, you don't know any more right now, so you don't have to lie. You can tell them the name of the company and that we provide worldwide security and consulting. You can tell them you named them as beneficiaries of your life insurance with the company. If you're killed in the line of duty, they'll get five times your annual salary. That's more than a quarter of a million dollars. Plus we'll pay for your burial. But we don't want you to get killed, Randy. We'll train you to stay alive. Now come on. We'll go down the hall and fill out the rest of your paperwork. Then someone will introduce you around. Tonight you go back to the club, and tomorrow you go home and prepare to move. You have ten days to get your affairs in order. Then you report back for training."

"Ten days? That's awfully fast, ain't it? I got things to sell and a lease to break."

"You can draw an advance to cover moving expenses. Pay off your lease, if you have to. But we expect you back here in ten days."

"What's the rush?"

"We're working under a deadline here, Randy. We need men ready to go before summer."

"Something big? A surge?"

"Something like that, Randy. Something like that."

CHAPTER THREE

After sealing all nine orifices against intrusion, the Ranger left his body.

"Spirit travel happens to everyone, although most people don't recognize it for what it is," Lokesvara had taught him. "It may happen spontaneously when driving a car or playing a piano or singing or listening to music or experiencing an orgasm. One is suddenly overcome with feelings of ecstasy and the spirit soars, separating from the body and leaving the body behind. The word ecstasy, you may remember, is derived of two ancient words—*ek statis* in Greek and *ex statio* in Latin—meaning to stand apart from the body. When you experience ecstasy, your body continues to operate without a spirit present; the heart continues to beat, lungs inflate and deflate, but your mind has gone elsewhere. Walkers between worlds learn to use rhythmic chants called mantras, or listen to the beat of a drum, to deliberately create ecstatic feelings allowing them to travel quickly and easily between the physical and spiritual worlds. I prefer mantras to drums, but you may use a drum if you wish. Or you may simply listen to the beat of your own heart in the stillness of meditation."

"But doesn't the body die without a spirit being present?" the Ranger had asked.

"Not if you are properly trained. If you are a true walker between worlds, the body keeps functioning while the spirit travels. Your heart continues to beat, your lungs continue to inflate and deflate, the metabolic processes go on, but after a while those processes slow down, as if your body were going into hibernation. The body doesn't move—isn't able to move—unless there is a spirit present to motivate it. If the spirit doesn't return to the living body within a week or two, the body dies of dehydration."

"What happens to the spirit when the body dies?"

"If the spirit is prepared for death, it moves immediately—within 72 hours—to one of the spirit realms. Depending on karmic debt, the spirit will naturally be attracted to the light of the upper worlds or to the darkness of the underworlds soon after it leaves the body at time of death. But if one is not prepared for death, if one has unfinished business one feels he must complete before moving on to the spirit realms, the spirit may remain in the physical world in discarnate form and never have an opportunity to be reborn. That sometimes happens if one is detached from the body and traveling in spirit form when the body is killed or dies of dehydration. Trauma, too, can separate the spirit from the body as easily as ecstasy. Battlefields around the world are filled with discarnate spirits that were shocked from the body by bomb blasts, or the result of sudden violence such as a bullet or a blade striking the body while the body still lived, and the spirit is propelled out of the body by the sudden shock before the body expires. You always know where battles have taken place by the number of discarnate spirits wandering around looking for a physical body to inhabit. Such dislocated spirits do not automatically progress to the spirit realm to eventually be reborn into a new body. They need to finish their work before they can move on. One of our missions as Bodhisattvas is to help discarnate spirits finish their jobs so they can move on."

"How do we do that?"

"First, we seal our own bodies so no discarnate spirit can take possession while we travel. Then we meditate. When the mind and body are calm, we begin to chant. Any chant will do, as long as it contains seed syllables that are rhythmic and melodious. I use Om Ah Ra Pa Tsa Na Dih. Others use Om Ma Ne Pad Me Hum. Western sorcerers use A E I O U M, and it sounds like aeeeeyiiiooyouooowmmmmm. They all work. It is the repetition of sounds in the mind that is important. Repeat your seed syllables until you feel your spirit soar from the body."

"Then what?"

"Then you have achieved the *Samten Bardo*, the third Bardo or transitional state of consciousness, and can travel freely in any of the spirit realms. You can walk between worlds. When you first learn to astral travel, you take it one step at a time, and learning to walk between worlds is like first learning to walk as a child. You take one tentative step, then another. If you fall down, you pick yourself up and take another step. Eventually, you won't have to think about each of the separate steps anymore, and you simply walk when you will yourself to walk. Begin now to meditate. Clear your mind of all things. When your mind becomes as clear as a pond without ripples, begin chanting your seed syllables. You may chant silently to yourself or out loud. Either works, but it takes practice. Be not dismayed if you are unsuccessful at first. Continue to practice until your mind is freed of the body."

After a year of practice, the Ranger was getting really good at separating the mind and body at will. Now he could soar over the entire world in an instant, viewing events, seeing and hearing as if he were physically present. He could see and hear and smell, but he couldn't touch. In order to touch anything—in order to act in the physical world—his spirit needed to be inside his body.

"When spirits meet on the astral plane," said the old man during the initial Pho-wa instruction, "they can communicate directly. Their spirit bodies often look the same as their physical bodies because that is how they are used to thinking of themselves. Now let us both meditate and meet on the astral plane. Then you will see with the clear light. I will be your spirit guide until you are comfortable moving about on your own."

Lokesvara's spirit body looked and sounded no different than his physical body, but the Ranger detected a glow, not unlike a halo, surrounding the old man from head to foot. "What you see is the aura of my astral body, the vital life-force that extends beyond each of us. You may have noticed how uncomfortable you sometimes feel when someone gets really close to you and invades your personal space. That is because the auras of both astral essences interact on a level neither of you recognizes consciously, but recognize nonetheless. When you encounter a kindred spirit—someone who shares the same values as you—your auras resonate and you are inexplicably drawn closer to each other. When you come in contact with someone of opposite polarity—a woman, perhaps, or a man with strong feminine energy—who also shares the same values as you, you feel compelled to interact with them because of mutual resonances. When you meet a person of the same polarity but opposite values, you are instantly propelled away from them as if you were natural enemies. Polarity plays an important role in the interactions of all beings, sentient or non-sentient. Negatives attract positives and repel negatives. Positives attract negatives and repel positives. Those of us who achieve a balanced polarity are able to interact without being pushed or pulled against our will."

"How do you achieve a balanced polarity?"

"Balance is only possible through compassion. When you learn to recognize that good and bad, light and dark, male and female, positive and negative, exist in all beings, you have taken the first step toward enlightenment. Understanding the suffering of others because you have suffered yourself is the second step. Seeking enlightenment for all beings and seeking to relieve their suffering is the third step. To want nothing for oneself but everything for others is the fourth step. To be truly balanced, one must empty oneself of all personal desire and become a vessel for the Dharma."

"Is such a state possible?"

"It is with practice. Such is the way of the Bodhisattva, my son. It is the path you are on. Come, follow me. I will show you suffering beyond belief. For there are many who have died and still suffer because they are filled with desire. Let this be a lesson for you."

Lokesvara took the Ranger to the battlefields of Afghanistan where thousands of discarnate spirits still lingered. They visited Iraq and Viet Nam and Hiroshima and Nagasaki. In all those places they saw spirits, hungry ghosts, whose lives had been suddenly and violently cut short before they had a chance to fulfill their destinies.

"They still remain focused on their intentions," said Lokesvara. "They remain blind to everything else. They were not prepared for death, and they were unable to see the clear light when it appeared to them. They cannot be reborn until they can see the light and become one with it."

They circled the globe and saw discarnate spirits everywhere. "They feel they still have unfinished business in this life," said Lokesvara. "They feel they cannot move on to the next life until they finish what they set out to do in this one. But they cannot complete their work, because they no longer have bodies with which to act in the physical world. They suffer with unfulfilled desire. And they are so filled with fear and anger that they are unable to recognize the light each time it appears."

"How can we help them?"

"By becoming their spirit guides and teaching them to let go of desire. By showing them the clear light again and urging them to move on into that light. By releasing them from the karmic illusions that now control them."

"But there are so many spirits. It will take forever to release all of them."

"Time has no significance for the dead. It will take as long as it takes."

"Where do we start?"

"Choose one spirit to help today. Recite the words of the *Bardo Thodol* to him. Help him to see the light. I'll choose another spirit to help. You learn by doing. Go and do."

"Excuse me," said the Ranger as he approached a soldier north of Kabul. The man looked to be about nineteen, wearing battledress and a Kevlar vest. "What happened to you, soldier?"

"Ambush," said the soldier. "Three of my buddies got it, and I was wounded. The rest of my unit is around here somewhere. I'm trying to get back to them."

"I got caught in an ambush near here once, too," said the Ranger.

"Where's your uniform? Why are you wearing those orange robes?"

"I'm a Buddhist monk."

"I thought you said you were a soldier. You a chaplain or something?"

"No. I was an Army Ranger. I received my calling and became a monk after I was discharged from the Army."

"Then what the hell are you doing back here in Afghanistan? Better not let any of the Taliban learn you're here. Taliban hate Buddhists worse than they hate Americans."

"I came here to help you."

"To help me get back to my unit? I have to get back you know. They need me. But I can't move. I've been trying for weeks to get back. But I'm stuck here, trapped."

"You can't move?"

"I've been trying to move, but it's as if I'm chained down to this one spot. Funniest thing. I can't get back to my unit. I can't even get over there to where the other guys were hit to see if they made it. I can't go anywhere."

"Then you don't know?"

"Know what?"

"That you're dead."

The soldier laughed hysterically. "I ain't dead. How can I be dead? Maybe I was shot. Okay, I *was* shot. But the wound's completely healed. Look, see? I feel fine. How could I possibly be dead? If I was dead, how could I talk to you? How could you talk to me?"

"We're both spirits. The shock of being wounded in an ambush sent your spirit out of your body before your body died.

We're talking now in the spirit realm. You're in the transition period from one life to another. You feel fine because you're beyond pain. But you died."

"I can't die. I've got to get back to my unit to help the other guys fight the Taliban and Al Qaeda. We lost too many men already. I can't die! I have to get back!"

"We all die. Don't be angry. Don't be frightened. Death is only temporary. You'll be reborn in a new body. I'm here to show you the way to move on to the next life."

"But I can't leave my unit short-handed. They need me. We lost too many men already. I can't die, too. I just *can't*!"

"They'll manage without you."

"I can't leave them. It would be like deserting."

"You must leave. I can help you move on to the next life."

"Help me get back to my unit. You say you want to help me? That's how you can help me. I need your help to get back to my unit. I can't move more than a few feet. Can you help me? Can you help me break free of whatever's holding me here? Can you help me get back?"

"Soldier, listen up," the Ranger snapped out in his best command voice. "You can't go back, you can only go forward. Your mission here is finished. Now pack up your gear and prepare to move out. Is that clear?"

"Who are you? You sound like my sergeant."

"I was the best damn NCO the Army ever had. But all things change, all things end. Your job here is finished, done, over with, ended, kaput. Get that through your thick skull, soldier. It's time to move on. Look around you now. Look for the clear light. You'll see it if you look for it."

"I do see a light," said the kid. "But I'm scared of that light. I seen it before. That's the same light I seen when they hit us with that RPG, the rocket-propelled grenade, that knocked me out. That's the light that took out my buddies. That's the light that killed them. That's the light I saw when they died."

"That's the light you saw when *you* died, you mean. Go into the light now, don't run away from it. It can't hurt you. Nothing can hurt you. I'll walk with you. C'mon, soldier. It's time to move forward. Get a move on."

As they walked together into the light, other spirit guides came to meet them. Surrounded entirely by light, the spirit guides appeared the way the Ranger imagined angels from heaven might look. Their auras glowed so brightly that their faces and forms were barely visible and didn't appear human.

"It is not your time," spoke a voice inside the Ranger's mind. "You may go no further. We'll guide him on from here, but you must go back."

They pulled the soldier into the light surrounding them, and the soldier disappeared. Then the light disappeared, too.

"You did well, my son," said Lokesvara a moment later.

"He didn't believe he was dead," said the Ranger. "He didn't even know he had died. Why didn't he know he was dead?"

"He felt no different than before. He could see and hear. All he knew was that he had been sent on a mission and he hadn't completed his mission. There were signs, of course, but he didn't want to acknowledge them. He saw the light not as something friendly but as something frightful. That's why he avoided going into the light each time he saw it, and he did see it. It appeared again and again to him, but he refused to go near it."

"They wouldn't let me into the spirit realm. I wanted to go into the light with him, but they stopped me. They wouldn't let me in."

"That is because while your spirit is still attached to a living body, your spirit can only enter the upper or lower worlds via the World Tree. All worlds are connected by a living tree whose roots descend into the underworlds and whose branches ascend to the upper realms. Access to the World Tree is only possible at one of four vortexes: at Angkor Wat in Cambodia, at Machu Picchu in Peru, in Lappland in northern Scandinavia near the North Pole, and in an old-growth forest in Wisconsin. You are not yet ready to climb the World Tree to enter the spirit realm."

"But you have?"

"Yes," said Lokesvara. "I have journeyed to the spirit realms. And someday you shall, too."

"But not today?"

"No," said the old monk. "Not today."

* * *

Bill Ramsey had seen that light before. It was a brilliantly beautiful, bright and clear light that suddenly appeared on the mountaintop at regular intervals like he remembered the doorway to his dark bedroom looked when the door opened only a tiny crack, letting in a small sliver of light, so his mother could peek inside the room to see if her children were already asleep. Each time the light had appeared, Bill had closed his eyes to it and pretended to be sleeping. Like he had done as a child when he worried that maybe it wasn't his mother peeking in at him after all. Perhaps it was really the boogeyman—disguised as his mother—come to consume him. Maybe if he ignored the light, like he had eventually learned to ignore the boogeyman, it would simply go away. And it did go away. But the clear bright light always came back to haunt him.

Bill had to stay focused on the mission. Though he knew he had no way to get down from the mountain and send word to America about the training camp, he was obsessed with getting a message through. He imagined reaching the short wave radio he had stashed just north of the mountain where he died, keying the radio transmitter, and broadcasting a signal that National Security Agency monitors might pick up. "I am a U. S. Army Ranger attached to INSCOM," he would say. "I have important information to relay regarding my mission. This information is vital to national security. Please respond."

He had no idea how long he had been dead. He had seen the sun rise and set multiple times, but he had lost track of time after forty-some days. The wristwatch he wore had stopped at 4:12, the precise moment of Bill's death. Time wasn't supposed to matter to the dead, but it still mattered to Bill Ramsey. He was running out of time. If he didn't get a message out soon, it might be too late. The people that had killed him were training for something big, and somebody needed to know about it before it went down.

So he increased his efforts. He concentrated his thoughts on the message. "I am a U. S. Army Ranger attached to INSCOM. I have important information to relay regarding my mission. This information is vital to national security. Please respond."

One day, when he had about given up hope, an apparition appeared in front of him. The apparition looked like a man, but it couldn't be human because this man was walking on air and there was a glow surrounding him like some kind of halo. He was dressed in saffron and red robes, and he wore bamboo sandals on his otherwise bare feet.

And he looked vaguely familiar.

The apparition had a shaved head like a monk or an Army Ranger or a gung-ho Marine. He had piercing blue eyes and a thick neck. The muscles in his bare arms were rock hard like he did five hundred push-ups before breakfast.

"I swore I would kill you someday, Captain Ramsey," said the apparition. "But it looks like someone beat me to it."

"You...you're...."

"The Lone Ranger. I'm the guy you had booted out of the Army for killing Afghan civilians."

"You've changed."

"So have you."

"What are you doing here? Are you dead, too?"

"Not yet. I heard your call and came to help."

"You heard my call?"

"On the astral plane. I was in neighboring Afghanistan helping soldiers cross over. I heard your distress call. You kept repeating the same message. 'I am a U. S. Army Ranger attached to INSCOM,' you said. 'I have important information to relay regarding my mission. This information is vital to national security. Please respond.' So I responded."

"You're not dead? You can relay my message to INSCOM?"

"If it's really that important."

"It is."

"Then tell me. Give me the message and I'll relay it to intelligence."

"How do I know I can trust you?"

"Do you have any choice?"

Ramsey didn't take long to make up his mind. "You're right," he said. "I don't have a choice."

"Then tell me, Captain Ramsey. Tell me what it is that's important enough to keep you here long after your body died and gave up the ghost."

"It's *Major* Ramsey now. I'm still with the 75th, but I've been assigned to do special ops for INSCOM."

"Go on."

"I work for Colonel McMichaels. He runs special ops in the field and puts boots on the ground. One of his intel people found a shitload of former military being trained in a camp down in the valley. All hush-hush. It didn't smell right to him, and McMichaels needed someone to go in and find out what they were up to."

"And you were that someone?"

"Yeah."

"And people from that camp killed you?"

"Yeah."

"Why? What did you learn you shouldn't have?"

"They're training more than a thousand men in special operations down in that valley. All are seasoned combat vets. Mostly Special Forces, Rangers, SEALS. A few ex-Marines. They have state of the art weaponry, and they've got their shit together. They'd beat the pants off the 75th."

"That would be hard to do. The 75th Ranger Regiment is the best of the best. You think the guys in that camp are working for the Taliban?"

"No. They're working for an American contractor. But they aren't being used for government contracts."

"Then what are they used for?"

"That's what scares me. They're being prepped for something big. Like a surge or a push of some kind. You don't keep that many combat-ready troops around for nothing."

"Wait here. I'll be right back."

The apparition vanished. Five minutes later, it was back.

"I took a look at their camp. You're right. They're preparing for combat."

"You can just move around like that without anyone seeing you?"

"I can. I can send my spirit almost anywhere."

"Why can't I do that?"

"Because you're not grounded."

"Grounded?"

"You're no longer attached to the physical world. You're in a transition between worlds. You can't go anywhere until you go into the light."

"I can't go anywhere because I still have work to do. I'm staying here until I complete my mission."

"Come on, Ramsey. You *can't* complete your mission. Your job here is done, finished, over with, kaput, ended. See the big picture. See the light. If I can see the light, you can, too. It's waiting for you to enter. It's time for you to move on."

"I won't go. Look, I know you were a good soldier once. Before you freaked out. I order you to help me complete my mission."

"I'm not in the Army anymore, Ramsey. Remember? You saw to that. You got me kicked out. But I promise I'll get word to INSCOM for you. I'll tell them what you told me. They can complete the mission without you."

"And lose how many other men? C'mon, Ranger. I'm already on top of the situation here. There must be some way I can infiltrate their ranks. I can't die in peace until I've done that. You hear me? I won't move on. I'll stay here forever. I'll find a way to stay. There must be a way."

"Too bad no one taught you about the Bardo while you were alive, Ramsey. Then you'd know how to transfer your consciousness from one living entity to another."

"You mean there's a way to do that?" Ramsey seemed excited now. "I *knew* there was a way. There had to be. I knew it! I just knew it!"

"There are two ways, actually," said the Ranger, remembering what Lokesvara had taught him. "One is to find a willing partner—someone who is still alive—who agrees to share his body with another spirit. You have to ask permission. You can't do that because you have no way to communicate directly with the living."

"And the other?"

"Taking possession of a living body when the spirit is out of the body. There are two windows of opportunity to do that. The first is within three-and-a-half days immediately following your death."

"And the second?"

"On the forty-ninth day after dying. That's the day you get to choose your new body. Depending on your karma, you may choose to enter a new body at the instant that body is conceived at the height of orgasm. Or you may enter an unprotected body that is experiencing the ecstasy of orgasm. Only those who know the Bardo are able to do the latter."

"Can you teach me?"

"Perhaps. How many days has it been since you died?"

"Forty-something. I'm not sure."

"Then we haven't much time. First you must learn to clear your mind of all earthly desires except this one thing."

"And then?"

"And then you have to find a body. It must be a body that has left at least one of its orifices open."

"How can I do that? I'm stuck here on this mountain. I can't move anywhere."

"If you properly prepare, then on the forty-ninth day you'll be drawn to that body no matter where the body is physically located in the world. Begin now to prepare. Empty your mind of all thoughts and desires except one."

"Thank you," said Bill Ramsey. "Thank you. I've forgotten your name. What is your name?"

"What my name once was is unimportant. My name now is Vajrapani."

"That's your Buddhist name?"

"It is the only name I have that matters, Major Ramsey. You may call it if you ever need my help again."

"Thank you, Vajrapani."

"Now listen up, Ramsey, and I'll explain what you need to do…."

CHAPTER FOUR

Randy Edwards felt like he was in lust. Truly in lust. If Randy had believed in love, he might have labeled what he now felt for this woman as love instead of lust. But Randy didn't believe in love. So he called his feelings lust. And desire. And need. He thought those labels as good as any.

He had chosen Doreen to fuck again tonight from among the dozen or so young girls available at the club, and this time he had forced Doreen into the S & M room, chained her naked and spread-eagled to an upright X-frame, and he was now sadistically teasing her backside with a peacock feather and occasional slaps to her butt with his bare hand. She squirmed and squealed with delight. She seemed to be enjoying this as much as he was, and that really turned him on. Anticipation was a great aphrodisiac, and his raging hard-on stuck straight out in front of him like a bayonet fixed to the end of a rifle.

They had all night to play, and Randy was just getting warmed up. It had finally dawned on him that he could do absolutely anything he wanted with this beautiful young woman and she would be forced to—would have to—let him. Anything short of killing her, that is.

Randy didn't want to kill her. Killing her was the last thing he wanted to do, certainly the farthest thing from his mind. All he wanted to do was take total possession of her, to dominate her body and her mind and her soul so completely that nothing else mattered to her but him. He wanted her to want him as much as he wanted her. He wanted to hear her beg.

He moved the feather between her thighs and eased it up very slowly to tease her secret center from behind. Her tight little butt wiggled with every stroke of the feather.

When he couldn't take it anymore, and he thought she couldn't take it any more either, he took her hard from behind. He rammed himself inside her and slammed her body so hard against the wooden frame that the frame splintered. She bucked and screamed. She begged him to stop, but he couldn't stop. He slammed into her, withdrew, slammed into her again, withdrew, slammed into her again.

"Please, stop! You're hurting me! You're really hurting me!"

But he didn't stop. He kept ramming and slamming until she screamed and screamed and screamed and he erupted inside of her like a volcano spewing hot lava.

After he had finished, he unchained her hands and feet and led her back to the room with the king-sized bed. Then he made her make love to him, first with her mouth, then with the rest of her body.

This time when Randy came, he felt total ecstasy. He felt like he had gone to another world. When he returned to the real world, he discovered he had company.

There was someone else inside his mind.

"Who are you?" he tried to ask the unknown entity that now cohabited his body like a siamese twin, but the words remained only half-formed, his thoughts interrupted by alien thoughts. It was as if his mind didn't work the same anymore.

Nor did his body. Despite Doreen's nimble fingers playing with his private parts, his body didn't respond, his member a wet noodle between his legs. He tried to move his hands to touch Doreen, but his hands didn't move where he wanted them to.

Instead, he abruptly pushed her away and sat up in the bed, looking around the room as if he had never seen that room or anything in it before. Suddenly, Randy began to notice things he had never bothered to notice before, ordinary things he had ignored because they were simply there and didn't matter to him. There were watercolor pictures of naked women on two of the walls, for example. And a large floor-to-ceiling mirror on the third wall.

He got out of the king-sized bed and walked over to one of the pictures and stared at the watercolor very closely. He moved a finger to one of the oversized breasts on the painting, touched each of the nipples in turn as if to caress the areoles and points with his fingertips. He felt a tiny hole in the paper, and he could feel the slightly larger indentation in the wall behind the painting that he suspected would be there. And it was.

He went to the second painting and did the same thing. This time he found a pinhole in one of the eyes.

Now he walked across the room and looked closely at the floor-to-ceiling mirror. He saw his own image reflected in the glass, saw his naked body all sweaty and sticky, and he saw something else, too. There were shadows moving behind the glass.

He couldn't see them when he looked directly into the mirror, but when he looked to one side he caught glimpses of vague movement with his peripheral vision which was better at detecting movement than looking straight on. There were several people in the next room watching them. Probably recording everything with cameras.

And there were cameras behind both of the watercolors.

He walked back to the bed, crawled under the sheets with the half-asleep Doreen, and closed his eyes as if he were going to sleep.

How long had they been watching him? All the time? Since the first night Doreen had brought him to this room and they had made love? And what about earlier tonight? Were there hidden cameras in that other room, too? Did they record every little thing he did to Doreen on the rack? Did they record her begging him to stop, pleading with him to stop, but he ignored her frantic begs and pleas and just kept right on pounding her and pounding her until he got his rocks off? Jesus! What kind of perverts were they?

And what kind of pervert did they think he was? Was what he did to Doreen any different than rape? She begged and begged him to stop, but he hadn't wanted to stop and he didn't stop. Not until he had finished. She cried and screamed, begged and pleaded. And he hadn't listened.

But wasn't that okay? Hadn't Wright told him he could do anything to the girls he wanted, anything his heart desired? Tonight he wanted to be in control, to prove something to Doreen and to himself. So he had kept right on pounding her even when she had begged him to stop, even when he knew he was hurting her, even when he knew what he was doing was wrong.

He raised the sheet over her sleeping body to look at the purplish bruises marring her tiny breasts and flat stomach. There were bloody scrapes and ugly scratches on both of her boobs and on her abdomen, too, where pieces of wood from the broken X frame had caused abrasions and punctured the skin. Doreen's body looked like autopsy pictures Randy had seen of rape victims in television documentaries about serial killers.

One part of him felt ashamed, while another part of him felt very proud. He had shown her he was a real man, hadn't he? Real men take what they want. Women beg and plead. Men take.

A third part of him seemed to be observing the other two parts. Jesus! How many parts of him were there?

Somehow his mind had expanded and he was more aware now than he had ever been in the previous twenty-three years he had been alive on this earth. Things Randy had never before thought important now very seemed very important.

It was if he had died and been reborn.

Didn't men die a little each time they came? Didn't the French call orgasm, "la petite mort," the little death? They did, but Randy didn't know French.

So how was it he now knew how to speak and read not only French, but German, Farsi, Urdu, and a smattering of Arabic?

Randy gradually became aware of a lot of things he had never known before. He knew what it was like to be really in love with a woman—to love her with his whole heart and soul—and he knew what it was like to have kids. And he knew the heartbreak of going through a bitter divorce caused by too many military separations over the years that changed love into something closer to hate.

And he knew what it was like to attend the Command and General Staff College at Fort Leavenworth, though he had never been to Kansas in his entire life and had never been in Eisenhower Hall nor seen the stars as clearly as they appeared in the skies over Kansas on a cloudless night. Nor had he been an officer, much less an Army officer. Only field grade officers went to C G and S. The highest grade Randy had attained in the Corps was lance corporal.

And Randy knew what it was like to die. He remembered the pain and shock as multiple bullets passed through his body and ripped out vital organs. He remembered floating above his own body and watching men mutilate his corpse with more bullets. Only it wasn't Randy's body. The dead body belonged to someone else.

Randy felt Doreen stir beside him, and one part of him wanted her again. That part of him had fond memories of plunging deep inside her until it found blessed release within the heart of her, and he wanted to do it all over again until she screamed and he screamed and he floated away on a cloud.

But now that he knew there were people watching them and cameras recording his every move from every angle, he had second thoughts about resuming lovemaking. It wasn't that he was shy or embarrassed.

It was more like he was concerned about what they would do with those recordings. Why had they put so much money and effort into such an elaborate set-up? It sure as hell wasn't just to make an amateur porno movie.

What if they sent copies of those pictures to his parents back in Minnesota? How would he feel about that? And what if they sent copies of the scene in the S & M room where he'd raped Doreen, despite her repeated protests and pleadings, to the local cops?

Doreen looked young, probably too young. Was he really certain that she was old enough to be in college? What if she had been lying about her age? What if she were under eighteen? Was he guilty of statutory rape, too? Could he go to jail? What was the penalty for statutory rape in Virginia these days?

None of these thoughts had ever occurred to him before. Why now? Why did it matter?

Randy saw the training camp in Pakistan in his mind's eye, and suddenly he understood how WLSCTC controlled all those men and he knew why it mattered. Wright had warned about the carrot and the stick. The women at the club were carrots. The recordings were part of the stick WLSCTC held over his head to keep him in line. Teddy Roosevelt had once said, "Speak softly, and carry a big stick." WLSCTC carried a very big stick.

And what was it Edie had said about Earl Wright on Randy's first visit to the club? "Everyone he brings here is a veteran. Or a politician. And you don't look old enough or pompous enough to be a politician." How many politicians had WLSCTC recorded doing things with underage women? And what would those politicians do to keep those recordings from becoming public knowledge?

What was WLSCTC really up to? Who were the big brains controlling this operation? Wasn't it part of his mission to find out?

Suddenly Randy knew the name of the entity who now shared his body and his thoughts. It was Major Bill Ramsey, U. S. Army Rangers, recently deceased.

And he knew that Ramsey had looked the whole world over for the perfect candidate to possess. Not only was Randy out of his body in the throes of orgasm at the right time on the one day possession was possible, but Randy was slated to leave for training at the very camp in Pakistan that Ramsey had died trying to infiltrate.

Ramsey had been attracted by Doreen's screams and Randy's first orgasm, and the second time Randy came Ramsey slipped inside Randy's empty shell as easily as Randy had slipped inside Doreen's wet cunt.

That was bad luck and bad timing on Randy's part, because he sure didn't want the extra baggage of another mind tagging along with him wherever he went. It was like having a conscience looking over your shoulder and watching everything you did and making you aware of all the mistakes you had ever made or were about to make.

But maybe that wasn't all bad. Maybe it was time Randy got a conscience. Maybe, just maybe, it was time for Randy to grow up and act like a man.

* * *

Her given name was Anong, which meant "beautiful woman" in the Thai language. Since her father had sold her for two hundred American dollars when she was eight, she hadn't used her family name. She was simply Anong.

She had turned twelve two months ago, and she expected she would bleed soon and become a real woman. Some of the other girls had shown Anong how to protect herself against pregnancy as well as disease, and she was already doing that. It was better to be safe than sorry.

Anong had lived in a house in Thailand that serviced men. She had been placed into service when she was eight, barely able to understand what was happening to her. She had worked as a sex-slave for four long years. She couldn't—or didn't want—to remember what life was like before she moved to that house. Some things were better forgotten.

She would still be working there except for a fortunate accident that had freed her. Eight days ago another group of men had flown in from somewhere, and they had the pick of the girls for the duration of their stay in Thailand. Anong was among the first to be chosen, as she always was. Men said she was very beautiful, but she knew better than to trust what any man said.

After two days of drinking and any and every which kind of sex the men could ask for, the visiting men took a handful of the girls with them on a sight-seeing cruise down the Mekong River. The men forced the girls to drink, and it wasn't long before everyone on the rented tour boat was too drunk to stand.

Anong had never consumed so much alcohol at one time before in her entire life, and she was practically out cold when she staggered to the railing at the back of the boat and attempted to relieve herself over the side. Anong quickly discovered that urinating off the side of a boat was far easier for a man than a woman, and she had to climb up onto the railing and balance precariously to lift her skirts to pee into the river.

That's when the accident happened. Anong lost her balance and fell overboard, dragged underwater by the wake of the rudder and the propeller. By the time she resurfaced and recovered her senses, the boat was nearly a mile upstream. Even if she were a strong swimmer— which she wasn't—she couldn't catch up with the boat. She barely had strength enough to reach shore before she collapsed.

It would take her two days or more to walk back to the house, and by the time she got there this group of men would be long gone, replaced by another group of groping hands and leering faces. If she went back, she would have no way to explain why she had deserted the boat and the men. She was sure to be beaten. Or worse.

So she went south instead of north. She had no money, and only the clothes she wore to her name. But she felt free for the first time in her life, and she liked the feeling.

Anong followed the Mekong River, walking south along the side of the river as it flowed from Thailand into Laos. She saw a two-lane highway just east of the river, and she crawled through the weeds and bamboo until she reached the paved road where she managed to hitch a ride on the back of a motor scooter driven by a boy of sixteen. She was able to ride on the back of the scooter down Highway 13 almost to the Cambodian border. Getting across the border presented a significant challenge to someone with no money and no identification. The boy with the scooter had told her she'd need a visa, and that the border guards on each side of the border charged thirty-five baht or one American dollar each to cross over. She had no money. She had to find a way to sneak across the border without being seen by any of the guards.

She chose to return to the river. She walked through the marshes at the side of the river and passed under rotting stilt poles supporting the guard shack where the river crossed the border. The lone armed guard watching the Mekong wasn't looking for a young girl on foot. She wasn't a rich tourist seeking ways to avoid paying the crossing fees, nor was she an armed enemy invading the country from the north. If the man at the guard shack did see the movement of her small body making ripples in the water, he simply ignored it as she slipped past the guard post in the dark.

She saw numerous snakes in the river or along the muddy bank and some were probably poisonous and deadly, but she left them alone and they left her alone. Snakes didn't frighten her half as much as some of the men she had known. Some bites poisoned the body, and some poisoned the soul. She would rather die of a poisonous snakebite than be bitten again by any man.

Once inside Cambodia, she was able to hitch a ride in the back of a Toyota truck filled with squawking chickens and bird dung all the way into downtown Phnom Penh.

Cambodia's capital was a huge and scary place. She had never seen modern freeways before, and the towering buildings of the teeming multi-million-population metropolis seemed to scrape the sky itself and blot out the sun. Besides being noisy, the place smelled bad.

She was able to steal some fruit from an outdoor fruit stand, and she begged some coins from wealthy tourists passing in front of the shops. She used most of the money to buy a small bowl of rice and noodles and a cup of Jasmine tea.

Though she recognized multiple similarities between the spoken Khmer languages and her native Thai, she couldn't understand much of the strange writing on signs or storefronts. She felt lost until she discovered a Buddhist pagoda on one of the side streets. She went inside and prayed, as much to seek refuge from the oppressing heat as to seek refuge in the Buddha, the dharma, or the sangha. She had never been particularly religious, but there was a certain comfort in the familiar surroundings and the smell of burning incense.

Anong had nowhere to go, no money, no home, no family, no hope of survival unless she became a cheap prostitute walking the bustling streets of this foreboding city like many of the girls she had passed on her way to the temple. She made a decision there and then not to return to her former life. It was better to die than allow herself to be used up and thrown away like trash.

Perhaps it was the influence of the incense that made her think of becoming a nun. She had seen the white-robbed Mae Jis with their shaven heads and shaven eyebrows begging near the house in Thailand, and she had asked some of the other girls about the nuns. No one seemed to know much about them except they were women who had taken vows of poverty and chastity, and they were housed at a nunnery inside one of the temple compounds in nearby Kong Chiam.

Since Anong owned nothing, a vow of poverty didn't frighten her. And a vow of chastity had an appeal all its own for a girl who had been exploited as a sex toy.

Anong sought out one of the saffron-robed monks and tried to tell him she wished to become a Mae Ji. None of the monks seemed to know what she was talking about.

Finally, after frustratingly trying to explain, another of the monks asked if "mae chee" meant the same as "doun chee," a Bhikkhuni. He explained that a Bhikkhuni was an older woman, usually a widow or gray-haired grandmother, who cleaned the temples and cooked for the monks. They sometimes taught children, especially females. "But," he explained, "you are far too young to become a doun chee. You have your whole life ahead of you yet. First you must become a householder and raise a family. Then you must know suffering and experience the death of someone close to you. How can one so young know anything of suffering? Or of death?"

"Surely, there must be a way," insisted Anong. "I have known suffering and I have seen death. My entire family is dead to me. How can I not become a nun?"

"We have no doun chees here," said the monk. "But at Angkor Wat there are some. Even some very young girls who have become *samaneras*, or novitiates. You must go to Angkor if you desire to learn more."

"I have no money. How do I get there? How far is it? Can I walk?"

"Oh, no. Angkor is more than three hundred kilometers from here. That's a good six hours travel by motor car or bus. Or you could boat the Siem Reap River northwest to Angkor. I know someone who could take you upriver by boat. He leaves Phnom Penh tomorrow."

"How much will that cost?"

"It will cost you nothing. He will do it only as a favor to the temple. It is how he earns merit in this life. He does lots of work for the temple when he has time, and his work pays some of his karmic debt. He has terrible karmic debt. He was a young officer under Pol Pot. He destroyed temples and schools. He killed many people, including many monks. He feels he owes us something for the suffering he caused. He will be glad to take you upriver."

Anong made wais with her hands near the top of her head. "Kup koon, ka," she said. "I thank you, sir."

"You may sleep here tonight, if you wish. You will be safe. Someone will take you to the river in the morning."

A tuktuk driver arrived at 5:30, and he was another man who did favors for the temple and charged Anong nothing for his services. Anong felt like a queen sitting alone in the large canopied compartment built behind the putt-putting motorcycle as the driver expertly negotiated city streets. She arrived at the docks well before the 6:00 AM scheduled departure.

The boatman's name was Rithisak, and Anong guessed his age at nearly sixty, despite the way he moved cargo around on his stooped shoulders like a much younger man. The boat itself was constructed of weathered wooden planks approximately thirty feet long and ten feet wide. There was an old Evinrude motor near the back. Stacks of cargo occupied every inch of the floor of the boat except for a very tiny space for the boatman to stand near the motor and almost enough room for Anong's legs to dangle between tightly stacked wooden crates if she sat atop one of the stacks of boxes.

Rithisak spoke little the entire trip. Anong could see he had his hands full navigating the river, poling through the narrows by hand, and Anong didn't bother him trying to make conversation. The boat crept slowly up-river until the river widened into a huge lake Rithisak said was called Tonle Sap. During the rainy season, he told her, the lake swelled to twice its present size, flooding the areas all around and depositing nutrient-rich silt perfect for growing rice. So, too, did the lake support a variety of fish and waterfowl. There were many peasant shacks—pole houses with thatched roofs—on both sides of the lake, and Anong saw hundreds of small boats and bare-chested men fishing with nets closer to the shore.

Rithisak threw the throttle on the old motor wide open and the boat moved quickly to the center of the lake where it raced north unobstructed by weeds and reefs. As the boat swung to the northwest, waves of water splashed back from the bow like a tsunami and dumped on Anong's head like water from a rinsing bowl when she washed her hair, drenching Anong's hair and dress as completely as if she had been caught outside in a sudden thunderstorm.

"The sun will soon dry you," said Rithisak, laughing.

And it did, in a matter of minutes. She got wet a dozen times more from the spray, but it didn't bother her. She was free, she was on her way to a new home where no man could touch her, and she would let nothing bother her ever again. She felt happy for the first time in her life.

After docking the boat at Siem Reap and unloading his cargo, Rithisak walked with Anong past the ruins of Angkor Thom to the temples of Angkor Wat.

"Because so many of the temples were destroyed by the Khmer Rouge," lamented Rithisak, "the monks have had to reclaim some of the ancient buildings that have been left crumbling at Angkor for centuries. There is now a lamasery inside the main temple at Angkor Wat, and that is where I will take you. The Abbot is a kind man and very wise. He will know what to do with you."

Ankor Wat was a city unto itself. There was a moat as large as a small river surrounding the temple grounds, and they had to cross that moat on a long narrow stone bridge on the west side of the complex in order to reach the single gate leading into the temple. The place was built like an enormous medieval castle with a moat and a high stone wall limiting access, and then the pagoda itself was located nearly another kilometer beyond the wall. Everything was built of sandstone, and it seemed to Anong that every stone had been carved and sculpted to depict stories from the holy books. She saw visages of ancient Hindu gods and goddesses, images of half-naked women dancing with snakes or making mudras with their fingers, and pictorialized stories of gods and goddesses and demons and nagas engraved on the walls.

Once they reached the main temple, they still had to walk up half-a-hundred steep steps to get into the building. The place was so huge that hallways branched off at right angles into other hallways on three levels. The temple was indeed like a small city, and Anong became quickly lost in the bustling streets of that city crowded with foreign tourists, tour guides, and small groups of saffron-robed monks with shaved heads.

But Rithisak seemed to know exactly where he was going. He walked purposely down a long corridor that led into what looked to be a school. She saw young monks now, and children in ordinary dress, and some older monks playfully herding the children through the halls. She smelled incense burning, and she heard chanting.

"This is the Lama's private chambers," said Rithisak, stopping in front of an open door. "He closes the door only when he is in meditation or disciplining a pupil."

The room was simple and humble, nothing like what she expected of an eminent Abbot of a lamasery. There was a cotton rug, reddish-brown in color, covering half the stone floor. There was no desk, no telephone, no chair. She saw a small wooden table against one wall that contained relics, burning incense sticks, and a stone statue of the Buddha. And there was a very old man, clothed in the saffron robes of the brotherhood, sitting alone on the carpet on the hard floor.

The old man opened his eyes and smiled warmly. He greeted them with a wais, and they returned the traditional greeting. He did not attempt to get up, but with an inviting gesture indicated they should join him on the floor.

"Who is this charming young lady that you have brought to visit us, Rithisak?" asked the old man.

"Her name is Anong, Master," said Rithisak. "She wishes to become a duon chee."

"I am Lokesvara," said the old man, turning his attention to Anong. His eyes were as kind as his smile. "Is it true, Anong, that you wish to study and live among us here?"

"I....I...." stammered Anong. She was so in awe of the man that she couldn't find words.

"Have you eaten after your long journey?" asked the Abbot. "Forgive me for asking silly questions before seeing to your needs. Let me show you to the washrooms and the kitchen. We can talk better while you are eating."

"How did you know I was hungry?" asked Anong.

"Everyone who comes here is hungry," said the old man. "The people of the community are generous with their donations of food and clothing. Come." He stood up easily and Anong was surprised how tall and straight he stood as he towered over her like a statue of the Buddha. Lokesvara offered her his hand and helped her up from the floor.

"I will leave you now," said Rithisak to his young charge. "I have business to attend before returning to the capital. You are in good hands here." He made a wais to Anong at heart level, and then he made a high wais of respect to the Abbot with his hands nearly above his head.

"Namaste," said Lokesvara. "You are a good man, Rithisak. Thank you for your trouble."

"It was no trouble," mumbled Rithisak. "I was coming to Siem Reap anyway."

"But you walked more than five kilometers each way to see me," said Lokesvara. "You went out of your way to help someone who needed your help. That makes you a good man."

Rithisak smiled and took his leave. Anong followed Lokesvara to the washrooms and then to the kitchen where the monk served her tea, noodle soup, and her choice of fruits.

"You, also, have come a long way to see me," said Lokesvara, seating himself at the table next to Anong. "Where do you come from? And why are you here? Leave nothing out."

So Anong told the kindly old man her story, relating how her father had sold her to the people who ran that house in Thailand where she had worked for four years. She told what men had demanded of her, and she told of the accident that had freed her. She spoke of the journey down the Mekong to Phnom Penh, finding the temple in the capital, and the monks who had helped her. She spoke highly of Rithisak and his skills as a boatman. She said she hoped he had earned merit by his actions.

"Do you know what taking holy vows demands?" asked Lokesvara.

"It means I must lose my hair," said Anong.

"It means you must lose yourself to find yourself," said the old monk. "You must give up all worldly goods and desires."

"That is easy," said Anong. "I have no worldly goods. And I have no desires."

"That may seem true now, but you are young yet. Someday you may want children. Do you like children?"

"I am a child myself. I like children better than grown-ups."

"To become a nun, you must agree to follow the gurudhamma, eight rules established by the Buddha. You can begin today as a sramaneri, a small renunciate. You may keep your hair while you study. You will remain a sramaneri for at least a year. If it is your true desire to enter the Sangha, the religious community, you may then become a probationary nun, a sikkhamana, for at least two years of additional study with a bhikkhunni and myself. It is then that you must give up your hair. You will follow the first six precepts of the gurudhamma. If, after two years of study, you still wish to remain with us you may do so. You are always free to choose to remain or to leave. If you decide to stay, you may seek to be ordained when you reach twenty years of age."

"Why must I wait so long?"

"So you may know your heart. First, you must learn to refrain from killing any living thing, refrain from stealing, refrain from unchastity, refrain from lying, refrain from taking intoxicants, refrain from taking food after noon, refrain from dancing or entertainment, refrain from wearing perfume or cosmetics, refrain from sitting on chairs or sleeping on soft beds, and refrain from accepting money. Can you do that?"

"I can."

"Good. Now tell me more about that house where you lived. Where is it exactly? Who was the proprietor? I would put an end to the suffering of so many women and children. But I must know more before I can do anything."

"It is a large house, built like many in the west, of cinderblocks and cedar. It has ten bedrooms and two other rooms on the main floor. But the girls all lived in one big room in the cellar where it was often wet from the rains. There were snakes that came in through cracks in the foundation, and sometimes girls were bitten and died from snakebite. We were always glad to be out of that room, even if it meant servicing men."

"What about the people running the place? What can you tell me about them?"

"There was a Thai woman who told us what to do and showed us how. We called her Maa. There was a man in the house all of the time guarding us, and there were two men who came regularly to examine the girls. One was a medical doctor. The other liked to put his hands on us and make us do things. They were all Thai. Another man, an American, came twice a year to look the place over. He never touched us, but he made us take our clothes off and display our bodies. Maa and the other men treated him with great respect. They called him Mister Right."

"And where was this house located?"

"Near Kong Chiam in the east of Thailand. Near where the Mun flows into the Mekong."

"I have been to Wat Tham Khu Ha Sawan on the hill above the river. It is a beautiful place."

"Not to me. We were seldom allowed to leave the house, and never the grounds. We never visited the temple nor saw the beauty of the countryside. And inside that house, there was only ugliness."

"You were beaten?"

"The men who came to the house could do with us whatever they wanted. Some of the men wanted to hurt us. And they did."

"And did Maa beat you?"

"All the time."

"And the men who worked in the house?"

"Yes."

"To do such a thing to a child is unconscionable. The people who did this to you will have to endure the same suffering eightfold in the afterlife. It is the law of karma. They have brought much suffering on themselves by their actions."

"Do you really believe that?"

"Yes. I know it to be true."

How could he be certain? wondered Anong. He sounded so certain, almost as if he really knew. But how could anybody be certain of what happened after death?

"Now that you have eaten and we have talked, I will show you to the women's quarters and introduce you to our doun ji. Then I must leave you. I have work to do."

"Thank you, Master," said Anong, making a high wais.

"Namaste," said Lokesvara, returning the wais at the same height.

* * *

Deb knew that many of the women who disappeared were simply runaways. They couldn't stand remaining with their spouses or their jobs or their children one more day, but they didn't have the resources—economic or emotional—to get out of their situations and relationships any other way. So they simply ran away and started a new life somewhere else. Or they committed suicide, usually with an overdose of pills or slit wrists.

Some men ran away, too, when their lives became unbearable, and they either started new lives somewhere else or committed suicide by putting a gun in their mouths and pulling the trigger. But there were other men who simply went crazy and picked up a gun or another weapon like an axe or a hammer and killed their entire family or they killed their bosses and co-workers or they took out people in a shopping mall or a movie theater or a restaurant or a school before killing themselves. Women seldom did that. They might kill themselves, but they rarely killed others.

When life became unbearable, people looked for, and often found, ways to escape.

The FBI maintained separate lists of missing persons and missing children, but those lists contained mostly Americans. Deb suspected most, if not all, of the women recruited, willingly or unwillingly, to service men in training camps for a private army would come from other countries. Some might be runaways, but most were bought-and-paid-for sex-slaves.

Deb knew from personal observation that women, especially young women and girl children, were often considered property to be bought and sold in various parts of the less-developed world. Women had few rights in some of the countries Deb had served in abroad, and girl children were often considered a burden on large families with more mouths to feed than available food. That was slowly changing, thanks to herculean efforts by the United Nations and other agencies or civil rights watchdog groups. But there were still dozens of places in Africa, Asia, the Middle-East, South America, and Eastern Europe where women and children were sold and traded like commodities. Those were the places Deb would search first, although she doubted few women or children were ever reported missing to the authorities.

But if WLSCTC's parent companies and subsidiaries were buying or abducting women, those women had to be housed and fed somewhere. And that somewhere or somewheres had to have access to transportation facilities that allowed men from the secret camps to visit on a regular basis. It was obvious there were no women near the one camp she knew existed in Pakistan, and Deb was willing to bet the women were kept safely locked away where men from the camps could get to them only with special arrangements.

WLSCTC owned or leased cargo planes capable of flying groups of men anyplace in the world, and they had secured landing rights at airports in many remote places, some Deb had never even heard of before. Two of the places were less than fifty miles apart, and WLSCTC paid exorbitant fees to maintain those landing rights. One was Pakse International Airport in Laos, and the other was Ubon Ratchathani Airport in Thailand.

Now why would they want landing rights in such far-away and strategically unimportant places? And why would they pay so much if they didn't use those places on a regular basis?

Deb drew a line on the situation map between Dubai and Pakse and one between Islamabad and Pakse. Pakse was on the east side of the Mekong River, just across the border from Thailand. Ubon Ratchathani was about 45 miles southwest of Pakse as the crow flies. She drew a line between the two places. Somewhere along that line was a primary destination for men aboard WLSCTC flights.

Thailand was notorious for providing women to service foreign men, and Deb suspected WLSCTC had established rest and relaxation facilities in eastern Thailand near the Laotian border. American servicemen had used Thailand as a center for R & R during the Vietnam Conflict, and Thailand had remained a haven for westerners seeking sex—especially sex with underage girls—ever since.

Deb told Eddie Morsay she needed information about all flights in and out of the two suspect airports, and Eddie did some magic with the computers and obtained lists of WLSCTC flights from Islamabad, Dubai, and Mafikeng in South Africa, near the Botswanian border.

Deb went back to the situation map and drew a red line between Mafikeng, which used to be called Mmabatko and was still called that on her map, and Thailand.

There were monthly flights from Islamabad and Mafikeng to Thailand, and semiannual flights between Dubai and Thailand.

What was the connection? Surely, there was one.

CHAPTER FIVE

Lokesvara asked the Lone Ranger to travel to Thailand in spirit form and visit the house where Anong had been held captive. If there were other girls in that house that were being mistreated, Lokesvara would intervene to stop their suffering.

The Ranger sat in lotus and sealed his body against intrusion. Then he left his body behind and traveled instantly to Kong Chiam in eastern Thailand and looked for the house Anong had described. He found the house about a mile out into the countryside, hidden near the edge of a forest.

It was a western-style house with solid cinderblock and wood walls and a real roof. And the entire house was air-conditioned. There were a dozen or more rooms on the main floor, all but one of them with beds. The room without a bed was larger than the others, and it had a bar and tables and was designed for entertaining.

All of the rooms were occupied, some with several men and women at the same time. Most of the girls looked far too young to be having sex with any man, much less full-grown westerners.

There were twice as many girls locked in the cellar, and two of the girls lying on mats on the floor were severely injured.

One had a broken arm and a broken nose, and the other had bruises and burns all over her body. Both were crying, and the injuries looked very fresh and recent.

While the Ranger watched, two burly men tramped down the wooden stairs into the cellar and picked the girls up and carried them up the stairs. They took the girls out into the woods, dropped them on the ground, and slit the throats of both girls as if they were sows. Then they fed the bodies one at a time into a wood chipper that ground them up and spit out their remains into plastic garbage bags. If the Ranger had been in corporeal form, he would have slit the throats of both those men. Only the fact that he was a spirit and could not act in the physical world saved him from breaking his vow to refrain from killing another sentient being. Some men deserved to be killed, and the Ranger didn't consider those two men sentient beings.

He had seen more than enough to report back to Lokesvara that Anong had indeed told the truth.

In the blink of an eye, the Ranger was back in his body at Angkor Wat. He immediately sought out the Lama and told him what he had seen in Kong Chiam.

"We must stop them," said the old monk. Lokesvara rose from his carpet and walked to the table in the corner. When he returned, he handed the Ranger three of the sacred relics that had been on that table. One was the Kris, a dagger or short sword with jagged edges that looked like a crawling snake or a bolt of lightning, depending on how the blade was held. Another was the

Vajra, two symmetrical spheres of five prongs and a compass point at each end to direct polarized energy, joined together by an ornate cylindrical shaft. The Vajra was said to have been created of two strong metals by Tvastar, the weapons-maker of the gods. The third was a coiled rope of braided hemp and cotton—a magic lasso or pasha noose—similar to ropes Sufi Faqirs used to climb to the heavens and disappear from sight. These were the tools of Vajrapani.

The old man walked back to the table one more time, and now he returned with a shining sword which had also been forged by Tvastar. It was the Sword of Enlightenment that cut down ignorance and duality. When Manjusri wielded the sword, it broke into flames bright as the sun that temporarily blinded any adversary who gazed upon it.

"We shall go as Manjusri and Vajrapani," said Lokesvara, his voice already changing, becoming deeper, more powerful. "I would not have you break your vows. If any killing is to be done, let Vajrapani and Manjusri do it."

The Ranger called Vajrapani to manifest in the physical realm, and Vajrapani instantly became real. Where moments ago the five foot-eleven inch Ranger had stood, now the seven foot Vajrapani stood. He held the Vajra in his right hand, the Kris and Lasso in his left.

So, too, had Lokesvara disappeared and Manjusri appeared in his place. This was not the visage of the youthful Manjusri, sweet and innocent and beautiful to behold, who carried the wisdom sutras in one hand and a lotus in the other. This was the visage of the wrathful Manjusri, ferocious beyond measure, and a dharmapala who met evil measure for measure. He held Chandrahrasa, the flaming Sword of Enlightenment, in his right hand, and the Book of Judgment in his left.

And then they blinked out of existence in Angkor and into existence inside the house in Kong Chiam.

"What the hell?" asked the startled woman standing next to the bar when the two giants suddenly appeared in front of her. "Who the fuck are *you*?"

"We have come to free the women and children imprisoned in this house," roared Manjusri.

"Phut! Kam! Get in here!" she yelled.

"If you value your life," warned Manjusri, "do not interfere."

Two men entered the room only to be stopped dead in their tracks when Manjusri held up his flaming sword to fill the room with the light of pure reason.

"They are the men who killed the girls," said Vajrapani as he recognized the men from the Ranger's memory. "They deserve to die the same way the girls died."

"Why did you kill those children?" Manjusri asked the two men.

"They were useless," said one of the men, compelled by the power of the flaming sword to speak truthfully. "There's plenty more where they came from."

"If you promise you will never again hurt another person," said Manjusri, "You may leave now and live to atone for your sins. Speak truly, for the sword will know if you lie."

Though he couldn't see because the light of the sword had blinded him, one of the men reached inside his coat pocket and brought out a Sig-Sauer automatic pistol.

And Vajrapani gestured with the Vajra and a bolt of lightning appeared as if from nowhere and struck the man squarely in his chest, stopping his heart and frying the surrounding flesh.

The other man made no move either to leave or to attack. He looked petrified.

But the woman swung a liter bottle at where she had last seen the intruders standing, and Manjusri struck the bottle with his blade and the bottle shattered. Shards of glass sliced the woman's hands.

"Enough!" said Manjusri, and his voice was as hard and firm as a diamond. "Bring the women and children here. All of them. He lowered the sword so they could see. "You," he addressed the man, "bring the children from the cellar. It will be your first act of repentance."

The man left the room and they could hear him clomping down the cellar steps like a zombie. "And you, Maa," he addressed the woman, "bring the women and children from the other rooms."

"They're with men," protested the woman. "I dare not interrupt. The men will kill me."

"Then we shall interrupt them for you," said Manjusri. "You will come with us and observe."

Manjusri and Vajrapani went into each of the rooms, and the reluctant Maa followed to observe the bloodbath. Not a single man in any of those rooms escaped his fate that day.

Fortunately, the girls were blinded by the flaming sword and they did not see the sword or the Kris do their work, slicing through flesh and bone like butter. But Maa was allowed to see, and she witnessed each of the decapitations as they occurred. It was a sight that would remain in her memory forever.

When all of the girls were assembled in the barroom, Manjusri turned to the evil man and the misguided woman and said, "Today you have seen the fruit of your actions. You have much to atone for."

"Who are you?" asked the woman. She had seen animals slaughtered like that, but never humans. "Who gave you the right to walk in here and kill everyone in sight?"

"You did," said the Bodhisattva. "I am Manjusri, and your past actions called out for retribution. Your evil deeds brought me here."

"Manjusri is only a myth, a legend. Something made up to frighten children. You don't exist."

"But Manjusri does exist. Have you yet any doubt that I am real?"

"No," agreed the woman, and she bowed down and made a wais above her head. "I have no doubt."

Vajrapani uncoiled the Lasso and asked each of the girls to grab onto the rope. Then he blinked out of existence in that house and took the girls back to Angkor with him.

"Do no more evil," Manjusri directed the man and the woman. "You already have much to atone for in this life. Do not make me come back."

And then he, too, was gone, leaving the man and the woman alone in the house with fifteen corpses.

* * *

Earl Wright was furious about something. Randy had returned to WLSCTC headquarters ready to leave for training, but Wright was too preoccupied to complete Randy's orientation.

"Of course, I don't believe her," Randy overheard Wright tell someone on the phone.

"Clean up the mess. The man and woman, too. Burn the house down with everyone inside."

Randy waited patiently outside Wright's office for hours while Wright rescheduled flights for personnel. Instead of sending men to Thailand, they would be brought to America. Edie would have to take up the slack, Wright told someone else on the phone, until another house could be built and staffed. She wouldn't like it but she would have to live with it. Randy heard enough to know Wright was worried.

"I think it's an isolated incident," Wright told yet another person on the phone. "Yes, I know about Ramsey. No, he didn't. How could he? Ramsey's dead. Yes, we've stepped up security. INSCOM is involved? Deb Johnson? Never heard of her. No, I'll take care of it. Yes, I'm sure. Personally? You want me to do it personally? Don't worry. I'll see it's done."

After Wright finished with the phone calls, he called Randy into his office. "I have a job for you to do while you're here," Wright said. "Before you go for advanced training. It's a little something I think you'll like."

"You're calling the shots," said Randy.

"That's right, I am. C'mon. Let me introduce you to some of the guys you'll work with. Then I'll brief all of you on your mission."

Wright took Randy down the hall to a room labeled "Security." Inside were a dozen or so desks with computers, a wall of video monitors that displayed various views of the outside and inside of the building, and a group of men, some in security guard uniforms and some in suits. He asked the men in suits to follow him to the briefing room.

"It's been brought to my attention," began Wright, "that we have a security problem. Her name is Deb Johnson and she works for INSCOM at Fort Belvoir. I want you to dig up everything you can on her and have it on my desk no later than 1900 hours today. Now let me introduce one of our new recruits.

Randy, stand up. This is Randy Edwards. He saw combat as a Marine in Afghanistan, and he's been to Edie's club."

A titter went through the group. Wright raised a hand and the room became silent. "I want LeRoy, Cal, and Tom to work with Randy on this. Four of you big, strong guys ought to be able to take care of one little woman. We'll meet back here at 1930 hours and I'll give you your orders. Meanwhile, start digging up dirt on Deb Johnson. I want to know everything about her. Where does she live? Is she married? Does she live alone? What kind of car does she drive? You know the drill. LeRoy, take Randy down to the armory and fix him up. Cal, you're the designated driver. Draw an old beater from the motor pool, something untraceable. Tom, you pick up pre-paid cell phones. I want the four of you dressed like bums, the kind of shit that pedals crack on street corners. If anyone sees you, they'll think you're looking to score drugs. I'll see you back here at 7:30. Any questions?"

"Yeah," said Cal. "We gotta kill her quick?"

"You can have some fun with her first. Any other questions? No? Then get on with it."

LeRoy Salter was an ex-SEAL, lean and wiry, full of nervous energy. He paced back and forth while an armorer fitted Randy with a holster harness and two Smith and Wesson Military and Police 9 millimeter automatics. Then they walked to the next room where they were both clothed in jeans, black t-shirts, and sneakers, plus an old Army field jacket to hide the weapons and harness.

"Where you from?" asked LeRoy.

"Minneapolis," said Randy.

"Me, I'm from middle-of-nowhere Tennessee. I joined the Navy to see the world. I did, too. I joined the Navy and I saw parts of the world I didn't like. So I got out of the Navy. But I couldn't find a job in Tennessee. So I took this job. It's a lot better than the Navy."

"You ever killed anyone before, LeRoy?"

"Yeah. And you?"

"Yeah."

"I never killed a woman before, though. That ought to be fun."

"Yeah," said Randy.

At 7:30, they met back in the briefing room and Wright gave each of them pictures of Deb Johnson. She was a cute blonde, older than what most of the men liked, but Johnson was shapely and LeRoy said she might still be fun to fuck even if she was over-the-hill old. The plan was to go to her apartment in Alexandria, break in, rape her, and kill her. They would plant drugs around the apartment and make it look like some whacked-out druggies broke in to rob her and decided to gang-rape her instead. The idea, according to Wright, was to make Johnson's death appear completely spontaneous and not a premeditated hit on a military officer.

"Our man at Belvoir says she works late. It will take you two hours to get from here to Alexandria. You should be there shortly after she gets home. Or just before."

"What if she's not there when we break in?" asked Tom.

"Then wait for her in the apartment. She'll get there eventually."

They left Richmond at 2000 hours, 8:00 PM civilian time. Their car was an old Oldsmobile that the owner had reported to the insurance company as stolen after he sold it to a drug dealer for a few hundred dollars worth of crack cocaine.

They were in Alexandria a little before 10. After circling the block several times to check out the neighborhood, LeRoy, Tom, and Randy got out of the Olds just around the corner from the apartment building, an old three-story brick on the west side of town two blocks from U. S. Highway 1. LeRoy ordered Cal to stay with the car.

Deb lived on the third floor. LeRoy picked the lock on the outside downstairs door, and the three men rushed inside and looked for stairs. At ten o'clock on a weeknight, the building was pretty quiet. They saw no one and no one saw them as they snuck into the stairwell and climbed two flights of stairs.

Randy now faced a major dilemma. Bill Ramsey had informed Randy that Deb Johnson worked for the same people that had sent Bill to Pakistan, and Bill Ramsey didn't want to see Deb hurt in any way. In fact, Bill had threatened to interfere if Randy attempted to rape Deb Johnson. "As much as I want you to be accepted by this group so I can infiltrate their camp in Pakistan," Bill had whispered insistently inside Randy's mind, "I can't and won't let you hurt a fellow Army officer. I'll take over your body completely. Then I'll force you to stop LeRoy and Tom. Or die trying."

"We'll both die," said Randy. "If I die, you'll die too."

"I'm already dead," said Bill. "If I die again, it's no big deal."

"It's a big deal to me," said Randy. "I'm not dead yet."

"We can make this easier on both of us if you just stay out of the way completely and let me handle things my way. If you try to interfere with what I'm doing, things could get messy."

"I really don't want to kill a woman," admitted Randy. "And I don't want to be part of a gang rape."

"Then it's settled. If you don't fight me on this, I think I can stop them."

"How?"

"When they jump the girl, I'll jump LeRoy. If I can chop his carotid hard enough, I can break his neck or cut off blood flow to his brain so he'll go out like a light when the switch is flipped. Then I'll do the same to Tom. If we time it right, we can make this work."

Deb's apartment was the first door on the right at the top of the stairs. LeRoy expertly picked the door lock, plus the dead-bolt lock, within half a minute, and LeRoy opened the door just a crack to peek in. They heard the woman talking to someone, but it sounded like a one-way conversation. She was probably alone and chatting on the telephone.

LeRoy signaled that they should wait until she ended the call before bursting into the apartment. He put the picks away and drew his pistol from the holster inside his jacket.

Tom and Randy drew their pistols, too. LeRoy would go in first, followed by Tom and then Randy. LeRoy would wave the gun in the woman's face, make her take off all her clothes, and force her face-down on the floor. Tom would rape her first, then LeRoy, and then Randy. LeRoy said he didn't mind sloppy seconds. They all had condoms, and they all wore gloves. They would leave their clothes on, unzip their flies, and whip it out. When they were finished, they'd beat the girl to death with something they'd find inside the room like a fireplace poker or maybe a vase or a broom handle, anything handy that would do the job.

LeRoy licked his lips and fidgeted impatiently. He looked like he was pumped with adrenalin. He was ready to go.

Finally, they heard the woman say, "I love you, too." Then she stopped talking and they waited two minutes more just to be sure she was off the phone before bursting into the room.

LeRoy moved too fast for Bill to reach him, and Bill had to settle for slamming the side of one hand hard against Tom's neck instead of LeRoy's. Randy heard a snapping sound and knew Bill had broken Tom's neck with the force of a single blow. LeRoy was already pointing his pistol at the girl's head, and he seemed far more interested in holding her attention than what might be happening behind him.

But when Bill tried to take LeRoy, the ex-SEAL spun and kicked, barely missing Randy's groin but catching Randy's hip with the rubber heel of the running shoe. Randy felt excruciating pain, and he nearly dropped his gun as he was knocked completely off balance and fell sideways to the floor.

LeRoy might have killed Randy then if he'd pulled the trigger fast enough. But the Johnson woman kicked out at LeRoy the instant his back was turned, and LeRoy's first shot went wild as the girl's right boot slammed hard into the small of his back, catching him completely unawares, pushing him forward into Randy. Bill squeezed the trigger of Randy's gun three times. The bullets entered LeRoy's stomach and exited out his back, barely missing the girl. LeRoy jerked in the air as the nine millimeter rounds literally blew him away.

Now the girl was coming for Randy. She was still fully dressed in the battle uniform she had worn to work, and she looked like she could do some serious damage with those desert boots. He didn't want to hurt her, so he threw the gun away and tried to protect his face with his hands.

"I'm Bill Ramsey!" Randy heard himself shout. "I'm on your side, Deb!"

Deb stopped the kick before it connected with the side of Randy's head. "You can't be Bill Ramsey. Bill Ramsey's dead," she said. "And, besides, you're much too young to be Major Ramsey."

"Is that what Eddie and the Colonel told you, Deb? That I'm an old man?"

Those names seemed to resonate with her, and he saw her boots back off a step or two.

"When no one heard from Ramsey after three days, the Colonel listed Ramsey as Missing in Action and Presumed Dead in Pakistan. If you're Bill Ramsey, how did you get here? And how come you look twenty years younger?"

"You wouldn't believe me if I told you."

"Try me," she said. "I've seen plenty of things I didn't want to believe, things I thought were impossible but weren't. Try me, or I'll punt your head across the room like a football."

"All right. I'll try. I was killed on a mountain in Pakistan five weeks ago. My body died, but my spirit didn't. Someone, he said he was a spirit guide named Vajrapani, showed me how to transfer my disincarnate spirit into a new body. I know it sounds impossible, Deb. But it's God's honest truth. I swear it is. Cross my heart and hope to die."

Deb smiled at the irony of his choice of words. "I believe you, Major," she said, sounding like she actually did. She backed down completely. "I really do believe you."

"You do?" asked Bill. "I'm not sure I believe it myself."

"I believe you because I've met Vajrapani. I worked with Vajrapani and the Ranger a few years ago."

"You did?"

"It seems like a long time ago now, and I've been too busy putting my life back together to think about it much. Are you okay? Can you stand?"

"My hip feels dislocated," said Randy.

"Then let me help you heal." Deb knelt and placed her left hand on top of Randy's head like a priest blessing a parishioner and touched his hip with her right hand. Suddenly, the pain was gone and Randy felt his hip bones slip back into place. The torn ligaments tingled as they began to mend.

"What the fuck did you just do?" Randy asked.

"I transferred a small part of the healing energy of the physical universe directly into your body," said Deb. "It might take a week to heal completely, but the healing has begun."

"How did you do that?"

"It's something I learned from the Ranger's mentor, a monk named Lokesvara. Everyone can do it if they know how. But it takes several lifetimes to learn, and few people can recall what they learned yesterday, much less several lifetimes ago."

"But you can?"

"Yes," she said. "I can."

"But you're just an ordinary woman. A soldier like me. You're not a healer. How the hell did you do that? I can't do that. Neither can anyone else. Not even a doctor. What makes you so special?"

"I was a healer in a past life. I'll tell you all about it sometime. But right now I want you to tell me what you learned in Pakistan. How many men do they have there? How well organized are they? Who gives them funding? What are they training for?"

"I'd guess a thousand or more men in a camp constructed in a long valley with a river running through it, hidden from satellite observation with camouflage and electronic countermeasures. They have effective command and control, and they are all undergoing intensive training for combat. More than that I don't know yet, but I still have a chance to find out. I'm going back there in my new body to learn more."

"Who sent the three of you to kill me? Why?"

"WLSCTC. We were ordered to rape and kill you. It seems WLSCTC has someone inside INSCOM who says you're a threat. They think you're getting too close. Something happened to one of their facilities in Thailand. They think you're responsible in some way. You better watch your back."

"I will."

Bill got to his feet. "I'm taking one of the dead men, LeRoy there, out of here with me. That'll be my cover for the blood on my clothes. I'll leave Tom, the other one, for you to handle after I'm gone. Report a break-in and attempted robbery to the police. Take LeRoy's gun and wait until I'm on the stairs. Then shoot Tom a half-dozen times. Fill him full of holes. Cal's down in the car and he'll hear the shots. I'll tell him you were waiting for us with a gun and caught us by surprise. LeRoy got hit bad and Tom stayed to shoot it out with you. But Tom ordered me to get LeRoy out while he covered me. So I did."

"You think they'll buy that?"

"They might. I'm new. I did what Tom told me. It's worth a chance."

The cell phone in Randy's pocket began to vibrate. "Cal's calling to see what's taking us so long. I better get out of here before he comes up those stairs." Bill hoisted LeRoy's body onto Randy's back in a modified fireman's carry, and headed for the door. His hip hurt, but it held up to the added weight. "Count to ten and start shooting," he said. "Then call the cops."

Cal had the car waiting in front of the building, the motor running and the passenger door and rear door open. Bill dropped LeRoy onto the back seat and climbed in next to him as gunfire erupted in the apartment building. "Drive!" he ordered.

"What about Tom?"

"He's hit, too. He's giving us covering fire to get away. He got hit bad. I don't think he'll make it."

"You hit?"

"Kicked in the hip. Knocked me down. Tom ordered me to get LeRoy out of there. LeRoy's gut shot."

"What happened?"

"The girl was waiting for us with a gun. LeRoy went in first and took three rounds to the belly. Tom went second and couldn't get a clear shot at the girl. I went in and the girl came out of nowhere and she tried to kick me in the balls before I could shoot. She missed and hit my hip instead. Knocked me to the floor and made me drop my gun. I think my hip was dislocated. But I pushed the joint back into place so I could walk. Hurts like a son of bitch."

"You let a woman do that to you?"

"She came out of nowhere, man. Slammed me with her boot before I saw her. I went down and she would have kicked my face in if Tom hadn't jumped her. She knows hand-to-hand and karate and Aikido and all that sort of shit. Believe me, she ain't no ordinary woman. Tom ordered me to get LeRoy out of there and said he'd give us covering fire. So I picked up LeRoy and left. I saw Tom get hit as I was going out the door."

"We got to go back," said Cal, pulling over to the curb. "Maybe we can still get the girl. Maybe Tom's still alive. We gotta *do* something! Wright will have our asses if we leave the girl alive."

"Don't be a fool," said Bill. "She already called the cops. Hear those sirens? They're coming this way. They'll be here before we can get up those steps. You want to talk to the cops?"

"Shit!" Cal said and put the car back into gear. He pulled away from the curb, tires squealing, picked up U. S. 1 south, and drove all the way back to Richmond without saying another word.

They reached Richmond shortly after midnight, and a doctor immediately pronounced LeRoy long expired from gunshot wounds to the stomach. The doctor took a good look at Randy's hip, and he said it was badly bruised but Randy would live. He gave Randy some pills for the pain.

Wright called Randy and Cal into the briefing room and questioned them both until the sun came up. Wright didn't want to believe Randy's story, but he had no other explanation. Either the Johnson woman was paranoid, or someone had tipped her off to the operation.

It didn't make sense, Wright said. If the Johnson woman knew she was about to be killed, wouldn't she have someone else in the apartment with her? The police maybe, or some guys from the Army? Why did she wait for them alone? Did she have a death wish? It didn't make any sense at all.

"She was on the phone when we got there," said Randy. "We waited until she was off the phone before we went through the door. I think whoever she was talking to must have tipped her off. I don't think she had time to bring in anyone from outside."

"Then we have an even bigger problem than I thought," said Wright. "We have someone inside INSCOM, but INSCOM must have someone inside this building who tipped her off. That's problematic. Real problematic."

"It wasn't us," said Cal. "We only had the phones you gave us. Besides, we were together all the time. I can vouch for Randy, and he can vouch for me. We didn't make no calls."

"You made one," said Randy. "You called me when I was carrying LeRoy down the steps."

"Yeah. But you didn't answer."

"How could I? I had my hands full with LeRoy."

"We'll check all the phones and cell phones in the building. No one leaves."

"What about the guys who got off duty last night?" asked Randy. "Could one of them have called after he left the building?"

"We'll check it out," said Wright. "You two will have to stay here for a few days. Security will show you to your temporary quarters. If everything you told me checks out, we'll return you to duty."

Randy and Cal were taken to a small room with two made-up bunks and an attached bathroom. There were two security men posted outside the door, and the door was locked.

The next morning Wright informed them that Tom had been killed in Johnson's apartment, and the police were investigating the break in at Johnson's apartment as an attempted robbery and rape. Wright kept them locked up for two more days. Then he sent Randy to Pakistan and Cal back to work in the security office.

CHAPTER SIX

Anong was happy to see her "sisters" again. Lokesvara and another man had brought them all to the women's quarters and had them examined by a woman doctor. Several of the girls showed signs of being repeatedly beaten, and all had visible scars on parts of their bodies where there should be no scars.

Lokesvara and the other man gently questioned the girls about the house and their captors, telling the girls that they were safe now here in Cambodia and they could choose to remain here or return to wherever they had originally come from. No one need ever know what the girls had been through, and they were free to begin a new life. Only one of the girls chose to return home. Lokesvara paid for her way by bus back to Thailand. He was able to obtain passports and identity papers for all of the girls. They were now considered official residents and students of the monastery school.

Anong had never gone to school before, but she quickly discovered she possessed a natural knack for learning. Within a few months, she felt comfortable enough with the Cambodian script to attempt to read some of the many books in the monastery library. She loved to read, and she buried her nose in books for hours on end.

The rainy season was beginning and, despite dark skies and torrential downpours, Anong began to love life again. She wanted to stay here and live and learn forever. It was as if she had lived here before in a past life. She felt she knew the language and customs like a native of Siem Reap. She felt like this was home. The wet mud even smelled like home.

Memories came flooding back to her now of a time long ago when she had been a full-grown woman living in Cambodia. She had full breasts, and she wore splendid jewels—opals and rubies and jade—in her ears, in her hair, and around her neck. The year was the eight hundred and second year of the Common Era, and Jayavarman Ibis was conquering and unifying all of Kambu, the land of the Khmer. Jayavarman called in from India a Brahman ascetic named Hiranyadama, the most powerful magician of the time, to use special magic to aid Jayavarman in uniting the country. They met at the Ku Len Hills, atop sacred Phnom Kulen, which some called "Mountain of Lychees," but once was called Mahendrparvata, the Mountain of Indra. It was also said that Mount Kulen was akin to Mount Meru, the most sacred mountain of Hindu scriptures. More than a hundred craftsmen were instructed to carve symbolic lingams and yonis from the sandstone of the sacred mountain, and plant the genitalia along the bottom of the Siem Reap River and its tributaries where running water passing over the carved symbols of male and female polarities might generate great power for Jayavarman. Two years later, Jayavarman Ibis was crowned Jayavarman II, king of the newly united Khmer empire and ruler of all Kambuja. He attributed his victories to the magic of Hiranyadama. Jayavarman asked Hiranyadama to stay on as a spiritual advisor and to perform the rites that legitimized his kingship.

Jayavarman kept many courtesans in his palace near Phnom Kulen, but the most beautiful woman of them all was the dancer Anong, and she was accorded special favor as the king's concubine. Her name then was Rukmini, and she was said to be as beautiful and talented as Lakshmi, wife of Vishnu.

Hiranyadama had lived a lonely life wandering the forests of India as an ascetic, learning the secrets of nature from the heart of the Great Mother herself, and gathering sacred herbs from which he concocted magical preparations of great power. When he saw Rukmini, he was smitten with lust for her. He had to have her, to possess her, to own her.

So blinded with her beauty was he that Hiranyadama forgot entirely his vows of poverty, chastity, and ahimsa. He devised a plan to kill the king and run off with Rukmini. During the great festival celebrating the king's ascension to the throne, Hiranyadama would infuse the fruit drinks with a potent herb that would kill any and all who imbibed. So, too, would Hiranyadama wear a special fragrance that would make him irresistible to Rukmini.

On the night of the coronation festival, Hiranyadama was seated on the carpet with Jayavarman and his consorts, a position of honor for his invaluable help in securing the throne. Rukmini, more beautiful than ever, was seated next to the king.

"A toast," said the king, "to the greatest magician in the world, Hiranyadama the Magnificent." As Rukmini raised her cup to drink of the poisoned liquid, Hiranyadama bumped her hand and spilled her drink all over her blood-red sari, soaking the silk and making her nipples clearly visible beneath the thin material.

"I beg your pardon, Princess," said Hiranyadama. "I am so clumsy tonight."

"An accident," said Rukmini, wiping the spilled drink from the front of her dress.

"Here, my sweet," said the king, "you must drink. Take mine."

"No," said Hiranyadama, trying desperately to swat the proffered cup from the lips of his beloved. But he was too late. Rukmini drained the cup, smiled her most beautiful smile at both the king and the magician, and collapsed into death.

All around the gathering those who had participated in the toast were falling like flies at the end of summer.

"What devilment is this?" demanded the king. "This must be the magician's doing. Guards! Slay him!"

Whether those memories were true memories of a past life or memories of stories Anong had read in books mattered little to the adolescent girl. They seemed perfectly real to her, and that was all that mattered.

She had other images, too, come to her in dreams. She was a man in one life. An old woman in another.

She knew the pain and joy of giving birth to a child, the love of a man who was completely devoted to her and she to him, the agony of losing her loved ones in war, the contentment of grandchildren. She grew wise beyond her years, and she knew she was in the place she was meant to be. If home was where the heart was, Anong had come home.

From time to time Anong talked with Lokesvara or the monk known as Vajrapani, and she was grateful for their friendship and support. Vajrapani taught her to speak and read English and he told her tales of America. She wanted to go to America someday. Just to visit. Then she would come back to Angkor. She belonged here. This was home. This was the home she wished she'd had when she was a child living with a dysfunctional family that didn't love her, didn't want her, that abused and beat her whenever they felt like it, that had sold her into slavery for four long years.

But Anong no longer thought of herself as a child. She was a woman now. She had begun her menstruation, and her breasts were budding. Even the duon chees treated her like a woman. They gave her women's work to do when her studies permitted. And they even let her listen as they gossiped about the monks, which they weren't supposed to do but they did incessantly any way.

That's how she learned that Lokesvara and Vajrapani were more than mere mortals. They were reincarnations of two of the Great Bodhisattvas. She had read about the Bodhisattva Manjusri and the Bodhisattva Vajrapani in books.

She couldn't imagine Lokesvara as anything other than a kindly old man. Wise, yes, and extremely compassionate. But Manjusri was said to be a mighty warrior, or so all the books claimed. Manjusri was the fierce Yamantaka, the slayer of death. How could an old man like Lokesvara be a mighty warrior? It didn't seem possible.

Vajrapani, on the other hand, looked precisely like the fierce warrior Anong imagined. He was big and strong, and Anong had seen him running laps between the stone wall and the moat every morning. The nuns claimed he was an American, an ex-Army Ranger, and he had appeared unexpectedly one day two years ago and asked to become a monk. He spoke several languages fluently, and he could recite the Sutras from memory before he even began his studies. It wasn't long before the other monks accepted him as a brother, though some remained jealous of the special relationship he had with Lokesvara.

It was rumored that the American had killed many men, some even after he took his vows.

Anong knew him only as a kind and compassionate teacher, an older brother who would look after her and keep her safe. Lokesvara was like the grandfather she had never known.

But she began to read about the Eight Great Bodhisattvas. She tried to learn all she could about Manjusri and Vajrapani. And that's when she began to remember who she really was, and that was when her childhood ended forever.

* * *

Randy Edwards was in the last cycle of advanced training in Pakistan when the shit hit the fan.

Someone at INSCOM, probably Deb Johnson or Eddie Morsay, had uncovered one of WLSCTC's minor sources of financing. Billions of American dollars in unaccounted cash that had been stolen from Saddam Hussein's secret stashes in Iraq during the war and had disappeared, along with millions of dollars from U. S. Commanders' emergency contingency funds, reappeared in WLSCTC overseas bank accounts. That money had been diverted into financing that expanded WLSCTC's secret operations, and a small portion was also being used to bribe local officials in Pakistan and elsewhere. Though similar thefts were now going on in Afghanistan, and had previously taken place in Bosnia, they were mere drops in the bucket compared to the money taken out of Iraq. More money went out than came in these days, and WLSCTC was rapidly running out of money.

When INSCOM asked the Justice Department to freeze some of WLSCTC's known accounts, the company was forced to dip into what remained of their hidden cash to remain fully functional. Much of the money used for bribes that hadn't already been used up had to be diverted to other uses.

And without their monthly bribes, the strongmen of Pakistan demanded the men in the training camp leave the country immediately.

"Listen up," said a senior NCO named Richard Sutton. Sutton was an ex-Ranger, tall and muscular. He had a scar across his entire forehead like the top of his head had been blown off—probably by an IED—and sewn back on. Sutton was known affectionately by all the men in his command as "Dickhead," a reference to his first name and the scar on his forehead. But no one dared call him Dickhead to his face, because Sutton would have torn the head off of any man who showed such disrespect. And he would have done it with his bare hands.

"We have a situation that we need to rectify," said Dickhead. "You guys get to see action sooner than you expected. But I know you're ready. If there's anyone here who doesn't think he's ready, please raise your hand." No one raised his hand.

"Okay. Your targets won't be easy. They're all Pakistani government officials or senior army officers. We take them out clean, we get out clean. We leave none of our people behind. Any of our people get hit, we bring them home. I want four backup teams for every hit team. Your NCOs will give you your individual assignments. We'll make it look like Islamic extremists made the hits on corrupt government officials. We paid off a few Taliban lowlifes who will make a public announcement claiming credit for the kills. They'll proclaim the same will happen to anyone else who takes bribes from American infidels. Now you guys get your asses in gear and be ready to move out in one hour."

They were assembled into four-man teams, issued sniper rifles and ammunition, and herded into Land Rovers. Their NCOs gave them pictures of their targets and maps of the area where the targets were sure to be the next morning. Under cover of darkness, they slipped into Islamabad or drove north to the major military compound where the generals were headquartered.

Randy was assigned to be a spotter for the sniper who would take out one of the politicians. Randy had been trained as a sniper, and he would be backup shooter if the first shooter failed. Both men had state-of-the-art scopes mounted on their rifles, and the rifles had laser targeting devices that would pinpoint exactly where each shot would go when the trigger was squeezed. It would be almost impossible to miss their targets with that kind of equipment.

They had back-up teams positioned all around them with automatic weapons, and one guy in each backup team had a grenade launcher. The grenade guy would create a flash-bang diversion while the others took out the politician and made their getaways. Police and Pakistani army responders would find themselves hit from all sides with massive firepower, pinning them down to allow the shooters to escape.

They would then rendezvous at a safe house until they could account for all of their men. If anyone were missing, they would search and find him and bring him back. No one would be left behind, and no one would know who was responsible for the hits.

Either Islamic extremists or CIA paid assassins would be blamed for the killings. But the message was clear to anyone who was in the know: We can kill you anytime, anywhere. Mess with us and you're toast.

Bill Ramsey could appreciate the accuracy of the intelligence behind acquiring exact locations for each of the targets because the politician emerged from his house right on schedule, within minutes of when they expected, and he had only two bodyguards with him. He made an easy target as he walked to a waiting car, and the primary shooter placed one round in the politician's forehead half-an-inch above the left eyebrow. Randy took out one of the bodyguards, and the primary shooter took out the other with a second round.

As they scrambled back to rejoin the rest of the team, a flash-bang grenade exploded right next to the politician's car, shattering all the car windows and rattling the windows of the house. Automatic weapons fire peppered the street so nobody in their right mind would come out to see what had happened until the team had disappeared.

Getting back to the safe house wasn't quite so easy. Two politicians and four generals had been murdered, and police and military units were quickly mobilized. There were helicopters buzzing around in the air, and there were roadblocks being hastily set up all over town. Islamabad was no stranger to violence, and Pakistani troops were well drilled in rapid response.

Once again the intelligence proved amazingly accurate, and the Land Rovers raced through side streets to avoid where the major checkpoints were set up and manned. They encountered only one small group of armed soldiers along the side streets, and they were able to shoot their way past without losing a single man.

When they arrived at the safe house outside Peshawar two hours later, Dickhead was already there waiting for them. He counted noses and made entries on a clipboard. Dickhead directed them inside the house for debriefing. After all of the teams were present and accounted for, Dickhead congratulated them on their success. All six of the primary targets had been terminated right on schedule, he informed them, and collateral damage to Pakistani property, bodyguards, and Pak soldiers was even greater than expected and that was good. None of the strike teams had suffered significant loss of men or materiel. One man had been wounded when his team ran a roadblock, but he had returned with the rest of his team and would recover in a few days. Two of the

Land Rovers had suffered minor damage, but they made it out of Islamabad and were still drivable.

"You have all been tested by live fire," said Dickhead. "And you all passed the test. Congratulations, graduates. Instead of going back to camp to complete your training, we're sending you all to South Africa for some R & R, and then you'll report to new assignments. Now listen up. We'll take the Land Rovers and drive straight across the border into Afghanistan. I'm going with you as your section leader. WLSCTC has a charter flight waiting at Kabul to fly us out as if we were contract employees of the U. S. Government. Instead of heading back to the good old U. S. of A., however, we're heading for a new campground. I'll brief you again after we're airborne. Grab your gear. Let's get going."

They drove overland on Taliban trails through the mountain passes with an Afghan civilian to guide them, easily avoiding border guards in Pakistan and American patrols in northern Afghanistan. Randy felt a strange sense of déjà vu as the convoy passed places where he had served in-country with the Marine Corps. He wondered if he would see any of the men he had served with. He wondered how many of them were still alive, if any.

They refilled their gas tanks from Jerry cans pre-positioned along the trails and rough roads, and they reached the airfield shortly after dark the next day. Dickhead showed fake IDs and authorizations at a NATO checkpoint, and they boarded a charter plane that was fueled and waiting for them at an airfield outside Kabul. An hour later, they were in the air and headed for South Africa.

Dickhead told them they were now part of an elite strike force, the kind he had always wanted to join. It might sound like blasphemy, he said, but they were better than the Rangers, better than the SEALS, better than the Marines, better than Special Forces, even better than Delta.

The world had changed drastically since 9/11, he continued, and large armies were now considered obsolete by anyone in the know. Small groups of well-trained and dedicated fighters proved more effective than huge armies. They always had been more effective, but politicians and generals couldn't admit it without losing power and prestige. Look at how Americans won the Revolutionary War against the British Army using hit and run tactics. Look at how Viet Kong sappers, hiding in booby-trapped tunnels and tall elephant grass, had defeated the U. S. Army in Vietnam, made us turn tail and run. Look at how the Taliban defeated the Soviets in Afghanistan and were defeating Americans now. Massive manpower and massive firepower wasn't necessary to win a conflict these days—hell, it never had been except maybe in World War II—and the logistics needed to support a regular army was too much of an encumbrance to be sustainable over long periods of time. What was needed today, Dickhead said, was accurate intelligence, small groups of well-trained and well-armed men organized into strike forces, and enough mobility to get in and out in a timely fashion that left the enemy shell-shocked and disorganized, wondering what the hell had just happened. With such strike forces prepositioned in strategic locations around the world, a select group of people could control the balance of power in world affairs, manipulate market conditions, and enjoy the fruits of war with little or no cost of men and materiel. They had just seen an example of that in Pakistan. They were about to see it work again.

"We are an army without generals," he said proudly. "We run a tight ship without interference from politicians, and we fight for no flag. We're in this only for ourselves. And we can kick butt better than anyone."

The men cheered and high-fived and hoo-hawhed.

After landing at Mafikeng, they were trucked across the border into Botswana where, on the southern edge of the Kalahari Desert, a huge concentration of prefabricated Quonset huts and several cinder-block bunkers suddenly materialized out of nowhere like a mirage. As they got closer, Randy saw each of the buildings had been effectively camouflaged with paint and netting to blend with the visual contours of the environment.

They passed several banks of solar cell panels installed to generate giga-watts of electricity powering air conditioners and communications satellite dishes and perimeter lights, and the camp sprawled, like a lazy lioness lounging in the hot African sun, over hundreds of acres of otherwise useless land that nobody else wanted, not even the natives. Dickhead pointed out training facilities that included rifle ranges and infiltration courses before the men were finally herded from the trucks to an administration building where they were processed in, issued clothing and supplies, and assigned sleeping quarters.

Randy shared a room in one of the Quonset huts with three other men, part of his strike team. Each man had his own bunk, a footlocker, an area for clothing and personal belongings, and a small writing desk. There was a modern indoor bathroom with two shower stalls attached to the room. They had a flat-screen television with a DVD player for entertainment.

The mess hall was in a separate Quonset hut, and teams were rotated in and out on a schedule that allowed several thousands of men to eat each meal without undue crowding. Meals were served buffet-style, and the food was more than adequate. Sometimes it even tasted good.

That first night, after dinner in the mess hall, the men were trucked to an undisclosed location about an hour away. There they were treated to drinks, allowed to choose from a variety of women of all ages and colors, and spent the rest of the night indulging in sexual fantasies. Randy selected a young black girl who looked about fourteen, if she was even that old, and Bill didn't say a word as Randy ravished her. Randy suspected they were being recorded, but he didn't care.

The men and their female companions of the previous night were treated to steak and fried eggs, toast, juice, and coffee served to them in bed the next morning. Then the men showered, dressed, and went back to camp in the trucks. If they wanted another R & R, Dickhead told them, they would have to earn it.

Now they began training as teams, living and eating and sleeping as one unit, building trust in each other and learning to watch out for each other exactly like brothers. Lester Radcliff was a former Army Ranger, and he was Randy's age, hard-muscled, hot-headed, foul-mouthed, and brash. Radcliff was an expert at devising and detecting booby traps and IEDs. Toby Jens was older, in his early thirties, ex-special forces, proficient in several languages and electronics, and had a college degree and a nervous tick he picked up during two tours in Iraq. Ward Anderson was an ex-Marine sniper who fired consistently-tight shot groups precisely where he aimed, but he was quiet and shy and kept to himself. Anderson had grown up in Montana where hunting elk was a way of life. He could hold position without moving or speaking for hours, and Randy really admired that about the man.

Randy was the backup shooter and spotter for Anderson. His job was to locate targets that Anderson would take out while Radcliff and Jens provided firepower and distractions. Radcliff was the designated flanker, and he watched their rears while they concentrated on the targets in front of them. Jens was the observer, or sensor, who watched for peripheral movement and listened for signs that the shooter had been detected. They learned to work together as a team, each man doing his job.

Randy and Anderson were issued M-21 sniper rifles, modified match-grade 7.62 millimeter M-14s with sniper scopes.

Randy also had an M-4 carbine, a spotter scope, and a small handheld computer for calculating the effects of wind, distance, humidity, and minute of angle on rounds fired downrange. He could actually see, through the scope, the vapor trail of the bullets as they sped to their targets.

One night, after they had worked comfortably together for almost a month, Jens asked, "Who do you suppose we're working for?"

"WLSCTC," said Radcliff.

"Yeah," said Jens, "they sign our paychecks. But this is way bigger than WLSCTC."

"What do you mean?" asked Randy.

"I mean we're being trained for something really big. There must be a thousand teams assembled here. Add in the support personnel, and there's at least five thousand people on someone's payroll. If WLSCTC is contracting us out to someone, I want to know who that someone is."

"The United States government?"

"Possible," said Jens. "But highly improbable."

"Does it matter?" asked Radcliff. "We've got it made, haven't we? We're doing what we were trained to do, and we're being paid good money that piles up in our bank accounts. We got everything we need here, including a little nookie on the side now and then. Why look a gift horse in the mouth?"

"I want to know who I'm killing for and why. Or who I'm going to die for, if it comes to that. Maybe it doesn't matter to you, but it does to me. If we don't work for politicians and generals, who do we work for? Who really gives the orders?"

"Then you should have stayed in the Army," said Radcliff. "At least then you'd know you're dying to defend Old Glory, a red, white, and blue piece of cloth that ain't worth shit."

"Quit talking about dying," ordered Anderson, surprising everyone by angrily interrupting the conversation. Anderson was a quiet guy who never said anything to anyone. "You'll jinx us."

"You superstitious, Anderson?" asked Radcliff.

"All snipers are superstitious," interjected Randy before Anderson could answer. "We have to be. It's what keeps us alive. If even one of multiple conditions isn't exactly right to make a lucky shot, we can easily miss the target by a whole mile. Luck is one of those conditions, plain and simple. The target might get a sudden itch and bend over to scratch at the same time a trigger is pulled. Someone else might choose that moment to step in the way of the bullet. A sudden wind can come up. A thousand or more things can go wrong, and if anything can possibly go wrong, it will. It takes as much luck as skill and patience to hit a target at 1,000 clicks, especially a moving target. Anything can jinx us, and if we run out of luck we die. So don't talk about dying or you could jinx us. And if you jinx us, we're all dead."

"Jesus," said Radcliff. "You guys are crazy. I'm cooped up here with a bunch of fucking loons."

"Shut up, Radcliff," said Anderson. "That's an order."

"You ordering us around now?" demanded Radcliff.

"I'm the designated shooter," said Anderson. "That gives me the right to tell you what to do."

"Maybe in combat. But not in cantonment. Here you're just another grunt like me, Anderson. I don't take orders from you."

Anderson took a step toward Radcliff with murder in his eyes, and Radcliff was ready for him with clenched fists. But Jens stepped between the two and kept them from slugging it out. If Anderson wanted to hit Radcliff, he'd have to go through Jens first. He obviously didn't want to do that.

"Hey," said Jens. "Knock it off, both of you. We're all friends here, so forget I even mentioned it. Okay? We'll see plenty of action soon enough. I heard we're moving out in a few days. Save the fighting for combat."

"Where'd you hear that?" asked Radcliff, suspiciously. "How come you know something we don't?"

"Mess hall. I overheard Dickhead talking with a few NCOs at their reserved table in the back of the room. He said orders came down from on high to move out within ten days. That's what made me wonder who's really running this show. I'm the designated observer, and it's my job to find out these kinds of things so Anderson can make informed decisions in the field. But I don't know who the fuck jerks Dickhead's chains and who pulls WLSCTC's strings. That's why I asked. Because I don't know, and I wondered if any of you guys did. So I asked you. Forget I asked."

"When I signed my contract," Randy said, "Wright at WLSCTC said there was a big surge planned for summer. This could be the start of it, the reason we're all here."

"Then we better get some sleep," said Anderson. "I have a feeling we'll need all the sleep we can get before this is over."

"You guys okay?" asked Jens. "Friends again?"

Anderson offered to shake hands with Radcliff and Radcliff gave him a high five instead.

CHAPTER SEVEN

Deb noticed increased activity at or near all of the airports where WLSCTC leased facilities, and that worried her. WLSCTC was frantically moving men and materiel around, positioning them for something. Whatever they planned to do, it was worldwide. And it was happening now.

Charlie@WLSCTC.com had sent another e-mail from Dubai. This one read, "Go 3." Who was Charlie? Was this "Charlie" the one giving the orders? Or was Charlie merely a go between, another layer between planners and players to isolate the people at the very top?

Deb hadn't heard a word from Bill Ramsey since Ramsey had left her apartment such a bloody mess back in January. Besides having to answer questions from the Alexandria police, Deb had been grilled by Army CID and MI for weeks about the incident. She told them nothing more than what Ramsey had instructed her to tell them.

And Bill Porter, the guy she called "my Bill" whom she intended to marry someday when life became more predictable for both of them, left New York State and came home as soon as he heard about what had happened. Bill had insisted the landlord replace the carpeting in the living room where blood stains had left ugly reminders of what had occurred. Bill said he was through with traveling. From now on there would be two people in the apartment in case the killers tried again. Deb was glad to have Bill Porter watching her back.

As far as local police were concerned, Thomas Huggins was an ex-Army Ranger who hadn't been able to keep a job since his discharge from the Army, especially after WLSCTC said Huggins had been fired from his job as a security guard in Richmond for failing a routine drug screening. Despite the fact there were no illicit drugs found in Huggins' system at autopsy, the local cops bought the story that Huggins and his friends had attempted to rob and rape a woman at random because of drugs. Deb didn't try to convince them otherwise.

Nor did she reveal any more to the Army criminal investigators or military intelligence interrogators who questioned her. She told them only that when three men with guns had broken into her apartment to rape her and rob her, she had used her military training to disarm one of the men, and she had killed one and wounded another of the three with the pistol they had waved in her face. The third man, she told them, had escaped with the wounded man while Deb was telephoning the police. She described the third man as clean-shaven, in his twenties, wearing ragged jeans, a black t-shirt, and an old olive-drab field jacket. That was all true as far as it went, and Deb refused to admit or speculate about any connection between the incident and her work for the military.

The only one she told, besides Bill Porter, was Eddie Morsay.

"Bill Ramsey's still alive?" Morsay asked incredulously when Deb related what really happened.

"More or less. He's in another body. His own body was killed in Pakistan."

"That's hard to believe, Deb. How could Ramsey obtain another body?"

"I didn't believe it myself. Not until Bill mentioned Vajrapani had helped him transfer his consciousness from one mortal shell to another after Bill's own body died of gunshot wounds. The Ranger told Ramsey he had learned the secret from Lokesvara. Then it made perfect sense."

Deb watched recognition slowly dawn in Eddie's eyes. It had been a while since Eddie, too, had worked with Vajrapani and Lokesvara. "Whatever happened to the Ranger after we left Rockford?" asked Eddie. "I've often wondered about him. And about Lokesvara."

"The Ranger became a Buddhist monk at Lokesvara's monastery," said Deb. "Can you believe that? He hung up his guns and took a vow to practice ahimsa, not killing another sentient being. I guess the Ranger must have been more spiritual than we knew or even he knew. Lokesvara opened him up to what had always been inside."

"To the Bodhisattva that is Vajrapani," agreed Eddie, remembering seeing Vajrapani manifest from the Ranger's body.

"I don't really understand this whole bodhisattva thing, Deb. It boggles my mind."

Deb smiled. She, too, had felt mind-boggled when Lokesvara revealed that Debra Johnson, the Ranger, and six other mortals, including Bill Porter, were all reincarnated Bodhisattvas. Deb didn't believe, not at first anyway, that she was an avatar of the Bodhisattva Sai Ngingpo, better known as Ksitigarbha, the Boundless Earth Matrix. How could she be? She had always been an ordinary mortal, a girl like all the other girls she grew up with. She had a mother, a father, and siblings. She had gone to school, graduated, attended college. The only thing different about her than most girls was Deb had entered the Army instead of getting married and having kids of her own. Raised Methodist, she believed in the Father, Son, and Holy Ghost. Reincarnated Bodhisattvas had no place in her world view. Bodhisattvas simply didn't compute.

Even after reading the *Sutra of the Past Vows of the Earth Store Bodhisattva* in translation, Deb didn't fully understand. It was only after Lokesvara helped Deb recall some of her past lives that Deb began to grasp the meaning of what a Bodhisattva was all about.

It was about feeling great compassion, not dissimilar to the compassion Jesus Christ displayed on the cross for his fellow man, even sinners. Compassion for those who suffered terribly from ignorance ("Forgive them, Father, for they know not what they do"), and disease, and the inevitability of death. Compassion meant finding ways to relieve the suffering of others, although it often meant enduring great suffering yourself. And that wasn't really too different than being a soldier, was it? Soldiers often suffered great hardships in order to relieve the suffering of others. Those who mistakenly thought that soldiering was only about killing enemies in order to capture territory and property, the spoils of war, had it all wrong. Soldiering was about protecting innocent people from all enemies, both foreign and domestic, including enemy soldiers and corrupt politicians at home and abroad. It was a tough job, but somebody had to do it.

Soldiers actually did take a vow to defend against all enemies foreign and domestic, much like Bodhisattvas took a sacred vow to eliminate ignorance and suffering. In order to achieve their vows, Bodhisattvas were armed with *satisampajannia*, the ability to analyze correctly according to the circumstances and according to the occasion. And they were given other tools to use, too, like special weapons.

Vajrapani had the Vajra, the Kris, and the magic Lasso. Manjusri had the flaming sword and wisdom beyond measure. Ksitigarbha had, besides the power of analysis, the power to heal living things and to make living things grow. Deb had laughed when she first heard the name. Ksitigarbha sounded so much like "shitty garb ah" that she thought instantly of dirty diapers.

"Ksitigarbha was once a Brahmin maiden we Buddhists call Sacred Girl," Lokesvara had explained. "Because she has been through hell herself and seen the suffering wrong thoughts and wrong actions can cause, she has vowed to act to relieve the suffering of others in each of her reincarnations. You are an avatar of Sacred Girl, Debra Johnson. You are the most recent reincarnation of Ksitigarbha."

Deb was surprised to discover that Bill Porter, too, was a Bodhisattva. Lokesvara said Porter would someday in the future become the Buddha known as Maitreya. But, in this life, Bill Porter was an electrical engineer, an ex-Air Force electronics tech, and the man Deb Johnson loved more than life itself. She had a hard time thinking of Bill Porter as a Buddha. And so, Bill claimed, did he.

Deb and Bill had gone on with their lives after the Eight Great Bodhisattvas had defeated Death and restored the Dharma. They so rarely thought about their other lives that they had forgotten how to astral travel and teleport and do all the other things Bodhisattvas were capable of doing.

Until now.

"Ramsey told me WLSCTC has a mole inside INSCOM," said Deb.

"Any idea who that might be?" asked Eddie.

"Someone who knows what I'm doing. When I uncovered a link between the training camp in Pakistan and landing fields in Laos and Thailand, WLSCTC decided I was getting too close for comfort. That's when they decided to take me out and make it look like a rape and robbery. Who sees my progress reports?"

"I do," said Eddie. "And the Colonel."

"I trust you and Colonel McMichaels," said Deb. "Who else?"

"Nobody."

"Must be somebody. Who has access to my office when I'm not there?"

"Just the cleaning crew."

"Cleaning crew?"

"Yeah. The base contracts facility cleaning to a civilian firm. They send in a crew after midnight, empty the wastebaskets, clean the toilets, dust the desks."

"Without security clearances?"

"I never thought about it. I assumed the base ran clearances, or maybe their employer."

"Can you find out who has the contract? I bet it's WLSCTC or one of their subsidiaries."

"I'll do that. But we're supposed to lock up everything at night so it shouldn't matter. The cleaning crew doesn't have access to classified files. You lock everything up, don't you?"

"I lock the office door and the filing cabinets. But the situation map is hanging on the wall. It doesn't get taken down and put away at night. I thought locking the office was enough. Obviously, I was wrong."

"I'll have your office put off-limits to the cleaning crew. It will mean you'll have to do your own cleaning. Think you can handle it?"

"I know how to empty wastebaskets and dust my desk."

"Right," said Eddie. "And from now on, you lock that map up before you leave at night."

That night, Bill Porter and Deb practiced teleporting from one place to another until they remembered exactly how to do it. Then they blinked out of existence in Alexandria, Virginia, and blinked into existence again inside the main temple at Angkor Wat. It was almost midnight in Alexandria, but it was nearly noon of the next day in Cambodia.

They surprised a young girl of about twelve who was leaving the classroom and on her way to the kitchen by appearing out of thin air in front of her.

"I'm sorry," said Deb. "We didn't mean to startle you."

"Where did you come from?" asked the girl in English. "You weren't there a minute ago."

"We came from America to see Lokesvara," said Deb. "You speak English very well. Did Lokesvara teach you?"

"Yes," said the girl. "But I learned most of my English from Vajrapani."

"We came to see them both," said Bill Porter. "We're old friends of both Lokesvara and the Ranger. Where will we find them?"

"I will guide you," said the girl. "Follow me."

Bill and Deb followed the girl down a long hallway almost to the end where she stopped in front of an open door. "Who shall I say is here to see the Lama?" asked the girl.

"I'm Debbie Johnson," said Deb. "And this is Bill Porter."

"I am Anong," said the girl.

"We're very pleased to make your acquaintance, Anong," said Deb, making Anong smile.

"I'm glad to know you, too," said Anong.

A moment later the girl emerged from the room with Lokesvara at her side. "Namaste," said the old man, making a high wais.

"Namaste," said both Americans, returning the greeting with their hands held at their foreheads.

"It is good to see you again, my friends," said Lokesvara. "You honor me with your presence."

"We need to talk," said Deb. "Can the Ranger join us?"

"Yes, of course. Anong, would you please ask Vajrapani to come to my chamber?"

Anong scurried off while Deb and Bill joined Lokesvara in lotus position on the carpet. A few moments later, Anong returned with the Ranger. It was the first time Bill and Deb had seen the Ranger with a completely shaved head and wearing the saffron robes of a Buddhist monk. He seemed more subdued than they remembered him to be.

"Thank you, Anong," said Lokesvara, dismissing the girl.

"I understand you helped Bill Ramsey get a new body," Deb said to the Ranger when he had seated himself on the floor in a lotus position.

"I did," said the Ranger. "He said he had vital information for INSCOM. How did you find out I helped him?"

"I work for INSCOM now. I ran into Bill Ramsey in his new body, and he told me he had met you."

"Bill Ramsey is the soldier you told me about?" asked Lokesvara.

"Yes," said the Ranger. "His spirit wasn't ready to move into the light. He had unfinished business that held him here. I helped him find a way to complete his mission so he might eventually move on."

"Is there any way to locate him? To contact him?" asked Deb.

"Yes. We can find him in his current body and we can speak with his spirit. Why?"

"I need a channel of communication with him," said Deb. "Can we open one?"

"Do you remember how to astral travel?"

"It's been a few years since I've done it. I may need some practice."

"Then let me contact him for you. Give me a few minutes and I'll find him for you." Deb watched as the Ranger sealed his body and entered meditation. After a few moments the Ranger's body went slack, and his facial muscles took on a waxy appearance.

Fifteen minutes later, his body returned to life. As he opened his eyes, he said, "Bill Ramsey is in Botswana."

"What's he doing there?"

"There's a large training camp with several thousand armed men at the edge of the Kalahari Desert. Ramsey is one of the men housed in the camp."

"Did you talk with him?"

"I said hello in passing," said the Ranger, grinning like a Cheshire cat.

Deb knew what that meant. She remembered the first time someone in spirit form had spoken directly to her mind. You understood the words and you recognized who was speaking to you, but it wasn't exactly a voice that you heard. If you weren't expecting to hear voices, you would think you were going insane.

"How did he react?"

"Ramsey recognized me immediately. But Randy Edwards had no idea who I was. His first thought was that he was going crazy because he heard voices inside his head. Wasn't it bad enough that he had to share his body with one other consciousness? Two carrying on an internal dialog was one more than he could handle. Fortunately, Ramsey took charge of Randy's body while I introduced myself and assured Randy my visit was only temporary. None of the men around them had a clue we were talking. The next time someone visits his mind, Randy should be able to deal with it better."

"What did Ramsey tell you?"

"They're all being trained to be snipers. They're broken down into four man teams and ready to assassinate politicians and generals."

"American politicians and generals?"

"They haven't been assigned targets yet. But Ramsey did say they took out a few generals and politicians in Pakistan a month ago as a training exercise."

"Holy shit!" said Deb, putting two and two together from intel about assassinations in Pakistan. "INSCOM thought that was perpetrated by a radical element of the Taliban. If we were wrong about that, what else are we wrong about?"

"I sense," said Lokesvara, "that there may be much more to this than meets the eye. Not being a military man, I must ask you to explain the significance of such assassinations."

"It could disrupt the balance of power in the world," said Deb. "It could change global politics the way 9/11 changed the world overnight if even half of the assassinations are successful. If key generals and politicians of a nation are eliminated, the country is left leaderless and floundering, vulnerable to further attack. People will panic if multiple assassinations occur simultaneously all over the world."

"It could destroy the world as we know it," said the Ranger. "It would throw the world into total chaos. People depend on politicians and generals to protect them, and they'll look for someone else to fill the vacuum if the usual generals and politicians aren't there to calm and lead them during crisis. That's how Hitler came to power. He set fire to the Reichstag, the German parliament, and claimed Jews and communists were responsible. While the Reichstag was still burning, Hitler persuaded President

Paul Von Hindenburg to declare a state of emergency and give the Nazis power to make mass arrests of Jews and communists, including all Jews and communists who were elected members of the Reichstag. Stalin came to power by assassinating or imprisoning all the generals and politicians who stood in his way, including Lenin and Trotsky. Stalin used the assassinations as a ruse to ban rival factions and ruthlessly begin a rule of terror. He executed or imprisoned millions of people. He ruled with an iron fist and lived up to his name."

"I see," said Lokesvara. "And who would want to do such a thing now? Who would profit by a world in chaos?"

"That's what I haven't quite figured out yet," said Deb. "I know a company called WLSCTC is involved, but they're merely a front for something else. I have no idea who is ultimately behind all this. But they've invested big money, and they have trained a secret army capable of killing lots of people."

"We must stop them," said Loksvara. "We cannot allow the world to become more chaotic than it already is. There is an order to all of existence, the Dharma, which allows this world and all other worlds to progress toward eventual enlightenment. If that natural order is suddenly disrupted or destroyed, all progress—and even this world itself—can also be destroyed. If that happens, the world must be created anew amidst the primordial struggle between good and evil, light and darkness. There are those who would destroy the world in order to remake it to suit their own ends. Such evil does exist, I assure you, and I have vowed to combat it. Will you join me?"

"Count us both in," agreed Deb. "But what can we do now? How can we begin to find a hidden enemy when we don't even know who he is?"

"As with all things," said Lokesvara, "we begin with the breath. Chant the following mantra: *Om Nishumbha Vajra Hum Phat Hum*."

"And what will that do?" asked Deb.

"Try it and see," said Lokesvara.

Deb did. At first, nothing happened. Gradually, however, her mind floated free and she saw a serpent, giant, deadly, sinuously winding its way through grass and weeds toward a tall tree in the distance which Deb recognized as a huluppo tree, part of the willow family. When the serpent reached the tree, it coiled its scales about the rough bark and ascended the tree, its coils snaking around and around again and again, relentlessly, until it reached the top of the tree, to balance on one of the branches where it remained hidden by copious twigs and leaves until unsuspecting prey passed by below.

It waited, patiently, for days, for weeks, for months, for eons. A variety of fauna—rabbits, mice, chipmunks, boars, even a lion—walked beneath the tree but the serpent seemed uninterested in feasting on their flesh. Perhaps it was still digesting its last meal and wasn't yet hungry. It continued to wait in hiding until a woman appeared.

She was naked. Young, perhaps nineteen or twenty, her breasts still pert and pointed. She was tanned all over by the sun as if she had never worn clothes. This girl reminded Deb of the way she had herself looked in college days, except for the missing tan lines, and the fact that the girl had flame-red hair.

When the woman walked beneath the tree, the serpent's head appeared as if from nowhere.

"Be not afraid," spoke the serpent to the woman. "For my name is Samael, and I am a messenger of the gods. I couldn't help but notice how beautiful you are, and I wanted to tell you I have chosen you for my bride."

"Be gone, serpent," said the woman. "I already have a husband, and his name is Adam."

"And what is your name, my sweet?"

"I am Lillith. I was created from the earth, and Adam was created after me to be my husband."

"For what purpose were you created, beautiful one?"

"To be fruitful and multiply."

"And how will you accomplish that?"

"I do not yet know. God will reveal how in His good time."

"And so He has, my sweet. I am sent as His messenger, and I am here to show you how to be fruitful and multiply. I will make your offspring legion."

"You can do that?"

"I can and I will," whispered the serpent. "It is all part of God's plan. God will be proud of you when you submit to me, and you do want to make God proud of you, don't you?"

"Yes," said Lillith.

"Then submit to me, my sweet. Open your legs and let me caress you."

Lillith did as she was told, and the serpent came down from the tree and caressed the girl's body with its forked tongue, and when the girl was ready, the serpent entered her and made her his bride.

As the scene faded, Deb tended to her breath. The sight of the woman violated by the serpent had so revulsed Deb that she had become agitated and found herself shouting out loud,

"Don't believe him! He's deceiving you! Oh, God! Oh, no! Don't let him!" And the sound of her voice had snapped her out of trance and brought her back to the world shouting, and sweating, and shaking, and finally sobbing.

Bill Porter was holding her now, soothing her with his gentle touch, and Lokesvara and the Ranger both looked at her with great concern as if they were worried she had suddenly gone mad.

"It seemed so real," she tried to explain. "I know it couldn't have been real, but I saw it so clearly as if I were actually there."

"What did you see?" asked Lokesvara.

She told them.

"Each of us," explained the monk, "interpret what we see with what we already know. What you saw was tempered with Judeo-Christian myth. Look beyond the myth to find the truth of your vision. Now what was it you saw that you know to be true?"

"I saw a red-haired woman seduced by serpent."

"A red-haired woman and a snake that talks like a man?"

"Yes."

"Then we must search for a red-haired woman. She is the one who plans to bring chaos to the world."

And the snake?" asked the Ranger. "What about the snake?" The Ranger hated snakes.

"Find the red-haired woman," said Lokesvara, "and we shall find the snake."

CHAPTER EIGHT

Anong didn't know whether it was simply because she was now living inside the ancient Buddhist monastery at Angkor Wat or whether it was a normal side effect of the overabundance of hormones from achieving puberty, but something made memories flood her mind like the Mekong and Lake Tonle Sap flooded surrounding lands when heavy rains came in May and June, leaving behind a thick, rich, fertile silt when they receded in summer.

Sometimes she felt as if she were literally drowning in an uncontrollable deluge of vivid memories from multiple lives, most of them long past. A few memories were so beautiful they took her breath away. Many, however, were such bitter memories that they often choked her and made her gag even worse than the thought of eating the meat of a dead animal. Some memories, long buried and best forgotten, were truly horrifying.

As Rukmini's spirit floated high above her poisoned body, Anong could see clearly now some of the more significant events surrounding the death of Rukmini that she had missed before or forgotten. She heard Jayavarman's command to kill the sorcerer, and she watched as Haranyadama's spirit voluntarily separated from his body a moment before the magician's mortal shell was hacked to pieces by the king's guards. Because he was already out of his body at the time of death, Haranyadama wasn't bound to one place the way Rukmini was.

And Rukmini saw not merely one spirit separating away from the magician's mutilated body, but two spirits, one light and the other much darker.

Haranyadama had been possessed by a double, a demonic spirit so terrible that Rukmini dared not look upon its form. And the double's name she instinctively knew was Mahesvara, the destructive aspect of Lord Shiva.

Mahesvara saw her and spoke directly to Rukmini's spirit, gleefully divulging, as if speaking to a co-conspirator, that he had conducted a parallel rite at sacred Mount Kulen. And while Haranyadama himself conducted the public rite that allowed Jayavarman to be crowned king, his *purohita*, or double, had performed the rite for *kamiraten jagat ta raja*, the *anak ta*, the god who is the real king. And the god who was the real king, the *anak ta* or spirit of the place, was not Vishnu but Shiva.

Shiva was known to all as the destroyer, for Shiva was the dancing god who created and then turned around and destroyed only to recreate and destroy some more, as if life were merely a game played to amuse the gods at the expense of everyone else. Shiva's greatest delight was the destruction of entire worlds, and Shiva's most evil and destructive aspect was the demon Mahesvara.

"I desire you, my pretty one," said the demon, "and I *always* get all I desire. I have performed the holy rites that will tie your spirit to mine for all eternity, and once I claim you, you will be mine forever. You will no longer be Rukmini. When I take possession of you, you will become Uma, my bride."

"Never!" protested Rukmini.

"Always," insisted Mahesvara. "I will have you, or I will destroy you. Either way, you will be mine and no one else can ever have you."

But before his spirit could touch her spirit and claim possession of her soul, Rukmini escaped into the clear light. And, after a time, she was reborn into a new body.

Rukmini was known as Maha Gauri, the Fair Lady, in her new life. Her birth name was Taleju, and it was said she displayed the kinder aspect of Durga, and her innocence had earned the protection of the mother goddess. She had reincarnated in Kasthamandap Mahanagar, the great city of Kathmandu, not far from where the Buddha himself had been born.

The year was 1345 of the Common Era, and Taleju grew up to become the most beautiful sacred dancer in the court of the Malla King. Malla meant "Man of great Strength" in Sanskrit, as it was a term usually applied to wrestlers in the arena. Jayaraja Deva, the wise but weak son of the prior monarch, had inherited the kingdom, and the land had remained peaceful and prosperous and almost like heaven on earth for but a brief time after the old king's death. Buddhists and Hindus lived and worked side by side, and there were as many Hindu temples as Buddhist pagodas in Kathmandu and the surrounding hills. But that was about to end.

Taleju, who was now the dancer called Maha Gauri, lived in the Malla palace, an opulent structure built nearly 800 years previously by the Licchavi princes who founded the great city after fleeing enemies in India. Near the entrance to the palace stood a statue of Hanuman, the monkey god of the Hindus, a symbol of fecundity.

When Shamsuddin Ilyas Shah, the Mogul ruler of nearby Bengal, invaded Nepal on an unholy mission of conquest, looting and destroying Hindu and Buddhist temples in the name of Allah, he moved swiftly with a thousand men on horseback, and before the young Malla King could mobilize his meager army and mount them on their war elephants, the Sultan was already breaking down the gates of the palace. The Sultan stormed inside, looted the palace, and burned half of Kasthamandap Mahanagar, the great city of Kathmandu, to the ground.

Besides gold, jewels, and elephants, the Sultan's loot from the conquered city included the royal courtesans and several Malla princesses. The king barely escaped the city with his own life while the Sultan was busily looting and destroying nearby Buddhist temples. After three days of looting and killing, the Sultan moved out of Kathmandu and took his loot with him. He was a master of hit and run tactics, and he had many more towns yet to destroy on his lightning-like sweep through Nepal.

Maha Gauri instantly recognized the Sultan as the reincarnation of Haranyadama. Fortunately for her, the Sultan had no memory of, nor interest in, past lives. Muslims didn't believe in reincarnation, and Shamsuddin Ilyas Shah had reincarnated as a devout Muslim. He believed in conquest, and collecting the spoils of war was considered a divine right of the conqueror.

When the Sultan returned to Pandua, he added the Malla courtesans to his personal harem. It wasn't long before the Sultan noticed the beautiful new addition to his harem, and he commanded Maha Gauri to dance for him.

She did dance for him, gladly, and it was a dance unlike any he had ever seen. In the intervening years between her rebirth and her capture, Maha Gauri had studied magic. When she was six, she had met an old woman of the forest who saw her potential—recognized the goddess within her—and tutored the young Taleju in the magic arts as if Taleju had been her own child.

Now Maha Gauri utilized all she had learned in the woods plus all she had learned since. There was power in the dance, magical power. It resided in the movements, and in the sacred hand and finger positions called hasta mudras. She knew all 108 mystic mudras used in tantric rituals, and she knew how to combine mudras to work magic.

And what magic did she work that day! She danced the sacred Dance of Creation Shakti once danced for Lord Shiva when the earth was created. There was pure magic in the dance itself, and magic in the movements of her fingers. Within moments, she had the Sultan mesmerized. When she was certain he was completely under her spell, she commanded him to forget all about her, forget who she was, forget seeing her, forget she ever existed. Henceforth, in this life and in all future lives, she would be invisible to him. He would not be able to see her in any form, physical or spiritual.

And then she set the command forever in his mind by tapping thrice on his forehead.

And then she walked out of the Sultan's palace, out of Pandua, and out of Bengal.

When next she met Haranyadama in another incarnation, it was as though she were invisible to him. He walked right past her and took no notice

But the original spell he had cast, the ritual his double had performed at Mount Kulen, would force them together again and again over the centuries until Mahesvara himself chose to break the spell that tied her spirit to his or Anong became powerful enough to break it herself. And though the mortal Haranyadama could not see Anong in any of her physical incarnations, the immortal spirits of Mahesvara and Uma and Anong remained intimately linked through all of time and space like lovers in an embrace.

* * *

Earl Wright had never met Charlie before. Earl had come to Dubai to receive new orders, and Charlie was the preferred delivery vehicle for orders from the Big Boss, whoever that was. In this day and age of radio and internet communication, important messages were still best delivered the old-fashioned way: in person, up close, and personal.

Earl had been instructed to meet Charlie in a room at one of the investment banks in Dubai's financial center, a secure location that had been swept for listening devices and was out of reach of U. S. intelligence. Dubai was Charlie's home territory, and Charlie had made all of the arrangements in advance. Earl had been told nothing more than to meet Charlie at the bank building. Once Earl was in the room, the bank would notify Charlie that Earl was waiting. Then Charlie would show up and pass on the orders.

Earl didn't mind waiting. He had been in the air for more than sixteen long hours, leaving Dulles before seven the previous morning, and he was glad to have some free time for himself. He could smoke in the conference room at the bank, something he hadn't been able to do on the plane, and the bank had graciously supplied him with a pot of strong Arabian coffee. Caffeine and nicotine were two of Earl's few remaining vices. He had only simple tastes remaining after too many years in uniform. Give him a cigarette and a cup of coffee, and Earl Wright was a happy boy.

Wright had been a trouble-shooter for the Army, a Special Forces officer who volunteered to get things done behind enemy lines when others couldn't or wouldn't do them. Earl was a hands-on kind of guy; he liked being in the thick of things, and he liked being in the know. He had been an embedded liaison with the CIA in northern Afghanistan twice, and he was used to relaying secure information between sources.

Earl had left the Army a disillusioned man. Corruption was more rampant today than ever in Afghanistan, and so many of the American and Afghan generals had turned blind eyes to what was going on that he wondered if any of them even gave a shit anymore about winning the war. Goddamned ticket punchers put in their time and got out, and the next bunch to come in weren't any better and nothing ever got done that needed to get done. They knew what needed to be done to win, and they didn't do it. Not even once. He considered all generals and politicians traitors. They were losers, not winners, and he hated them all. In a perfect world, the politicians and generals would get out of the way and let soldiers do their job. Wright dreamed of creating a more perfect world.

When Colonel Brakken told Wright about an opportunity to be on the winning side for a change, Earl had listened. "I'm going to retire," said Brakken, "and head an organization that can use men like you, Earl. We're going to build a new army from the ground up, and I want you to be my right-hand man. How would you like to fuck the politicians and generals real good?"

"You got my attention, Colonel. What's the deal?"

"Parallel forces, a shadow army," said Brakken. "Small units trained to infiltrate and kill selected targets. Kind of like what you and the CIA were training hill people to do. I need an operations officer who doesn't mind getting his hands a little dirty, a little bloody. You mind blood on your hands, Earl?"

Earl had looked down at his hands, turned them over, examined them closely. They were big hands, callused and powerful. But his hands were seldom clean after weeks in the field. Earl's hands hadn't been clean in a long time, and he had a feeling they never would be again. "No, Colonel," he said. "What I mind is spinning my wheels."

"I can guarantee you won't be spinning your wheels with us. When we move, we move forward. None of this two steps forward, three steps back bullshit. But it's all irregular warfare, Earl. Hit your target and move on to the next target. The kind of thing you were trained to do. Do you want in?"

"Who do I work for?"

"You'll work for me."

"And who do you work for?"

"Someone who appreciates what real power is all about."

"Name?"

"No names. Not yet. Trust me, Earl. This is someone who can change the world. Forget about all that patriotism bullshit and help us take down the structure that holds us back. We're going to remake the whole world in our image. Join us."

"Let me think about it."

"Don't think too long. We're moving ahead with or without you."

Earl went on one more mission for the U. S. Army before he was finally convinced that everything in Afghanistan was FUBAR—fucked up beyond all repair—and he resigned his commission to begin work for John Brakken and WLSCTC as chief operations officer.

That had been four long years ago, and Wright had done lots of things with his hands during those intervening years. He was proud of his accomplishments. He had helped set up new training camps in Pakistan and Botswana, and he had personally trained many of the NCOs that would lead the shadow army. He had beefed up security at WLSCTC headquarters with state-of-the-art equipment, and he had established rest and relaxation centers in Richmond, Poland, Thailand, and South Africa. Besides servicing the troops, those R & R centers had proved useful in compromising several politicians, including some prominent members of the U. S. Congress and three state governors.

Two things still bothered him though: the bloody incident that shut down the house at Kong Chiam, and the constant interference by Deb Johnson at INSCOM.

Had he underestimated Johnson because she was a woman? Probably. He needed to keep in mind that she was still a soldier and a very good one, even if she was a woman. And a superb intelligence officer. Johnson had successfully plugged the leaks at INSCOM. None of the cleaning crew could get anywhere near her office now, and Wright had no idea how much she knew or didn't know. He suspected Johnson had been directly responsible for the massacre at Kong Chiam, and for shutting down most of the auxiliary funding sources WLSCTC used for special operations. It still bugged him that Johnson was alive and posed a significant threat to plans and operations. He intended to personally rectify that situation when he got back to the states. Johnson's days were numbered. Wright could count those days on the fingers of one hand.

Charlie was taking his good time getting there, but Wright had expected Charlie would make him wait. Charlie would certainly double check security before entering the room, and Charlie would want to personally observe Wright before making an approach. For all he knew, Charlie was observing him right now with hidden cameras. He looked around the room and tried to detect where cameras might be located, where he would place them if the situation were reversed. He decided the cameras were inside the light fixtures in the ceiling.

Finally the door opened, and a young woman entered with another pot of coffee. She was medium height, about five-five, and shapely despite a plain black dress and a black hijab covering her hair and most of her head. Earl smiled at her, and she smiled back.

"I'm Charlie," she said. "You're Wright?"

"You're....Charlie?"

"You were expecting a man?"

"Yes."

"Sorry to disappoint you. I'll have to do. I've always been a woman, and it has always been to my advantage."

"Your name is Charlie?"

"We named ourselves Alpha, Bravo, Charlie, and Delta. I am Charlie."

"You have orders for me?"

"Yes. While Alpha and Bravo are directing other operations, I have the privilege of overseeing WLSCTC. Do you have a problem taking orders from a woman, Mister Wright?"

"No," said Wright. "It's not a problem."

"Good. I want you to personally take these instructions to our camp in Botswana." She opened the top of the coffee pot she had brought with her into the room. Wright was surprised to see the pot contained no coffee. She removed several papers from the otherwise empty pot and spread the papers out on the conference table. "The first targets are selected senior officers serving in Afghanistan. Your men know the terrain and they may even recognize some of the officers. Make it look like Taliban snipers were responsible. Will your men carry out these orders without question?"

"I'll see that they do."

"Good. The second hit list contains names and locations of politicians, some American, some British, some Israeli. You have one week to prepare. When I send the fourth e-mail, you will accomplish all the hits within twenty-four hours. Is that clear?"

"Yes. But I'll need time to gather intelligence on each target. Or can you provide Intel?"

"Of course. Prelim intel is in the package. Details will follow by courier. You will have everything you need by tomorrow."

"I'm impressed."

"Do your job, and I'll be impressed with you. Fuck up, and you're dead."

Earl stared at the woman. Although she was young, maybe twenty-five, her blue eyes were cold as ice. He suspected she was harder than nails and twice as tough. Not someone you could toy with. Her eyebrows were light colored, and he suspected her hair likely was, too. She was either blonde or a redhead. Eastern European, perhaps, and multilingual. She spoke English with barely an accent, as if she had schooled in London. Though her body was covered with that baggy, non-descript black dress, he knew the flesh beneath that dress was hard and firm with muscles wound tighter than a metal spring. She was a fighter, a warrior. Like he was.

"Any questions?" she asked.

"How do I get to the camp?"

"There is a plane already waiting for you at the Dubai airport. It will take you to Mafikeng, then a truck will take you to the camp in Botswana. You will select the appropriate men for each assignment and arrange transportation to the targets. Weapons and equipment are being prepositioned in each location. Here," she removed a cell phone from a hidden pocket in her dress and handed it to him. "Each team will have two phones similar to this one. They have been programmed to send and receive so only you and I can communicate with each of them. Press star and one, and you'll get me. Press star and two, and you'll get everyone else. They have no ringers. They only vibrate. So keep the phone on your person at all times. I'll monitor your calls. And I'll call you with further instructions twice a day."

"Just how big an operation is this?" asked Wright. "You already have people and equipment in place at each of the target locations? How can you keep anything this big under wraps? How do you keep control of so many people?"

"We are ruthless in achieving our goals, Mr. Wright. No one betrays us. Ever. Besides, we won't need to keep anything under wraps after next week. Once the assassinations begin, we'll continue killing until we are perfectly positioned and ready to assume control. We'll move so fast that no one will be able to stop us. We act because we can, and we can because we will it."

"But this is worldwide," said Wright. "How can you coordinate something this big? Just how many people do you have working for you?"

"Enough questions, Mr. Wright. You have a plane to catch and you have orders to implement. I will stay in touch with you. Have a good flight."

Wright gathered up the papers from the conference table and slipped them inside his jacket. When he looked up, the girl had opened the door and was halfway out of the room. Then she surprised him by turning around and saying, "To answer your question, Mr. Wright, we are legion."

And then she was gone as if she had disappeared into thin air.

CHAPTER NINE

His name was Temujin, and he was a conqueror. He swept into Anong's tiny village with his tartar hoards and slaughtered every man, woman, and child in sight, Anong among them. Nearly a century later, the grandson of Temujin's own grandson, a man named Buqa Temur, swept through Tibet and killed ten thousand Tibetans. Again, Anong was among them.

Avatars of Mahesvara killed Anong's reborn bodies fourteen additional times before Anong, in her Maha Gauri incarnation, cast the spell of invisibility that protected her spirit from the wrath of the destroyer. For nearly nine centuries, she managed to slip through his fingers like fine grains of sand. When he looked for her, he couldn't see her. But she couldn't help but see him.

He was legion.

She saw Mahesvara's spirit at work everywhere in the world where death and destruction, wars and invasions, revolutions and insurgencies, even earthquakes and natural disasters, tsunamis and floods, existed. He tore down temples and churches, mosques and synagogues. He looted and defaced, stole and slaughtered. He tore asunder the fabric of entire civilizations the way a rapist ripped away clothing and delicate undergarments, with delight and great anticipation of what he was about do next.

His name was Gonzalo Pizaro, and he was a Spanish Conquistador. He was the bastard son of a Spanish colonel and the half-brother of Francisco Pizaro, the man who led the invasion of Peru to conquer the Incan empire and steal its gold. Gonzalo was more ruthless than any of his brothers. The year was 1533, the Incan emperor Atahualpa had been captured and executed, and the Pizaro brothers marched on Cusco, the capital city of the Incas. If they took Cusco, Machu Picchu would be next. Then the Incas, as a distinct civilization, would be no more.

For the moment, Machu Picchu remained an inaccessible fortress. To reach the sacred site all the way up at the very top of a craggy mountain that towered nearly 8,000 feet above the Urubamba River, the conquistadores would need to make the long climb on foot. Their horses would never make it that far, nor would their cannon. And the altitude would slow the men down so Incan archers or dart blowers, their darts tipped with poison from plants gathered near the Amazon River, could pick them off one at a time along the narrow trail up the mountain. Despite the firearms they carried, the conquerors were vulnerable. Machu Picchu was momentarily safe.

But the Spaniards had brought with them a weapon the natives could not defend against: the dreaded smallpox. None of the American natives had any immunity to the virus, and the deadly disease was spreading through the countryside like wildfire through dry grass. People were sick and dying everywhere. And Cusco was no exception.

Anong was a bruja, a healer. She treated as many people as she could with the last of the herbs that remained from her frequent trips into the Amazon jungle. When the herbs finally ran out, all would be lost. People would get sick, and they would die, and she wouldn't be able to cure them with herbal medicines because her herbs were all used up.

She heard frequent gunshots as the Spaniards entered Cusco, and she knew they were killing women, children, and old men with impunity because all the young men were gone. There had been more than enough warriors to repel the conquistadors when they had tried to enter Cusco once before, but now there were too few able-bodied men left to defend the city and most of those were sick with the pox. Many of the warriors had left with Quizquiz to protect Machu Picchu from assault, and the royal court and temples at Cusco had been abandoned. Solid gold ceremonial masks and sacred icons of the sun, so prized by the Spaniards only as booty, were too heavy to take into the Andes so they had to be left behind. The Spaniards would surely melt them down to send as ingots of raw metal back to Spain aboard ships anchored off the coast, keeping a third for themselves as a reward for their labors. Conquerors, it seemed, had no respect for any religion other than their own, and sometimes they didn't even have that. Gold was their god. Gold and silver and the spoils of war.

When the wooden door to the room at the Temple of the Sun housing the sick and injured was kicked open and Gonzalo Pizaro himself stood right there directly in front of her in his tin monkey suit with a shiny steel helmet covering half his bearded head, Anong felt great fear. This man was pure evil. She could sense the evil of Mahesvara within him. Mahesvara had absolutely no compassion, and neither had Pizaro. They cared nothing for beauty nor truth nor love. They existed only to destroy, to take away, to burn, to steal, to rape, to kill.

It seemed he could sense her, too. He couldn't see her, but he knew she was somewhere very close. He sniffed the air like a hungry wolf sniffing for scent of prey. She was so close he could probably taste her.

"El Capitan! El Capitan!" shouted one of Pizaro's men from another room. "Come quickly! We have found gold! Lots of gold!"

Pizaro hurried from the room. Anong knew he would soon return, and she knew the sick she had so carefully attended would be slaughtered without mercy. There was nothing she could do. If she remained, she would be killed, too.

She went out the back way, sneaking through the streets like a thief to avoid soldiers on horseback. Machu Picchu was fifty miles to the northwest, and the roads were filled with soldiers looking for loot. A lone woman didn't have a prayer.

But Anong was no ordinary woman. She had skills acquired over many lifetimes of diligent study and practice. Besides being a healer, she was an enchantress. Her extraordinary beauty held men's attention while she weaved spells around them.

She could work her magic easily on one or two men at a time, but she had not yet learned to entrance crowds of large numbers. There were far too many soldiers to enchant. If she were going to survive, she would have to avoid them.

She hid in the city until dark. There were soldiers everywhere now, and they were no longer killing people randomly. Some natives, the few young and healthy able-bodied men still alive, were allowed to live as slaves to work the mines or do menial labor. Some women were enslaved to cook and wash for the soldiers. Some women were taken as wives. Others were simply raped or killed on the spot. Children were either killed or held hostage, depending on their status in the community. All this had been accomplished in less than a day as Anong was forced to watch in horror from her hiding places in the shadows.

How could anyone be so cruel? How could any human being inflict such terrible suffering on another human being?

And how long would it be before Mahesvara's men found her and inflicted the same or worse sufferings on her?

Sickened by all the atrocities she had witnessed, Anong felt almost equally sickened by her inability to stop the bloodshed. But what could a lone woman, unarmed, untrained in warfare, do against brutal men like these? She felt powerless and helpless, and she hated the feeling. She wanted to change that. She wanted to become more powerful than any man so she'd never feel this way again. She swore she'd search until she found a way to fight back. Even if it took forever.

She waited in the city until the campfires and funeral pyres began to flicker out. After a day of killing and a night of revelry, most of the men were now asleep. She could easily slip past the remaining guards at the periphery of the city. Individual men were easy to enchant, and no man would be able to stand in her way.

Three days later, an exhausted Anong stood next to the Intihuatana stone near the highest peak of Machu Picchu, her arms raised to the heavens.

"Hear me, gods and goddesses," she intoned. "I swear this day I will become as one of you. Grant me the power to fight like a god, the power to defeat all men and demons. Though I am a woman, give me a weapon I can use."

And she heard the gods answer her. "You are already as one of us, my child," said Lord Vishnu. "Look not to the heavens but within yourself to find your own power. For inside you resides the Sudarshana Chakra which I have granted unto you. When you awaken the sleeping Kundalini inside your center channel, when the head of the serpent of power rises beyond your human heart, you will activate the Sudarshana Chakra to use as a weapon. The Sudarshana Chakra will defend you against all men and demons. This is a gift of the gods. Learn to use it wisely. The Sudarshana Chakra is made of pure light, and it will not harm creatures of the light. But creatures of the dark will feel its power and fear its wrath."

"If I am already as one of you, then who am I?"

"Why, child, the answer should have been obvious to you long ago. You are an avatar of Lady Durga, and your spirit was born in a sea of light, created of the combined energies of all the gods, to defeat the darkest demons during a time of need. You yourself are not a goddess, but you have the powers of the gods and goddesses at your disposal. Now go, child. Go inside yourself. Find your own power. Someday you may need to use it. Farewell, child of light. Farewell."

Vishnu's revelation had occurred many lifetimes ago, and Anong was still searching for her power. Each incarnation brought her closer.

But each time she was reborn, she had to learn all over again. The accumulated memories of past lives manifested only with maturity. After puberty, she was able to recall some, but not all, of what she had learned before. Anong was often killed as a young woman, dying before she could realize her full potential. Life and death became a vicious circle for Anong. Each time she was about to uncover her power, death would take her and she would need to start again from the beginning.

She had tried to do it on her own for many lifetimes, and it had proved far too difficult. What she needed, she decided, was a mentor, a guru, a teacher who could guide her into power.

The Buddha had once said, “When the student is ready, the teacher shall appear.” Where was her teacher?

“Good morning,” said Lokesvara cheerfully, finding Anong sitting alone in the library with her face buried in a book. “Do you need any help with your lessons today? I am free all afternoon. How may I assist you?”

* * *

Bill Ramsey had been expecting Earl Wright to show his smiling face at the camp, and Bill wasn’t at all surprised to see Wright arrive because Wright was a hands-on kind of guy who seemed to have his hands in everything WLSCTC did. If Wright wasn’t one of the top bosses, Ramsey reasoned, Wright most likely knew who was. Ramsey had tagged Earl Wright as a person of primary interest, and a potentially dangerous adversary. Wright’s arrival didn’t bode well.

Career Army officers recognize other career officers miles away, and Ramsey had immediately recognized Wright as airborne qualified from his strac haircut, the way he walked with a spring in every step, and the supreme confidence he exuded. The guy was a lean green killing machine who didn’t take shit from anyone.

But he did take orders from someone, and Wright was the best—maybe the only—link Ramsey had to the higher ups in the shadow organization that ran this elaborate dog and pony show.

Ramsey wanted to get the information about Wright's arrival to Deb Johnson and the others at INSCOM as soon as possible, and he was impatiently waiting for Deb's spirit to pay him another visit. Not long after Vajrapani had spoken with Ramsey's mind inside Randy's head, Deb had surprised him by doing the same.

"I had to learn to do this all over again," said Deb. "I'm sorry it took so long."

"How do you do that?"

"Detach from my body and astral travel? I just picture in my mind where I want to go. And I'm instantly there."

"You pictured the camp?"

"No, I pictured *you.* Vajrapani did the same when he located you earlier today. He zeroed in on your spirit, not your body."

"And you're here inside Randy's body with me?"

"No. My spirit is actually on the astral plane, adjacent to where you and Randy exist on the physical plane. I'm here only in spiritual form, and I'm not physically anywhere near here. I can see and hear and I can communicate directly with your spirit, but I can't touch anything or change anything. I'm far from an expert in how any of this works. I'm still learning. All I know is that it does work, and my spirit can travel on the astral plane any where in the world without disrupting the balance of energy in the universe. Astral travel is different from teleportation. Teleportation works on the physical plane and moves energy around."

"You're way ahead of me. I believe you, but I don't understand anything of what you just said."

"Any word yet on what they're planning?"

"They split us down into four-man sniper teams and trained us to be assassins. Each team can take out multiple targets."

"Any idea who those targets might be? Or when they'll be hit?"

"Not yet. Scuttlebutt has it that we're about to make a move."

"I'll check back with you in a few days. Maybe you'll have something more to tell me."

"Did you hear about the politicians and generals that were hit in Pakistan two months ago?"

"The ones the Taliban shot?"

"That wasn't Taliban. That was us."

"You? You personally?"

"My team and six other teams like mine."

"That's impossible. The Taliban claimed credit for those kills. Why would they claim credit if they didn't do it?"

"They were paid to do that. It enhanced their position with the populace to take the credit. But we did the hits with six four-man sniper teams and twenty-four back-up teams. We were told it was part of our training, kind of a final exam."

Deb had departed with the promise she would check back every few days, but Ramsey hadn't heard from her in almost a week. He was beginning to worry.

"We got orders," Anderson announced, returning from a meeting with Dickhead and Wright. "We move out tomorrow."

"Where we going?" asked Jens.

"The good old U.S.A.," said Anderson. "We're going home."

"Home?" said Radcliff. "I ain't got no fucking home. The Army was my home and they kicked me out like my old man kicked me out of his house in Cincinnati. This is the closest I have to home."

"They giving us leave?" asked Jens.

"No fucking way," said Anderson. "We got targets."

"In the U.S.?" asked Randy.

"Washington, D. C., area."

"We're going to hit our own people?" asked Randy.

"We're going to hit politicians," said Anderson. "Politicians ain't people."

"Which politicians?" asked Jens. "Do you have names?"

"I got names and pictures," said Anderson. "Here." He handed Jens a handful of papers. "Memorize the targets."

"Pictures, addresses, habits," said Jens, looking through the papers. "Everything except which hand they use to wipe their asses and which hand they use to beat off."

"Let me see," said Randy.

Jens handed Randy some of the papers. The list included two U. S. Senators, one four star general, and an intelligence analyst at INSCOM named Edward Morsay.

"Did the other teams get assignments?" asked Randy.

"Everyone got assignments," said Anderson.

"Any idea who's on their hit lists?"

"Some of the other guys are going to Afghanistan, some to England, some to Palestine."

"Anyone else going to America?"

"Yes."

"How many?"

"Maybe a hundred teams."

"Jesus," said Jens. "If each team takes out six targets, it'll create chaos all over America. The country will be leaderless."

"That's the plan," said Anderson.

Bill hoped Deb made contact soon. If she didn't, it would be too late to stop the wholesale slaughter of the political and military leadership of the United States and its allies.

He wondered if the President was on one of the hit lists.

And if Eddie Morsay was on one of the lists, was Deb Johnson on one, too?

CHAPTER TEN

Deb Johnson had been kept so unusually busy, just with posting all the data that flowed incessantly now from all over the globe, much less attempting preliminary analyses of data, that she felt she didn't even have time to take a shit. Not only did her situation map show new activity between Dubai and London, Dubai and Tel Aviv, Dubai and Kabul, but there was now significant movement between Dubai and Moscow, Tokyo, Beijing, and the capital cities of most—if not all—of the major players in world politics. Colonel McMichaels had asked to confer with the CIA, and he had met with top-level CIA and DIA case workers several times. New data was being uncovered daily. Weapons were being stockpiled at strategic locations all over the globe. Everyone agreed that something big was brewing, but nobody who was supposed to be in the know knew what.

Deb's walls were covered with situation maps. Not only did she have the big map of the entire world covered with different color lines and pins, but she had recently installed regional maps and geospatial imaging maps. She also had armed MPs guarding her door 24/7. No one went into or out of Deb's office and the two adjoining briefing rooms, also covered with maps, without the Colonel's written permission.

Dubai was obviously the center of operations. Weapons, procured from numerous middle-eastern black markets, were being smuggled out of Dubai's port aboard cargo ships almost daily. WLSCTC and a handful of other private contractors provided the security for those ships. One CIA informant said weapons were hidden inside oil tankers bound for Tokyo and Shanghai, but the agency had yet been unable to confirm that information as accurate. There were rumors of a new spy network—made up of ex-KGB, ex-Mossad, ex-MI6, even ex-FBI and CIA operatives—watching our own operatives from the shadows and sometimes compromising intelligence. Someone had just upped the ante in this already high-stakes game even before the deck was cut, and now the dealer was getting ready to deal a new hand off the bottom of the deck.

Deb knew it was time to pay another visit to Bill Ramsey, but she had been so exhausted when she got home each night that she had even neglected her relationship with Bill Porter in favor of sleep. She showered in the morning before heading back to Belvoir, instead of bathing at night, and she was putting in fourteen and fifteen hour days at INSCOM with an extra hour added for the commute. Tonight, she promised herself, she would talk with Ramsey. She really needed to learn if he had anything new to report.

It occurred to Deb during her drive to work that she had the ability to visit Dubai in spirit form and personally observe the loading of weapons. But she had no clue of where to look. She could go to the port, but what good would that do? Unless she knew exact locations, her spirit would see and hear nothing more than normal shipping port operations.

Eddie Morsay was anxiously waiting for her when she arrived at the office. Eddie had news of significant new developments. “WLSCTC has flights scheduled to leave from Mafikeng for Dulles this afternoon,” Morsay told Deb the moment she walked through the door. “They moved dozens of planes to Mafikeng overnight. It looks like they’re flying four or five hundred men back home, and sending the rest to other locations.”

“Giving their troops R & R?” asked Deb.

“It’s possible,” said Eddie. “But highly unlikely. Since the people they’re bringing back to the states are U. S. citizens, we have no cause to detain any of them. They’ve never given all personnel R & R at the same time before. Why would they do it now? They’re moving *everyone* out of the camps, Deb. Everyone.”

“So we have to assume there must be some military operation underway, and they’re pre-positioning people out of operational necessity. Whatever this operation is, it’s big enough to send all their personnel out to multiple locations at the same time. That requires a lot of planning, Eddie. Do you have flight plans for the other aircraft? Do we have their final destinations?”

“Some, not all. I have flight plans for Heathrow and Haneda.”

“They’re sending people to London and Tokyo?”

"And to Tel Aviv. They've also scheduled flights to Ben Gurion International. Two plane loads."

"Shit!"

"What do you think they're up to?"

"I have no clue. But it can't be good if they're sending sniper teams to major cities."

Deb looked at the big situation map with its colorful criss-crossing lines, and she asked Eddie to help her stick colored push-pins into the map, marking each of the destinations with red or blue pins to indicate their relative tactical significance.

"I bet they're also sending a group to Moscow," Deb said. "If they're concentrating on the power centers, they'll send teams to Moscow."

"And Rome," added Eddie. He used a yellow pin for Rome. "If they're assassinating world leaders, they'll hit the Pope."

"Better notify the Colonel," said Deb. "This is much bigger than you and I can handle by ourselves. I'm going to the ladies' room to meditate. I'll be back in twenty minutes."

"Going to talk to Ramsey?"

"I should have done it before. I'll leave my body in a locked stall. If I'm not out in twenty minutes, come check on me."

Deb found a stall, locked the door, and sat down on the toilet seat, still fully dressed, in a modified lotus position. She sealed her body and entered meditation. Then she focused on Bill Ramsey's essence.

She found Ramsey bouncing around in the back of a truck with a dozen other men. The truck, one of nearly a hundred cargo trucks moving in convoy formation, had already left the camp and was almost half-way to the Mafikeng airport.

"Hello, Bill," said Deb inside Bill's mind.

"Where have you been?" asked Bill. "I've been waiting for you to return. I thought you were going to check back with me every couple of days. I was beginning to think you didn't love me anymore and forgot all about me."

"I've been busy," said Deb.

"So has the opposition," said Bill. "Do you see that guy riding shotgun in the lead truck? That's Earl Wright. He flew in two days ago from the states with orders. Written orders that we burned after we memorized them word for word. Each team received their own set of orders from Wright. None of us knows what any of the other teams are doing. But Wright does. He's the closest thing to a general this army has. If anyone knows the whole battle plan, it's Earl Wright."

"Who does he get his orders from?"

"He works for WLSCTC."

"In Richmond?"

"In Richmond. He has an office on the second floor of the WLSCTC building. His official title is Operations Director, and his office is on the floor directly below the executive suite and the board room. Capture Wright, and you get the best information source I know of in the organization."

"Anyone else?"

"Dickhead."

"I beg your pardon?"

"That's the guy's name. His real name is Richard Sutton, but we call him Dickhead. He has a long scar across his forehead, an inch above the eyes, probably from a battle wound. Maybe from an IED or a rocket blast. He's one of the guys who trained us, and he's one of the guys who killed me in Pakistan. I have a score to settle with Dickhead. Leave a piece of him for me."

"Tell me about your orders. Who are you assigned to kill?"

"Two U. S. Senators, one American four-star general, one government official in the State Department, and Eddie Morsay."

"Eddie? You've been assigned to kill Eddie?"

"Eddie and his whole family. His kids are away at college, so we'll only need to hit Eddie and his wife. We have his home address, and we'll take Eddie out in his house some night after he gets home from work. I wouldn't be surprised if another team has your name on their hit list. I know they have your address."

"When? When is this supposed to happen?"

"Soon. When we get back to the states, we'll pick up weapons and wait for a go signal. Each team leader—the sniper—has a cell phone. So does the observer on each team. When they text the first go signal to the sniper, we'll move into position. When we get the second go signal, we'll take out the targets in order. The Senators are first. Then the generals. Eddie's last on the list."

"I'll have to stop you."

"I hope you do."

"Give me the names of your targets."

Bill gave her the names. "You can bet the Speaker of the House is on one of the other hit lists," Bill added. "Probably half the Senate and the senior Representatives, too. Secretary of State. Secretary of Defense. Military Chiefs of Staff. Some key cabinet members. Maybe the President and Vice President. You won't be able to protect them all."

"Maybe we can save some. I'll relay your information to the Colonel."

"Does he know I didn't die? Well, I did die. At least, my body died. But I'm still around and I have a new body. Did you tell him?"

"I don't think the Colonel would believe me if I did tell him. So I haven't told him yet."

"How about Eddie?"

"Eddie knows."

"What did he say when you told him?"

"Eddie has worked with Lokesvara and Vajrapani before. He's seen some pretty amazing things."

"Warn Eddie. He's a nice guy. I'd hate to see him die."

"I'll tell Eddie as soon as I get back. Do you know what they're planning for London? Or Israel?"

"Everything is too compartmentalized and targets are kept on a need-to-know basis. I only know the names of the targets my team is assigned. But Wright is moving all of us into position. No one is left in camp. Rumor has it that some guys are going to England, some to Afghanistan, some to the Far East, and some to the Middle East."

"Who's going to Moscow?"

"None of us."

"Then they have men in more than one training camp. I know they plan to hit Moscow."

"The camp in Pakistan has been shut down. So has the camp in Africa. I don't know of any others."

"I'd bet a month's pay that they have teams from other camps already on their way to Moscow, Paris, Berlin, and a few more places. There must be a camp somewhere in eastern Europe that we don't know about."

"I won't bet against you."

"I'm going back to warn Eddie and tell the Colonel. But I'll return tomorrow."

"Promise?"

"I promise."

When Deb emerged from the ladies room, Eddie was waiting outside the door.

"You took longer than twenty minutes," Eddie said. "I was beginning to worry."

"There's plenty to worry about," said Deb. "You and your wife are on their hit list, Eddie. I probably am, too. And the President. And most of the Senate. And God only knows who else. We've got to tell the Colonel."

"He's waiting in the briefing room."

Colonel McMichaels had read all of Deb's reports, and Eddie had briefed the Colonel weekly on developments. When Deb told the Colonel she had just spoken with one of the trained assassins and confirmed the threat, the Colonel demanded to know the name of the informant. "It's Bill Ramsey, Sir," said Deb.

"Bill's *alive*?"

"No, Sir. Bill was killed in Pakistan. But his spirit took over another body. Right now he's in South Africa with about four thousand trained assassins. They're coming here to kill the President and half the members of Congress."

Deb had expected the Colonel to react with disbelief, but McMichaels barely lifted an eyebrow. "Tell me, Chief, how did you manage to talk to a dead man in South Africa while you used the ladies room? I'd really like to know."

"I traveled to South Africa in spirit form," said Deb, knowing how crazy that must sound. "It's called astral travel, and I'm not making this up, Colonel. Ask Chief Morsay. He's seen it done."

"I've seen it done, too," said the Colonel with a straight face. "My wife does it all the time."

Eddie and Deb both felt their jaws drop open with surprise. “Your wife astral travels?” asked Deb, realizing she knew so little about the Colonel’s personal life. McMichaels had never spoken about his wife before, and Deb had never met the woman at any of Fort Belvoir’s social gatherings. The Colonel had no pictures of his wife on his desk, and he wore no wedding ring. Deb had assumed the man was divorced or never married.

“I’ll tell you about it sometime,” said the Colonel. “But now you have the floor. Tell me what Ramsey told you. Don’t leave anything out.”

Deb told the Colonel everything she knew, including the names of the Senators and the general on Ramsey’s hit list. She said Eddie and his family were also on the list, and she suspected her own name was on one of the other lists. Maybe the Colonel’s name, too.

“How much time do we have?” asked the Colonel.

“A few days,” said Deb. “Less than a week.”

“I’ll notify the Director,” said McMichaels, meaning the Director of National Intelligence. “I’ll tell him we have confirmation from an asset on the ground to support your analysis. We have contingency plans in place, but it will take time to get everybody on board and implement those plans. Our first priority will be to protect the President and members of Congress. You and Eddie will have to look out for yourselves. Get your families someplace safe.”

After the Colonel left to notify the DNI, Eddie phoned his wife and told her to pack for an extended stay out of town. Deb phoned Bill Porter and told him to do the same. Bill flatly refused to leave Deb alone. "We're in this together, my love," he said. "The Ranger taught me how to kill with knives and guns. I think I still remember how. And I can always teleport out of danger if I need to. I'm staying here."

Deb didn't waste time arguing. She told Bill she loved him now more than ever.

After she got off the phone, she teleported to Angkor Wat. It was time to tell the Ranger and Lokesvara that she needed their help.

* * *

Anong was not a Kuli. Anong had always been a Quli. Until now.

The Sanskrit word "kuli" originally meant an itinerant worker or day laborer, one who had left home to work for people who were neither family nor countrymen. In Urdu, Kuli became Quli, which came to mean a slave from conquered lands. The words sounded the same in both languages, but the subtle differences were immense. Kulis were paid for their labor. Qulis were not.

Americans pronounced the word exactly the same, but they had Americanized it to “coolie” in the last half of the nineteenth century and applied the term indiscriminately and derogatorily mostly to Asian workers who laid railroad track west of Kansas and worked the mines in northern California. Some coolies were kuli who came to America to work for better pay than they could get in their own country. Some were quli, and they had been shanghaied and forced to work like slaves in the mines. Few quli survived the harsh conditions for long, and many were killed in frequent mine cave-ins. Some were killed outright or simply disappeared when they became sick or injured or too frail to work, their mutilated bodies buried under tons of rock, some of them not yet dead when they were buried.

In each of her previous lives, Anong had no acknowledged country because she had so often been taken or driven from her home by evil men who seemed to pursue her relentlessly. She had sometimes been forced into slavery, forced to entertain men and service them without compensation, not unlike a quli. She had been beaten and tortured, and she had been slaughtered like an animal. She was a Quli, and Qulis were victims.

Now Anong was Quli no longer. Lokesvara helped her to see the goddess within herself, to use the powers of the mind and spirit to free herself from quli bondage.

Not only did Lokesvara teach her to systematically relive past lives to regain accumulated knowledge that had been clouded by numerous rebirths, he taught her to awaken the sleeping Kundalini that was her core essence.

And he taught her the Tummo breath.

"Coiled about the base of the spine like a snake," said Lokesvara, "the Kundalini resides within every spirit body as a subtle energy. Most of the time, as we mindlessly move through the mundane world, Kundalini sleeps to store energy for when it's really needed. But when we awaken the sleeping serpent through will or desire, through mindfulness, it rises up from the center of our being. It ascends the various energy channels of the subtle body to release unbelievable energy, setting the chakras to spinning like wheels of light, firing the dan-tien, opening all the subtle centers. As the Kundalini rises, it becomes a powerful force."

"I have read of the Kundalini," said Anong. "And I have heard about the chakras. Lord Vishnu said my power resided in the Sudarshana Chakra and that power would manifest when the Kundalini serpent awakened."

"Just so," said the monk. "You may begin meditation now. When the mind is still, listen to my words."

Anong closed her eyes. After a moment, her breathing slowed.

"First, go inside yourself," instructed the old man, "And my words will go with you and follow to your core. Go deep inside yourself to find the very center of your being. Now place yourself in that exact center and continue silent meditation. Focus all of your awareness there at that center, about four fingers below the navel. Ignite the fire in your belly by holding your awareness at that exact point until you see flames flare up. Begin repeating a single *Bija* or seed syllable inside your mind like a mantra. You can use Om, or Ah, or Dhih, or Hum. They all work, so pick the one that feels most comfortable to you. Repetition is the key. Allow one part of your mind to continue the mantra as another part focuses on the breath. Breathe in. Hold the breath inside for a count of five. Breathe out. Picture prana—the sacred energy resident in air— entering your body through every pore. See prana as a color. White, red, blue, yellow." He paused until Anong's breathing slowed and her muscles went slack. "Once again," he said. "Breathe in. Hold the breath in for a count of five. Breathe out. Feel the *Drod*, the fire in the belly, grow hotter and brighter with each and every breath. Begin the Tummo exercises. Tummo fans the flames of the fire with the bellows breath. Take quick, short intakes of breath through both nostrils as if you were pumping a bellows, which is what your lungs are. Feel the flames rising from your center. As you continue the bellows breath, the flames rise higher and higher, hotter and hotter, brighter and brighter. Now the intense heat you are generating awakens the sleeping Kundalini. The serpent of power uncoils from around your center and rises up with the flames. As the serpent's hooded head and the heat of the flames pass each of your chakra centers, those chakras become infused with Kundalini energy. Each chakra, in turn, begins to spin. Faster and faster. Faster and faster. Faster and faster. Feel the heat expanding now. Feel the glow increasing. It begins in the belly and rises all the way to the top of the head. But don't release it yet. Keep it in. Circulate that heat and light through the Ida and Pingala, the male and female meridians on each side of your spine. Keep that heat circulating in your body like a modern heat pump. Keep it circulating, keep it moving. Now open up your third eye—the Ajna—and allow the light to shine forth."

"I can feel the fire in my belly," said Anong.

"Good," said Lokesvara. "Now fan that fire with the bellows breath. Add Tummo. Kindle the fire in the dan-tien, fan the flames higher with the bellows breath, and release the Kundalini."

A beam of blinding white light, as pure as the snows of Mount Meru, emerged from a spot on the girl's forehead, engulfing the room and all in it.

"Now visualize, within the light, a disk with 108 serrated points like the sharp points of an arrow or the blade of a kris. Use the Kundalini energy to set the disk to spinning. As it spins faster and faster, you control the disk with your will. You can hurl the disk at an enemy as if thrown from your hand. Repeat this mantra: *Om sudarshanaya vidmahe mahajwaalaya dheemahi tannaschakra prachodayath.* Add *Swaha* at the end to fix your intention and make it so. Feel the power of the Sudarshana Chakra. With this power, you may slay your enemies. Do not release the disk until you face an enemy. Save your strength for when you need it. The Kundalini is like a battery. When the Kundalini power is used up, the serpent needs to sleep to recharge the battery. Now you must reverse the process. Allow the power to pass. Allow the Kundalini to rest. Be still and meditate."

When Anong finally opened her eyes, she said, "Thank you master. I am no longer afraid."

"A little fear may be not be unwise, my child," said the monk. "Our enemies possess weapons as powerful or more powerful than we. The universe seeks balance in all things, and if we are aspects of the gods so do our adversaries represent equal and opposite aspects of the same gods. Now tell me, who was it you feared?"

"A demon. His name is Mahesvara."

"I know of Mahesvara," said the old man. "His is the destructive power of Lord Shiva. And it is said that before Lord Gautama's enlightenment, Mahesvara misled the world with the five poisons: lust, greed, desire, ignorance, and pride. He is a dangerous adversary. How is it you know of him?"

"He wanted me for his wife."

"He already has a wife. Her name is Uma."

"He said he would take possession of me and I would become Uma."

"I wonder what Uma would say about that. She is almost as powerful as Mahesvara. She is a jealous goddess and wouldn't take kindly to being replaced by a mortal."

"Mahesvara put a spell on me. He said if he couldn't have me, he would destroy me."

Lokesvara lapsed into silent meditation. Anong waited patiently for the old man to speak again. When he did, he said, "We must prepare. Please ask Vajrapani to join us."

Anong found Vajrapani in the classroom teaching geography to children. "The Lama Lokesvara requests your presence," she announced. Vajrapani gave the children an assignment and immediately left the classroom with Anong at his side.

When they arrived at Lokesvara's chamber, the American woman named Debbie Johnson was waiting with the Abbot.

"Deb has come to us seeking our help," said Lokesvara. "She has talked again with Bill Ramsey, and he informed her that evil men plan to assassinate the world leaders, all of the world leaders, within a few days. I have spoken with Anong, and she tells me that Mahesvara, whose power to work in this world directly was greatly reduced by the Enlightened One, is at work in the world once again. I believe Mahesvara intends to unleash chaos on this world through his avatars, ignorant men and women who are motivated only by lust and greed. He wants nothing more than to rule the world. And if he can't rule the world, he will destroy it."

"Who is Mahesvara?" asked Deb Johnson.

"He is the destructive side of Lord Shiva. He is a prideful spirit who takes possession of mortal men through lust and greed and ignorance. He would be the ruler or the destroyer of the three worlds, but he has been limited by the Powers that Be, the

Dharma, to the two lower realms of desire and form. He is the demon of Arrogance, Anger, and Delusion. He is pure evil."

"But who is he exactly? What does he look like?"

"He is legion, and he has more than a thousand faces, ten thousand forms. He takes possession of mortals, and he could look like anyone or be anyone. He is a most dangerous adversary who deludes mortals by appearing to do one thing or be one thing while doing or being another."

"Is he a god? And if he is a god, how can we mortals fight him?"

"Mahesvara likes to think he is a god," said Lokesvara. "It is said that gods exist only in the third realm, the world without form. They exist as pure spirit, and thus they cannot work directly in this world without help. For a spirit to work in the physical realm, avatars are needed that have physical form. It is said that Jesus was an avatar of El, or Yahweh, and Mohammad was an avatar of Allah. Mahesvara is said to be an emanation of Shiva. He represents but one attribute of Shiva, and his spirit can manifest in the real world only though the use of avatars. Avatars are manifestations of aspects of the divine in the physical world. Avatars may be incarnated spirits or they might be ordinary human beings possessed by the spirit of a god."

"Jesus was God incarnate?" asked Deb. "The Gospels were correct?"

"Jesus was a man, an ordinary mortal, possessed by the spirit of God," said the Lama. "Jesus was a way for God to act in and through the world. He was God's avatar."

"That makes perfect sense to me," said Deb. "Didn't Jesus say he was possessed by the Holy Spirit? He often said God was in him. As Jesus said in John 14:10, 'Believest thou not that I am in the Father, and the Father in me? The words that I speak unto you I speak not of myself: but of the Father that dwelleth in me, he doeth the works.'"

"Mahesvara may not be a god but a demon, because he cannot exist in the third realm, the realm of formlessness and enlightenment. He is a demon contained by the worlds of desire and form. He is not an enlightened being, and he may never become one. His selfish pride, arrogance, and anger hold him back. All beings may become as gods when they become truly enlightened, when they shed desire and pride and become truly selfless, when they allow compassion to trump ego. Those are the rules of the game, the Dharma. Without compassion, one is trapped forever in the lower realms of desire and form. Ego prevents transcendence to formlessness, and Mahesvara is pure ego. It is Mahesvara's ego that we must vanquish if we are to win this battle."

"But," said Deb, "if Mahesvara is an aspect of Shiva and has the destructive power of the gods, how can we battle him and win?"

"Mahesvara can only be vanquished by using the venom of humiliation as an antidote for the poison of pride. We must meet him on the field of battle and soundly defeat him. We must strip him of his pride and arrogance and delusion, allowing all to see him—himself included— for what he truly is. It will not be easy, but we must prevail. The Dharma depends on it."

The old man rose from lotus and walked to the table at the far end of the room. He picked up the Vajra, the Kris, and the Noose and handed them to Vajrapani. Then he returned to the table and picked up the Vajra sword of enlightenment, the sharp sword of prajna with the power to slice through delusion and ego. He also picked up a book, and he plucked a lotus blossom from a brass bowl. "I, too, would join this fight as Manjusri," said the old man, his soft voice becoming like a lion's roar as Manjusri manifested in the physical world.

Anong couldn't believe her eyes. As she looked in amazement at the transformed Lokesvara, she sensed other transformations happening around her as well. Vajrapani was now no longer the Lone Ranger but the Bodhisattva Vajrapani, and the Johnson woman had disappeared and in her place was Ksitigarbha, the Sacred Girl.

"Maitreya, too, shall join us," said the woman, "when it is time."

Anong felt privileged to be in the presence of three of the Eight Great Bodhisattvas. But she was also frightened. If three of the most powerful protectors of the Dharma were armed for battle and uncertain of victory, how great must be the threat they faced!

But whatever the threat, no matter how great it might be, Anong made up her mind to stand and fight with her friends. For she no longer felt weak and powerless. She was no longer a victim, a quli. She was Anong, and she carried within her the gift of the gods.

CHAPTER ELEVEN

Earl Wright positioned his men in safe houses scattered throughout the greater Washington, D. C. area. One of WLSCTC's subsidiaries had purchased the buildings—houses, apartment complexes, and commercial properties—as investments after the real estate bubble burst in 2008, picking up foreclosures for pennies on the dollar. They even owned a couple of motels in Maryland, perfect for housing transient personnel.

Wright was amazed by the quantity and quality of complicated advance planning that had gone into this entire operation from the very beginning. Someone had obviously orchestrated the purchase of those strategically-located properties years before they were needed. Someone had purchased weapons and munitions on black markets in various corners of the world and pre-positioned them for pick-up where and when they were needed. Earl recognized the hand of John Brakken in some of the weapons acquisitions and real estate deals, but Brakken was a doer and gofer, like Wright was, and not the kind of thinker and planner it took to pull off something as enormous as this. Whoever it was that planned this decades ago, he had the unique ability to see the big picture and exactly how to fit all of the pieces of the puzzle together to make it work over time.

And it was that same someone who had the foresight to hire Brakken, who in turn hired Wright, who in turn hired Edie. It was Brakken who acquired most of the girls who serviced the men. Brakken had lots of connections in black markets, and Wright knew Brakken ran parallel networks of drugs out of Afghanistan and Turkey that supplied off-the-books operating capital for acquiring women and weapons and munitions. Brakken was an undeniable asset to the organization because of his connections.

So far everything had proceeded perfectly, right on schedule. When the guys had landed at Dulles in WLSCTC cargo planes, the TSA and customs people had treated them like returning warriors from Afghanistan, thanking them for their service to their country. If only they knew!

Homeland Security had grown lax in the decade and a half since 9/11, and the death of Osama bin Laden made it seem like there was nothing to fear anymore. Even the CIA and INSCOM operated like lasting peace, except for a few brush-fire wars, was just around the corner. If only they knew!

The people who did know, or at least suspected, had been added to the hit lists. Deb Johnson, Eddie Morsay, and Colonel McMichaels would be dead within days. That would be a big load off Wright's mind. There was something about those three that triggered warnings in Wright's subconscious. The fact that Johnson had survived one attack didn't sit well with him. She should already be dead, but she wasn't. And that bothered him a great deal.

But what could Deb Johnson do at this late date to throw a monkey wrench into the works? Absolutely nothing. Even if she knew their exact plans—which was impossible—who would believe her? And even if someone did believe her far-fetched conspiracy theories, it would take weeks or months to get the military bureaucracy off their butts and into motion. Within a week, everything would be over and Johnson could be counted among the dead or permanently disabled. The Secretary of Defense and the Chair of the Joint Chiefs would be dead. The military bureaucracy would be leaderless and ineffective.

One other thing did worry Wright and that was the aftermath of the assassinations. With the leadership of the country out of the way, politicians that WLSCTC owned or had compromised would be in charge of American policy, foreign and domestic. What were those political puppets being asked to do? What kind of country would the U. S. become? Who would pull their strings?

What was this all about anyway?

Wright had never concerned himself with such thoughts before. He was a doer, not a thinker. His job was to accomplish the mission, and when his job was done he simply moved on to the next mission assignment without looking back. It didn't pay to look back or to look too far ahead.

Earl Wright was the kind of guy who thrived on removing obstacles to mission accomplishment. When there was a mountain in his way, he went through the mountain, or over the mountain, or around the mountain, or under the mountain, or he blew up the mountain. No mountain ever stood in his way for very long. That was the way Earl had been trained, and that was the way he operated.

Earl Wright had a one-track mind: accomplish the mission. Like a vicious attack dog who had been given the scent, he had been trained to run his prey down until he could tear it apart and eventually kill and devour it. It didn't matter what or who or where the prey was. Once he caught the scent, he was off and running.

But this was different. This was more than just the hunt.

Everything was too perfect. Everything so far had gone exactly according to plan, just like magic, without a hitch of any kind. Wright sensed there was more at work here than met his eye, something he couldn't quite put his finger on. He shook that thought off and concentrated on the mission.

His troops were all in position waiting for the go signal. He knew Charlie had similarly-trained troops positioned in other countries also waiting for her signal to proceed. Charlie had called Wright on the special cell phone twice a day with accurate updates on targets. Her intel was impeccable, and Earl suspected she had a network of operatives shadowing the targets on the ground almost constantly. The sheer size and complexity of this operation still boggled Wright's mind, and he had to admire a woman who could keep it all straight in her head.

Wright had never met a woman like Charlie before.

Earl Wright didn't take time to think about women very often. He kept far too busy to have much of a personal life. Besides, women were a needless distraction he felt he couldn't afford. Wright had long ago learned to sublimate his sexual urges into military action, and sinking a knife into warm flesh, slicing a throat with a garrote, felt more satisfying to Earl than stuffing his penis into a woman's vagina. Sex, after all, was meant primarily for procreation and not for personal pleasure, and Earl Wright had no time in his busy life for wife or children. Not now. Not ever. Sex might be a primary motivation for most other men, but it wasn't something that made Earl Wright tick.

But Charlie had stirred something within Earl that wouldn't do away. Thoughts of her spring-taut body, business-like demeanor, and icy-cold eyes rudely intruded when he least expected them, and he wondered what it would take to seduce such a woman, to subjugate her to his will, to make her moan, to make her beg for more. Was such a thing even possible? Did she find him as attractive as he found her?

Each time he had forced her image from his mind she would call on that damned telephone, and her sexy voice—so precise, so directive—would make him imagine her all over again. He imagined her tied to a bed, naked, waiting for him, wanting him, while he took his sweet time paying attention to all the little details others called foreplay before finally turning his full attention on her most pressing need.

He imagined her ordering him to enter her, and he would tell her, "No. Not until you beg." And he would make her beg and say "please, Earl," and he would make her squirm, and when he finally entered her he would make her scream.

That was all just fantasy, of course, and Earl Wright knew it was just fantasy. But he couldn't help fantasizing about her.

Where was she now? he wondered. In Dubai? In London? In Paris?

Where would he find her when all this was over?

And then the phone in Wright's pocket vibrated, and he took the phone out of his pocket and answered it, and Charlie's voice said, "Go," and Earl Wright forgot all about his infantile fantasies as he pressed star and two and ordered his men into action. Within two hours of the call, the first shot would be fired and the world would change forever. It was all over now except for the shouting.

BOOK II

The wolf shall dwell with the lamb, and the leopard shall like down with the kid; and the calf and the young lion and the fattling together; and a little child shall lead them.

Holy Bible, King James Version, Isaiah11:6

CHAPTER TWELVE

Anderson and Jens got the calls on their vibrating cell phones at the same time, and the team immediately grabbed their weapons and headed out the door. They had been quartered for three nights in a boarded up storefront in downtown Washington, only blocks from the White House and the U. S. Capitol, and they could be in position within minutes. They planned to take out the first Senator right outside the Hart Senate Office Building, named for deceased Michigan Senator Philip A. Hart, when the target Senator was picked up by a limousine to go to a scheduled dinner speaking engagement at the Washington Hilton. They wouldn't be able to reach the target in the Capitol itself nor in the underground subway tunnel connecting the Capitol Building and the Senate office complex, but when he left the Select Intelligence Committee meeting at the Hart Building at 1630, the Senator would be vulnerable.

The second target had offices for himself and his staff in the connecting Dirksen Building. Anderson and Jens would take out the main target, and Edwards and Radcliff would take out the second Senator simultaneously. Randy was the designated shooter, and Radcliff was the spotter-observer. Their target, too, was a member of the Senate Intelligence Committee. They expected both Senators to leave at the same time, by different doors, the second Senator to attend a different dinner party.

Randy and Radcliff took up positions in Lower Senate Park, across C Street from the office buildings. They had direct line-of-sight across First Street NE, and intermittent traffic on the street posed the only impediment to a clear shot. Anderson and Jens had positions outside a Catholic church a few blocks away.

Their escape route was simple: discard the weapons, a quick run through the park, cross D Street and Columbus Circle, and disappear into the Metro station where they would board a train to a safe house out in the suburbs. They would pick up fresh weapons at the safe house, and someone would drive them to the new target locations where Anderson and Jens would hit the general and Randy and Radcliff would hit the State Department guy. Then all four would go after Eddie Morsay.

Randy chambered a round in the sniper rifle and took aim through the scope. A Senate staff member had brought the Senator's car around, and Randy had the passenger door in his sights, centered in the crosshairs, ready to squeeze the trigger as soon as the target's head appeared in the crosshairs.

Randy and Bill Ramsey had already discussed what they would do. Neither wanted to kill a U. S. Senator, and Ramsey intended to turn the rifle on Radcliff a moment before Randy pulled the trigger. Radcliff was armed, and it would be a dangerous move. Randy had to ensure Radcliff kept his eyes on the target. Radcliff would kill Randy without blinking an eye if Radcliff smelled betrayal, so Randy had to kill Radcliff first.

"Distance and windage check," Randy said.

"Eight hundred meters," replied Radcliff. "Northeast wind one click."

"Roger that," said Randy. "Tell me when you see the door opening and the target comes out."

"Hold position," said Radcliff. "Any minute now. Wait for the target to clear the door."

Radcliff was lying prone about four feet to the right of Randy, and Randy mentally calculated how he could swing the rifle 90 degrees and get off a round before Radcliff could react. It would be difficult, but not impossible, if he rolled quickly to his left. Was it doable? Yes, with a little luck. He hoped he wasn't jinxed.

"Door opening," Radcliff said. "Target coming out."

"I got him in my crosshairs," Randy said.

"You're all clear," said Radcliff. "You're good to go. Fire at will."

"Keep your eye on the scope," said Randy. "Tell me where this first round hits."

Randy rolled to the left and brought the muzzle around quickly, squeezing the trigger at the same time as Radcliff reacted to the sudden motion by looking up from his scope and directly into the muzzle. Radcliff's head exploded like an overripe pumpkin as the 7.62 millimeter steel-jacketed projectile hit Radcliff's face at close range.

As Randy came up into a sitting position and chambered another round, he heard gunfire erupting to the east and assumed it was Anderson making a kill. He heard other shots, too, and he knew other teams were carrying out their assignments all over the city. He had to make a move while he still had a chance to get away.

"Find Deb Johnson and protect her," Bill Ramsey said inside Randy's head. "Get to the Metro and take a train to Alexandria. Wait for Deb at her apartment. Phone her at INSCOM and tell her what just happened. Tell her the locations of the safe houses. Tell her to tell Colonel McMichaels. Tell them to get the FBI and Homeland Security moving ASAP."

Randy dropped his rifle and stood up, removing his gloves, shirt, and pants as quickly as he could. Beneath the bulky camouflage clothing, he wore jeans and a black t-shirt with an "I heart Washington, D. C." logo on the front. He could easily pass as a civilian tourist taking in the sights on foot. He shoved the gloves into his pants pockets. As Radcliff had said, he was good to go.

Though he carried no identification, he did have a roll of one dollar bills in his right pants pocket. If he got to the Metro station, he could afford a train. But he'd take a train south to Alexandria instead of a train north to the safe house.

Now he heard sirens in the distance, and he knew he had to move fast before police shut down the transit system and set up roadblocks. As he sprinted through the park, he caught sight of frantic activity to the east and west of him as Capitol security responded to shots being fired in the area.

D Street was being blocked by snarled traffic as panicked drivers also reacted to sounds of gunfire by running red lights and creating accidents at every intersection. He knew he'd never get past all those cars without being seen. If D Street was blocked by traffic, Massachusetts Avenue would be worse. He abandoned plans for the Metro station, turned left on D, ran past the Japanese American Memorial and kept running. He continued west on D Street, slowing to a less-conspicuous jog, until he found a Washington Mass Transit Authority station near Pennsylvania Avenue. The Metro was still running. He paid the fare, and boarded a southbound train.

Forty minutes later, he got off the Metro in Alexandria. Fifteen minutes after that, he was knocking at Deb Johnson's apartment door. The guy who opened the door was about forty, slim, nerdy-looking, wearing wire-rimmed glasses. He was unarmed, but he didn't seem afraid.

"I'm Bill Ramsey," Randy said. "I'm looking for Deb Johnson. Does she still live here?"

"She's at work," said the nerdy-looking guy. He had a soft voice, and kind eyes.

"I'm an Army officer and I need to speak with her. Can I use your phone?"

"What did you say your name was?"

"Ramsey. Bill Ramsey. Major, U. S. Army."

"Come in, Major Ramsey. Deb has spoken highly of you. I know all about you and your death and resurrection."

"Who are you?"

"Porter. Bill Porter. I'm Deb's fiancé. You can use my cell phone, if you'd like, to call INSCOM. The cell is over there on the desk."

"Thanks, Turn on the TV, will you, please? I expect there will be breaking news on all the broadcast channels."

Randy asked for Deb's office phone number and then dialed it. Deb took a moment to answer.

"I can't talk now, Bill. All hell is breaking loose."

"Wrong Bill. It's Major Ramsey, Deb. The first shots have been fired."

"Where are you, Ramsey? Are you okay?"

"I'm okay. I'm in your apartment up here in Alexandria. Bill Porter let me in and let me use his phone. "

"Did you shoot the Senator?"

"No. I shot another guy on my team instead. But I think the rest of the hits are going down as planned. I couldn't stop them, so I didn't try."

"Fourteen Senators have been assassinated in the past hour. Plus the Secretary of Defense and all his deputies, the Secretary of State, and dozens of other ranking government officials. Maybe twenty percent of the House of Representatives. Several of the Joint Chiefs of Staff including the Chair of the Joint Chiefs. We're getting reports now from overseas. The British Prime Minister is dead. So is the German Chancellor. No word yet from Israel. Or China. Or Japan. Russia is in a panic. We have no intelligence on casualties there, but shots have been confirmed fired in Moscow and Saint Pete. Two American generals, one NATO general, and several of the Afghan security force commanders are dead in Afghanistan. It's a real mess."

"Any casualties on the other side?"

"A few. We haven't received reports from civilian law enforcement yet. The FBI is pretty busy right now, and so is Homeland Security."

"What about the President and Vice President?"

"They're safe. The President cancelled out of a political fundraiser after we informed him of a potential threat. The Secret Service will keep the President and Vice President under wraps for the time being at an undisclosed location. We managed to save a few who listened to our warning. Fortunately, the Secret Service took the threat seriously. Many other agencies didn't."

"Deb, listen. I think you're on one of the hit lists. Stay inside your office. Don't come home tonight. You're in danger."

"Eddie and I will be working on this all night. I might not be home for a day or two."

"Good. I'll stay here and guard Porter. Do you have any weapons stashed in the apartment? I had to leave mine behind."

"Negative. The police confiscated the two handguns you left behind the last time you visited. I never felt I needed firearms in my apartment. I'm sorry."

"Don't worry, I'll improvise something. I want to be ready for them when they come for you. And I will be."

"You sure they'll come to the apartment?"

"I'm sure."

"Tonight?"

"Tonight. After they have taken out their primary targets. You're near the bottom of their list. But I'm sure you're on someone's list."

"What are they after by creating all this carnage?" Deb asked. "What will they do next? What is their ultimate objective?"

"I don't know," said Ramsey. "Ask Earl Wright. Did you get him?"

"The FBI raided WLSCTC and shut it down, but Wright wasn't there. None of the staff had seen him or John Brakken for more than a week. Wright's obviously gone into hiding."

"I can tell you about some of the safe houses. Maybe you'll find him there."

Ramsey gave Deb the addresses of four of the safe houses he knew about. Deb promised to relay the information to Homeland Security and the FBI. Then Deb went back to work assessing the devastating impact to national security, and Ramsey went to search for household chemicals he could use to make improvised explosive devices.

"Why?" asked Bill Porter, sadly shaking his head in disbelief as a national news anchor named dozens of known dead including the Secretary of State. "Why are they doing this?"

"I don't know," said Ramsey.

"You really think they'll come here to kill Deb?"

"They will."

"What can I do to help?"

"Find all of the caustic chemicals you can. Toilet cleaners, drain openers, anything with acid or lye in it. Then bring me any thin glass containers with lids, the kind of glass that will shatter on impact. The thinner the better. Do you have any alcohol in the apartment? Rubbing alcohol? After shave? Cologne? Vodka? Bring anything you have with alcohol in it. And I'll need some pillow cases from the bed and a pair of scissors or pinking shears."

"I'll bring what I can."

"And matches. Every sulfur match you can find."

"All right."

Ramsey went into the apartment's kitchen and searched the refrigerator and cupboards for the rest of what he needed. He found a dozen eggs, a bottle of salad dressing, a bag of sugar, a container of salt, a bottle of vinegar, and a rack of assorted spices. He mixed the eggs and other ingredients into a two quart saucepan and set it on the gas stove to slowly boil into a gel. When it reached the desired consistency, he put the jelly into the freezer to cool quickly. When it was cool enough, he added the sulfur heads cut from wooden kitchen matches into the mixture.

Ramsey used the kitchen table to make two kinds of weapons from the assembled materials: incendiaries from the alcohol-based fluids, and caustics from the acidic fluids. He cut strips of cloth from the pillowcases and stuffed the cloth in the tops of the containers filled with alcohol. When lit, the cloth would act as a fuse. When the flames burned down to reach the alcohol gel, the bottles would explode. The caustics would burn as surely as flames when thrown on bare flesh or into open eyes.

Ramsey told Porter to toss the acid bottles at the first person through the door. There would probably be four men in the assault team, and they'd all be heavily armed. But they wouldn't be expecting resistance. Ramsey and Porter had the element of surprise in their favor, and they needed to capitalize on it if they expected to survive.

They had barely completed their preparations when the door burst open, splintered by a steel battering ram. Porter's reflexes were superb, and he had a jar of acid in each hand before two men came through the open doorway with assault rifles. He hit one of the men in the face with a jar, hurled hard enough that the jar shattered on impact and coated the man's face and eyes with drain opener and shards of broken glass. The other jar missed, and the second man opened fire at Bill Porter, sending a volley of 5.56 millimeter rounds straight for Porter's exposed mid-section.

But the bullets passed through empty air and hit the wall behind where Porter had been standing. Chips of plaster flew from the wall as the bullets chewed up the paint.

Ramsey couldn't believe his eyes as he saw Porter reappear right next to the assassin. Porter held a steak knife with a six-inch blade against the assassin's neck and made a quick slice through the carotid artery. Blood pumped out of the gaping hole in the man's neck, and the man immediately dropped his weapon and fell to the floor. Porter disappeared before the blood could touch him.

Ramsey dove for the rifle and had it in his hands when the third man came through the doorway. He placed two rounds in the third man's gut before a fourth man charged into the room. Ramsey rolled out of the way as a barrage of bullets tore up the carpet on the floor where Bill Ramsey had been only a moment before. Once again, Bill Porter appeared from nowhere next to the assassin, holding the knife grabbed from a Chicago Cutlery set to the man's throat. One quick slice, and it was all over.

Ramsey levelled the rifle at the first man who was still alive but trying to desperately to clear glass from his eyes with his left hand while holding onto his weapon with his right.

"Drop it, Carl," Ramsey ordered. Ramsey had recognized the guy as Carl Rossiter, an ex-Ranger he had known in Afghanistan. "I'll kill you if you keep holding that weapon." Carl let the rifle fall to the floor. "I can't see," he said. "I'm blind. I got glass and acid in my eyes. It hurts like hell! Help me!"

"Lie down on the floor, face up. Keep your hands where I can see them. We'll flush your eyes as soon as we can."

"All clear in the hallway," said Bill Porter.

"Good," Ramsey said. "Can you bring some baking soda and hot water, Bill? We'll flush the acid and glass out of this guy's eyes. Then we'll ask him some questions."

Porter carefully bathed Carl's eyes with the mixture of baking soda and water. The baking soda helped neutralize the acid. Then he soaked a towel in warm water and laid it across Carl's eyes.

Ramsey found a roll of duct tape and bound Carl Rossiter's wrists and ankles.

"How are you feeling, Carl?" Ramsey asked him. "Any better?"

"It doesn't burn as much now," Carl said. "But I still can't see a goddam thing."

"I'm Major Ramsey, Carl. We rangered together in Afghanistan. Remember?"

"Ramsey's dead," said Carl. "You can't be him."

"You're right, Carl. I am dead. Dickhead killed me in Pakistan. But I came back from the dead to stop you from killing innocent civilians."

"You're too late then. We already made the kills."

"Who did you kill, Carl? Who was on your list?"

"I ain't telling you squat."

"Bill," Ramsey said to Porter, "would you bring me another bottle of drain cleaner? And remove the towel from Carl's eyes so I can pour it where it will do the most damage."

"No!" Carl shouted. "You can't do that!"

"I can, and I will," said Ramsey. "You better start talking before Bill gets back with the drain cleaner."

Carl told Ramsey everything, babbling on incessantly to keep Ramsey from carrying out his threat. Carl's team had assassinated the Secretary of State, he said, and two other government officials before coming to Alexandria to take out Deb Johnson.

"Why?" asked Ramsey. "Why did you do it?"

"Because they paid me," said Carl. "They paid me more than the Army ever did."

"But why did you target the Secretary of State?"

"Because we were ordered to," said Carl.

"But why were you ordered to kill the Secretary of State? What did you hope to accomplish?"

"I don't know," said Carl. "That's the truth. They paid me and I did what I was told. I don't know why the Secretary of State was important. They told me to shoot him, and I did."

"Who told you?"

"Dickhead Sutton. And some guy named Wright."

"You worked for WLSCTC?"

"Yeah."

"WLSCTC is out of business, Carl. And you're out of a job. What were you supposed to do after you made the hits?"

"Go to the safe house and wait for orders."

"What kind of orders? Who were you to kill next?"

"I don't know. You got to believe me. I don't know nothin'. I only follow orders. Like I did in the Army. Like you did, when you was in the Army."

"Okay, Carl. I believe you. Relax. I won't put anything more in your eyes. Just tell me the location of the safe house, and I'll stop asking questions."

While Ramsey was interrogating Carl, Bill Porter had gathered up the weapons and ammunition. He dragged the bodies of the dead assassins to a corner of the room.

"How did you do that, Bill?" Ramsey asked. "How did you disappear and reappear like that?"

"Teleportation," answered Porter. "I moved a quantum of energy from one point in space-time to another. It's a natural phenomenon, not unlike electricity. I created a difference of potential with my mind, and energy flowed from one point to another because nature seeks equilibrium. Negative to positive and positive to negative, cancelling each other out. Anyone can do it, once they know how."

“And just where did a civilian like you learn to cut a man’s throat?”

“The Ranger taught me. The guy you call Vajrapani. He trained me the way he was trained in the Army.”

“You know Vajrapani?”

“I know him quite well, as a matter of fact,” said Porter. “I consider him a close personal friend. I saw him just last week.”

“Where was your friend when we needed him?” asked Ramsey. “I thought Deb said he would prevent the killings from happening. But he didn’t.”

“He can’t be everywhere all at once,” said Porter. “I’m sure he did his part.”

“But isn’t he supposed to be a god? How could a god let this happen?”

“Vajrapani isn’t a god. He doesn’t control the universe, not by a long shot. He’s a human spirit who seeks to restore balance to the universe when things get too far out of balance. He’s been around a long time, and he knows how to do things we don’t. But he isn’t a god.”

“Too bad,” said Bill Ramsey. “We could use a god about now.”

* * *

Vajrapani stood between the killers and their target, the Prime Minister of Japan. He deliberately became a target himself.

Bullets could kill a reincarnated Bodhisattva if they touched him. He had to make certain bullets didn't touch his mortal body.

The Ranger's spirit had observed the men moving into position, and he had watched them until he was certain of their intent. Then he had returned to his body at Angkor Wat. A moment later Vajrapani had physically teleported back to Tokyo.

It had become increasingly difficult for the Ranger to think of himself as separate from Vajrapani. Both spirits shared the same values as well as the same human body. It was impossible to tell where one stopped and the other began.

Lokesvara had taught the Ranger that, at a level most humans could never fathom, the universe was One, an interconnected expanse of pure energy that continued almost forever. There were many levels of existence, and each interacted with the others. What we thought of as reality was mostly an illusion. Reality itself was beyond human perception.

At one level, matter and energy were interchangeable. By making a quantum leap from one level to another, matter became energy. That's what made teleportation possible. Energy could move matter from one point in space-time to another as matter converted to energy and back again.

Vajrapani, who was a spirit of pure energy, existed on a different level—or plane—of existence than humans. But in order to manifest in the physical world—in order to affect things in the human realm—Vajrapani needed the help of a human incarnation who was grounded to this time and place.

Vajrapani's energy was so powerful that his manifestation physically changed the Ranger's body into what appeared to be a seven-foot giant. Sometimes Vajrapani manifested as a fierce warrior with fangs and multiple limbs. He had a third eye in the middle of his forehead, and he wore a serpent necklace around his neck, a tiger skin robing his body, and a five-pointed hat atop his head. That's what happened now as Vajrapani appeared in Tokyo. He was known in Japan as Kongo Shu Bogatsu, or simply Nio, and he was sometimes called Fudo-Myo, the holder of the Vajra. As Vajrapani manifested in Tokyo, he held the Vajra in his right hand, the Kris in his left.

The Lasso was tied around his waist like a belt. He stood squarely in the shooter's sights, half-way between the shooter and the Prime Minister of Japan, effectively blocking the shooter from hitting his assigned target.

The shooter recovered quickly from the surprise intrusion, and he aimed his rifle at Vajrapani's torso and squeezed the trigger. At this range, and with a target so huge, the shooter couldn't miss. He intended to take out the intruder first, then return to the primary target. Vajrapani saw that the observer was also reaching for his M4, and the observer intended to follow the first shot with shots of his own.

Thunder roared in the heavens and drowned out the sounds of gunfire as separate bolts of lightning struck each of the bullets, knocking them out of the air half-way to their target. Both the shooter and the observer were instantly blinded by multiple white-hot flashes spiking in front of their eyes.

"Drop your weapons," Vajrapani bellowed in a voice as loud as the thunder. "I have no desire to harm you."

Panicked, the two men fired their weapons blindly. The wrathful Vajrapani raised the Vajra and both men vanished as lightning struck their positions.

Now the flanker and the observer emerged from hiding and fired at the giant. Again, Vajrapani raised the Vajra and twin bolts of lightning sent the men someplace else, someplace far away and dark where they could contemplate their actions and learn to repent before being reborn.

With the Prime Minster safe, Vajrapani went to the home of the Finance Minister where another team of assassins were in position to open fire. Again, Vajrapani gave them an ultimatum, an opportunity to lay down their weapons and leave. Again, they refused.

And, once again, the skies filled with thunder and lightning as the wrathful Vajrapani directed their spirits to a far-away place.

Before the night was over, Vajrapani had saved the lives of fourteen people in Japan without taking a single human life himself.

Because he couldn't be two places at the same time, he couldn't save more and that worried him immensely. Each life was precious, each person had a role to play in the great drama of human interactions. Every life that was cut short changed the dynamics of the way the world worked.

Manjusri had chosen to go to China to save lives, and Vajrapani was certain that Manjusri had saved many there, too. Would it be enough?

If every death affected the way the world worked, how had the deaths this night affected the Dharma? What subtle changes were already taking place?

Dharma sustained the harmony of the universe. Dharma was the universal law or rules by which the game of life was played. Dharma held this world—and all worlds—together in a symbiotic relationship, a natural order of things that was knowable by enlightened beings. Chinese philosophers had called Dharma the "Tao," the way. Christians called it the "logos," the meaning or purpose or raison d'etre. Dharma maintained the natural order of things through a cause and effect relationship. Every cause had an effect, every action a reaction.

One aspect of Dharma was karma, the consequences of one's actions dictating the future. Not only your own future, but everyone else's, too. The universe was in a constant state of change, of becoming. What it would become, was dependent on the actions of the present. Today's actions changed the future dramatically. Nothing would ever be the same again.

How much the Dharma would be affected was still to be seen. If Mahesvara's intention was to rip asunder the fabric of society, the basis of civilization, by demonstrating the rule of law was ineffective, then he was partially successful. The rules by which people lived, the safety they felt in their own homes, the ability of the police and the military to protect them from harm, had fallen by the wayside with the deaths of so many people. When high-profile leaders the world over were murdered on the same day while going about their ordinary business, what could prevent the same thing from happening to other people? Was anyone safe anywhere anymore? People would know the rules civilized people had played by all their lives no longer applied because death and destruction were present now everywhere and couldn't be stopped. Once the commandment "Thou shalt not kill" had been violated, no other commandment could be considered sacred. The old rules no longer applied. New rules would take their place.

Fear made people irrational, and irrational people often acted irrationally. Some people might become violent, seeking an eye for an eye. They would demand retribution, not just for the killings, but for destroying their innocence and trust. And when retribution wasn't immediately forthcoming, they would explode in violent behavior that was totally irrational. Vajrapani had seen it happen before, time after time, throughout human history. The French Revolution and the Russian Revolution were just two examples. Unruly mobs of desperate people could create such chaos that the last remnants of civilization would fall away, exposing the vulnerable underbelly of society. Naked humanity wasn't always pretty. Sometimes it was downright scary.

Once started, violence would continue escalating. Round and round the wheel would go, and where it would stop nobody could know.

Mahesvara thrived on violence. As the violence increased, so would Mahesvara's powers.

For the past two thousand or more years, the Dharma had placed limits on Mahesvara's destructive abilities. Consequently, civilized people had been able to band together and agree to rules that kept unbridled greed and lust and violence somewhat in check.

But this time, Mahesvara possessed an avatar that had managed to change the whole world practically overnight. Not only was this avatar smart, he had patience and foresight. From what Deb had told Lokesvara, this whole thing had been in process since before 9/11/2001.

It made one wonder if Osama bin Laden and the 9/11 terrorists had somehow fit into Mahesvara's overall plan.

Who was he, this avatar of Mahesvara? And just as important, *where* was he?

And what was he planning to do next?

CHAPTER THIRTEEN

Earl Wright was not pleased. Though most of the hits went off exactly as planned, there were some notable failures. Deb Johnson was still alive, and that certainly wasn't good. More than a dozen men had been killed or captured, and that wasn't good, either. Lester Radcliff was dead, and Randy Edwards was missing, either captured or killed. Radcliff and Edwards had failed to complete any part of their mission, and all of their targets remained alive. The four men sent to Deb Johnson's apartment to kill Johnson had been presumed dead when they didn't report to the safe house within a reasonable time. The team that had been assigned to take out the Vice President of the United States had been captured by Secret Service. A team assigned to hit the Treasury Secretary had been shot at the scene after shooting the Secretary. Another team had been killed by police, but only after successfully taking out a U. S. Representative at his house in the suburbs. It was a mixed bag, but Wright didn't take any failure lightly.

Wright had moved all of his men—nearly five hundred of them—to new safe houses in Maryland, addresses unknown to any of the men who had been captured. Wright had his own personal safe house in a Baltimore suburb, fully furnished, an hour's drive from D. C. He had made it his new headquarters. When

Wright reported the results to Charlie, she congratulated him on a job well done. She confided that operations in Japan and China had not gone nearly as well as the ones in America or Afghanistan. Charlie told Wright to sit tight and wait for further instructions. She said she would get back to him in a day or two.

Wright turned on the television and lit a cigarette as he watched the news, switching between CNN and Fox News and back when a commercial came on either station. The President of the United States had urged the country to remain calm, assuring the American People that Homeland Security and the Federal Bureau of Investigation were rounding up the killers—which he described as a disaffected para-military group—even as he addressed the nation. The President said it was too early to tell for sure yet, but it seemed these were home-grown terrorists, not foreign-born jihadists. The President said he was in constant contact with the leaders of most foreign nations trying to sort this out, and he had sent condolences to the British and German peoples on the loss of their Prime Ministers and other officials. He promised that the perpetrators of these heinous crimes would be brought to justice. If it were true that American citizens were indeed responsible for the deaths of those foreign officials it was not with the official sanction of the U. S. Government. Meanwhile, he urged calm and asked people to pray for the dead and injured. He announced that emergency measures were now in place that would prevent anything like this from happening again.

Fox News reported the Secretary of State and the Secretary of Defense among the dead, along with sixteen U. S. Senators and forty-two members of the House of Representatives.

CNN ran a sidebar segment on para-military groups in various parts of the United States, including interviews with leaders of some of the more radical militias. Naturally, they all denied any involvement with what had happened. They claimed to be as surprised and horrified as everyone else.

The Director of the FBI and the Secretary of Homeland Security repeated the President's pledge to bring the perpetrators to justice. A state of emergency had been declared, and Washington D. C. had been cordoned off. No one got into or out of the nation's Capital without authorization. Roads were closed, airports were shut down, mass transit had armed soldiers with flak jackets and loaded automatic weapons riding every train.

"Too little, too late," Wright told the TV.

One of the Senators who was shot but survived was interviewed at Bethesda Naval Hospital. He told how he was walking from his car to his home when he felt a sharp pain in his left side that doubled him over. Then he was knocked from his feet by a second bullet that slammed into his abdomen. Then the pain hit and he passed out. He was lucky, he said, that both bullets missed vital organs. "Whoever trained those boys to shoot, did a lousy job," said the Senator.

"Bullshit," said Wright. "You were just plain lucky."

BBC reported widespread panic in London, a city that had survived the Nazi blitz but couldn't defend itself against a handful of modern gunmen. The entire city was in shock over the loss of the Prime Minister and several members of Parliament. Heathrow had been shut down, and cab drivers were urged to report suspicious activity to the police.

Japan had fared far better than most other industrialized countries, losing only a few minor officials who could be replaced. A sudden lightning storm had prevented the perpetrators from assassinating the Prime Minister and the Finance Minister, interrupting the attempt on the Prime Minister's life and frightening the assassins away. They had left behind their sniper rifles and scopes in their hurry to escape. A nation-wide search was underway in Japan for the would-be assassins. Both China and Russia had declared martial law. Information from those countries remained scant, and no details were forthcoming from either government. It was as if the old Iron Curtain had suddenly descended to block sight of what was now happening on stage from an audience sitting entirely in the dark.

Europe was in complete chaos. Germany and France had suffered heavy losses. The Italian Prime Minster and two government officials were dead. NATO was on full alert. An attempt had been made on the Pope's life, but through some unexplained miracle the Pope's secretary and three Swiss guards had taken the bullets meant for the Pontiff. The old man was still alive and in seclusion inside Vatican City.

Only half the hits in Israel were successful, thanks to quick moves by the Shabak, the Israeli Internal Security Agency. The Mossad, the Israeli Institute for Intelligence and Special Tasks, had alerted the Shabak that assassination attempts on government officials were imminent. The President and the Prime Minister, as well as most Knesset members, were shuttled to safety and afforded additional security. In a land where terrorist attacks were an everyday occurrence, all security threats were taken very seriously by the government. The few deaths that had occurred were attributed to Palestinian extremists, and Israel promised prompt retaliation against Hamas and others.

Now that this mission had been accomplished, even if not completely successful, Earl Wright was ready to move on to the next assignment. He knew his men were as impatient as he was to be doing something useful. Sitting around and waiting for orders was a big waste of time.

Though they had all learned to "Hurry up and wait" in the military, the men would certainly grow restless and unruly after only a day or two of doing nothing. Wright understood the need to keep a low profile while the military and every police force in the country were looking for them, but it still frosted his balls to sit around with his thumb up his ass. He knew his men felt the same way.

He phoned Dickhead and ordered the non-com to have the men clean and lube their weapons. They would need them again as soon as orders came down.

Earl wished he'd had the foresight to bring Edie and her girls to Maryland to entertain the troops. If he could be certain Edie's place hadn't been discovered when the FBI confiscated the records at WLSCTC headquarters, he would call her and have the girls here in a couple of hours.

That would keep the men happy and fully occupied for a day or two.

But women were always a liability in a combat situation, and the United States had become an active war zone after the first shot had been fired. This was now enemy territory for Wright and his men. He had to remember they were at war, and one wrong move could get them all killed.

Wright refilled his coffee cup, then sat back down and lit another cigarette. The mistake the United States had made in both Iraq and Afghanistan was to have no workable plan for what to do next after the initial battles were won. Brakken and Wright had planned to get the men to the safe houses after the assassinations, but they had made no plans for a long-term confinement to those safe houses.

Wright had distributed cash to the non-coms so they could send men out to buy food when the current stockpiles ran out. He suspected the men would be able to subsist on frozen TV dinners heated in the microwaves for about a week without complaining. Then he would have to find another solution for obtaining an adequate mess at each of the safe houses. They could have pizzas delivered a few times a week, he supposed. But long-term subsistence required proper prior planning. The Army always said, "Proper prior planning prevents piss poor performance." He was surprised Brakken hadn't thought of that. Brakken was supposed to be an expert at logistics and logistical planning.

Wright found a tablet of legal-sized paper and a ball point pen, and he began jotting down contingency plans for the future. If they were kept in place for a week or less, no further planning was necessary. If their confinement to the safe houses exceeded a week, the men would need a variety of fresh food, fresh clothing, and a way to keep from going stir crazy. They could do calisthenics in the house—men were used to doing sit-ups and push-ups indoors—but they would need to go outside to run. He decided early morning runs would attract the least attention, and he'd need to supply all the men with jogging shorts and running shoes to keep them inconspicuous in residential areas. No more than two men outside at a time. He'd ask the noncoms to work up a schedule. That would keep the non-coms busy, anyway.

He had no clue what the men in other countries were doing. He assumed they had their own safe houses, and he had to assume Charlie and her cohorts were on top of the situation. Hiding assassins in Russia and China would be a real challenge. He was glad he didn't have to think about that. But he did have to think about the hundreds of men he had under his own command. They were his responsibility, and Earl Wright took his responsibilities seriously.

Dickhead—Richard Sutton—had a hundred men squirreled away in an apartment complex not far from Johns Hopkins University in Baltimore. Their cover story claimed they were a group of visiting students who would begin research at the eastside campus in the fall. The other three hundred men were in scattered-site housing up and down Interstate 95, ten teams or forty men per safe house. Each house had multiple vehicles—SUVs and pick-ups—parked at various locations for quick getaways.

As Wright worked on contingency plans, he tried to second-guess Deb Johnson and her people at INSCOM. Right now, he bet, Johnson was analyzing satellite images of the Washington area immediately after the shootings, looking for fleeing assassins and trying to track them. It wouldn't be long before Johnson discovered the safe houses where the men had rendezvoused prior to dispersement. If she was lucky, she'd get makes and models of vehicles and maybe even license plates from satellite views of the city. Then she'd be able to track the vehicles to their new locations.

It would be a painstaking and time-consuming chore, but he knew Johnson was not unlike him, another mean bull dog who sunk her teeth in all the way to the bone and wouldn't let go no matter what. She would keep at it for weeks, months if necessary, and would eventually find them, fix them, fight them, and finish them.

Unless Wright found a way to take her out first.

He phoned Dickhead and asked him to drive over right away. Dickhead and Wright were the only ones who knew all of the locations of the various safe houses, and Dickhead could be at Wright's house in less than twenty minutes.

When Dick Sutton arrived, Wright let him in, sat Sutton down in a chair at the kitchen table, and immediately said, "I need someone eliminated. Take four teams and find her, feel her, fuck her good, and finish her off. You have forty-eight hours. I can give you her work location and home address. Consider her armed and dangerous, and expecting you to come for her. Here's her file with a picture of what she looks like."

Dickhead read the file and looked at the picture. "Consider it a done deal," he said.

"Don't be fooled by her looks, Sutton. She survived two previous attempts by our men. She survived tours in Iraq and Afghanistan. She's a trained army officer with combat experience."

"I'll bear that in mind."

"Do that. Call me when you're sure she's dead."

"Want me to bring you her head?" Dickhead asked, half-jokingly.

"That would be nice," said Wright. "Or at least an ear."

"I'll bring you both ears," said Dickhead. "You want me to bring you both tits, too?"

"The ears will be enough," said Wright.

* * *

Deb no longer took time to drive back and forth between Alexandria and Fort Belvoir. She teleported instead.

Carl Rossiter had been taken into custody by military police to be interrogated by military intelligence, and the bodies of the three dead assassins had been removed by police. Randy Edwards/Bill Ramsey now shared the apartment in Alexandria with Deb and Bill Porter, sleeping on a blanket on the floor in the spare bedroom Bill Porter had formerly used for a home office.

The landlord had replaced the broken wooden door and doorframe with a much sturdier steel door, and both locks had been changed. The landlord examined the carpet and agreed to replace it one more time. "Last time, though," said the landlord. "If something like this happens again, you'll have to pay for it from your own pockets. I can't afford to keep replacing carpet."

"They will try to kill you again, Deb," Ramsey said after the landlord left. "They don't like loose ends or loose cannons, and you're both to them. They won't stop until they're sure you're dead."

"I hope they do try again," said Deb. "I'd like to question one of them about their future plans. And I want to know where they've moved."

"WLSCTC owned lots of real estate. They owned the safe houses in Washington where we assembled."

"Homeland Security found most of those, thanks to the information you gave us and what we learned from Carl Rossiter.

They're all deserted. I want to know where Wright moved all those men."

"Can't you check real estate records? Find a list of all the properties owned by WLSCTC?"

"The safe houses we found were held by various blind trusts established at foreign banks. These people have successfully covered their tracks with lots of legal loopholes. Wherever Wright's men are hiding now, those properties are owned by other entities with fictitious names. It will take forever to trace them through real estate records. If we eventually do find them, it won't be through real estate records."

"Wherever they're hiding," said Ramsey, "they're within a fifty mile radius of D. C."

"How do you know?"

"This is where the action is, Deb. Besides, they wouldn't want to be on the road any longer than absolutely necessary. The father they travel, the greater their chances of being stopped by a roadblock or getting into an accident. They would want to get off the road as soon as possible, and I'm sure they did. You can't move hundreds of men without something eventually going wrong. Wright is too smart to let that happen."

"Maybe they're still in D. C.," said Porter.

"Maybe."

After teleporting back to her office at INSCOM, Deb looked at satellite shots of traffic leaving Washington on the night of the shootings. She found several late-model SUVs traveling northeast on Interstate 895, and similar convoys of SUVs moving parallel on Interstate 95.

She followed those vehicles from the safe houses she already knew about up into Maryland. One by one, vehicles dropped out of convoy and stopped. Men got out of the vehicles and disappeared into ordinary houses in residential communities.

She went back and looked for other SUV convoys on the satellite pictures, found them, and tracked them to their new locations.

"They're in Maryland," she told Eddie Morsay. "They all went to Maryland driving SUVs."

"You sure?"

"I will be. I'm going to visit the ladies room and take a look at those houses."

Deb locked herself in an empty stall, sealed her orifices, and allowed her spirit to go to one of the houses she had seen men entering on the satellite shots. Inside, she observed forty men cleaning their weapons.

She went to another of the houses and also found men cleaning weapons.

She returned to her body, and then went back to her office.

"They're there," said Deb. "They have a variety of weapons, but they aren't expecting a visit. They only have two men on guard at each house. The others are sleeping, watching television, or cleaning their weapons."

"Mark the sites of each of the safe houses on a map and I'll get it to the Colonel. He'll forward copies to the FBI and Homeland Security. Let them handle this, Deb. You've already done enough."

"No, Eddie, I haven't done nearly enough. I should have been able to prevent the shootings from happening in the first place. But I didn't. I was too busy playing analyst, piecing together pictures of a puzzle like some stupid kid. I had my head stuck in a computer when I should have been out there doing something to stop them in the real world before they killed so many innocent people. I feel terrible about that."

"There was nothing else you could have done, Deb."

"No. But there is something I can do now. Or, maybe I should say, something Ksitigarbha can do now."

Deb took time to mark a map of the District of Columbia area that included parts of Maryland and Virginia with pins to indicate the locations of five of the safe houses. Then Deb blinked out of existence at INSCOM, and an instant later Ksitigarbha, the Sacred Girl, materialized in the first house she had marked on the map. Before any of the forty men could raise a weapon to fire at her, she became a ball of fire as bright and hot as the sun, turning the room into a blazing inferno.

Some of the gun barrels actually melted from the intense heat. All of the ammunition rapidly overheated, and the bullets in the chambers and magazines exploded and rendered the weapons entirely useless, sending pieces of metal flying every which way like shrapnel.

None of the men could see. Some were permanently blinded, and some blinded only temporarily, but all became blind. Many reflexively dove to the floor at the sound of exploding ammunition. One curled up into a ball and cried like a baby. One wet his pants, certain he was about to die. One tried to flee, but he couldn't see and ran into a wall.

As the floor and ceiling caught fire and hungry flames spread to consume the whole house, the men stumbled over each other before finding the nearest exit. Two of the men would have died of smoke inhalation if Deb hadn't led them out of the house to fresh air.

When she heard sirens in the distance coming her way, she blinked out of existence in that location and blinked back into existence at the second house on the map.

She did the same thing there. She borrowed energy from the sun, and she burned the house down.

Because Ksitigarbha was a healer, not a killer, she made certain all of the men made it out of the house with only minor burns. She regretted leaving the men blinded, but it was the best way to keep them from hurting anyone else. She vowed she would restore their sight and heal their scorched flesh after the police had taken them into custody.

She went to a third house and torched that one, too. Then she returned to INSCOM, and a moment later Deb Johnson emerged from the ladies room, satisfied that nearly a hundred of the enemy, twenty-five percent of their total force in the area, had been taken out of commission. She'd let the FBI and Homeland Security round up the others. She had done enough.

"You were gone a long time," said Eddie when Deb re-entered the office. "I was getting worried."

"I got a few of them, Eddie."

"You killed them?"

"No. I rendered them harmless."

"I passed your map on to the Colonel. He asked the FBI to visit the sites you marked on the map. They're already on the way."

"Three of the houses are burned to the ground. Some of the men inside suffered minor burns, but they're all still alive. The last two houses on the map are still intact. The men inside those houses are armed and dangerous."

"The FBI is sending SWAT teams. They'll be there within an hour."

"I didn't see Earl Wright at any of the houses. I was hoping to catch Wright in one of the houses because Ramsey said Wright knows more than the others. If I can nab Wright, maybe I'll finally get some answers."

"Keep looking. You'll find him."

Deb returned to the satellite images and painstakingly searched. If Earl Wright was somewhere in Maryland, she'd eventually find him.

Unless Earl Wright found her first.

Either way, she'd finally come face-to-face with the elusive Earl Wright. Maybe then she would learn the answers to those burning questions that had bothered her for months. That is, if Wright were still alive and able to talk.

CHAPTER FOURTEEN

It was December 13, 1937, and Anong was a thirteen-year-old girl living in Nanjing, China's capital city, with her parents, grandparents, and half a dozen siblings. The city was on fire, and Anong was afraid they'd all die.

When the elderly Japanese General Matsui Iwane became extremely ill and traveled back to Japan for medical treatment, his lieutenant Prince Yashuhiko Asaka—the uncle of Emperor Hirohito—and Asaka's ruthless aide-de-camp, Lieutenant Colonel Isamu Cho, assumed control of the Japanese military that had already conquered Shanghai. Prince Asaka laid the city of Nanjing to siege for four days and nights, surrounding the ancient walls of the capital city with Japanese troops and artillery to cut off any and all hope of escape. Yesterday, when the rag-tag Chinese army refused to surrender and vowed to fight to the last man, Japanese planes and artillery began bombing and shelling the city itself, killing thousands and injuring thousands more. Prince Asaka then ordered his troops to "Steal all, burn all, and kill all." Anong's entire family—mother, father, six siblings, and her grandparents—had been killed in the shelling by heavy artillery. Anong had been on her way home from a visit to the library at the time of the heaviest shelling, and she had returned to find her home still in flames and the charred remains of her parents, brothers and sisters, and her grandparents buried in rubble.

Anong tried to flee for her life, but there was no place left to go. Most of the city was in ruins, and everyone Anong knew—family, friends, neighbors, teachers, local merchants—were already dead or dying.

This morning, Japanese troops had entered the city and brutally massacred everyone in sight, sparing no one, especially none of the children. If children were the hope of China's future, China had no hope left.

Bodies littered the streets, and the naked corpses of women who had been tortured and raped were scattered everywhere. Many of the women had their nipples or breasts cut off, their bloody torsos mutilated beyond recognition. Some of the women had broken bottles protruding from their torn vaginas after being gang raped, and some had sharpened sticks of raw bamboo or other objects shoved deep inside their centers with their legs remaining grotesquely spread wide apart for all to see their shame. Though the dead knew no shame, the living who saw them did.

Anong knew the same fate awaited her if she were found by the invading Japanese.

Whether Mahesvara had infested the Prince or resided inside Asaka's aide didn't matter. Mahesvara was certainly behind the atrocities, because Anong recognized Mahesvara's tell-tale hand directing the destruction she saw all around her. It was Mahesvara—acting through a human avatar—who had given the orders to pillage and plunder, rape and kill. Some things never changed, and she had seen similar carnage in Kathmandu, Tibet, Peru, and a hundred other places where she'd sensed Mahesvara's presence.

Had the demon somehow managed to follow her spirit to its current rebirth in Nanjing? Or was it simply coincidence that he was here at the same time she was? Did it matter which?

A bomb exploded nearby, and Anong sought refuge amid the rubble of a bombed-out storefront. Her only hope was getting to the safety zone established for foreigners in the western part of the city where diplomats and missionaries from other countries were sheltered before she was captured or killed. The Japanese had promised to spare the safety zone from bombardment and invasion. Though she didn't trust the promise of Japanese generals, it was the only hope she had of remaining alive.

She emerged from the rubble and ran westward, hiding from soldiers—both the last of the Chinese defenders of the city and the invading Japanese hoards—whenever she saw them. Many of the Japanese were too busy looting and burning, stealing anything of value before torching houses and stores, to notice the small figure darting down smoke-filled alleys and side streets like a shadow. The few who paid any attention to her were easily enchanted and forced to look the other way. They wouldn't remember ever seeing her.

She continued to flee westward, avoiding the growing number of Japanese troops, until she reached the area outside the International Safety Zone.

But the foreign compound was surrounded by Japanese soldiers, far too many for Anong to mesmerize. No one could enter or leave the safety zone without written permission from Prince Asaka or Colonel Cho. And she certainly had no permission from either.

Where could she go? What could she do?

Several of the soldiers saw her now, too many to enchant, and they pursued her like dogs chasing a rabbit as she ran into what had once been a Roman Catholic mission and now lay entirely in ruin, the many-colored stained glass windows all broken to pieces and the bell tower and cross blasted to smithereens. More soldiers followed on the heels of others, and she was trapped on the church grounds with no way to escape.

Anong took her own life that day, preferring a quick death at her own hands to witnessing what might be done to her body when the soldiers finally reached her and laid their hands on her. She plunged a long sharp shard of stained glass from one of the broken windows deep into her abdomen, angled it upward toward her heart, and freed her spirit to flee into the protective light. She didn't look back, and when she saw the clear light appear she went immediately into it. After a time, she was reborn, died, and was reborn again.

And now, Lokesvara informed the twelve-tear-old Anong, the ancient evil was at work once again in China. The old monk, in the form of Manjusri, had confronted some of Mahesvara's minions in China and sent them elsewhere. But China was a big country, and not even Manjusri could be everywhere at once. Mahesvara was certain to send others to take the place of the missing men.

"I need your help to find Mahesvara himself," said Lokesvara. "Mahesvara is hiding someplace in the world where I cannot sense his essence. He will continue this mischief until we find him and show him the error of his ways. I believe there is a tie that binds you to his spirit, and that you may be able to locate Mahesvara and his current avatar. Are you willing to help?"

"How can I do that? How can I find him for you?"

"It will be risky for you to do this. He may sense your spirit searching for his and retaliate. If he takes possession of your spirit while it is out of your body, you may never be reborn. That is a fate worse than death. You will have no way to reach enlightenment."

"Is it important that we find him?"

"Yes."

"Then I will find him for you."

"You are very brave, Anong."

"I am frightened, Master. I am not brave. But I will do what needs to be done."

“Then let me teach you to release your spirit and travel on the astral plane. Let me show you how to recognize the energy signatures of spirits in this world and others. Let me aid you in locating Mahesvara wherever he may seek to hide from you.”

“I am ready to learn, Master.”

“Before we begin, you must first seal your own body so Mahesvara cannot take possession of you while your spirit journeys,” said the old man. “Now pay attention. There are nine ordinary gates, called *buga*, through which the spirit may enter or leave the human body. They are the gates you must close to protect yourself when your spirit travels outside the body: two eyes, two ears, two nostrils, one mouth, two nipples, one navel, one genital, one urethra, and one anus….”

* * *

It was close to midnight when Deb teleported home from work. She had labored over the satellite images until her eyes were seeing double. She needed sleep, and she needed it badly.

If there had been additional convoys leaving Washington on the night of the shooting, Deb had missed seeing them. She decided it was time to get some much-needed sleep and tackle the images again in the morning with fresh eyes.

Randy Edwards and Bill Porter were still awake when she materialized in the apartment. They were watching the latest developments on ABC’s Nightline. The Director of the FBI and the

Secretary of Homeland Security had announced the successful capture of more than a hundred of the alleged assassins earlier in the day, and SWAT teams were currently engaging nearly a hundred more in firefights at two houses in southwestern Maryland. News footage showed the burnt-out houses Deb had visited earlier in the day where blind men were being herded into FBI vans. The reporter commented the FBI attributed the house fires to exploding defective ammunition, and the reporter interviewed a doctor who speculated that the violent explosions caused such severe concussions to optic nerves that all the men went blind from the shock. Though several men had said the fires were set by a young girl who seemed to appear from nowhere, authorities said those men were delusional as a result of their ordeal.

Then the scene switched to live coverage of a shootout near I-95 where a dozen Federal trucks and two armored personnel carriers were parked in a residential area surrounding a large two-story brick house. Camera crews were kept at a safe distance behind steel barriers erected at the end of the block, too far from the action to record more than brief glimpses of the operation in progress, but the sound of gunfire indicated the men inside the house and federal agents were actively exchanging fire.

"They were inadvertently tipped off when the feds began evacuating residents from a three block area around the house," said Randy Edwards. "They killed six agents and a handful of civilians before the area was secured. The men inside that house won't go down without a costly fight. Even with APCs, the feds can't get close. They tried using tear gas, but we've all been trained to survive in a gas chamber without protective masks. Their best bet is to use incendiaries to burn the house down and drive the men outside."

"Is that what the feds did this afternoon?" asked Bill Porter. "Or did Ksitigarbha have a hand in that?"

Deb smiled. "I got tired of doing nothing," she said. "I was hoping to find Earl Wright, but he wasn't in any of the three houses I visited."

"Wright is holed up someplace by himself," said Randy. "He's a loner. You won't find him with any of the others."

"Where do you think he is?" asked Deb.

"Close enough to direct operations," said Randy. "But separate from the others. Wright's too smart to be trapped with any of his men."

"I'm going to bed," said Deb. "It's been a long day, and I need my beauty sleep."

"I'll join you," said Bill Porter. "We'll see you in the morning, Randy."

Deb undressed and collapsed naked into bed. When Bill tried to cuddle, she was already half-asleep.

She had slept for less than an hour when the front door exploded from a shaped charge of Semtex, sending the steel door flying inward as a dozen men burst into the apartment with automatic weapons. Caught completely unaware, Deb couldn't find her center and raise the energy to teleport before the men entered the bedroom and held guns on her and Porter.

"Look what I found in the other room," said one of the men shoving Randy Edwards into the bedroom at the point of an assault rifle.

A tall, muscular, older man with an ugly scar across his forehead came into the room right behind them. "Kill the bitch," ordered the man with the scar. "Do it now. And then cut off both her ears and her tits. While you do that, I think I'll have a little man to man talk with the traitorous Mr. Edwards."

Deb dematerialized as a dozen bullets riddled the bed, sending stuffing from the mattress flying high into the air. She hoped Bill had done the same, but she didn't have time to see before she teleported away from the bed.

She rematerialized next to the man with the scar and hit him hard on the side of the neck with all the strength she could muster. He barely winced at the blow.

As he turned to face her with a wry smile twisting his mouth, he squeezed the trigger of the nine millimeter Heckler and Koch MP5 machine-pistol he held in his right hand. The barrel inched upward as the weapon emitted a loud URRRPPPPPPPPP and peppered the bedroom wall with bullet holes, raining plaster and paint chips all over the place.

Deb had again teleported out of the way just in time to avoid being ripped to shreds like the wall. When she rematerialized, she instantly assumed the form of Ksitigarbha.

Her essence shone so bright that the man with the scar had to close his eyes and fire his weapon without being able to see the target. Two of his accomplices and Randy Edwards were hit by stray rounds before the magazine emptied and the bolt locked to the rear.

Ksitigarbha stepped forward and forcibly removed the MP5 from the scarred man's big hands before he could reload, grasping the weapon by its hot barrel and almost effortlessly prying it free of the man's fingers. She heard some bones in the man's index finger snap as the trigger housing twisted around a knuckle. He grasped the injured hand with his other hand as pain brought the blind man to his knees.

The other men were stumbling blindly all around the room now, trying to get their bearings after losing their sight. None of them dared shoot for fear of hitting each other. Ksitigarbha easily disarmed each of them and shoved them off balance. They fell to the floor and struggled to get up, but Ksitigarbha shoved them back down.

"Stay down," she ordered. "I don't want to have to hurt you."

Randy Edwards, too, was himself temporarily blinded by the Bodhisattva's pure essence, but Randy had been knocked to the floor when he was hit in the shoulder by a stray 9 millimeter.

He was bleeding, but he'd survive. He would be okay where he was while Deb checked on Bill Porter.

Porter lay on the blood-spattered bed, his naked body riddled with bullet holes. He was unconscious, and he was barely breathing. But if he was breathing, he was still alive. Deb knew she had to act quickly or Bill would bleed out.

Ksitigarbha threw the gun she held away and went immediately to the bloody bed, placing one hand on Bill's forehead and another on his abdomen just below the navel. She drew the healing energy of the earth's unlimited store of energy into her own body and let it pass freely through both her hands into Bill's bloody body.

After a few minutes, Bill's breathing became more regular. Deb held her hands in place until the flesh mended completely, the holes in his chest knitting closed and essential internal organs resuming their ordinary functions as if nothing had happened. Bill had lost a lot of blood, but the earth's healing energy would quickly restore blood levels to normal. Ksitigarbha was the Earth Store Matrix, and she had access to all of the healing energy Mother Earth had to give.

Bill opened his eyes and smiled up at her.

Ksitigarbha walked to Randy Edwards and touched his shoulder. Randy's eyes popped open and he stared up at her in terror. She took away his pain, and sent new energy though his body that stopped the bleeding and healed his wound.

"Fear not," she said. "I'm Deb in another form. I won't hurt you. Gather up all the weapons and take them to the other room and lock them up. Keep a rifle for yourself. Do it now."

Randy picked up the rifles and pistols and carried them to his own room. Then he returned to stare at the man with the scar.

"That's Dickhead," he told Ksitigarbha, pointing to Sutton. "He's one of the honchos. He's the guy who killed Bill Ramsey."

She walked over to Dickhead and touched his left shoulder, taking away his pain and mending the broken bones in his hand.

The look of relief on the man's face was priceless.

"I can inflict pain, and I can take it away," Ksitigarbha said. "I wish only to free you from all suffering, past, present, and future, and I will vow to save you from yourself if you give me your solemn vow that you will not attempt to harm anyone. Give me your word and I will return your sight."

"And if I refuse?" said Dickhead.

"Then you will remain blind until you see the light. Do not make a vow unless you intend to keep it. If you break your vow, I will see you go straight to hell without passing go and without collecting two hundred dollars. Do you understand?"

Dickhead smiled. "Okay," he said much too quickly. "Give me back my sight and I promise not to hurt anyone."

Ksitigarbha touched his right shoulder and his eyes opened.

He stared at the form of Sacred Girl, trying to make sense of what he saw. Ksitigarbha appeared to him as a beautiful teenaged girl, dressed in a simple sari, looking helpless and harmless.

Around her neck she wore a string of precious jewels worth a king's ransom. He recognized emeralds, rubies, and pieces of jade. Each jewel seemed to glow with a radiance that was mesmerizing.

"Who are you?" he demanded. "You can't be Deb Johnson. You're much too young to be Johnson. Who the fuck *are* you?"

"I am an incarnation of Ksitigarbha, the Earth Store Matrix. I am part of the Earth's limitless bounty. I can either be your best friend or your worst enemy. I told you who I am, now tell me who you are. Be truthful."

"My name is Richard Sutton."

"Why did you come here to kill Deb Johnson, Mister Richard Sutton?"

"I was ordered to."

"Who ordered it?"

"That I can't say."

"Of course, you can. It was Earl Wright, wasn't it?"

Deb saw the truth in Sutton's eyes. Wright had indeed sent him. That meant Sutton knew where Wright was hiding.

"I suppose that traitor Edwards told you all about Wright."

"He did. And what Edwards didn't tell me about Wright and your organization, Deb Johnson did."

Dickhead looked nervous. "How much does Johnson know?"

"Everything. She knows who you are and where your men are located. Do you realize that Homeland Security and the FBI are rounding up most of your men even as we speak?"

"Impossible!"

"No, it isn't. Deb Johnson discovered the safe houses in Maryland this afternoon. She furnished a map with their exact locations to the FBI."

"I don't believe you."

"Believe me, it's true. By tomorrow at this time, all your men will be in custody. Including Earl Wright."

Something changed in Sutton's eyes. Sutton suddenly lunged at Sacred Girl with a knife he had hidden inside his sleeve, but Ksitigarbha had read Dickhead's intent in his eyes a moment before he made his move. She glowed bright as the sun as she moved energy around, and the knife melted before it reached her body.

Dickhead was once again deprived of sight by the sudden brightness, and half his hand was now badly burned where it had entered Ksitigarbha's aura. He howled with pain as his clothes suddenly caught fire and flames devoured his flesh.

"I am sorry you chose to break your vow," said Ksitigarbha, her voice filled with genuine compassion. "Every action you make seals your fate. It is the inevitable law of karma. Now you must suffer the consequences. That, too, is karma and I cannot prevent what is about to happen."

Ksitigarbha took a step backwards as three female figures appeared. They wore diaphanous white gowns that were so sheer that nothing was left to the imagination. One of the women raised her hand and Dickhead's burning body simply vanished. One moment he was there, and the next moment he wasn't. Then the women vanished, too.

"Where did they go?" asked Edwards, frantically looking around the room. "And who were those women?"

"Sutton went to hell," said Ksitigarbha. "The Erinyes took him straight to hell. Hell is where he belongs."

There really is a hell?" asked Edwards, still not believing what he had just seen.

"Nine of them, actually," said Ksitigarbha, matter of factly, as if she had personally visited each of them. "And because Sutton was escorted directly to Hades in both body and in spirit, he will spend seven torturous years there learning to repent his sins before he can hope to be reborn on earth. The Erinyes have special tortures in store for oath breakers. I tried to save him from going through that needless suffering, but he brought it on himself. He will receive appropriate punishment."

"Who are the Erinyes?" asked Randy.

"Three sisters, sometimes called the Furies, but I prefer to call them the Fates. For it is fate that oathbreakers be punished. I could not stop them from taking Sutton to hell once he broke his vow. I warned him, but he didn't listen."

"What will we do with the others?"

“Though blind, they have heard all that has happened. None of them has made a threatening move since I disarmed them, and they now know what happened to Richard Sutton could also happen to them if they raise a hand to hurt us. I will heal those who are wounded, and then we can simply call the police and have them arrested. Maybe the FBI can learn something from them. I regret Sutton was taken away before we could learn more.”

Ksitigarbha disappeared in the blink of an eye, and Deb Johnson reappeared in her place. Randy openly stared at Deb’s naked backside as she walked to a chest of drawers, grabbed a t-shirt and jogging shorts, and put them on. She smiled at the thought that she could still turn a young man’s head. Maybe she wasn’t over the hill, after all.

“Thank you, my love,” said Bill Porter, sitting up in the bed now, looking much like his old self. Other than the pool of blood surrounding him, here were no visible signs that he had been shot multiple times.

“For getting dressed?”

“No. For saving my life.”

“I couldn’t let the future Buddha die before his time. Now could I?”

“Is that the only reason?”

“No, Bill,” she said, sitting on the edge of the bed and looking into his eyes. “I love waking up with you next to me.”

"Looks like we'll have to replace the bed," Bill said. "This one is full of holes."

"But this time, at least," said Deb, "we don't have to replace the carpet."

* * *

Earl Wright was furious. He kicked the table, swore, and threw his coffee cup against the wall where it shattered and left a stain. Not only had Dickhead not reported back within 48 hours, but Wright's calls to Dickhead's phone went unanswered. It was as if the stupid fool had disappeared from the face of the earth

Did that mean Dickhead had been compromised? Was he dead or had he been captured by the feds? If the feds had him, Dickhead might reveal the locations of the safe houses. He was the only one, besides Wright, who knew where all of them were located. It was a mistake to send Dickhead instead of someone else. But who else was left who could do the job?

Wright had stayed up all night watching news coverage of the FBI shootouts with his men at two of the safe houses. Three other safe houses had been burned to the ground, the occupants taken into custody. Six of the twelve safe houses had been discovered. Which of the six safe houses remaining would be next?

Wright phoned the men at the remaining safe houses and ordered them to leave immediately, just get in their vehicles and go to nearby shopping center parking lots where there were lots of civilians present and wait for further orders. Even if they were tracked to the shopping centers, the feds wouldn't try to take them in the middle of a crowd of civilians for fear of collateral damage.

He had expected Charlie to call long before now, but Charlie had remained dangerously silent. Had Charlie and her mysterious partners in crime abandoned Wright and his men? Had the men served Charlie's purpose and were about to be fed to the wolves like helpless sheep? Was she really such a bitch? Why the hell hadn't Charlie called?

Wright paced back and forth while he analyzed options. He knew he had to leave his own safe house before Deb Johnson found him. He had to assume, since Dickhead hadn't reported otherwise, Johnson was still alive, still at work, and still tracking him. Damn that woman! What the hell did it take to kill her anyway? An atomic bomb dropped right on her head?

Wright gathered up his essential papers, including his detailed contingency plans, and burned them. From now on, he would have to travel light.

He packed a change of clothes, toiletries, and two assault rifles broken down into parts. He packed ammunition for the rifles and the two Smith and Wesson MP 40s he wore in a shoulder harness. He also packed six boxes of nine millimeter ammo for the Beretta M9A strapped to his hip. He was ready to go.

The phone in his pocket vibrated. Only two people had his number: Dickhead and Charlie.

It was Charlie.

"I hear you're having some difficulties. Anything you can't handle?"

"I've lost half my men. The feds are on us like stink on shit. I ordered my people out of the safe houses ASAP. We need new accommodations right away. Meanwhile, we're all going to be mobile."

"Brakken will take care of accommodations. He'll contact you within the hour."

"Good."

"Here are your new orders." She gave Wright a list of federal judges in New York, Chicago, Denver, Seattle, and LA. "Assign your men to each location and get them on the road. Brakken will have housing for the men both before and after the shoot. Repeat the list back to me. Then make your assignments. I'll call you with a go signal when you have your people in place."

Wright recited the list of names and locations back to her. "Brakken will have new weapons waiting in the new safe houses when you get there. Have your men destroy their current weapons and bury the remains before they get on the road. Tell no one the targets until the men are in place."

"Roger," said Wright.

"I'll phone you in two days to monitor your progress. Expect the go signal in five days. That will give your men time to get across country. Don't call me, I'll call you."

"Roger," said Wright. He heard her click off the phone.

It was time to get the hell out of Dodge.

CHAPTER FIFTEEN

Anong's spirit could go anywhere. She discovered she could easily soar over the buildings of Angkor or peaks of mountains like Phnom Kulen, walk through solid walls, enter other bodies with the permission of the resident spirit. She might even be able to sneak inside bodies when the resident spirit wasn't minding the store. Lokesvara told her she wasn't limited just to earth—she was no longer earth-bound—and she could easily astral-travel to other planets, other solar systems, other galaxies, even other universes.

All without being seen by mortal eyes.

Spirits could see other spirits on the astral plane, however; and one spirit could find another spirit anywhere in the universe simply by searching for an energy signature. Each spirit possessed a recognizable aura of electro-magnetic energy, an energy signature, which was entirely unique. Once your spirit had come into contact with the aura of another spirit, you could locate it again on the astral plane. If the spirit were embodied, you could learn the location of the physical body by seeing the aura on the astral plane.

Spirits could sense other spirits. Mortal eyes could not.

Powerful spirits—those that had learned over many remembered lifetimes how to manipulate the subtle energies from which was woven the very fabric of the universe—were easy to find when they acted in the world. Even when hidden in a human body, they had a unique eminence that was recognizable by an adept. Their power was discernible.

Bodhisattvas, like Manjusri and Vajrapani, had auras as bright as the sun.

But spirits that had not been born into this world were very different, and they were difficult to detect by human spirits. Mahesvara was said to be an essential aspect of Shiva, a shadow self or doppelganger, just as Satan was said to be an aspect of Jehovah or Angra Mainyu an aspect of Ahura Mazda, and they were never born into a physical body of their own. Never had they personally experienced death, suffered from karma in the afterlife, and been reborn as human. Nor had they ever forgotten who they were nor what they had learned. They were capable of remembering every thing they had ever seen or done, and that made them extremely dangerous.

They had emerged as separate and distinct entities because the universe required balance in all things. They were the polar opposites—the equal but completely opposite counterparts of another entity—existing solely to balance the power of the entity they emerged from. Without shadow selves, some spirits might become so powerful they could upset the balance of the universe. The universe wouldn't allow that to happen. So the universe created opposites to impose limits on power. Not even gods were omnipotent.

When such beings became enlightened, they gained not omnipotence but omniscience. Those that did not become enlightened were demons, and their knowledge, though great, remained limited.

It was out of this duality—the struggle between opposites—that life itself emerged. Life couldn't exist without death, man couldn't exist without woman, light couldn't exist without darkness, the firmament couldn't exist without the waters, creation couldn't exist without destruction. Everything came from something. Because the universe required balance in all things, when any one thing became too powerful, its counterpart emerged to usurp its power. Such was the Dharma, the way of the world, a continuous cycle of balance and counterbalance, of beginnings and endings and new beginnings.

Some entities, however, developed egos so selfish that they possessed neither conscience nor compassion. Such an entity was Mahesvara. He sought unlimited power at the expense of all else. He wanted unlimited power for himself, and he would destroy the Dharma to get it. Mahesvara was a creature of impure spirit. He was limited to the realms of desire and of forms because he was a creature without compassion and enlightenment. Because Mahesvara had never actually been born, he could not act in the material world to acquire such unlimited power without human help, an avatar or avatars to act for him.

Mahesvara could act in the physical realm only by taking possession of a physical body, human or inanimate, and he could take possession of a human body in one of but three ways: take complete possession of a body while the resident spirit was astral traveling, provided that body had not been sealed, and denying the owner re-entry; take total control of a human body while the resident spirit was temporarily apart from the body to experience ecstasy; or co-occupy the body of a person who gave explicit permission, who invited the entity in, usually in exchange for material possessions or an extended lifetime or power over others.

And once Mahesvara had possession of a body, he could act in the material world.

Obviously, Mahesvara had been invited to share a body with another spirit, as Mahesvara had once done with Haranyadama, and that other spirit was used to mask Mahesvara's energy signature from anyone searching on the astral plane. Lokesvara and Vajrapani had both searched for Mahesvara, but his whereabouts somehow eluded them. They had never come into contact with Mahesvara's aura before, and they had no idea what his energy signature looked like.

If there were indeed a psychic link between Mahesvara and Anong, Anong could follow that link as surely as Theseus followed Ariadne's tiny thread through the length of the labyrinth. All she need do was picture Mahesvara's aura in her mind.

Her spirit followed the subtle link to Dubai's International Financial Center. Somewhere here, in the heart of Dubai, was a man with Mahesvara's spirit attached to human form. Though she knew which of the tall steel-and-glass buildings he was in currently, she was unable to enter the building in spirit form. Something blocked her way.

She went back and reported what she had learned to Lokesvara and Vajrapani.

"He has set wards of protection against spirit intrusion," said the old man. "He is being cautious. We cannot see what he looks like, nor what he is doing, while the wards are in place."

"But at least we know where he is," said Vajrapani. "We can teleport there and confront him in person."

"The wards will prevent Manjusri and Vajrapani from entering," said Lokesvara. "Wards prevent fluctuations of energy within set boundaries, making manifestation and teleportation impossible. We would need to go there in human form. And we would need Anong to accompany us to identify the man who houses Mahesvara's spirit once we meet him face-to-face."

"I will go, Master," said Anong. "I am not afraid."

"Nor am I," said the Ranger.

"It will be dangerous," said the old man. "You must be ready to kill or be killed. Are you prepared to do that?"

The Ranger considered the implications of his Master's words. He had vowed never to kill again. Killing was always bad for karma. Breaking a vow not to kill could prove disastrous.

But, the Ranger had learned over many lifetimes, doing nothing while others killed with impunity was just as bad, if not worse.

He had to make a decision.

"Vajrapani is a protector of the Dharma," he said at last. "And I am Vajrapani. If the Dharma is threatened, I will kill those responsible unless there is another way."

"Then let us go to Dubai," said Lokesvara. "I will pretend to be a representative of a Hong Kong banker seeking to make profitable investments in the Middle East. Anong can pretend to be my great-granddaughter whom I brought with to show her parts of the world she has never seen. And Vajrapani can pretend to be my American bodyguard. We will find suitable civilian attire in the donations available to the poor in a room down the hall. After we have changed, we can teleport to Dubai and begin our little charade. It should prove a most interesting game."

"This is not a game," said the Ranger.

"Mahesvara may not think so," said Lokesvara. "To him, everything is a game."

* * *

Wright drove northeast on Interstate 95. He was already well on his way to New York City, behind the wheel of a stolen Subaru Forester with Maryland plates, when John Brakken's call made the cell phone in Earl's pocket do a dance. This was the call

Charlie promised would come within an hour. Earl glanced at the clock on the dashboard. Fifty-seven minutes. Brakken was cutting it close.

Wright put Brakken on speaker and kept driving.

Earl Wright had chosen to steal the sage-green Forester, a cross between a station wagon and a suburban utility vehicle, because it sported all-wheel drive, heavy-duty all-terrain tires, had built-in Wi-Fi and Bluetooth, was less of a flashy police-attention grabber than other vehicles of its class, and had been parked in long-term patient parking at the Johns Hopkins Medical Center where the owner had likely been admitted for surgery. With a little luck, the vehicle wouldn't be reported missing for several days and by then Wright would have reached New York and obtained alternate transportation. By the time the cops found the Forester, Wright planned to be long gone.

Though the Jersey turnpike had cameras positioned everywhere along the tollway, he wasn't too worried about it. He wore a blue Orioles baseball cap with the bill pulled down to hide his face from overhead camera views, and by the time authorities looked at the camera footage—if they ever got around to it—he would be long gone from Jersey.

Wright kept to the posted speed limits, staying in the right or middle lanes, and blending seamlessly into the flow of traffic. The chances of him being stopped were slim.

As Brakken listed the locations of safe houses in all of the cities where targets were located, Wright took in the information while driving, organizing the addresses with mnemonics. Wright had an excellent memory, trained through years of discipline, and he seldom relied on written notes. If it was worth knowing, he would remember it exactly as he heard it.

Brakken said each location had a laptop computer with internet access, and a dozen email accounts had been established at Yahoo.com. Details about the targets would not be emailed to each team but would be saved as drafts on the various Yahoo accounts. Wright had been given the logins and passwords for all of them, and he was cautioned to write additional instructions merely as drafts on each account and not actually send them. Each team could then log into their individual account, read the draft messages, and none of the information need go out over the internet where it might be intercepted. After the drafts were read, said Brakken, they should not be deleted from Yahoo's server but simply overwritten three or four times with useless messages. Even if NSA gained access to Yahoo's archives, the messages would seem like meaningless drivel.

It took four and a half hours to reach the new safe house in a New York suburb. Wright found the car Brakken's people had left for him where Brakken said it would be, and he ditched the Subaru for a rented charcoal black Ford Taurus. He entered the safe house, checked it out from top to bottom, found the laptop computer, and sent instructions to his men.

Then he phoned his team leaders and gave them the locations of their own safe houses and individual log-ins.

Each of the safe houses had been a foreclosure bought by one of WLSCTC's blind real estate trusts after the real estate bubble burst and houses were put on the market for pennies on the dollar. Real estate investments helped finance WLSCTC military operations, and Brakken had teams of people snapping up properties and reselling them or renting them out. Brakken had once bragged to Wright that the investment bankers in Dubai were making money from similar deals all over the world, money that paid for weapons and training facilities, R and R activities, personnel, and bribes to politicians. Some of the best financial brains in Dubai were working for the Big Boss, manipulating markets in order to fund secret operations that were part of some mysterious master plan. They bought and sold, invested and divested, and made money from every transaction.

"We're talking trillions of dollars here, Earl," Brakken had said. "These guys aren't penny-pinching paupers. This is big. This is real big. And they've been doing it for years with no one noticing. They're everywhere, and they have their fingers into everything and everybody. They made billions when the real estate bubble burst, and they're buying up properties left and right. They'll sit on them until the economy comes back, then they'll make billions more."

Wright remembered Charlie saying something similar when he'd met her in Dubai. "We are legion," she had said, and an image of a giant squid with long, sinewy tentacles extending into every nook and cranny of the modern world immediately sprung to mind. He saw himself and his men as a single sucker on one of those million-mile-long tentacles. If he and his five hundred men were but one sucker on one tentacle, how many other suckers, tentacles, and men were there?

Wright was aware that America was only a small slice of the whole pie. Europe, Asia, the Middle East, and Africa were big slices in their own right, and they required lots of men, money, and materiel to conquer.

Was that what this was all about? Conquering the whole world? World domination? He hadn't thought about it in those specific terms before. But that's what this guy really wanted, He planned to take over the world.

What kind of nut wanted to rule the world? Hitler had tried to do that and failed. So had Attila the Hun, Genghis Khan, Alexander the Great, Tamerlane, and dozens of others. They had spread death and destruction far and wide, but in the end they had failed. The world was just too damned big, too complicated, for any one man to rule.

But this guy, whoever he was, had all his ducks in a row. He had recruited excellent lieutenants—Charlie and Wright and Brakken were prime examples—to do the dirty work for him. He had amassed a fortune to finance his army, and he spared no expense to arm, equip, and train them. He had a good chance of succeeding where others had failed.

It was a huge undertaking, and Wright had to admire the guy's low-profile long-term ambition. Would anyone know who he was until he had assumed absolute control?

Charlie knew. Earl was sure of that. Wright sensed that Charlie knew the guy personally, intimately. Were they lovers? Wright was surprised to feel a pang of jealousy tug at his heart.

Charlie was way out of Wright's class, yet Earl couldn't get her out of his mind. He realized his chances of ever meeting her again were slim and none, but the chances of ever meeting another woman anything remotely like her were even less.

He had never known a woman, nor many men for that matter, who exuded such absolute confidence in her own abilities. She assumed complete control the minute she walked into a room, and she left no doubt that anyone who challenged her authority would be dead in an instant.

She could be deadlier than a coiled rattlesnake because she would give absolutely no warning before she struck. Getting involved with her would be like a child playing with nests full of poisonous scorpions and black widow spiders both at the same time with his bare hands. Charlie was pure poison, and Wright knew it.

And therein lay a good part of Charlie's appeal. A man like Earl Wright, who had faced death thousands of times and survived, thrived on the adrenalin rush that facing certain death always brought. Conquering Charlie was the kind of challenge Wright couldn't ignore. One of them would emerge a winner and the other a loser. And then the winner would move on to face the next challenge, leaving the loser behind, defeated and deflated, to waste away.

Of course, there was also the rock-hard body that was so well hidden beneath the dress she wore that Wright could only imagine what it looked like. He fantasized about ripping that dress away from her bare flesh, pinning her squirming torso to the bed or the floor with his superior upper-body strength the way a lepidopterist pinned a butterfly, running his hands and lips over every part of her, dominating her will until she gave him what he wanted.

Or killed him in the process.

He knew he had to see her again. Maybe, just maybe, after he had successfully completed his latest mission, she would want to see him again, too.

He put aside those thoughts and focused once again on the mission. New York City had learned a hard lesson from 9/11, and getting teams of armed assassins close to federal judges would not be an easy task. The city had security cameras everywhere these days, and most of those cameras were manned 24/7. If he was going to be successful, he had to plan this out.

The Federal District Judges of the Southern District of New York, those assigned to the Daniel Patrick Moynihan building in downtown New York City instead of the Charles L. Brieant, Jr., building in the easier-to-get-to White Plains, were located in the heart of the city, only blocks from City Hall, the NY

Daily News, and the devastated World Trade Center site where there were tons of cameras and lots of cops. To take out Federal District Judges and Federal Magistrates in the center of the city was suicidal. Charlie's intel gave home addresses for each of the judges, and Wright concluded the best bet was to take them out near their homes.

Obviously, Charlie had come to the same conclusion because she had provided maps and photographs of each of the neighborhoods where the judges resided. With only one exception, they all lived in luxurious homes in the suburbs. The one exception had a condo on the near east side, close enough to walk to work.

Why some judges were targeted and others weren't, Wright never thought to ask. Obviously, Charlie and her partners had a reason for wanting these particular individuals dead. Wright would do his best to oblige her.

Wright put on a pot of coffee, then sat down at the kitchen table and lit a cigarette. He logged onto the laptop, went to Google, and did a search on each of the judges. He had time to kill, and verifying Charlie's intel would keep his mind off women.

After years of not thinking much about women at all, he now found himself obsessed with two of them: Charlie and Debra Johnson. He knew what he wanted to do to each of them, and there was no doubt in his military mind that someday he would do them both, each in their own way. There were winners and losers in this world, and Earl Wright planned to be a winner.

CHAPTER SIXTEEN

Unlike Phnom Penh, Dubai City seemed sparkling clean. It was daring and beautiful and spectacular, rising up from the burning desert sands of the southeastern Arabian Peninsula like the mythological phoenix from the ashes of its predecessor.

Dubai City looked impeccably clean. It smelled impeccably clean, too. Maybe, thought Anong, that was mainly because everything in this part of the city was literally brand new. The streets were new, the skyscrapers were new, the shopping areas were new. Construction continued unabated as the city spread into the Persian Gulf itself, and new buildings emerged daily from the waters like giant leviathans surfacing to feed on the myriad human trespassers who were attracted by the siren song of the sea.

Everything seemed so incredibly orderly and well-planned. It was almost as if one single person had designed the city and built it entirely from scratch, putting things precisely where he imagined they belonged and no place else. There was a place for everything, and nothing would ever be out of place. Like a miniature doll's house she had once seen pictured in a magazine.

But this was a giant city, not a doll's house. Real people lived here and worked here. The city was bustling with activity, alive like no place she had ever seen before in this life or any of her previous lives.

If Mahesvara were present here, he was well-hidden. There was no sign that death and destruction lurked just around the next corner.

It was a beautiful bright summer day in Dubai, unlike the rainy day Anong had left in Ankor. The sun was shining high in the clear sky, with no clouds in sight, no hint of rain on the horizon. Though it was extremely hot and humid, more than forty degrees Celsius or a hundred and eight degrees Fahrenheit, there was a brisk breeze off the Gulf that made the temperature seem almost bearable. If this place wasn't the Garden of Eden, it was the closest place to it, a virtual paradise on earth.

Because Anong was new at teleportation, she had clung tightly to the Ranger's huge hand when they left Cambodia so her energy and his energy displaced together as if they were one being. Lokesvara had explained that teleportation created a disturbance—an imbalance, a difference of potential—in the subtle energy fields of the universe at two distinct places, and energy flowed seamlessly from one point to the other as if by magic. By holding hands, the disturbance Vajrapani's mind created included Anong by natural extension. As energy instantaneously shifted from one point in space-time to another, she was part of the shift. Her physical body, clothes and all, moved from one place to another quickly and seamlessly. One moment she was physically standing in Cambodia, and the next moment she was standing in Dubai.

She wore a simple blue and white flowered dress, appropriate for a modest twelve-year old girl. Lokesvara and the Ranger both wore suits, complete with white shirts and ties. She had never seen either of them in other than their holy robes before, and it made them look strange to her. The Ranger had even taken the time to spit-shine his black oxfords before they left Ankor, and the shoes gleamed in the noon-day sun like black pearls.

"It is that building," said Anong, pointing to a very tall structure that housed several investment banks and financial services companies. "That is the building where I sensed Mahesvara's spirit."

"Then that is the building we shall enter," said Lokesvara. "But a word of caution before we do. There are powerful wards here that prevent us from entering in spirit form, and those same wards will prevent Manjusri or Vajrapani from manifesting inside that building. We will be limited solely to what we can do in our own physical forms. Please remember that you are mortal and can be easily harmed or killed. Once inside the building, you will not be able to teleport because of the wards. You will not be able to escape bullets by teleporting out of their path. Mahesvara will have many armed guards positioned throughout the building who are trained to kill, and if they shoot us while we are inside, we may die and never be reborn to new bodies. The wards will prevent our spirits from seeing the clear light and moving into it.

Under no circumstances should we attempt to confront Mahesvara inside that building. It is too dangerous."

"Then why are we here?" asked the Ranger.

"Merely to learn what Mahesvara's avatars look like," said the old man. "Mahesvara's wards are powerful, but they have their limits. Their power extends only a few meters, for example, from where they are set in place. They cannot be moved without revoking their purpose and re-invoking it elsewhere, and that takes time and energy and Mahesvara will be vulnerable during the transition. When any of the avatars leave the protection of the wards to act in the world, we want to be able to track them and confront them away from the wards. But first, we need to know who the avatars are and what they look like. That is why we are here."

"How will we recognize Mahesvara or his avatars if we see them?"

"By their actions. Within the field of the wards, we will not be able to sense their spirits nor can they sense ours. We will know them only by their actions."

"What kind of actions?"

"Actions directed by a supreme ego," said Lokesvara. "Mahesvara wants—needs—to be worshipped. He seeks to be acknowledged as the most powerful presence on the planet, and his avatars and acolytes will reflect that need. They will all be leaders in their respective areas of expertise, and they will have destroyed anyone who stood in their way during their rise to power. They will have underlings, yes; but only people who are non-competitive and pose no threat because they have no power. Consequently, we must tell underlings that we will speak only with the top man. And to see him, we will need to offer something he wants."

"And what," asked the Ranger, "could we possibly have that he wants?"

"Positioning," said the old man. "We thwarted his plans in China and Japan. He needs someone with contacts in the orient. I will convince him I can supply those contacts for a price."

"Can you?"

"I can, if necessary. I know enough names to impress him. I have Buddhist friends in both countries who keep me informed. Shall we walk into the lion's den?"

They entered the steel, concrete, and glass building through its main revolving door. The lobby was as large as an entire airport terminal at Chicago's O'Hare or Boston's Logan, and there were entrances to various shops and businesses from the lobby, including several restaurants. The inside of the building was cool compared to the outside, but it was brightly lit by sunlight coming through huge tinted glass windows and recessed fluorescents that made the building's exotic exoskeleton seem practically nonexistent.

Lokesvara located the directory of businesses and selected a financial services company on the thirty-fifth floor. They rode up in an elevator with three glass walls that ascended the side of the building and afforded breathtaking views of the city and the Gulf, including man-made islands in the shape of a palm tree. Other islands were being constructed in various shapes, some recognizable and others mysterious. Anong stared transfixed at the enormity of the undertaking.

"Quite a sight, isn't it?" said the Ranger.

"They are rebuilding the world," said Anong. "They are moving mountains to make Dubai look like the center of the earth."

As the door of the elevator swished open, Anong turned to see a large reception area, tastefully decorated and color-coordinated in rich earth tones. In the center of the reception area was a large desk with a fancy telephone. Behind the desk sat a smiling young blonde woman, perhaps twenty-four or twenty-five years old, dressed in a navy-blue blazer and matching skirt.

"Hi," said the woman in flawless American English, as if she were born and raised in the states and only recently transplanted to Dubai. "I'm Laura. Whom do you wish to see? Do you have an appointment?" She glanced down at a calendar on her Samsung tablet screen. "I don't see an appointment at this time. Are you sure you're on the right floor?"

"I never make appointments," said Lokesvara in perfect BBC English. "Appointments leave a record that can be traced. For reasons I won't disclose but will be obvious to your boss, I do not wish to leave a record of this visit."

The woman arched an eyebrow. "I understand," she said, as if she were used to dealing with the need for confidentiality. "Whom do you wish to see?"

"Whoever is now director of your operations in China and Japan. I understand the former director has been replaced."

"How did…how could…you know that?" she asked before she caught herself. "I mean, it just happened, and we don't publicize personnel changes."

"I know many things," said Lokesvara. "That is why I am here. I wish to sell my knowledge."

Laura pressed an intercom button on her phone. A door opened and two big burly men, Arabs from the look of them, entered. Both men wore identical black suits and red and white striped neckties.

"Please take these people to conference room two," said Laura. "Search them for weapons."

"We are unarmed," said Lokesvara.

"Search them anyway," insisted Laura. "I will talk to Charlie and see if they are to be escorted from the building or interviewed."

"Follow me," said one of the men. Anong could barely understand his heavily accented English. The other man held the door open and then followed the four into a small conference room with a rectangular wooden table in the center of the room and six comfortable-looking leather chairs equally-spaced around the table.

The men braced Lokesvara and the Ranger against a wall and searched their bodies for hidden weapons; then one of the men searched Anong. Both men were very thorough and very professional in conducting their full-body searches. Anong was grateful they searched only for hidden weapons and appeared to have no interest in copping a feel. Nevertheless, she gritted her teeth as the man's hands passed over her private parts.

After completing the search of Anong, that man punched a button on a special telephone mounted on the wall and said, "They're clean."

Anong grew increasingly nervous as the minutes ticked slowly by. Lokesvara retained his usual calm, and the Ranger appeared equally nonchalant, leaning back in his chair with his hands loosely clasped in front of his chest. He never looked directly at either of the two men, but Anong knew his peripheral vision took in every move they made. Had either man acted inappropriately in his search of Anong, she had no doubt the Ranger would have violated his vow and killed that man on the spot.

After an hour passed, Lokesvara stood up and said, "We have waited long enough. Obviously, they find no value in what we have to offer."

"What do you have to offer that might possibly interest us?" asked a voice from the speaker on the telephone before they could attempt to leave. It was a woman's voice, Oxford-accented, and definitely not Laura's.

"I will speak only with the top man," said Lokesvara. "You are not a man."

"You will speak to me or to no one," came the woman's voice, its tone cold and commanding.

"And you are who in this organization?"

"I am a senior vice president. Who are you?"

"A businessman from Hong Kong who has useful contacts in China and Japan. It has come to my attention that you recently suffered a setback in both those countries. I offer my services for a price."

"What kind of price?" she asked immediately. "And what kind of services?"

"One hundred billion dollars, or one third of the current value of the Chinese gold and jewels you salvaged from sunken Japanese ships after the Second World War."

The woman was silent for what seemed an eternity. Then she asked, "Who are you? And how did you learn about that gold?"

"My name is unimportant. My information is invaluable. Do we have a deal?"

"You have my interest. Tell me more."

"When we speak face-to-face. I do not negotiate over a speaker phone."

"Bring him to my office," the voice instructed the guards. "The old man only. Keep the other man and the girl in the conference room."

"You will meet with all of us or none of us," said Lokesvara. "I will not leave my granddaughter alone."

"Why have you brought a child with you to conduct business?" asked the voice.

"I would teach her the fine art of negotiation," replied Lokesvara. "She will someday be my heir."

"A girl? Have you no grandsons?"

"None worth teaching," said Lokesvara.

"Bring all three to my office," said the voice. "Do it now."

They were herded from the conference room into a stairwell and marched up a flight of steps to the thirty-sixth floor where an armed guard waited, blocking their entrance to the floor.

"Charlie wants to see them," said the man who had searched Anong. The guard nodded his assent and stepped aside, and they proceeded down a hallway to an unmarked door where the man gently knocked with his big knuckles.

"Entre," came the woman's voice, muffled by the thickness of a solid steel door so it was barely audible. Anong knew from books she had read that this was a special type of fire door, a safety precaution, something capable of keeping fire from spreading from room to room or from floor to floor in skyscrapers like this. The insulated door also served to muffle or silence sounds. She heard two clicks as the door was electronically unlocked from inside.

This room was huge, more than twenty times the size of the conference room on thirty-five. One entire wall was solid glass, very thick and slightly tinted with a metallic hue, looking out on the Gulf from thirty-six stories up. Three walls were decorated with weapons, both ancient and modern. Besides a variety of swords and knives, a bow and quiver of arrows, several automatic rifles and a dozen handguns, Anong noticed bolas and garrotes and hangman's nooses and even a double-bladed executioner's axe from the middle-ages.

There was nothing feminine anywhere in the room except the young woman sitting between a massive oak desk and a credenza filled with high-tech communications equipment. The woman had long fiery-red hair, natural and not a dye job, a figure to die for, and cold blue eyes that appeared more piercing and deadly than any of the swords or knives on the walls.

"I'm Charlie," said the woman without getting up from behind the desk. "Please take seats in front of me."

There was something vaguely familiar about the woman that made Anong's breath catch in her throat. Had they met before? Where? When? How? The woman was very beautiful, and surely Anong would have remembered had they ever met. No, it wasn't the way the woman looked that was familiar. It was the woman's demeanor.

"I am called Wenshu Wutai Shan," said Lokesvara, bowing slightly. Anong knew that Wenshu was the name given to Manjusri in China, and Wutai Shan was the sacred mountain in Shanxi said to be one of the earthly abodes of the young Manjusri.

"This is my granddaughter Anong," introduced Lokesvara, "and that is my associate Mr. Schweitzer."

"How did you hear about us, Mr. Shan?" wondered the woman.

"It is my business to see and hear many things," said Lokesvara. "My eyes and ears are legion."

The woman seemed startled by Lokesvara's choice of words. "It appears you may know more than is healthy, Mr. Shan. We do not take kindly to people who pry into our affairs. But I suspect you already knew that before you came here. Didn't you?"

"Knowledge is power," said Lokesvara. "It is my main stock in trade, and I'm willing to trade my knowledge for your money."

"Then let us negotiate a trade," said the woman. "What do you know about our recent enterprises?"

"I know your attempts failed in China and Japan. Do you know why?"

"Someone interfered. Someone who was in the wrong place at the wrong time."

"That's correct. Do you know who?"

"No. I know it was neither the police nor the military. They may have mopped up after the fact, but they were not the ones responsible."

"That is correct. If I can identify the ones responsible, what might it be worth to you?"

“Not a hundred billion in gold.”

“Are you certain?”

“Why should I pay you, Mr. Shan, when there are other ways of obtaining the same information at lesser cost?”

“My extensive contacts in the Far East can stand in your way or stand at your side. The choice is yours.”

“Big talk for such a little man,” said the woman. “You look old and frail. You might have a heart attack at any moment. Have you thought of that? These things can happen, you know. I can make them happen. Or what if you simply disappeared? What would your contacts do without you?”

“Believe me, they would track you down and take revenge. They can be relentless when seeking revenge.”

“How would they even know?”

“The same way I know. We are legion, Ms. Charlie. My eyes and ears are everywhere. You will never escape their notice. You cannot hide, no matter how hard you try. If I die, someone will take my place. We can be allies or adversaries. The choice is yours.”

Anong saw the woman’s eyes widen again at Lokesvara’s choice of words, and in that moment Anong remembered where she had seen the woman before.

“Who are you really?” demanded Charlie. “You look like a harmless old man, but I sense you are much more than you appear and you are far from harmless, though you may be old. *Who the hell are you, Wenshu Wutai Shan*?”

"Grandfather," Anong whispered at that precise moment, tugging desperately at Lokesvara's coat sleeve.

"What is it, child?"

"I need to use the washroom. Can you take me to a washroom? Please?"

"Can't it wait?" asked Charlie. "I asked your grandfather an important question, and I demand an answer."

"No," said Anong. "It cannot wait. I have waited too long already. Do you want me to have an accident that may spoil the leather of this fine chair?"

"I shall answer your question when we return," promised Lokesvara. "Where is the nearest restroom?"

"One of my men will show you," said Charlie. "Must you go with the child?"

"She is in a strange land among strangers she does not trust," said Lokesvara. "We would both feel better if I accompanied her. I will wait outside the restroom, and we will be back momentarily."

"Very well," agreed Charlie. "Hassan will take you."

As they walked down the hallway behind Hassan, the man who had searched Anong earlier, Anong whispered in Khmer, "I have met that woman before, and I am afraid."

"She is an avatar of Mahesvara?"

"She is not an avatar," whispered Anong. "She is something much more sinister, much more dangerous, much worse than an avatar."

"More dangerous than an avatar of Mahesvara? How can that be?"

"Yes, much worse," said Anong, shaking as if a sudden chill had passed through her body despite the heat and humidity. "Charlie is not merely an avatar of Mahesvara. She is his most powerful wife. She is the dreaded Uma herself made flesh."

*   *   *

The people of Ethiopia called her Gudit, the pagan queen of the Bani al-Hamwiyah; but she called herself Judith. It was the year 979 of the Common Era, and Anong—barely fourteen—was but one of thousands of girls Gudit had captured after crossing the Red Sea to conquer what remained of the once-mighty Aksumite Empire, including the southern tip of the Arabian Peninsula, all the way east to the Persian Gulf.

Along with hundreds of other slave girls in service to the Queen and her army, Anong was forced to trek through the desert carrying water. Though her own tender body was blistered and scorched by the incessant sun, her lips dry and cracked, she dared not drink even a single drop of the remaining water she carried in heavy gourds and skins strapped to her back and shoulders. Water was more precious than gold in the desert, and it was strictly reserved for the horses and the camels and the soldiers. Slaves could drink only, if they were still alive to drink, when they reached an oasis. Half of the girls had already fallen, dead or left to die in the burning sands, and their heavy loads were equally distributed to the remaining water bearers. New slaves would surely take the place of the fallen after the next raid on a village, and anyone not strong enough to continue on would be fed to the dogs for sport.

How long could a person survive without water? Not long. A few days at the most.

Anong feared she was a dead woman walking.

Six young Nubian eunuchs transported the Queen's canopied carriage on big broad black shoulders rippling with bulging muscles and glistening with acrid sweat, and even the Nubians were denied more than a sip or two of the precious water before they reached the next oasis, whenever and wherever that might be.

Anong could see the Queen's flaming red hair, half-hidden in the shadows cast by the colorful canopy above the Queen's head, not more than forty feet in front of her. Queen Judith lounged naked on soft pillows in cool shade, and she sucked noisily on grapes and figs, carelessly tossing the seeds and pits out the open sides of the carriage almost as an affront to starving slaves fed slop barely once a day. Judith was an incredibly beautiful woman, said to be the illegitimate daughter of a Jewish woman and the Christian king of the former Ethiopian fiefdom of Damat. It was also said Judith used her unparalleled beauty to conquer the hearts and minds of powerful men who became her fervent allies. She claimed to hate Christians, Jews, and Muslims equally, and she had set out to destroy all of the holy places she could find as she ravished all of Abyssinia, all of Aksum, and all of the known world. She was ruthless and unrelenting. Her gods were bloody and terrible, and some people said she thought of herself as a goddess, beyond the mores of any civilized religion. Anong could believe that was true, for had not Judith rained down more death and destruction than any of the many gods who had come before her?

As night brought blessed relief from the heat, the caravan halted before sighting the next oasis. That meant another day without water for the slaves. Men erected tents for the comfort of the Queen and her officers, and campfires were started and torches lit. Sentries were posted, and scouts were sent out to locate the nearest watering hole. If they didn't find water soon, what little water remained would be completely exhausted. Soldiers who were severely dehydrated were of little use in battle, and Judith needed a strong army to loot the towns between here and the Gulf.

They would camp here until the scouts located an oasis, hopefully by morning.

Anong overheard rumors, while serving food to officers in one of the big tents, that Judith next planned to march north along the Arabian coast. Sacking and looting along the way, she intended to destroy Baghdad and its environs, doubling her strength with new recruits. Judith added to her already-sizable strength with every tribe and village she conquered, pressing men into military service and women into sexual servitude, and those who wouldn't submit to her indomitable will were slain without mercy, their broken bodies left to bleed out in the desert sands. Then, after taking Baghdad, she would lead her massive armies east across all of Persia, Afghanistan, and India. She would leave a path of destruction thousands of miles wide. It was all part of her plan.

Why? Didn't the bloody Queen have more than enough already? Didn't she possess more than enough gold? More than enough land? More than enough soldiers? More than enough slaves? More than enough power?

Why keep killing? Why keep looting? Why keep destroying? Why?

"No one can stop us now," Anong heard the Queen boast to her generals inside the command tent. "Wherever we go, we will spread such terror in our approach, leaving such death and destruction behind in our wake, that even the stoutest hearts will tremble when word of our coming reaches their ears. Soldiers will flee before us like scared jackals, knowing we are merciless and spare no one in our path who does not submit. Those who do try to oppose us will die horrible deaths. Those who choose to serve us will be rewarded with their lives, paltry though they me be, at least for one more day. No one will ever dare to stand in my way because these fools value their own worthless lives above all else. They know I have both the power and will to end their miserable lives at my slightest whim. As long as all men fear me—fear us, my loyal generals—we are unstoppable."

"O, Mighty Queen, your name will be known among all peoples for generations to come," said one of the generals, bowing low. "Already you are well-known in the region. Your fame will be universal. It will spread like flames fed by the fiercest of winds. You are the stalking lion feeding on human flesh. You are greater and more beautiful by far than Cleopatra and even the fabled Helen of Troy ever were."

"Someday they shall know my true name," said the Queen, seeming pleased by the man's words. "Then the entire world shall quake in fear."

What did she mean? wondered Anong. Was not Gudit, or Judith, the Queen's true name? Why would she allow her name to be hidden? What was it about her name that was so important that she would want to hide it?

Not long after midnight, after all the camp fires were put out and the torches extinguished, Anong was awakened from a sound sleep by a noise coming from the Queen's tent that sounded like a combination of laughter mixed with the running water of a rapidly-flowing stream. Several of the servant girls, Anong included, were forced to sleep close to the Queen so that they might respond to the Queen's commands throughout the night, but Anong was the only one awaked by the sounds at this late hour. Fearing the Queen's wrath if none of the girls responded quickly, Anong crept closer to the tent to hear better if the Queen made demands.

Had it only been a dream? No, she could clearly hear movement and laughter within the tent, and she could see the tiny flicker of the flame from a lit oil lamp cast wildly-dancing shadows on the thin fabric flaps. The Queen was definitely awake and moving about. Was she alone? Or were there others in the tent with her?

Had she called for one of the girls to assist her? Would all of the girls be punished for not hearing the Queen's commands? Anong moved nearer to the tent and listened more attentively.

Then she heard water. The sound made her lick her lips, though her tongue was drier than sand.

Splash! More water. *Splash! Splash!* Lots of water. *Splash!* Again more water. *Splash!*

Splash!

Her fear forgotten now, driven forward only by unquenched thirst, Anong crept ever closer to the tent. Closer and closer she moved on skinned hands and knees, until, finally, she could see, in the tiny space between the flaps, the ceramic lamp held in the huge hands of one of the Nubian eunuchs, while another eunuch stood over a wooden tub and poured water from a tall ceramic vase onto the naked breasts of Queen Judith who sat in the tub surrounded with gallons of precious water.

Splash! Splash!

Judith was bathing! While people were dying of thirst, Judith was bathing!

Just the sight of so much water made Anong crazy.

Without thinking, she found herself lifting the flap and struggling to her feet inside the tent, stumbling toward the water, so surprising the Nubian pouring water over the Queen's back that the man dropped the vase and it splintered, spilling the precious contents all over the sand.

The other Nubian calmly placed the oil lamp on the ground, and grabbed the girl by the wrists and her slim waist before she could get any closer to the Queen and the tub. He effortlessly hefted her from the ground, hoisted her high above his head, and was about to throw her down to her death when the Queen commanded him to stop.

"How dare you!" spat the Queen, as if the girl were no more than a squirming scorpion who had raised its stinger in her direction and would soon be trampled underfoot by the Nubian. "How dare you violate my space with your presence?"

"How dare you squander water when so many die of thirst?" asked Anong, her voice as dry and cracked as her parched lips. The words emerged unbidden from her throat, as if it were someone else speaking. She knew she was already dead, and it mattered little what she said to anger the Queen.

"Do you know who I am, you worm? Do you know what I can do to you?"

"Yes," said Anong. "I know who you are. I know your true name."

Queen Judith seemed startled by Anong's choice of words. "Who are you that you know my true name?"

Once again the voice emerged unbidden from inside Anong. "I am the one chosen by the gods to defeat you."

Judith laughed. Her whole body seemed wracked with raucous laughter. Her face lit up and her eyes filled with amusement. She splashed around in the tub like a little girl, kicking her feet and sending water gushing over the sides. What a waste! What a terrible waste!

"You amuse me, child," said the Queen. "If you continue to amuse me, I may yet let you live."

Anong felt the Nubian's iron grip begin to loosen a little. Though he still held her wrists clamped in one iron fist while the nails of the other hand dug into her thighs, he was no longer crushing her bones with his bare hands.

"Let us play a game, child," said the Queen. "You like games, don't you? It amuses me to play games, especially when we play by my rules. Here are the rules. If you can say my true name, do so now and I shall let you live. You have my word. If you cannot, I shall have Hamad snap your spine like a twig. Speak now, and speak truly. Or you die."

"Your name is Uma," gasped Anong.

Once again, Anong saw the look of surprise on Judith's face as her words struck home and all mirth disappeared from the Queen's eyes.

"Who are you?" demanded the Queen, quickly rising from her tub to look directly into the face of the girl, searching her eyes for hidden secrets. "Who are you and who sent you?"

“I already told you,” said Anong. “I am the one sent by the gods to defeat you.”

“Then you are too dangerous to let live. Hamad, tear her to pieces.”

As the Nubian’s grip snapped her wrist bones and tore at her thighs, Anong gasped, “But you promised….”

“I lied,” were the last words Anong heard as her frail form was brought quickly down to smash hard against Hamad’s raised knee, snapping her spine and stilling her beating heart.

“Did you not know that Uma is the Queen of lies?”

CHAPTER SEVENTEEN

Deb tracked Wright to New York City. It was a long and painstaking process, and Eddie and a team of analysts from NSA helped. So did Bill Ramsey, after the Colonel arranged special clearance for Randy Edwards as a consultant.

They accessed GPS data from the stolen Subaru after FBI agents found the car abandoned in a New York suburb. Noting the date and time the engine had last been shut down from the Forester's factory built-in computer chip that recorded engine performance, Deb accessed concurrent satellite shots of the area and saw the Subaru being parked. Then she tracked the man who left the car as he slipped around the corner, walked straight for two blocks more, and climbed into a Ford rental, a late model black Taurus with plates she couldn't read because they were deliberately mud-splattered to obscure the numbers. She followed the Taurus to a house in an affluent suburb where it parked in a garage adjacent to the house. The man disappeared into the house.

Was it Wright? She wasn't sure with that baseball cap pulled down over his face, but the man she was tracking was about the correct size and build. What was Wright doing in New

York? Did he hope to hide amid the comings and goings of millions of civilians in the country's largest city? If that's what he thought, he had another think coming.

"I found Wright," Deb informed Eddie. "He's in NYC. Or, at least, he was yesterday."

"What about the rest of his people? They with him?"

"Negative."

"How many do you think are left?" asked Ramsey. "A hundred? Two hundred? Some were killed, and a hundred and eighty are in custody. But the rest are still out there."

"Maybe close to two hundred. But they're scattered hinter and yon. We tracked a half dozen or so going west, but we don't know where the others may be hiding. They could be anywhere."

"How far west?"

"We lost them on the interstate. Last we saw them, they were on I-70 heading northwest toward Pittsburgh. Four vehicles, all dark-colored SUVs."

"I'm on it," said Eddie. "If they pulled off for a rest stop, I'll be able to pick them up in future satellite shots when they get back on the intestate."

"Good," said Deb. "Randy and I will concentrate on Wright. Once we have an exact address, I'll send Ksitigarbha to pay Wright a little visit."

"Why can't you just find him the way you found me in Botswana?" asked Randy.

"I've never met Wright in person. I can't identify his aura on the astral plane unless I've had personal contact with him. It would be worse than searching for a needle in a haystack looking for an individual aura in a city filled with millions of human auras. But if I know exactly where he's located, I can find that place on the astral plane. Then I can physically go there and see if anyone there looks like the picture we have of Earl Wright from his 201 file. If it is Wright, Ksitigarbha can teleport there and confront him."

"Take me with you. I've met Wright before, and I'll identify him for you."

"Get me an address. Then we'll go get the man."

"Consider it done," said Randy Edwards.

* * *

"Tell me now," commanded the woman called Charlie as soon as Lokesvara and Anong returned to their seats in front of her. "Who are you really?"

"I am, as I said," said Lokesvara, "called Wenshu Wutai Shan, and my eyes and ears are everywhere. That is the truth."

"And the girl? Who is she, really?"

"Her name is Anong."

"She is your granddaughter?"

"She is my ward. I take care of her as if she were my granddaughter. That, too, is the truth."

"I have the feeling I know you from somewhere a long time ago. All three of you. I know I have seen the girl before, but I cannot place her. I do not believe her name is Anong, nor do I believe your name is Shan nor your companion's name is Schweitzer." She turned to face the Ranger. "Is your name really Schweitzer?" she asked. "What is your first name?"

"Schweitzer is the name on my passport," said the Ranger, speaking for the first time. "Why is it important to know our names?"

"I like to know with whom I do business," said Charlie. "Before we can do business, I need to know your real names."

"So you can check up on us?" asked the Ranger. "Don't you trust us?"

Charlie laughed. "No more than you trust me, Mr. Schweitzer."

"Then tell us your full name. I bet your first name isn't Charlie. You tell me your name and I'll tell you mine. You go first."

"Do you think this is a child's game, Mr. Schweitzer? Do you think if you offer to show me your peepee, I'll show you mine? We're all adults here, with the exception of the girl, and we're playing for keeps. You will tell me everything I want to know and you will tell me now, or you'll never leave here alive."

"Is that a threat?" asked the Ranger.

"Oh, no," said Charlie with a smile. "That's a promise. I have people with weapons on every floor of this building, and I will have you killed if you try to leave without answering my questions."

"And if we do, what will prevent you from killing us after you have everything you want from us?" asked Lokesvara.

"You have my word," said Charlie. "Is not my word good enough for you?"

"Don't believe her, Master!" shouted Anong. "She is a liar. She is the queen of lies."

Charlie responded as if she had just been slapped in the face by Anong's words. "Kill them," commanded Charlie, and Hassan and his partner reached for their guns. "Kill all three. Kill them now."

Anong saw the Ranger spring like a lion at Hassan, slamming Hassan hard against the wall and grabbing at Hassan's gun as it slipped from his fingers. The other man instantly opened fire, but not before the Ranger had dropped to the floor and rolled around to fire a bullet straight into the man's chest where a bright red rose seemed to blossom. He fired again, and another rose appeared next to the first. Then he reversed direction and grew a rose on Hassan's abdomen, but not before Hassan had managed to reach a phone on the wall and pressed one of the buttons.

Charlie reacted almost as fast as the Ranger, darting across the room and snatching what looked like a sub-machine gun from the wall to her left. She pulled back on a lever and Anong heard the solid-steel bolt fly forward and lock into place as the first round entered the chamber from the drum-type magazine. She knew the weapon was loaded and ready to fire, and it was aimed directly at her.

But Lokesvara had not sat idle. He was on his feet and pivoting, moving swiftly through the beginning Tai Chi forms, entering Parting the Wild Horse Mane, flowing effortlessly into the White Crane Spreads its Wings, then performing a high Pat on Horse before executing a perfect left heel kick that sent the machine gun flying from Charlie's hands to clatter nosily across the floor without discharging.

Just then the door flew wide open, and the guard they had seen out in the hallway stepped through the open doorway with pistol in hand looking for targets. The Ranger fired a shot before the guard could even take aim, and another red rose appeared, this one in the exact center of the guard's forehead, as a rain of blood and brains splattered the hallway floor behind him.

Anong stared wide-eyed at the fallen bodies, aware the Ranger had thrice broken his sacred vow never to take the life, neither deliberately nor inadvertently, of another sentient being. Although this was clearly a case of kill or be killed, she knew nowhere did any of the Sutras allow an exception for self-defense. Like Rithisak the penitent boatman, the Ranger now needed to devote the rest of his life to deeds of exceptional merit that might somehow offset some of the bad karma he brought upon himself by his actions. It would be a terrible burden to bear, and Anong saw it as an omen signifying bad things to come.

More men rushed through the door with guns, and the Ranger fired again and again until the slide on his pistol locked all the way to the rear. Anong knew that meant all rounds in the magazine had been fired and the handgun was empty. She watched the Ranger throw the useless pistol away and launch himself forward to plow face-first into the line of men, knocking some of them to the floor, but none of the men dropped their weapons and the Ranger fought them unarmed. Anong watched in horror as one of the men aimed at the Ranger and pulled the trigger, and a red rose erupted on the right side of the Ranger's suit coat. Another man fired, too, and this time the Ranger went limp as an even bigger flower blossomed and a rip appeared in the fabric of the coat where the round exited.

As if totally oblivious to the battle at the doorway, Charlie and Lokesvara were engaged in a deadly battle of their own, a desperate duel with broadswords they had simultaneously plucked from the display on the far wall. Their swords clinked and clanked as each effectively parried the thrust of the other and made counter-thrusts that were then parried in turn. Anong could tell that Lokesvara was fighting solely on the defensive. Charlie seemed to act much more aggressively, more decisively, because she had no reservations about killing her opponent, while Lokesvara sought only to disarm his foe and subdue her without killing. It was merely a matter of time before the old man's strength was depleted and Charlie ran a sword through his chest or cut off his head. That is, if one of the gunmen didn't kill him first.

Anong felt helpless. She thought about trying to retrieve the machine gun from where it lay on the floor, but she had no familiarity with firearms and absolutely no idea of how to aim or fire the weapon even if she could get to it and manage to lift it from the floor. She felt so very helpless and afraid, knowing that the evil ones were winning the battle and would soon be in perfect position to kill not only the two most important people in Anong's current life but also Anong herself. There must be something she could do. But what? She was only a girl. What could she possibly do against men with guns that would matter?

And then she remembered the Kundalini. She had been practicing for days, raising the Kundalini serpent and firing up the dan-tien with the bellows breath. It was almost second nature to her now. All she had to do was close her eyes and let it happen.

So she took a deep breath, held it, and then exhaled, willing the sleeping serpent to awaken. She felt the Kundalini stir from slumber, felt its hooded head flare as it rose up in anger, and she began Tummo breathing almost immediately. She pumped air into the fire in her belly, and the serpent rose ever higher with each breath, its hood flared as it prepared to strike.

She paid no attention to the horrible sounds coming from her left where there were men kicking the Ranger's limp body with their heavy shoes. She ignored the sounds of sharp swords clashing off to her right where Charlie and Lokesvara fought their deadly duel. She concentrated only on the fire flaring in her center as, one-by-one, each of the chakras began spinning, going faster and faster, faster and faster, faster and faster.

She opened her third eye, the Adjna, and a beam of blinding white light, as pure as the snows of Mount Meru, emerged from a spot on the girl's forehead, engulfing the room and all in it.

She visualized, within the light, a disk with 108 serrated points like the sharp point on an arrow or the blade of a kris, and she used the Kundalini energy to set that disk to spinning, too, controlling the speed with her will. She began to repeat "*Om sudarshanaya vidmahe mahajwaalaya dheemahi tannaschakra prachodayath*" over and over again in her mind. Then she added "*Swaha*" at the end to fix her intention and make it so, and she felt the power of the Sudarshana Chakra spew forth as she released a blast of pure energy and sent the disk with 108 serrated points spinning toward her enemies.

The spinning disk sliced through the men in the doorway like a runaway buzz saw splintering pine. It severed heads from shoulders, limbs from torsos. It hacked and tore and ripped asunder. Blood rained down everywhere as the Sudarshana Chakra did its work.

She brought the disk back, bade it return to her, and it was still spinning as it reentered the room from the hallway.

Charlie and Lokesvara seemed frozen like statues, frozen in place by the blinding light. Neither could see to move against the other. She thought about sending the disk flying at Uma, but something held her back.

"Save your strength for when you need it," Lokesvara had warned. "The Kundalini is like a battery. When the Kundalini power is used up, the serpent needs to sleep to recharge the battery. Now you must reverse the process. Allow the power to pass. Allow the Kundalini to rest. Be still and meditate."

She knew she had almost depleted her power. If she sent the disk at Uma, she would be completely spent, used up. She had to decide which was more important: Killing Uma or getting Lokesvara and the Ranger out of the building. She decided to save her strength, and she called the disk back inside herself and began to meditate.

As she closed her third eye, the light in the room returned to normal. Within minutes, she heard the clash of steel resume as Lokesvara and Charlie regained their sight.

Anong ended her meditation and rose from her chair. She recited a spell of enchantment as she approached the duel, gratified that neither Lokesvara nor Charlie seemed to take notice.

Despite the terror she felt as she moved closer and closer to Uma, Anong continued inching forward until she reached the wall displaying garrotes and a hangman's noose. The noose was made of thick braided rope, knotted, with a wide loop and about five feet of additional rope left dangling. She slipped the noose off its hook on the wall.

Charlie and Lokesvara were moving fast, paring, thrusting, dodging, ducking, equally matched except for age. Obviously, both had been trained in swordsmanship. What Lokesvara lacked in stamina, he made up in superior technical competence. But Anong could see he was tiring. It was only a matter of time before the sword became too heavy to lift again. Then Charlie would move in for the kill.

Anong moved in instead, matching her speed to Charlie's, standing on tiptoes to slip the noose over the taller woman's head. Lokesvara saw the noose moving through the air as if it were magically moving of its own accord, and he distracted Charlie's attention from seeing the movement until the noose was firmly in place.

Anong yanked back on the end of the rope and the hangman's noose slid tight around Charlie's throat, bruising the windpipe and choking the breath from the woman before she knew what was happening. Charlie dropped the sword and brought both hands to her neck, wedging her thumbs beneath the noose to try to release the pressure on her windpipe.

Lokesvara touched the tip of his sword to Charlie's chest. "Yield," he said. "I do not wish to harm you."

"I….I….aghhhhhh….yield…ggghhhhhhh."

"Release the pressure, Anong," Lokesvara said.

Anong allowed the rope to grow slack in her hands.

"Our business here is finished," said Lokesvara. "We are leaving now, and you will help us get out of the building."

"Never."

"You will help us or I'll...."

"You'll do what? Kill me? I think not, old man. You could have killed me many times over but you never pressed your advantage. You are a true master of the sword. That was evident during the first few minutes of our duel. But you stayed your hand. I must admit I admire your complete control. Not many men have that ability. But you are not a killer, Mr. Shan, or whatever your name is. You won't kill me. Your actions demonstrated that."

"Maybe *he* won't kill you," said Anong, pulling on the noose. "But *I* will. You killed my friend. For that you deserve to die."

"And you killed my men. You were the one who tore them apart, weren't you? I don't know who you are, child, but I know you are no ordinary mortal."

"Nor are you, Uma."

Charlie blanched. Her face turned whiter than if she had seen a ghost. "What did you call me?"

"Uma. That is your true name."

"You have me at a disadvantage, child. I still do not know who you are."

"I told you once, but you did not believe me. I am the one sent by the gods to defeat you."

"No more words," said Lokesvara. "I will pick up my friend's body and we will leave. You, Uma, will go with us to ensure our safe passage. Come. Do not argue, or I'll let Anong have her way with you."

Lokesvara bent his knees and wrapped his arms around the Ranger's body. Then he stood up, cradling the monk gently, affectionately, and stepped over the remains of Charlie's guards. Though the Ranger looked to weigh two hundred pounds and the Lama to weigh barely half that, the old man walked straight as if his burden were light as a feather. Anong never ceased to be amazed by Lokesvara.

They walked down one flight of stairs to the thirty-fifth floor and passed through the reception area to reach the elevator.

"Is everything all right?" asked Laura from behind her desk.

"Fine," said Charlie as an invisible hand tugged at the rope around Charlie's neck.

"We heard gunshots," said Laura. "I sent security up to investigate."

"I was showing our guests one of my antique guns and it discharged," said Charlie. "Nothing to worry about. Mr. Schweitzer was slightly injured, and we're taking him to the hospital. But I'm sure he'll be okay."

Laura obviously noted the noose around Charlie's neck, but the receptionist made no comment. "When will you be back?" she asked Charlie.

"Shortly," said Charlie, stepping into the elevator.

They rode down in the elevator in silence. No one commented on the view through the glass. Fortunately, no one else called for, or got onto, the elevator.

When the elevator doors opened on the lobby concourse, Lokesvara walked purposely toward the nearest exit. People stopped and stared at the old man carrying a blood-spattered body but no one offered to help and no one stopped them. Several people noticed the woman wearing a hangman's noose around her neck and the teen-aged girl following with the other end of the rope in her hands. Anong's enchantment didn't work on crowds.

Was this spectacle part of a play? Anong heard people ask their companions. Street theater, perhaps? Were they making a motion picture? Where were the cameras?

Few people could believe what they were seeing was real.

But before Lokesvara could get through the doors, two men stopped him. They stood directly in his path, blocking the exit.

"What y'got there, mate?" asked one of the men with what sounded like an Australian accent. "Looks to me like a dead body."

"My associate is badly injured," replied Lokesvara. "I must get him to a healer immediately. Please step out of the way. Let me pass or you will answer for his untimely death."

"He looks dead already, mate. What's your hurry?"

The other man noticed the rope around Charlie's neck. "You okay, ma'am?" he asked.

"No," said Charlie, and Anong quickly jerked back on the rope.

Both men, either security guards for the building or thugs in Charlie's employ, brought guns out of hidden holsters.

"Tell them to back away or I'll snap your neck," Anong whispered to Charlie. She tugged hard on the rope and Charlie made choking sounds.

"Back away," Charlie gasped as Anong let up on the rope. "Do as I say."

"We can't do that, ma'am," said the man without an accent. "Security protocol requires us to detain you."

"Do you know who I am?" asked Charlie.

"Yes, ma'am. But we have our orders."

Anong closed her eyes and willed the serpent awake. She gave one last tug on the rope and choked Charlie into unconsciousness before dropping the rope and opening her third eye.

It seemed to the people in the lobby that the sun had suddenly come down from the sky to take residence inside the building. No one could say what happened next because no one had actually seen it happen. They were momentarily blinded by the brightness.

But Anong saw the 108 sharp points of the spinning Sudarshana Chakra slice through the two men before they knew what had hit them. Body parts flew upwards and sideways, blood flowed like rivers. A severed head rolled across the lobby floor like a bowling ball. Anong saw everything. She was the one who guided the spinning disk of death to specific targets. She would have included Uma as a target if her energy wasn't nearly depleted. She spared Uma not out of compassion, but of necessity.

Lokesvara stepped over the mess and went out the door and Anong followed closely behind him, recalling the disk and closing her third eye before stepping out into bright sunlight that seemed dim compared to the light that was only now beginning to fade inside the building.

* * *

Randy Edwards held Deb's hand as Deb entered the ladies room. Deb had explained that the ladies room was one of the very few places in the building without security cameras, and she didn't want the government to see what she was about to do. She didn't mind if someone viewing the cameras in the hallway thought Deb and Randy had entered the room for an afternoon quickie, but she did mind if someone saw both of them disappear when they teleported, only to reappear when they came back. It might open up a whole new can of worms.

Randy felt nothing different as his body disassembled in the ladies room at Fort Belvoir and simultaneously reassembled in a New York suburb. He was still himself, and Bill Ramsey was still with him in spirit.

But Deb had definitely changed. Now she had become Sacred Girl, the reincarnation of the Bodhisattva Ksitigarbha.

They were inside the house Randy had identified from satellite images as the last known location of Earl Wright. This was the house where they had seen Wright leave his rental in the attached garage, and they were reasonably certain he had to be inside the building.

But where was he? The living room was completely empty, and there was no indication anyone had permanently occupied the house for months, maybe years. There was a for sale sign planted in the front yard. They searched through the rest of the house just to be certain Wright wasn't hiding somewhere. The bedrooms and kitchen were empty, though there was a coffee maker that had been used recently and coffee grounds were still in the basket. The coffee grounds were cold and looked about a day old.

Wright's rental car was indeed still parked in the garage where they knew he had left it, but it appeared to have been abandoned there. Wright must have gone elsewhere on foot. As a former Special Forces officer, he was an expert in camouflage and concealment and knew many ways to move about without being singled out by eyes in the sky or eyes on the ground.

"We'll never find him now," said Randy as they searched the back yard for any sign of where Wright might have gone.

Suddenly, a man appeared out of nowhere less than ten feet away. Randy was sure it had to be Wright, and he reached for his pistol. Wright must have known they would come for him, and he set a trap. They had walked straight into the ambush without suspecting a thing.

Ksitigarbha stopped Randy before he could shoot.

"Put your weapon away," said Ksitigarbha. "He is a friend."

Now Randy could see that it wasn't Wright but an old man, an oriental man wearing a suit and tie, and he struggled to carry another man in his arms.

And Randy saw a girl had also appeared alongside the old man, and the girl looked oriental, too. She wore a dress with colorful lotus flowers printed on the fabric.

"We need your help," said the old man, his knees beginning to buckle. "The Ranger has been shot multiple times and he is barely alive. I have been keeping him alive by sharing my energy with him. But I'm quickly burning out. Soon, we will both die."

"Let me restore both of you," said Ksitigarbha, and she touched both men with her hands. "The earth has need of you yet."

Randy watched in awe-struck silence as Ksitigarbha drew energy from the earth beneath her feet and the sky above her head, married the two, and transferred the result to the two men through her hands. Her hands began to glow with an eerie golden light, and then the golden glow spread to encompass each of the men like a halo.

She kept at it for what seemed like an hour, but was probably no more than a few minutes. The younger man stirred, moaned, and finally opened his eyes. "Where am I?" he asked.

"*Swaha,*" said Ksitigarbha. "It is done."

The old man set the younger man on the ground, and Randy now recognized the younger man's face from Bill Ramsey's memory. It was Vajrapani, the spirit guide that had sent Bill Ramsey to possess Randy. He hadn't recognized him before because he'd never seen Vajrapani wearing a suit instead of the saffron robes of a monk or the battledress of a soldier.

"Namaste, Anong" said Ksitigarbha, bowing to the girl.

"Namaste, Mistress," said the girl, putting her hands together at her bowed forehead.

"You're in New York," Randy told the Ranger.

"How did I get here?" Vajrapani asked. "What am I doing in New York?"

"The old man brought you. He saved you. The old man and Sacred Girl. They saved you."

"I remember being shot in Dubai. That's the last I remember. What happened?"

"Charlie is Uma," said the old Chinaman. "Uma is Mahesvara's wife. Anong knew Uma in a previous life and recognized her. If Uma is in Dubai, it is likely Mahesvara is also."

"Who is Uma?" asked Randy. "And who is Mahesvara? And who are you?"

"I am Lokesvara," said the old man. "And who are you?"

"This is Randy Edwards," said the Ranger. "He and Bill Ramsey cohabit the same body."

"I see," said Lokesvara. "To answer your question, Randy Edwards, Mahesvara is a demon. Uma is his bride. They are the ones responsible for the discord the world now faces."

"A demon? A real demon? Do such things exist?"

"We see Mahesvara as a demon, but he is more like a force of nature. He is as real as the wind when it becomes a hurricane, or as real as the volcano when it erupts to bury a nearby village with ash and lava. He is the destructive side of creation."

"And he's the one behind Wright and the sniper shootings?"

"I believe so, yes," said Lokesvara. "But we were unable to see him. We found, instead, his wife."

"Did you kill her?"

"No," said Lokesvara. "I do not kill, if it can be prevented."

"But I heard you killed some of the men who went on R and R to Thailand. That was you, wasn't it?"

"That was Manjusri and Vajrapani, not Lokesvara and the Ranger. The names of the men Manjusri and Vajrapani killed that day had already been recorded in the Book of Judgement. Those men had sealed their own fate by their own actions: raping young girls, taking the girls against their will, physically and emotionally injuring them in the process. Those men may someday be reborn, but first they have much to learn about compassion and the consequences of their actions. They will experience the same suffering they inflicted on others. Killing them was necessary that they might themselves feel the pain their own actions had caused. It is the law of karma. Think of Manjusri as an agent of the law."

"Kind of a cosmic U. S. Marshal?"

"Something like that. Manjusri is seldom judge or jury, but oftentimes he does act as divine executioner."

Anong and Ksitigarbha joined the men. "We were looking for Earl Wright," said Ksitigarbha. "But he eluded us."

"Who is Earl Wright?" asked Lokesvara.

"He's the guy who hired me to work for WLSCTC," said Randy. "He set up the training camps and the R and R centers. He's not the Big Boss, but he might know who is."

"And he knows where the assassins are hiding," said Ksitigarbha. "We think he knows what they are planning next. If we can capture Wright, we may be able to foil their future plans."

"I think," said Anong, "that is the same Mr. Right that came to the house in Thailand to inspect us. Maa afforded him great respect."

"We will leave now and allow you to continue your search for the elusive Mr. Wright," said Lokesvara. "We need to go back to Ankor and rest. The Ranger is still healing, and Anong needs time to recharge her batteries."

"Master," whispered Anong, "I am worried about the Ranger."

"He will heal," said Lokesvara. "Ksitigarbha has mended his wounds and restored his life force."

"That is not why I worry," whispered Anong. "He has killed three men. Did he not take a vow to refrain from killing?"

"Yes," said Lokesvara, looking at the Ranger with the greatest of compassion. "He will someday need to answer for that."

"Is there nothing we can do to help him?" asked Anong.

"No, child," said Lokesvara. "The only one who can absolve him is the Ranger himself through future actions. It is his karma, and he must deal with it in his own way. Not even the gods can help him now."

* * *

Earl Wright watched them through a spotting scope from his hide on the second floor of the alternate safe house three blocks away. When he saw Randy Edwards and a young girl come out of the house and look around the back yard, he quickly assembled an assault rifle and loaded a full magazine. Though the range was a thousand meters, he had a clear shot at the two figures. He rapidly calculated wind direction and drop, and used Kentucky windage to compensate for both instead of adjusting the iron sights.

He braced the weapon on the sill of the open window, found his spot weld, and took up slack on the trigger.

He recited the shooter's mantra in his mind: BRASS. Breathe, relax, aim, sight, squeeze. Something in his peripheral vision alerted him, and he took his finger off the trigger. There were others now in the yard. How many? Were any of them armed?

He put the rifle down and looked through the thirty power spotting scope which made things appear thirty times larger. He could clearly see three new arrivals on the scene: an old man carrying what looked to be a younger man who was obviously badly injured, and a young girl of about twelve.

The old man and the girl looked Chinese.

Wright watched as the girl who had been with Edwards walked to the two men and touched their shoulders with her hands. Even from this distance, he could see something strange happening as the girl's hands began to glow.

And then both men began to glow. They became surrounded by the strange light that pulsated with some kind of weird energy.

What the fuck?

Wright kept his eye glued to the scope. Within minutes, the injured man began to revive.

This can't be happening, thought Wright. *I've got to be hallucinating.*

The old man laid the revived younger man on the ground and the others gathered around, blocking Wright's view, and they all talked about something Wright would give his eye teeth to overhear.

Wright had half-expected Deb Johnson to show up at the house, and he had asked Brakken to put him in a safe house within a block or two of another property. Brakken had just the thing, a vacant house with an attached garage where Wright could store the car, and another house three blocks away. Both houses were on the market, and the keys were kept in locked boxes with combination locks that were secured to the buildings near the rear doors. Wright had parked the car on the drive, walked around back, opened the lock box with the combination Brakken had given him, removed the key, entered the house by the back door, and opened the garage. Then he drove the car into the garage, parked it, went back inside the house, made a pot of coffee, and used the computer. Then he exited the building by the back door, dropped the key in the box, and used available cover to conceal his movement to the real safe house two blocks away.

Then he had waited for Johnson or the FBI to show up. He was surprised to see Randy Edwards still alive, and he was extremely disappointed not to see Deb Johnson. But he now knew Edwards and Johnson had to be working together, and he wanted nothing more than a chance to blow Edwards away. If he couldn't get Johnson in his cross-hairs, he at least could get Edwards. He would have had him, too, if the others hadn't interrupted the shot.

Unfortunately, he didn't have a clear shot with the old man and the young girl in the way. Shooting them would only alert Edwards to his present location. He had seen that Edwards was armed with an M9 Beretta, a standard military-issued sidearm, and he knew Randy had been trained to take cover and return fire. Though the maximum effective range of the Beretta was only a little more than 500 meters, the lead would travel more than three times as far. If Edwards was as good as his records had indicated, he might hit Wright with a lucky shot before Earl could isolate and kill him.

Wright had taken fire before, and he wasn't worried about being shot at. But the mission came first, and he didn't dare blow his cover until he had a clear shot at Edwards. He decided to wait and watch. If he got a clear shot at Edwards, he'd take it.

But he didn't get a clear shot. The two other men and the oriental girl suddenly disappeared right before Earl's eyes. One minute they were clearly visible in the scope's view, and the next they were gone.

And before he could raise the rifle to take a shot at Randy Edwards, Edwards and the other girl disappeared, too.

Wright moved the scope frantically this way and that, adjusted the focus, and still couldn't find them. They had simply disappeared, as if the earth had opened up and swallowed them whole.

That, of course, was impossible. Yet, his peripheral vision had detected no sudden movements, no mad dashes for concealment. They had to still be there. Why the hell couldn't he see them?

None of the five human beings he had observed in that yard only moments before remained visible. Not to the naked eye. Not to the spotting scope. He used his peripheral vision to check the edges of things in the yard: bushes, trees, a birdbath. If they were hiding in that back yard, they blended so perfectly with their environment that not even a trained intelligence expert like Earl Wright could detect an anomaly. There were no abnormal shadows on the lawn, no pieces of colorful clothing mixed with the green and brown of the shrubs, no toes sticking out from behind the base of trees.

The only way he could be certain they weren't there, however, was to blow his cover and go there in person. Sometimes you just had to get up close and personal in order to get the job done right.

Wright went back to the scope and checked out the entire area, not just the back yard. He looked in the neighbors' yards, into the windows of the neighbors' houses, scanned the streets as far as he could see.

Earl checked the two pistols he wore in a harness across his chest. Both were fully loaded, chambered, safeties on. He checked the M4. Thirty round magazine, two more mags in his pants pockets, and safety off. He was ready to rock and roll.

And then the telephone clipped to his belt began to vibrate.

"Mr. Wright," said Charlie, her voice sounding hoarse as if she had a sore throat from a bad cold, "we have a problem."

"Oh?"

"My office in Dubai has been compromised, and I must relocate immediately. All operations will go on as planned, but I want to alert you to possible complications."

"What kind of complications?"

"Two. A man and a girl."

"Both Orientals?"

"How did you know?"

"I saw them."

"They were there? When?"

"Just now."

"Impossible. They were just here in Dubai."

"I saw them here less than ten minutes ago. They had another man with them who looked like he had been injured. But he recovered."

"He was dead. He had been shot multiple times and bled out. I am certain he was dead."

"I saw him stand up and walk."

Charlie said nothing, and the silence was deafening. Wright knew she was thinking. Finally, she said, "Are they still there?"

"I don't think so. I was just going to see if I could find them. It looked like they disappeared into thin air, but I know that's impossible."

"Do nothing," said Charlie. "You are not to interact with them in any way. Do you understand me, Wright?"

"I hear you."

"Stick to the timetable. All your men should be in place by tomorrow. Then we act."

"We'll be ready."

"Good. I'll call you tomorrow. Don't do anything foolish. Leave those people alone. I'll take care of them when the time is right."

"Do you know who they are?"

"Yes," she said. "I didn't know them when I met them earlier today, but I do now. Not only do I now know who they are, but I know where to find them."

She clicked off.

CHAPTER EIGHTEEN

After eight hours of uninterrupted sleep and a breakfast consisting of three kinds of fruit, the Ranger felt almost human. His entire body still ached, and he had dark bruises on his chest and stomach from where he had been kicked, but most of the bullet wounds had mended completely and he could barely see slight scars where he had been shot in the chest, side, and back multiple times at close range.

He had passed in and out of consciousness after the second round tore a huge hole in his chest, and he barely recalled clinging to life by the thinnest of threads. He knew he had work yet to do in this life, and he wouldn't—couldn't—let himself die. Too much depended on Vajrapani, and the Ranger's body provided the perfect vehicle for Vajrapani to act in the world.

If the Ranger died, Vajrapani would have to find another vehicle. He could enter a fetus at the moment of conception, cohabiting the developing cells along with another reincarnated soul, but then he would need to wait until that body matured to adolescence before he would be able to fully manifest in the world again. That would take precious time they didn't have to spare.

Besides, the Ranger had lots to make up for before he could go into the light. He had far too many human deaths on his hands—three added just yesterday—and the only thing that might offset the bad karma of his past actions would be the number of lives his future actions saved, the number of deaths he prevented.

But even if he saved a thousand lives, he had again broken a sacred vow, a trust, and for that, he knew, he would pay dearly in the life between lives. Perhaps it was the fear of facing that punishment that kept him from dying.

He had clung desperately to life while Lokesvara and Anong had battled Uma. But even the Ranger's diamond-hard resolve wasn't enough to keep him alive. He felt the last of his strength leaving him as he bled out on the floor. It would be only a matter of minutes before he saw the clear light or the eternal darkness. There was nothing more he could do, and darkness closed in upon him as he took his last breath.

And then he had felt a sudden surge of new strength that pulled him back from the abyss as Lokesvara cradled him in his arms like a child. He knew the old man was voluntarily sharing his own life force with a dying man—an act of compassion beyond compare. Though Lokesvara's life-force was strong, it would not last forever. He would be depleted in less than an hour. The old man was willing to die in order to save another. It was an act of supreme sacrifice, one few men were willing to make. Lokesvara was willing to lay down his life for his friend.

But Lokesvara was like no other man the Ranger had ever encountered. His wisdom and compassion were legendary.

The Ranger felt himself being carried out of the building and into the bright light of late afternoon, and then he felt a subtle shift of energy as Lokesvara teleported elsewhere. Now it was mid-morning on the other side of the world. There were smells of flowers and recently mown grass. It reminded him of his boyhood home in Oak Park. He heard voices.

Then he felt a gentle touch on his shoulder and suddenly he was filled with energy. The pain in his side and his chest and his back momentarily increased as his flesh moved about to fill in the holes, and then the pain was gone. It had simply vanished.

He opened his eyes. Ksitigarbha, the Sacred Girl, stood in front of him with one hand on his shoulder and the other hand touching Lokesvara.

"Where am I?" he found the strength to ask.

"You're in New York," said a man the Ranger recognized as Randy Edwards, the vehicle where Bill Ramsey now resided.

But now that the Ranger was back in Angkor, teleported there by Lokesvara, he felt alive and ready to return to work.

There was much work to do.

If Charlie was Uma, then Mahesvara was indeed active in the world because the two were said to be practically inseparable. The Ranger knew very little about Mahesvara, and he decided he needed to learn more. He went to the library, and there he found Anong, her nose buried, as usual, in a book.

"Good morning, Master," she said, looking up from the book. "Are you well?"

"Better than can be expected," said the Ranger. "What are you reading?"

"It is the Padhana Sutta. It tells of Prince Siddhartha, when he was but a Bodhisattva and had yet to attain Buddhahood, and his encounters with the demon known as Mara. I believe Mara is Mahesvara in another form."

"The Padhana Sutta is the story of Mara tempting the emaciated Gautama to return to worldly ways, is it not?"

"Yes, Master. Mara tried to unleash the ten armies of temptation to deter the Buddha from seeking liberation."

"And why do you think Mahesvara is Mara?"

"He is a deceiver. He pretends to be kind and compassionate, and he urges Gautama to live as a mortal so that he might gain merit by his actions. When the Buddha sees through Mara's lies and defeats his ten armies, Mara sends his three daughters—the three poisons—Confusion, Lust, and Pride, to seduce Siddhartha under the Bodhi tree. But the Buddha's resolve remains steadfast."

"Did you not know that Mara is the Sanskrit word for destruction as well as the word for demon?"

"No, Master."

"Mara is said to be the king of demons."

"So is Mahesvara the king of demons," said Anong. "And the Master of Deception."

"And you do not believe there could be two demon kings?"

"No, Master. Mahesvara's pride would not allow that. I believe they are different aspects of the same being."

"Tell me more of what you have learned about Mahesvara and Mara. And about Uma."

"They wish to destroy the Buddha, the Dharma, and the Sangha."

"Why?"

"Because they love to destroy. It makes them feel powerful to destroy what others have built."

"How will they try to destroy us?"

"Through greed, lust, and ignorance or delusion."

"Come. Let us tell the Lama what you have learned. I would seek his wisdom."

They were half-way between the library and Lokesvara's chamber when a powerful explosion knocked them from their feet. The Ranger recognized the whoosh of another RPG, a rocket-propelled grenade, being fired and shielded Anong with his own body as the second explosion ripped a huge hole in the wall at the end of the hall, right in front of Lokesvara's meditation room and filled the hallway with flying shrapnel and sandstone.

The Ranger was on his feet in an instant, racing toward the end of the hall, when a barrage of bullets hurtled through the hole in the wall. The Ranger hit the floor and low-crawled to the end of the hallway and crawled through the open door of Lokesvara's chamber on his right as bullets flew thirty-six inches above his head.

The whole outside wall was missing, blown to bits by the blasts. The top half of the other walls and part of the ceiling were pock-marked with bullet holes and pieces of flying shrapnel, but the bottom halves of those walls seemed to be untouched. Because the shooters were shooting up from the courtyard two stories below, all their bullets had entered at a 45 degree angle. Anything above three and a half feet would have been pulverized.

Lokesvara calmly sat on the floor in lotus, the thumbs and forefingers of both hands resting on his knees in mudra. The top of his bald head was only three feet above the floor. The bullets had passed above him, but only inches away from his head.

"They missed," said the old man. "They expected me to be sitting in a chair or standing. I did neither."

"You knew they were coming?"

"I sensed their approach. I knew what they would do."

"I will send Vajrapani after them."

"Let them go," said the old man. "Let them report to Uma that they have killed both you and me. I want her to think we are dead."

"You think Uma sent them?"

"I think she wanted revenge for what we did to her yesterday."

"How did she know where to find us?"

"She has spies everywhere. Once she knew what we looked like, it wasn't difficult for her to track us. We are not the only ones who astral travel."

"You should have killed her when you had a chance."

"Uma cannot be killed. Uma is not mortal, though her spirit now occupies a mortal body. If we had killed Charlie, Uma's spirit would only have taken possession of another hapless human, and then we would have no idea what her avatar looked like. Is it not far better to know your adversary? Now she knows us, and we know her. But, if she believes we are dead, she will not be wary."

"Have they stopped shooting?" asked Anong as she crawled into Lokesvara's chamber on hands and knees.

"I think so," said the Ranger. "I'll take a look."

He duck-walked to where the outside wall once was and cautiously peered down to the courtyard. Hundreds of brass shell casings gleamed in the morning sun.

"They're gone," he said.

"Good," said Lokesvara. "Soon they will make their next move. If they are successful, Mahesvara will come out of hiding. Then we can confront him and put an end to this madness."

"How can we do that without killing?" asked the Ranger.

"When Mahesvara and Uma reveal themselves for whom they truly are—and they will because they want people to bow down in fear before them—then we, also, shall reveal ourselves for who we truly are. Manjusri and Vajrapani will be armed with truth and enlightenment, and Mahesvara and Uma will have only pride, lust, and lies. If we conquer them, we shall help them to see the light."

"And if they conquer us?"

"Then," said Lokesvara, "there shall be no more light."

* * *

Earl Wright vibrated. That is, the cell phone on his waist vibrated, but Wright felt the vibrations run through his entire body like an electric shock from touching a live wire while standing in a puddle of water.

"It is time," said Charlie's voice when Wright answered the call.

"What about complications?"

"There are no more complications," said Charlie. "You may proceed as planned."

Wright clicked off and called his men. "Go," he said.

He wished he were with them. Earl Wright was a hands-on kind of guy, and sitting around and waiting to hear if the operations were successful or unsuccessful stressed him more than if he were in the middle of a firefight. If something went wrong, there was nothing he could do to make it right from a distance.

His guys in Seattle, Los Angeles, Denver, and Chicago were entirely on their own now. He was close enough to the guys in the Big Apple, but they were scattered throughout the metropolitan area like ants at a picnic and he doubted he could get to any of them quickly enough to help in a crisis. He yearned to be with one of the teams, content to be only a spotter or an observer or a flankman. He hated not being in the know.

Instead, he was stuck here in a house without even a coffeemaker. He had no television, but he did have the laptop he'd brought from the other house. He could use the internet to keep up with the news.

Today was the middle of June, less than a week to go before the Summer Solstice, and sunlight would remain until well after nine. Sunlight meant his men could see their targets without nightvision scopes, but sunlight meant his men might be seen also.

If Deb Johnson were still alive, she'd be watching for his men to make a move. If Deb had traced him to New York, had she traced the other men too? Did she have any idea what was about to happen?

And what about Randy Edwards? Had Charlie eliminated all of the complications or only the oriental ones? Did she even know about Edwards? Did she know that Randy Edwards had successfully infiltrated Wright's operation and was still alive to tell about it?

By eight-thirty, he expected to get some reports by phone, and shortly after that news of the shootings would begin to appear on the internet. He could monitor operations only after the fact. It bugged the shit out of him that he couldn't do more.

He wondered what the hell had happened to Dickhead. He had sent the man on a fool's errand, and the man hadn't come back. One by one, Deb Johnson was whittling away at Wright's command. The girl was good, he had to hand her that. But she definitely had to go. Wright made up his mind to take care of her personally.

He lit another cigarette and balanced it on the lip of an empty Coca-Cola can while he checked Google News, CNN.com, ABC.com, CBS.com. Some Senator, one of the men he'd escorted to Edie's club and who was not among those targeted for killing, called the current administration totally ineffectual. "The American people demand protection," said the Senator at a news conference earlier today after the funerals of some of his assassinated colleagues. "The American people deserve protection. If the American government can't protect its citizens, maybe it's time for a new form of government." He advocated stricter controls on guns, and he went so far to suggest that all guns be taken away from private citizens. "The First and Second Amendments to the Constitution of the United States were a mistake," he said. He called for the immediate suspension of the Bill of Rights.

Other Senators, and a handful of Representatives, were clamoring for immediate action to stop the terror. They were fear-mongering, preying on the public's fear for their own political ends. No one knew what to do, so everyone did nothing. Lots of rhetoric and wheel-spinning but no action. It sounded to Wright like business as usual in Washington. He wondered what the politicians would have to say after the latest round of assassinations.

Other countries, too, were posturing and fear-mongering. Russia and China had both armed nuclear weapons and threatened to retaliate if they felt they were being attacked. Israel had already sent air strikes to bomb Hamas and Hezbollah strongholds in neighboring countries. Suicide bombings had increased ten-fold, and the Middle East threatened to erupt in full-scale violence at any moment.

Where was all this leading? wondered Wright. What would happen after the latest round of shootings became known?

His phone vibrated. Seattle was successful. All targets down and no complications.

LA wasn't nearly as lucky. One of the targets had changed his routine, and they had missed him entirely. They did get two of the targets, but one of the men was wounded in a shootout with police during a high-speed chase on the freeway. California law was all over them in minutes, and the men had gone to ground, hiding like mice in some hole in the wall while angry cats prowled around trying to sniff them out.

Denver and Chicago were yet to report in.

Almost immediately, an internet post appeared from the LA times about a massive manhunt for killers in the Los Angeles area. Two federal judges had been murdered in cold blood, and the police had responded quickly. They had drilled for this a thousand times, and they had been on high alert since the first round of assassinations a week ago. Within minutes, police had executed a huge dragnet that closed down the city.

Video cameras had picked up a dark-colored SUV fleeing the scene, and state police had cornered the van shortly after it entered a freeway. After a brief shoot-out with police, all suspects had fled on foot into a densely-populated suburban area. Police were still looking for the suspects, one of whom had obviously been wounded in the shoot-out. A door-to-door search was currently underway.

Wright's phone vibrated, and Denver reported in. All targets had been successfully eliminated, and the men were now in a safe house in the mountains near Idaho Springs.

That left only Chicago and New York yet to report.

Suddenly, the internet erupted with a blaze of new activity. There was breaking news from Seattle, LA, and Denver. Wright scanned the posts, but he learned nothing he didn't already know. What about Chicago? Wasn't anything happening in Chicago? And what about New York? Jesus! New York was the news capital of the world. You'd think they would be on top of this before anyone.

Unless something went wrong.

Wright went to the *Chicago Tribune* website. Nothing about attacks in New York or Chicago. He went to the NY Times website. Nothing there either. He went to the TV news networks websites. Nothing.

Something *was* wrong.

He knew he couldn't be everywhere at once, but he wished he could be on-site with his teams and know what was happening and maybe do something to make everything right. His men had always referred to him as "Mr. Right," because he had the uncanny ability to see what was wrong and make on-the-spot corrections before things got too far out of hand. Things went wrong in war, they always did. If anything could go wrong, it would. That was a fact.

Wright had been wrong a few times in his life. He had been wrong about Randy Edwards.

Everything he knew about Edwards indicated he was a perfect recruit for this kind of work: young, immature, disillusioned about society, money hungry, sexually compromisable. His psych tests showed no indication he'd betray his teammates under any circumstances. What changed him between the time he was recruited and the time Wright sent him to take out Deb Johnson? Something had.

Obviously, Deb Johnson had gotten to him. Perhaps she had appealed to his sense of patriotism. Not possible. He wasn't inherently patriotic. Or maybe she had simply seduced him with her body. Did Edwards have a penchant for older women? No, the psych evaluations showed he preferred girls his own age or a year or two younger. It had to be something else.

Wright had been wrong about Deb Johnson, too. She was a formidable foe, not some dipshit blonde who didn't know her ass from a hole in the ground. Wright had underestimated her twice. He wouldn't underestimate her again.

What the hell was happening in New York and Chicago?

He had no idea, and that worried him. In this case, no news couldn't be good news.

He thought about calling Charlie, then thought better of it. He thought about calling the team leaders, but he knew they were either in a firefight or dead or in custody. If they were in a firefight, they didn't have time to answer their phones. If they were dead or in custody, the Feds might have possession of the phones, and if he called, they could trace him and track the phone and his location from the cell's built-in GPS. He was better off doing nothing.

But doing nothing went against his grain. He needed intel, and he needed it now.

He tabbed through each of the web sites on his screen. The guys in LA were still eluding authorities. His men were well-trained in survival, evasion, and escape. They would have split up and made themselves scarce, something relatively easy to do in an urban environment. He'd hear from them once they reached the safe house, if they made it out alive. He had to wait.

And he had to wait to learn about Chicago and New York. His men would either call, or they wouldn't call. Either way, he'd know what had happened.

But Earl Wright was not a patient man. He wouldn't mind waiting so much if he'd had coffee, but he had no coffee. He did have cigarettes, though, and he lit another off the butt of the last.

Earl had a brass-plated Zippo lighter, engraved with his initials—E. A. W. for Earl Anton Wright—and he twirled the Zippo around in his fingers to keep his hands occupied. He flipped the lid, spun the wheel, watched the wick ignite, and snapped the lid closed. He had purchased the Zippo in a PX as a graduation present to himself when he'd completed Officer Basic. Earl was a former Special Forces enlisted man who had been selected for Officer Candidate School based on his high GT on the ASVAB, the Armed Services Vocational Aptitude Battery, plus a college degree. He had attended MIT on a full scholarship before enlisting, graduating near the top of his mechanical engineering class. But he knew he wasn't cut out to be an engineer, starting at the bottom of the corporate food chain, working nine to five in a corporate office where he would have been bored to death in a year. He craved excitement, and the U. S. Army had promised plenty of that. 9/11 had just happened, and the Army was gearing up to go into Afghanistan.

As a second lieutenant and then a first lieutenant, and even sometimes as a captain, he went where his men went. First to Afghanistan, then to Iraq, then back to Afghanistan. He was the back-up guy, the one who rushed in and pulled his men out of the fire when things got too hot. He had competent NCOs, and he let them do most of the hard work, the heavy lifting. He gave the orders, and his men carried them out. But Earl Wright was always around when he was needed, always ready to pitch in and get his hands dirty with the best of them.

And then he made major. As a staff officer, he had to hang around headquarters sipping coffee and smoking cigarettes while others saw all the action. Every day became just one of many hurry up-and-wait days where he'd see the men off in the early mornings to perform their missions and then have to wait anxiously all day behind a desk for them to return and report. Sometimes, when they didn't return, he sent out a detail with body bags to recover what was left of the bodies. He felt then that he should have been with his men when he sent them out on a mission. And if he couldn't bring them back alive and whole, he would have—should have—died with them. It wasn't right that he was still alive and so many of his men weren't.

But the generals, those assholes he saw sitting around headquarters doing nothing constructive to win the war, wouldn't let him go out in the field. They said he was too important—just as they thought they were too important—to risk his life being a grunt. He was a staff officer now, they said, and he needed to learn to relax more. After all, rank had its privileges. He should be glad his ass was safely ensconced in a chair behind a desk.

When Wright couldn't stand being a cardboard soldier anymore, he requested a transfer. The Army assigned him to the only duty position they had for someone of his grade and skill set: liaison to a CIA nation-building operation up in the mountains near the Pakistani border.

Earl's assigned job was to use his engineering skills to first determine building requirements for improving the life of the northern tribes, then go to the Army to request construction materials and contract employees, and finally help train the Afghan populace to improve sanitation facilities, create better and more modern living conditions, and become self-sustainable, independent of Taliban support or drug money. The idea was to win the hearts and minds of the people. Then the people would turn on the Taliban and betray the Taliban's secret hiding places in the hills to the CIA operatives who worked with Wright.

And some of the people did. The CIA collected the information they provided and verified its accuracy, and Earl would relay that information back to headquarters so special ops units—Special Forces, SEALS, Marine Recon, Rangers—could raid those hiding places and supply trails. Earl would sometimes accompany those special ops units into the hills and kill the enemy himself.

Wright also trained locals to be snipers. The idea was they would be able to protect their villages after the Americans left.

Sometimes the Taliban would retaliate by blowing up the water purification plants or even destroying entire villages, and then Earl would need to help the people rebuild.

But, eventually, the generals decided it was useless to throw good money after bad. Did it make sense to have to keep rebuilding only to have to do it again and again, ad nauseum? Earl's request for more materials came back denied.

Earl complained to John Brakken, and Brakken had listened sympathetically. "My hands are tied, Earl," Brakken had said. "I'm only a colonel. If it was in my power to give you these things, I certainly would. But the generals said no more, and I have to follow orders. They scratched your line items out of the budget. I think they're getting ready to pull the plug on the whole operation because there's no money left to support your project. Talk to the CIA boys. Maybe they can pull some strings. Maybe they can sell some poppies or something. You know, find a back door to getting your supplies. These things are done all the time. There's more than one way to skin a cat, especially in the 'Stan."

What the hell was happening in Chicago and New York?

And then the phone vibrated and he answered, and at last he knew.

BOOK III

"Greater love hath no man than this, that a man lay down his life for his friends."

Holy Bible, King James Version, John 15:13

CHAPTER NINETEEN

Deb had alerted the FBI and Homeland Security of a possible terrorist attack in or around New York City. If Wright was in New York, his men were there, too.

Eddie and the other analysts had picked up the SUVs traveling westward, and they watched their progress in real-time satellite images projected on a big screen in INSCOM's tactical operations center. Colonel McMichaels watched with them, along with CIA and FBI liaisons.

"They're headed for Chicago," said McMichaels as the vehicles left Indiana and took I-90 northwest toward the loop.

"Ten teams," said Randy Edwards. "Forty men, four men to a team."

"What do you suppose is their target this time?" asked Eddie Morsay. "Last time they took out federal officials. There aren't any federal officials in Chicago, are there?"

"Plenty," said McMichaels. "Besides the Dirksen Federal Building on LaSalle, there's the Chicago Federal Reserve Bank and a federal office building downtown on Congress. And the Illinois Senators and Congressmen have offices in the city."

"Watch where they go to ground," said Randy. "They'll be within close striking distance of their targets."

So they watched the convoy of SUVs progress up the Dan Ryan, pass the loop, and turn off at the Ohio Street exit. Then the convoy split up, each vehicle going its own way.

"Split screen," directed McMichaels.

As techs worked their magic on a keyboard, the big screen spit into ten separate images. Each image zoomed in on an SUV.

One by one, the SUVs found parking spaces. Four men got out of each parked vehicle, looked around, and walked down the street to enter houses with for sale signs out front.

"Those houses are all in up-scale neighborhoods," said the Colonel.

"Close to their targets," said Edwards. "They'll hole up now until they get the go signal from Wright. Then they'll all move on all the targets at the same time."

"Do we have street addresses for those houses they entered?" the Colonel asked a tech.

"Got 'em all, Sir."

"Give them all to FBI and Homeland Security. It's their ballgame now."

"Sir," said Deb, "I couldn't help noticing that all of those houses the men entered were up for sale. There were for sale signs in the front yards of each. Wright's safe house in New York also had a for sale sign."

"Good point," said the Colonel.

"Can we go back and get a close-up on each of the signs?"

McMichaels directed the tech to go back, and the tech moved some dials so the big screen zeroed in on one of the for sale signs. Then the image switched to another of the signs. The name of the realty company was the same on all of the signs: Good Hunting Investment Company.

"That's the same name I saw on the sign in front of the New York house," said Edwards.

"They must be a national company," said the Colonel.

"International, Sir," said one of the techs from his live computer terminal. "Good Hunting's owned by an obscure company headquartered in Dubai. They have holdings all over the world, including real estate investments in the continental US."

"Bingo," said Deb. "Can you bring up a listing of their properties in New York?"

The tech clicked his mouse and the networked printer spewed out ten pages of property listings.

"Wright must be holed up in one of the houses on this list," said Deb. "And I bet his men are squatting in one or more of the others."

"Then we'll send people to get him," said the Colonel. He turned to the FBI liaison.

"Can you have your New York office check out all the houses on the printout?"

"It may take us a while."

"What's a while?"

"Three or four days."

"Why so long?"

"Twenty-four hours to get agency approvals and clearances, request search warrants, then another day or more to run accurate surveillance on each building and assemble, coordinate, and brief SWAT teams. Once we locate the perps, if we do, then another day or two to stake out the entire area and clear the area of residents. Those are all heavily populated residential areas, Colonel. We can't just go in with guns blazing. There would be too many civilian collaterals, and we won't allow that to happen."

"Any way to expedite operations?"

"That is the best-case expedited timetable, Colonel. And that's with assuming, of course, nothing else breaks that siphons off SWAT personnel before we get them in place."

"Then you better get the ball rolling," said the Colonel.

After the meeting broke up, Deb asked the tech to run another set of the Chicago and New York printouts for her. She took the list back to her office, and Eddie and Randy followed her.

"Let the FBI handle it," said Eddie.

"They'll take too long."

"You really want Wright, don't you? You think he's still in New York and hiding in one of those houses?"

"Yes," said Deb.

"Which one? There are hundreds of houses on the printout. You can't go to all of them."

"I will if I have to."

"Take me with," said Bill Ramsey, speaking through Randy. "I want Wright as badly as you do."

"All right," said Deb. "I'll come back for you after I locate Wright."

Colonel McMichaels stuck his head in the office and said, "I want to see all three of you in the briefing room next door right now."

"What's up, Colonel?" asked Eddie.

"Chicago," said the Colonel. "The FBI thinks they know who the next targets will be."

"Who?" asked all three simultaneously.

"Judges," said the Colonel. "They ran the list of safe houses against the work addresses of federal employees in the Chicago area, and came up with nothing. Then they ran the list against home addresses of the same employees. Guess what they found?"

"What?" asked Eddie.

"A correlation between the safe houses and the home addresses of a dozen federal judges."

"Jesus!" said Deb. "First they take out the country's ability to make laws, then they take out the ability to interpret laws."

"Into the briefing room now," ordered the Colonel. "Forget about New York. We already know where they're hiding in Chicago and what they plan to do next. I want you to help me figure out how we can stop them before they can pull the trigger."

"They'll make their move real soon," said Edwards. "They're already in place. I don't think the FBI will be able to round them up in time to stop them."

"Then I guess it's up to us," said the Colonel. "Into the briefing room all of you, and we'll put our heads together and figure out how to do this on our own. I've ordered a flight from the Air Force to take us to the military terminal at O'Hare. We can be in Chicago in two hours."

"We?" asked Eddie.

"I'm sending the three of you to Chicago. And I'm going with you. Now into the briefing room and we'll go over the details."

"What can the four of us do against forty armed men?" asked Eddie.

"We'll think of something," said the Colonel.

* * *

It was Charlie on the phone. "You fucked up, Wright," she said.

"How?" Earl asked.

"Chicago's a mess. Not one single target down."

"How do you know? There's nothing on the internet."

"I have people everywhere. Do you think I depend on the internet to tell me what's going on?"

"No."

"All of your men in Chicago are now in FBI custody."

"I thought you said you eliminated the complications."

"I did. There are new, unforeseen complications that now have to be dealt with."

"Deb Johnson," said Wright.

"Who?"

"Deb Johnson. She's a complication that keeps getting in my hair. It had to be her. You didn't know about her?"

"No."

"She's an analyst at INSCOM. Regular Army. Sharp. Very sharp. I've tried to kill her twice, and she survived."

"Interesting," said Charlie.

"What about New York? Any news about New York?"

"Someone tipped the FBI in New York City, and they had people protecting the judges all day long. Most of your men were captured or killed when they tried to get close for a kill shot, and only two hits were successful. You better get out of there, Wright, before they come for you, too. I have it on good authority the FBI has the addresses of all the safe houses."

"I'm out of here now," said Wright, closing the laptop and shoving it inside his war bag. He grabbed his rifle and headed out the door without waiting for Charlie to end the call.

He was barely two blocks away when the SWAT teams arrived at the house. There were two van loads filled with FBI agents and a tactical truck with armed men in assault gear. They all had FBI stenciled in yellow letters on the backs of their flak jackets.

Earl Wright ran through the manicured back yards of the upper-middle-class neighborhood, carrying his war bag in one hand and the rifle in his other. He didn't try to hide, didn't bother keeping a low profile. If the lengthening shadows of night weren't enough to protect him, nothing could.

He ran like his life depended on it.

Because it did.

* * *

Waiting patiently for the men to leave the house and head for their vehicle before they moved in and cornered them, Deb was with a dozen heavily-armed men from the FBI's tactical team, wearing an FBI flak jacket over her BDUs. She was unarmed, and the FBI let her accompany them only as an interested observer.

Eddie, Randy, and the Colonel were with other teams in a similar capacity.

Theodore Ferris, the Special Agent in Charge of the tactical operation, had met them at the military terminal on the north side of O'Hare when their Air Force jet touched down. All of O'Hare Field had belonged to the military during World War II, and the federal government had kept a small portion of the base alive, despite turning the rest of the land and runways over to the

City of Chicago after the war ended. The military part of O'Hare was now used mostly as a training facility for Air Force Reserve personnel and Air National Guard.

The Tactical SAC had thanked them for their wonderful intelligence work, but he said he didn't understand why they wanted to go along when the FBI raided the safe houses. He reminded Colonel McMichaels that members of the United States Armed Forces were prohibited from carrying out tactical operations against U. S. citizens in the Continental U. S., unless or until the President and Congress jointly declared martial law and suspended the Posse Comitatus Act of Title 18 U. S. Code.

"We're all experienced combat officers," said the Colonel. "We can offer special insight if any situations develop you haven't encountered before. Randy here went through training with most of the men we're after, and he knows how they will react when cornered. Chief Morsay and Chief Johnson have been on top of this situation from the very beginning, and Chief Johnson has survived two prior skirmishes with them. We're here only to advise and observe, and to learn as much as we can first-hand and in real time. We suspect there will be simultaneous attempts on federal judges in other cities tonight, and whatever intelligence we gain might save some lives if we act quickly enough."

"You think they'll hit judges in other cities tonight, too?"

"We've alerted the New York field office to that possibility. We think New York is definite. LA is a real possibility, and Homeland Security is carrying the ball there. But Chicago is the only place where we know exactly where we can find these guys before they come out of hiding. Now please tell us your plans for getting the bad guys, and we'll tell you if we think your plans might have a snowball's chance in hell of working."

"We've had all of the locations under discrete surveillance since noon. We have tactical teams and equipment stationed close by and ready to move in when ordered. We'll hit the front doors with battering rams and take the perps in the houses by surprise without needing to evacuate the entire area."

"And all your men will be killed before they get through the door," said Randy.

"All my men have body armor," snickered Ferris. "They'll be in the house and shooting before the men inside know what happened."

"These guys are trained snipers," said Randy. "They know all about body armor, and they'll do head shots." He reached out and tapped the SAC on the forehead. "Right about here, an inch below the helmet. And they'll pick off your men before they reach the door. These guys have sentries posted who can scramble the other guys in an instant. These are highly-trained combat soldiers, Mister. They'll kill your guys and go on to complete their assignments."

"What do you suggest then?"

"Take them down when they leave the house for the car. They'll have their weapons under wraps, and they won't expect you. If you move fast enough, they'll be vulnerable. But you must move on them from all sides at once. They're not suicidal, and they won't fight if they know they haven't a chance. But if you give them an opening, they'll take a shot and make it count. Give them no opening, and they'll surrender. We want them alive so we can question them."

"Do you agree, Colonel?" asked Ferris.

"I agree. Randy went undercover to train with them for months. He knows what makes these guys tick."

"Washington said I have to listen to you, Colonel. The boys in the Hoover Building think you walk on water."

"Sometimes," said the Colonel, "I do."

"Okay. I'll take your advice. You can be my scapegoat if anything goes wrong."

"I've been a scapegoat before," said the Colonel.

"I'll get you flak jackets and helmets. You'll all have radios and headsets. But no weapons. I can't let active duty military fire on civilians, even if the civilians are armed. Not without an order from the President of the United States, and I have no such order."

"I understand," said the Colonel.

"Then let's go and suit up."

Deb had waited in an FBI van until the radio said all the men had left the house, and then she'd scrambled with the tactical teams to surround the assassins and take them without a fight. Only one of the four drew a weapon, but he didn't fire when he saw he didn't have a chance against all that federal firepower.

The other teams weren't quite so successful, and several of the assassins had been killed or injured while being apprehended. None of the assassins got away.

Neighbors were told that the FBI and DEA had executed routine drug busts and not to worry. Such things happened in Chicago with some regularity, though seldom in such up-scale neighborhoods.

They all went downtown to the FBI regional headquarters at 2111 West Roosevelt Road, near the University of Illinois Chicago campus and the Rush-Presbyterian-St. Luke's Medical Center. There, in the large steel-and-glass building, the men were fingerprinted, photographed, and read their rights. Deb was allowed to question each of the suspects, but they had all clammed up except to ask to call a lawyer. Then Randy Edwards walked into the holding area were the suspects waited for their lawyers to meet with them. Randy wore a blue windbreaker with F. B. I. in large yellow letters on the front and back.

"You goddamned traitor!" shouted one of the men when he saw Randy Edwards wearing an FBI jacket.

"You're the traitors," Randy told them. "I want Wright. It will go easier on you if you give him up. Where is Wright? Give us Wright and we can cut a deal for a lighter sentence."

"We don't know where he is," said one of the other men. "You know how this works. We get a phone call and we go where he tells us. He doesn't go with us."

"Where are the phones Wright gave you?"

"The FBI took them."

"The FBI can trace all calls," said Eddie Morsay. "We'll use the phones to locate Wright."

"Where are Anderson and Jens?" Randy asked the men.

"West coast," one of the guys said. "You going to go after your old partners now? How low can you get?"

"I just wanted to know if they were all right," said Randy. "But I'll go after them, if I have to."

"You'll never take Anderson alive," said one of the men. "He's a shooter, and a damn good one. He'll get you first. Or he'll die trying."

"I hope it doesn't come to that," said Randy.

"It will," said the guy. "You know it will.

"Yes," said Randy. "I guess I do."

CHAPTER TWENTY

Anong had a headache that hadn't gone away since the bomb blast had knocked her to the stone floor. What few scrapes and scratches she had received from flying sandstone had scabbed over, and the bruises had turned purple and ugly. But the headache refused to go away.

Lokesvara had moved his meditation chamber to another room in the temple, and he had remained in meditation, keeping a low profile, since the vicious attack two days ago. The Ranger, likewise, had spent an unusual amount of time in meditation.

Anong suspected they were actually astral traveling, not merely meditating. Although their bodies remained here, their spirits were off searching for Uma and Mahesvara. Now that they had seen Charlie, they knew what Uma's energy signature looked like. They wanted to watch for Uma when she left the protection of the wards, follow her, and maybe catch a glimpse of Mahesvara.

"Soon now," Lokesvara had said, "Mahesvara's spirit will emerge from the human it hides within. It will manifest in its true form, just as Manjusri and Vajrapani manifest. Then we may challenge him, and the real battle will begin."

"How soon?" Anong had asked.

"During the night of the Summer Solstice. It is a most propitious time, a time of the changing of the guard, when new seeds planted in the spring have flowered and thus begin their slow descent into death and eventual rebirth. For a period of seventy-two hours, the sun appears to stand still, to stop in the heavens, before reversing its course. It is a time that tests the strength of all living things. Doors open and others close. After the Solstice, light begins to wane. Death and destruction are on the ascendant. It is then that Mahesvara will emerge. It is then that we must confront him, before he becomes too powerful to overcome."

"The Solstice is but four days away," Anong said.

"Just so," said Lokesvara. He retrieved the relics and handed the Vajra, Kris, and Noose to the Ranger, keeping the sword for himself. "We must be prepared."

"Master, what can I do to help?"

"Practice," said Lokesvara. "Practice meditation. Practice raising the Kundalini. You must be ready when the time comes."

"I shall be ready, Master."

"Remember, the Kundalini has not only the power to kill, but the power to heal. When you learn to control it, Kundalini can work miracles."

"I will remember, Master."

Anong had practiced. She had raised the sleeping serpent and breathed fire into her belly.

She had set her chakras to spinning, their speed increasing, nearly reaching the speed of light. She had opened her third eye and the light emerged.

And her headache went away.

Just like that. One moment she was in pain, and the next she was pain-free. And the scratches and bruises on her arms quickly faded as if they had never been there.

"The Kundalini has not only the power to kill, but the power to heal," Lokesvara had said. Now she knew it was true.

The powerless little girl who, for so many lifetimes, had lived in such abject fear, now knew she possessed all the power she'd ever need, and she'd always had it but just never knew it before. She had looked to acquire power in so many of the wrong places—looked to the heavens where it was said the mysterious and omnipotent gods of the universe resided, to strong men like Jayavarman in Cambodia and the Malla Kings in Kathmandu who had ruled entire nations on earth, even looked to the Buddha and the Sangha for the power of protection—and hadn't found in others the power she yearned to possess herself.

She knew now the power to conquer one's demons resided only deep inside oneself, but she had never thought to look there before Lokesvara had taught her to meditate.

The serpent had been asleep inside her all along, waiting to be awakened. Even as a child the serpent had been inside her, as the Kundalini resided inside each human being from birth, but nothing could arouse the serpent from sleep until one reached a certain propitious age. Children have no fire in their bellies to fan with the Tummo breath. And without fire, the Kundalini serpent remained asleep, coiled in hibernation like any cold-blooded reptile, conserving its energy.

But after adolescence, whenever the fire was stoked in the belly and the internal temperature reached a certain critical point, the serpent awakened and rose up. Anong wasn't certain whether it was the rising heat from the fire or the position of the head of the serpent that set the chakras to spinning. Maybe it took both. But the wheels of light within the subtle body spun faster and faster with each Tummo breath, and when the third eye opened and the light within entered the physical world it carried incredible power.

The power to kill or the power to heal, the power to destroy or the power to create.

Unleashing the serpent power, however, took an inevitable toll. Nothing lasted forever, and when the power was used up Anong felt drained and even more helpless than before.

"It is important to learn the limits of your power," Lokesvara had cautioned. "Many have burned themselves out or burned themselves up. If you drain the battery completely, the serpent may die an untimely death and you with it. You must allow the battery to recharge while enough juice remains to do so. Moderation is the key to all things."

So Anong practiced and practiced. She brought herself to the point of exhaustion, then retreated. She slept, and the serpent slept along with her.

Now she was rested and ready. Let the battle begin.

* * *

Earl Wright didn't dare sleep.

He lay, exhausted after his long run, face down in the dirt of a flower garden in someone's back yard. It was well after midnight, and there were still sirens in the city and police cars everywhere.

He disassembled the assault rifle and shoved the parts and the loaded magazine in his war bag. He did this while remaining prone, in complete darkness, recognizing from long practice the familiar touch of every separate piece of metal on an M4 carbine, so similar to the M16 that he had memorized in basic training.

He felt the phone vibrate on his hip, and he reached down and found the phone, brought it up to his ear.

"You'll find a car waiting for you in the parking lot of a convenience store six blocks west of your present location," said John Brakken's voice in his ear. "Drive up to Greenwich, Connecticut, and I'll tell you where to find a safe house."

"How did you know where I was?" Wright asked.

"I have ways," said Brakken. "The SIM chip in your cell phone, for example, can be tracked. I have taken the liberty to secure for you an XM2010 ESR, enhanced sniper rifle, from the Picatinny Arsenal in New Jersey. You qualified with the M24, didn't you? Well, this is essentially the same rifle, a bolt-action Remington 700 chambered in Winchester .300 magnum, with a Leupold Mark 4 6.5–20×50mm ER/T M5 Front Focal variable power scope and sound suppressor with muzzle brake. It's the newest and best. It's so new, the Army is only now bringing it into inventory."

"I qualified a long time ago," said Wright. "I haven't fired a sniper rifle in years."

"You never forget. You retain muscle memory forever. Fire a few rounds and it'll all come back."

"Who do you want me to kill?"

"Charlie will phone with the names and locations of your targets. Your mission now is to get out of town and get to that safe house in Greenwich. Move out now."

Wright resheathed the phone, grabbed his war bag, and walked west. He found the rental car exactly where Brakken said it would be, the keys in the ignition.

An hour later, he was in Connecticut. True to his word, Brakken phoned and gave Earl the location of the safe house.

Inside, he found the rifle and two boxes of match-grade ammunition waiting for him. Brakken had also left a change of clothes to woodland-pattern battle dress uniform in Wright's size, a disposable razor, a bar of soap and a towel, a tube of camouflage paint, and a camouflage ghillie, the kind of yowie suit hunters wore to hide in the woods.

The phone on his hip vibrated.

"You have an hour to shit, shower, and shave," said Brakken. "Then drive somewhere and take a few practice shots, zero the weapon. Charlie will call you with your assignment."

"I could use some sleep," said Wright.

"You can sleep when you're dead," said Brakken. "Find someplace to get coffee and chow, maybe a McDonald's or a Burger King. Then get on the road. We're running out of time."

"What's the hurry?"

"You'll know soon enough." Brakken clicked off.

Wright felt better after a shower, more like his old self. But the adrenalin rush of last night had long since dissipated, and he really did need to get some sleep. Even an hour or two would help.

Maybe you're getting too old for this kind of shit, he thought to himself.

But Brakken was right. He would have plenty of time to sleep when he was dead.

And Earl Wright felt very much alive, more so than he had in months. He had evaded, escaped, and survived. He lived to fight another day, even if most of his men had not.

What went wrong? How could the feds have interfered so effectively in Chicago and New York? How could they have known?

Deb Johnson, his intuition told him. It had to be her doing that wised the feds to the hits before they happened. Damn that woman! She was too fucking good for her own good. She must have used satellite surveillance to track his men, and then put two and two together to come up with federal judges as the next targets. After this next assignment, he promised himself, he'd take care of Deb Johnson personally. He'd blow her brains out and scatter the remains to hell and gone.

He used a McDonald's drive-thru and ordered two Big Macs and two large black coffees. He wolfed down one of the Macs while driving into the country looking for an abandoned gravel pit. He finally found one.

He used the empty coffee cups as targets, placing them downrange approximately five hundred meters from where he had positioned the XM2010.

He thought about using a large rock to brace the weapon instead of the usual sandbag, and then he noticed the rifle had a built-in bipod. He unfolded the bipod, assumed a good supported prone position, wedged the stock between his shoulder and his cheek, and sighted through the twenty-power scope. He moved the weapon until the cup was squarely in the crosshairs. Then he took a deep breath, let half of it out and held the rest in as he squeezed the trigger.

He fired three groups of three, making slight adjustments to the scope after each group. The rifle was a shooter's dream. It had the familiar Remington 700 bolt action, but the bolt operated much smoother and moved a shorter distance than he remembered. He had a five round box magazine loaded with Sierra MatchKing .300 Winchester Magnum Hollow Point Boat Tails, and he had firmly tapped each of the rounds to align the powder before loading them in the magazine. The Titan sound suppressor effectively deadened the noise of the discharge and prevented an echo, something that had concerned him when firing in the natural echo chamber of a civilian gravel pit near an urban area.

Though the two coffee cups bounced around and were practically obliterated by the time he finished, he hit the cup he aimed for each time he fired. Satisfied that he could make a head shot at up to a thousand meters, he dropped the magazine, emptied the chamber, policed his brass, and put the weapon away, folding down the bipod and the stock for easy storage in his war bag. He planned to clean and lube the rifle the first chance he got.

He returned to the car and was half-way back to the safe house when his phone vibrated.

"Get on the turnpike and head for DC," said Charlie's voice. "Drive carefully, and don't get pulled over."

"Is DC safe?" he asked.

"Safer than New York," she answered. "There's still elevated security around the Capitol and most public buildings, but you aren't going into the city itself. Your first target lives in Alexandria and works at Fort Belvoir."

"Oh?" said Wright, feeling a shot of adrenalin because he knew what Charlie would say next.

"Her name is Debra Johnson, and she's an intelligence analyst at INSCOM. I believe you are already familiar with her?"

"Yes," said Wright. "I am."

"After you mentioned her name yesterday, I learned she was one of four people responsible for the debacle in Chicago."

"How did you learn that?"

"I told you we are legion," she said. "We have people everywhere. We really are legion. Anyway, we know from our sources in Chicago that four army officers from Fort Belvoir flew into O'Hare and instructed the FBI how to capture your men. Debra Johnson was one of those officers. The others were Colonel Robert McMichaels, Chief Warrant Officer Edward Morsay, and Major William Ramsey, who is now going by the name of Randy Edwards."

"Major Ramsey is dead. We killed him in Pakistan more than six months ago. Randy Edwards is an ex-marine lance corporal. He's nobody."

"My source cannot be wrong. If he says Ramsey is still alive, then Ramsey is still alive. If he says Ramsey is Edwards, then Ramsey is Edwards."

"Jesus! That would explain some things that didn't make sense before. But I still say it's impossible."

"Impossible or not, Ramsey, Morsay, and McMichaels are your other targets. All four targets must be dead before midnight tomorrow. You have a rare opportunity to get all of them at the same time if you hurry, because they will depart the military terminal at O'Hare tomorrow morning to return to Joint Base Anacosta-Bolling. Then they will drive from the Bolling Air Force base, south of Washington, back to Fort Belvoir. They will be together in the Colonel's Toyota Prius. The Colonel will be driving and Johnson and Ramsey will be in the back seat. The best place to catch them is after they turn off I-95 onto the Fairfax County Parkway. There are several wooded areas that should provide excellent cover."

"That's why you gave me the woodland camo and ghillie."

"Very perceptive."

"Jesus! You plan for everything. How do you do it?"

"I'll tell you in person after midnight tomorrow."

"You're coming here?"

"Yes," she said. "I will come to reward you. You will be in for a nice surprise."

"I look forward to seeing you," he said, but she had already clicked off.

Wright drove straight through with only two stops for fuel and a quick bite to eat. He was on the beltway shortly after dark and scouting the area around Belvoir before midnight.

Now all he had to do was wait until morning. Then he would kill Deb Johnson and her three companions and make his getaway. He had his getaway route planned out, and he could be back on the expressway and miles from the scene of the shooting before anyone knew what had happened. He hid the rental car, walked into the woods, put on the ghillie, set up his hide with a perfect view of the road, and settled in for the night with the XM2010 loaded, aimed, and ready. All he need do was reach his thumb up from his spot weld to the release the safety, and he'd he good to go.

He wondered what kind of surprise Charlie had in mind for tomorrow night, and he let his imagination carry him away to a fantasy world where he was on top and Charlie was on the bottom and his perfect reward was hearing her beg to be fucked by Mister Right.

* * *

Randy picked up a *Chicago Tribune* and a *Chicago Sun-Times* from coin-operated vending machines and read them on the long drive to the airport. Both papers reported the deaths of federal judges in Seattle, Los Angeles, New York, and Denver on their front pages and offered additional inside pages of details and photographs. There was a small filler article in the local section of the *Tribune* that mentioned successful drug raids in Chicago by DEA and FBI agents, but nothing about an attempt on judges in Chicago.

An editorial in the Trib urged the people to demand immediate action. "Violence in Washington is one thing," the editorial writers said, "but violence in middle-class neighborhoods across the country, including Chicago, is yet another. People aren't safe anywhere anymore when law-abiding citizens—law makers and interpreters of the law among them—are brutally gunned down in or near their own homes. In Los Angeles, where an ongoing gun battle still rages between law enforcement officers and trained killers, dozens of innocent people have been caught in the cross-fire and some died as a result. In New York City, where FBI and Homeland Security foiled attempts on all but two federal judges, sixteen people were killed in shootouts. This cannot be allowed to continue.

"People everywhere are afraid even in their own homes. When law and order cannot protect us, we naturally look elsewhere for other solutions. Within the past few weeks, Washington D. C., and New York City have become virtual police states. Will Chicago be next?

"Other countries have declared martial law, and freedom of the press has been suspended in Russia, China, Japan, and Germany. We cannot let that happen here. Some have suggested that if our government can't protect us, maybe we need to abolish government and arm ourselves. There may be a new American Revolution brewing, and we're not sure that's so bad."

"News pretty awful?" asked Eddie Morsay.

"People are afraid," said Randy. "I can't say I blame them. I'm afraid, too."

"We'll stop the bad guys, and things will settle down eventually. You'll see."

"Not this time," said Randy. "I have a bad feeling that things are about to go from bad to worse."

"Relax. We'll be back at INSCOM in a couple of hours," said the Colonel. "Then we can assess the damages and decide what to do next."

"We've got to get Earl Wright," Randy said. "As long as Wright is still out there, we'll see more killing."

"We've got to stop the man or men behind Wright," said Deb. "Wright might help us find them, but he's only an errand boy. He's not important except to lead us to the others."

"I agree," said Bill Ramsey, speaking through Randy. "Unless we cut off the head, the organization will only grow new tails like most worms or some reptiles. There's a whole den of poisonous snakes buried deep underground and we can't fight them all even if we find them. So we've got to get the head man and make the rest leaderless, or they'll just come back and bite us in the butt."

"Whoever he is, he's well entrenched," said the Colonel.

"We'll find him," said Eddie. "Sooner or later, we'll find him."

Randy wasn't so sure. He kept thinking about it all the way from Chicago to Washington. He thought about it again as they climbed into McMichaels' Prius, the Colonel and Eddie in the front seat, Deb and Randy in the back. He thought about it as they drove from Anacosta to the beltway, all the way around Washington, and then south on I-95.

Whoever the Big Boss might be, he was practically invisible. It was almost as if he didn't exist.

But he had to exist. There had to be somebody behind this whole mess. Somebody behind the scenes was definitely pulling the strings and making the puppets on stage dance their deadly danse macabre.

Did Wright know who that someone was?

Chances were, he did. So maybe Randy should make finding Earl Wright his first priority.

They turned off I-95 and drove down Fairfax County Parkway, State Route 286. They were almost back to Belvoir.

Randy was still thinking about capturing Earl Wright when the window exploded, filling the car with fragments of flying glass.

And then Randy's head exploded and Randy was surprised he could still think at all.

He floated above the bloody remains of his ruined body. Bill Ramsey was there, too, floating right alongside him.

A second shot came through the open window two seconds later. It plowed into the back seat where Deb Johnson's head had been a second ago. It ripped apart the upholstery, sent tufts of stuffing into the air, and exited the rear window at an angle.

High powered hollow points, magnum load, thought Randy. From a sniper rifle.

A third round took out the front window on the driver's side, and Colonel McMichaels slumped forward in the driver's seat, constrained only by the stretched-taut seat belt. The car careened off the road and rolled into a ditch.

A fourth round flew through the shattered window and missed Morsay by less than an inch. Morsay had released his seat belt and ducked down under the dash, and the angle of the car in the ditch had prevented a clear shot.

Randy waited for a fifth round, and when it came it shattered the dash and glove compartment and ripped Eddie Morsay's left shoulder apart.

There was no sixth shot.

Randy heard an automobile ignition, and he saw a black Ford Taurus drive away. He tried to follow, but found he couldn't move more than few feet from where his shattered body lay in the Prius' back seat.

"What the hell happened?" he asked Bill Ramsey.

"You died," said Ramsey.

"I'm dead? I don't feel dead."

"Your body died, but *you* didn't. Your essence continues to exist."

"You're dead, too?"

"Yes."

"How come I can see you? How come you look like you have a body? How come I can talk to you and you can answer?"

"We're spirits, Randy. We don't really exist in the real world anymore. We're on the spirit plane somewhere between worlds. Because we're on the same plane, we can see and hear each other. Nobody in the real world can see or hear us."

"I can," said Sacred Girl.

"Deb! You're still alive!"

Ksitigarbha materialized in the front seat between Colonel McMichaels and Eddie Morsay. She placed a hand on each. Within minutes Eddie was able to sit up. The ragged flesh of his shoulder began to morph back to a recognizable shape.

Bob McMichaels moaned. The part of his face that was missing started to fill in.

"We nearly lost both of you," said Ksitigarbha. "I had to let Wright go in order to come back to help you."

"You saw Earl Wright?" asked Randy.

"Yes. He was the shooter."

"Why didn't you stop him?"

"I couldn't stop the first shot, the one that killed you, because I didn't know he was there before he fired. After the second shot, I was able to deflect the bullets with the subtle energy of my presence. I thought it was better to let him shoot and think he killed us all. Now that I know what he's like, I can track his energy signature. We can keep tabs on Mister Earl Wright and track him to his boss."

"What about us?" asked Bill Ramsey. "We want to stick around and see how this plays out."

"Ask Eddie and the Colonel if they'll let you share their bodies. If they give permission, you can become part of them. If they don't, you should go into the light."

"They can hear us? They're still alive and they can hear us?"

"As long as I touch them, they walk between worlds. They can hear you and see you. Ask them now."

Randy asked Eddie Morsay, and Eddie agreed. Randy felt his spirit move into Eddie's body.

Bill asked the Colonel, and got no response.

"He's not fully conscious yet," said Sacred Girl. "Ask him again in a few minutes."

While Bill Ramsey waited, he saw the light, the beautiful, bright, clear light appear and beckon to him as before. For just a moment, he felt himself drawn into the light. He had completed his original mission. He had contacted INSCOM, and he could let others take it from here. He could go, couldn't he? He deserved a rest, didn't he? What more did he need to do?

He still didn't know who was behind it all, who pulled the strings. Deb was correct. Wright was only an errand boy. The elusive master mind remained more elusive than ever.

"Please, Bob," he asked. "Let me go along for the ride. I know I can still help."

"Just for a little while," said the Colonel. "Just until this is over."

“Thank you,” said Bill Ramsey as his spirit joined with McMichaels. “A little while is all I need.”

* * *

One down, Wright said silently to himself as he saw Edwards’ head explode. His right hand moved from the trigger to work the bolt. Three to go.

He lined Deb Johnson’s head perfectly in the crosshairs, took a deep breath and let half out, and touched the trigger.

Johnson’s head disappeared from the scope.

He worked the bolt again and chambered another round. Suddenly, he felt he was being watched. He took his eyes from the scope and looked around. He saw no one.

He returned to the scope and sighted in on Colonel McMichaels. As he squeezed the trigger, he felt something—a wind? There was no wind to speak of—move the barrel slightly to the left.

Blood flew from McMichael’s ruined face. Not the dead-on head shot Earl had wanted, but close enough for government work.

He worked the bolt again and sighted in on Morsay. The car was at an angle off the road, its rear wheels spinning on air. He fired.

And missed. Goddamn it! That sudden wind had come up again and deflected the round. He quickly worked the bolt, sighted, and fired at what he could see of Morsay's back.

Not a head shot, either, but he was gratified to see flesh, blood, and bone fly from the left shoulder as the .30 caliber round passed completely through Morsay's body. The wound looked bad enough that Morsay should bleed out in a matter of minutes.

He worked the bolt again, and touched the trigger. He heard the hammer strike the firing pin, but nothing happened.

He was out of ammunition. He had fired all five rounds, and he'd have to reload if he wanted to take another shot.

"Fuck it!" he said aloud and scrambled to his feet. The bastard would bleed out soon enough, and Wright needed to get out of there before another car came along. He remembered to police his brass. He picked up the five empty shell casings and shoved them in his pocket. Then he ran to his car.

Within minutes, he was back on I-95 heading south toward Richmond.

He was elated that he'd finally done it. He'd blown Deb Johnson completely away. He'd had her in his crosshairs when he'd pulled the trigger, and when he looked again her head wasn't there. Not only was he certain he had killed Deb Johnson, but he had taken out Randy Edwards, Colonel McMichaels, and Eddie Morsay, too. When Charlie called, he'd tell her there were no more complications.

He thought about Charlie. He couldn't believe he'd actually see her tonight, but she had promised and he knew she'd keep her promise. She had promised him a reward, and he wondered what his reward might be. He knew what he wanted. But collecting that from Charlie might be a challenge.

He smiled. It was the kind of challenge he loved, and Earl knew he was up for the challenge of conquering Charlie, of making her beg. The difficult he accomplished immediately, the impossible sometimes took a little longer. He felt he had all the time in the world now, and he would take as much time as he needed to make her beg.

He felt really horny. Killing always did that to a man. He supposed it had something to do with the primal instinct to procreate in the face of death, to replace the life he had taken away by generating new life. It was a balance thing. Killing made one feel out of balance, like something was missing, until one had sex. Sex restored the balance and made everything seem all right.

Wright thought about Edie's place near Richmond and wondered if it still existed. If the feds hadn't closed it down, it might make a good place to hole up while he waited for Charlie to arrive. Maybe he'd even sample one of the girls while he waited.

It occurred to him that neither Charlie nor Brakken had arranged a safe house for him after the hits, and that bothered him a bit. They should have had a safe house ready for him. Maybe they did, and they just hadn't told him yet.

He bypassed Richmond, and traveled west. Then he pulled off the main road and traveled back roads to the big old house surrounded by the tall fence. He had no remote to open the gate. He parked the Taurus, took his warbag with him, vaulted the stone fence, and walked up the driveway to the house.

Edie was surprised when he rang the bell. "I wasn't expecting you," she said opening the door and inviting him inside. She wore a housecoat and no makeup. "You didn't call. You usually call ahead."

"I thought maybe the feds had busted you," he told her.

"Oh, they were here with their search warrants. They nosed around, but they didn't find anything. We're incorporated as a charm school, you know. Our cover is we teach southern girls old-time manners and ways to entertain men in social situations. We actually do that on weekdays from nine to five. In the evenings and weekends, however, we service men. Fortunately, there were no men being serviced when the FBI came to visit."

"You're in the clear then?"

"Except for the fact that the FBI had us tied to WLSCTC. I admitted WLSCTC had invested in this place, but I said the relationship was strictly financial. That seemed to satisfy them."

"What about the digital recordings? Did they find them?"

"They found the cameras, but the recordings are stored on the cloud. They're on a secure server in Dubai where the feds can't get to them. We told them the cameras were to record students for training purposes. I think they bought it because there was no evidence to the contrary."

"And the fantasy rooms?"

"Dismantled before the feds got here. We made the bedrooms look like classrooms, and told the feds that's where we show girls how to make hospital corners on sheets when making up a bed."

"Good. Now how about showing me some of that famous southern hospitality you're famous for and getting me a drink?"

"I've never seen you drink before, Earl."

"I'm celebrating."

"Then have some champagne. I always keep a bottle or two on ice."

"No, thanks. Bourbon and branch water, please. Easy on the water."

She went to the bar and poured three fingers of Maker's Mark. Then she threw in a couple of ice cubes.

"Branch water's in the ice," she said.

He smiled and took a sizable drink. "I could use some sleep," he said. "I've been on the go two days running."

"I had to let all the girls go home," she said. "I'm the only one here. I'm available, if you want company."

"Thanks, but no thanks. I really need the sleep. You'd only keep me awake."

"Take your pick of the rooms upstairs."

"Wake me at ten, if I'm not up before then. I'm supposed to meet someone around midnight."

"Of course. And, Earl, I'm glad you're here. I was real worried about you."

"I'm okay. I'm glad to see you're okay, too."

He walked upstairs and went straight to the king-sized bed in the room at the end of the hall. He knew he needed to clean his rifle, but he was far too tired. He flopped back on the bed, removed his cell phone from the holster on his hip, and cradled it in his left hand. If Charlie called, he wanted to be able to feel the vibrations of the phone right away. He knew that once he fell asleep, he'd be totally out of it. If he kept the phone holstered, he might miss the call.

And this was one call he didn't want to miss.

He closed his eyes and let the bourbon numb him completely. Within minutes, he was asleep and dreaming of Charlie.

CHAPTER TWENTY-ONE

"It's time," said Lokesvara as he emerged from his chamber. He held the flaming sword in his right hand and a bound book in his left.

Anong had waited patiently in the hallway, practicing meditation and raising the Kundalini for two days, camped between Lokesvara's closed door and the closed door to the Ranger's meditation chamber.

Today was the day when the sun promised to stand still. In the far north, the sun wouldn't set at all for three days and three whole nights. In the far south, the sun wouldn't rise. In Cambodia, the sun seemed hotter and closer than at any other time of the year, and solstice marked the end of the long humid rainy season that followed the spring monsoons.

"Uma's on the move, and so must be Mahesvara," Lokesvara told them when the Ranger came into the hallway carrying the Vajra in his right hand. He had the Noose tied around his waist like a belt, and the Kris was tucked beneath the Noose. Instead of his usual robes, he wore jeans, a black t-shirt, and running shoes.

"I saw," said the Ranger.

"Where have they gone, Master?" asked Anong.

"To America. To the United States. And we shall follow them and confront them there."

"I have wanted to see America, the Land of the Beautiful."

"Then let us go. We shall join Ksitigarbha and Maitreya at the place where Deb works. It is nearly midnight, the beginning of the solstice in America, and we must hurry. When the new day dawns, Mahesvara will try to take control of the country and its nuclear weapons. Then, if the world does not submit, he will rain down total destruction on the entire world."

"Nuclear Armageddon?" asked the Ranger. "That's what this is all about? Mahesvara wants to destroy the world with nuclear war?"

"He will issue an ultimatum. If the nations of the world do not submit to him, he will destroy them all."

"Of course, they won't submit. Especially not Russia and China. They'll meet threat with threat. How did you learn this?"

"I overheard Charlie—Uma—giving orders. She moved from the protection of the wards to meet with avatars in various locations in Eastern Europe. I followed her in spirit form and listened as she directed her secret armies. They will add to the upheaval when they attack Moscow."

"She has more than one secret army?"

"She has many. Her armies are legion."

"Why didn't you send Manjusri to stop her? If she is outside the protection of the wards, Manjusri could have materialized and captured her."

"It is Mahesvara we want, not Uma alone. We must catch them together. I sense that Mahesvara has gone to America to join with his avatars there because Uma, too, has left Europe for America."

"Then let's go to America," said the Ranger.

* * *

Deb was back in her office at INSCOM. She had telephoned Bill Porter and told him about the sniper attack that killed Randy Edwards and nearly killed her and the others.

"They may try again," said Porter. "Stay there and I'll join you."

"You don't have clearance to enter the building," said Deb.

"I don't need clearance," said Bill, as Maitraya materialized next to Deb.

Deb clicked off the cell phone and hugged her fiancé as tight as she could. "I'm glad you're here," said Deb. "I'm scared."

"I'm scared, too," said Bill. "How are the others? Eddie? The Colonel?"

"Randy died. I couldn't save him in time. His spirit is inside Eddie now. Bill Ramsey migrated to the Colonel. They're all trying to adjust to the changes, but it will take time."

"Where are they now?"

"Down the hall in the situation room," said Deb. "The country's gone completely crazy after the last round of shootings in civilian communities on both the east and west coasts on the same night, and the President is considering declaring martial law."

"What good will that do?"

"It will give the military the authority to act directly within the United States. We can bring a lot of firepower to bear without waiting for Congress to act, as if that alone could discourage further attacks. Congress has been decimated and is totally ineffectual, and all they want to do is talk and point fingers at political rivals. If all hell breaks loose, there won't be time for deliberation or politics as usual. We need to be able to respond to force with force, immediately and without hesitation. Everyone thinks martial law is the answer."

"Is that a good idea? The Secretary of Defense is dead, and so is the Chairman of the Joint Chiefs. Whoever heads the military will have a lot of power, far too much for one person. Who will that person be? Who will call the shots?"

"I don't know," said Deb.

"Kieffer," said the Colonel as he and Eddie entered Deb's office. "The President is recalling Lieutenant General Roger Kieffer, giving him a fourth star, and making him the new Chair of the Joint Chiefs."

"What! Whose stupid idea was that?" asked Deb.

"A half dozen of the remaining Senators. They agreed to confirm him first thing in the morning, and then the President will impose martial law. Kieffer will be our new boss."

"But can't the Senators see Kieffer's part of the problem? Roger Kieffer was Chairman of the Board at WLSCTC."

"He claimed he had no prior knowledge of what WLSCTC was up to, and I guess the Senate believed him. Congress has absolved him of any responsibility, and they insist he's the only man for the Joint Chief's job since all the other generals have either been killed or are indispensable where they're currently assigned. Some have flatly refused to take the top job because they think it would make them the assassin's next target. The President has no choice. Kieffer agreed to take the job."

"No!" said Deb. "It's a trick. We've got to stop them."

"Too late," said the Colonel. "It's a done deal."

"Then we're all in trouble," said Bill Porter.

Suddenly, the air shimmered as if an invisible door had opened from nowhere and then three people stepped through that doorway into the middle of Deb's office as if they had been out walking in the neighborhood and simply dropped in to chat. One was an older man carrying a sword in one hand and a book in his other. Another was a younger man wearing a rope belt with a jagged knife shoved in the belt and what looked to be an ornate scepter in his right hand. And the third was a young girl of about thirteen.

"Lokesvara!" exclaimed Deb. "What are you doing here?"

"It is time for us all to be together," said the old man. "Allow me to make quick introductions so we all know one another. I am Lokesvara. I know Colonel Bob McMichaels through his wife, Diane Groves. I know Eddie Morsay because we have worked together before. Bill Porter is also the Bodhisattva Maitreya, and we have worked together many times. This is the Ranger, a former Army Ranger turned Buddhist monk, who is also the Bodhisattva Vajrapani. And may I present Anong, the newest member of our group, who is the chosen of Durga and Vishnu? We are all together because a great evil is at work in the world tonight, and it is pre-ordained that we alone can fight this evil with a slim chance of defeating it. I speak of the demon Mahesvara and his avatars, who are evil incarnate."

"His avatars?" asked Eddie Morsay. "What is an avatar?"

"A human being that Mahesvara's spirit possesses," explained Deb. "It's the only way his presence can work in this world."

"Kind of like the way I now possess the spirit of Randy Edwards and the Colonel possesses the spirit of Bill Ramsey?"

"Yes," said Lokesvara. "Except Mahesvara can take possession of many people simultaneously, and his spirit may be in one or all of them at the same time. He has promised them power beyond imagining plus unlimited wealth, and they have agreed to do his bidding in return."

"Mahesvara is here?" asked Bill Porter. "In America?"

"His spirit has been here for some time now," said Lokesvara. "That is why I have been unable to pin down his spirit in Dubai, though he has avatars hiding there, too, as he has avatars everywhere. Now he has taken control of the most powerful men in this country with promises or threats, and by tomorrow morning he will be ready to destroy civilization as you currently know it. He will begin by dismantling your most cherished institutions, including organized religion and its rituals. He wishes to rule this world, and if he cannot rule it, he will destroy it and build a new world from the ashes."

"Where is he?" asked Deb. "Where will we find him?"

"He will be at Mount Sumeru tomorrow to claim his power. There will be a secular ritual where his avatars hand him the power to control the country. Mount Sumeru will be a mountain or a hill, not unlike the seven hills of Rome, near the seat of power."

"The Capitol," said Deb. "He'll be on Capitol Hill!"

"Kieffer," said Bill Porter. "Kieffer will be on Capitol Hill. That's where the Senate will confirm Kieffer as Chairman of the Joint Chiefs in the morning."

"And where," said Deb, "Kieffer is scheduled to hold a press conference after the President declares martial law. It all makes sense now. Kieffer must be an avatar of Mahesvara. The assassination of the Senators, the Secretaries, the generals, were all designed to give Kieffer control of the U. S. military and its weapons systems."

"Who is this Kieffer?" asked Lokesvara.

"A retired general who has been recalled to take charge of America's defenses," said Colonel McMichaels. "No one took him seriously until now."

"Tomorrow, he will be made the most powerful man in America," said Deb. "When the President declares martial law, he'll take over Homeland Security as well as the military. He can impose curfews, put churches and synagogues and mosques off-limits or close them up as threats to national security, do all kinds of things. And the worst part is Colonel McMichaels, Eddie, and I will all have to follow his orders."

"But Ksitigarbha, Randy Edwards, and Bill Ramsey don't need to follow his orders," said Lokesvara. "Nor does Bill Porter. I will teach Randy and Ramsey to spirit travel, and they can aid us on the astral plane while Ksitigarbha, Maitreya, Vajrapani, Anong, and I fight Mahesvara and his minions on the physical plane. The Colonel and Eddie will physically remain here. Time grows short. Let us enter lotus and gird for battle. Please take a seat on the floor."

When they were all peacefully sitting on the floor, Lokesvara began to instruct them. "Find a position that is most comfortable for an extended time. You may wish to cross your legs and distribute your weight equally over both your sit bones. Close your eyes. You may think about anything or nothing. You don't have to listen to my voice, because my voice will go with you and you will hear everything I say regardless of where you are or what you are doing. Take a deep breath and hold it for a count of five. Exhale for a count of five…."

* * *

Earl Wright awoke at ten minutes after ten. No one had phoned him, nor had he heard Edie quietly enter the room and crawl into bed with him. He discovered she lay sound asleep next to him, naked, and snoring.

Even over sixty, Edie was still a beautiful woman. She had kept wrinkles and blemishes at bay by avoiding the sun and by eating right and exercising daily. Only the slightest hint of aging showed on the back of her arms where her triceps had begun to atrophy. Edie had never born children, and her stomach remained flat and her breasts still looked lush as if they were still defying gravity. He felt a slight stirring in his loins as he looked at her.

But Charlie had promised to be here tonight at midnight, and he wanted to be ready and waiting for her when she arrived. Still dressed, he slipped from the bed and walked to the bathroom where he undressed, showered and shaved, and looked at himself in the mirror.

He wondered if Edie was still recording everything that happened in the house. Probably, he decided. The digital cameras didn't save images to a hard drive but transmitted them immediately to the cloud, a server somewhere in Dubai. The entire process was automated, and it would go on forever without anyone needing to push a button or be there to direct the cameras.

His own body was middle-aged hard, but he was aware he hadn't done his exercises today. He dropped and knocked out fifty push-ups, fifty sit-ups, and flipped upright with a contraction of his quadriceps and buttocks. He may be getting older, but he wasn't over the hill yet.

He dressed in the woodland fatigues he had worn all day yesterday. If he stank of perspiration, he couldn't smell it.

He splashed on a dab of Realm cologne to mask any body odor with pheromones. He was as ready as he'd ever be to meet Charlie and collect his reward.

Edie was awake when he returned to the bedroom. "I heard the shower," she said. "What time is it?"

Earl checked his tactical wrist watch. "Eleven-thirty," he said.

"Sorry I fell asleep. It felt good to have someone to sleep with again. It's been a long time."

"Fix me breakfast?" asked Earl. "I could eat a whole cow. I haven't had a good meal in two or three days."

"Steak and eggs okay?"

"Perfect."

Wright was in the kitchen watching Edie cook when Charlie arrived.

Charlie appeared out of nowhere, and Earl wasn't too surprised. Somehow he knew she would do that. Charlie had an uncanny ability to find anyone anywhere.

What surprised him was who she brought with her.

John Brakken and Roger Kieffer were both in uniform. Brakken wore ACU multicam battledress and Kieffer was in Class A's.

"We have come to give you your reward," said Charlie. She was dressed in a white blouse and tailored navy blue skirt with matching jacket. Her face and long red hair were bare, and she looked absolutely gorgeous.

"I wasn't expecting a …."

"A reward? But surely, Mr. Wright, you deserve a reward for your good and faithful service."

"I was going to say, I wasn't expecting a crowd."

"Oh, don't mind them. They're just my husband."

"Your husband? You're married?"

"Of course. We have been united forever. We belong together."

"You're married to Brakken?"

"I'm married to the god who occupies his body."

"The *god*?"

"Yes. He's a god."

"And I suppose you're going to tell me you're a goddess?"

"I *am* a goddess."

Wright couldn't help laughing, couldn't stop laughing, though he saw his laughter had angered Charlie. He laughed so hard his side hurt. He actually heard himself guffaw.

"You doubt me? How dare you!"

"Lady, you may look like a wet dream, but you're crazy if you think you're divine."

Earl should have seen it coming, but he was still laughing too hard to notice. The pain hit him like a ton of bricks had fallen squarely on his head.

"Relax," said John Brakken. "Just let him inside your mind. It doesn't hurt unless you try to fight him. His name is Mahesvara, and he'll give you everything you want. You want money? It's yours. You want power? It's yours. It's so incredibly easy. Just accept him. Just let him in. He'll give you everything you ever wanted, anything and everything your heart desires."

"Like he gave you everything, John?" asked Wright through clenched teeth.

"Yeah. He came to me more than ten years ago when I had just been passed over for promotion the second time. I was a real mess. I started to drink heavily. My wife had already left me for some dumbass civilian who made lots of money in real estate and owned a big house and drove fancy cars. I had nothing more to lose at that point, so I gave it a try. I made light colonel in record time, got my eagle and could have had a star, if I'd wanted one. But I opted out for the money. I became president of WLSCTC, made investments for the company and for myself, and now I drive a fancy car, own lots of real estate, and I can have any woman I want."

"And what did you have to give up to get all that, John? Does he own you, body and soul?"

"I got used to following orders in the army, Earl. Just like you did. It's not really any different than being in the Army. He tells me what he wants done, and I do it for him. I tell him what I want, and he gets it for me. Fair exchange. The army never gave me anything. Did it you? Tell him what you really want, Earl. He'll give it to you. He's inside Roger and me, and it feels good. He'll hear your wishes and your prayers and give you what you want before you even know you want it. This is your reward, Earl. Take it. You've earned it."

"He'll give me anything?"

"Anything."

"And what do I have to give him?"

"Just yourself. Body and mind. Forget the soul part. You let him use you whenever he wants in whatever way he wants. Accept his presence in your life. Allow his spirit to enter you. It's all so easy."

"And I can have anything I want? Anything my little old heart desires?"

"Yes."

"Then tell him I want Charlie," said Wright, puffing out his chest. "I want to fuck his wife, and I don't want him to watch."

"That's impossible," said Charlie. "I won't allow it, and neither will Mahesvara."

"No," said Brakken. "He says he will allow it, but only after Earl accepts him fully and completely."

"No," said Wright. "Then it will be him that fucks Charlie, even though it's my body. I want to be the only one who fucks her. Me alone. I want to have my way with Charlie before I'll give him permission to enter. He can have her back when I'm finished with her."

"Be reasonable, Earl. He'll let you go along for the ride, but it must be him—not you— who makes love to Uma. It's a matter of pride."

"Is that your real name?" Wright asked Charlie, ignoring Brakken and Kieffer. "Uma?"

"Yes," she said.

"Make up your mind, Earl," said Brakken. "I don't want to have to kill you, but I will. He who is not with us is against us. You choose."

"Don't do it, Earl," said Edie from where she stood half-hidden behind the stove, holding a hot skillet filled with eggs, meat, hash browns, and cooking grease in her gloved hands.

Brakken pulled a nine millimeter Glock from his cargo pocket and shot Edie four times in the face and neck. She dropped the skillet she had taken from the stove and collapsed to the floor amid a puddle of blood and spilled cooking grease. Her face looked like ground hamburger.

Earl didn't take time to think. His own hands had dropped to his cargo pockets, and he had the safeties off, the hammers cocked, and both pistols spitting flames as the M & P 40s cleared the pocket flaps. John Brakken fell face forward onto the kitchen table, hitting the wooden table hard enough to break it in two.

Roger Kieffer glared at Wright with hate-filled eyes, and Earl felt a hammering in his head. Kieffer was trying to take control of Earl's body without having permission. Earl tried to raise the pistol toward Kieffer but suddenly his arms felt too heavy to move, as if his wrists were chained to leaden weights.

And then Charlie was on him, knocking the guns from his hands, shoving him to the floor, clawing at his face and eyes with her fingernails. Red-hot blood flowed down his cheeks as he sank under the weight of her writhing body and her powerful thighs clamped around his midsection and squeezed. He felt as if he had been ambushed by a python that dropped from a tree along a jungle path in Southeast Asia and held him locked in its coils.

This wasn't exactly what he had had in mind, but he had dreamed so often of Charlie on top of him and all the ways he could flip her over and get on top of her while beating the shit out of her to make her compliant that he managed to easily flip her onto her back and wrestle her hands away from his face.

For the briefest of moments, their eyes met and locked. As she peered into his soul and he into hers, he saw himself reflected in her eyes and didn't like what he saw there.

She had incredible strength, and she broke free of his hands, and at the same time she tried to knee him in the groin. He bitch-slapped her face with the back of his hand until blood gushed from her nostrils, but she struggled even more and wouldn't stay still.

Now the headache became unbearable as Earl felt Mahesvara's mind look for ways to worm inside his head, found an opening, and attempted to take control of his motor cortex and turn off his muscles, including his heart muscle that was partially controlled by another part of his brain. He was fighting life or death battles on two entirely different fronts now, the physical battle with Charlie and the mental battle with an unknown entity, and he might be able to win one battle but he had no hope of winning both. He knew when he lost, he was a dead man. Charlie would be merciless. He expected no less of her husband.

He had to end this quick while he still possessed strength to move his muscles. He felt like he was trying to swim against the current in deep water, feeling the water's resistance holding him back, feeling the weight of the water dragging him down, dragging him under, all the way under, feeling his lungs fill with dank fluid instead of fresh air, feeling like he was drowning...drowning...drowning….

He remembered people he had seen water-boarded in Iraq. He remembered how they had struggled. He remembered the choking sounds they had made as he added more water to the towels clamped over their noses and mouths. He heard himself making the same sounds now.

And he knew it was all in his mind. Whoever had invaded his mind was playing tricks on his psyche. He wasn't really drowning. He couldn't be.

He fought harder on both fronts. He was Earl Wright, and he told himself he was a winner, not a loser. With a herculean effort, he forced the intruder from his mind.

Charlie had amazing strength for a woman, and she managed to break out of all of his holds. She had punched him in the face and in the ribs multiple times, and she had broken his nose and probably cracked a rib or two.

He, in turn, had punched her in the stomach, but her rock-hard abs had absorbed the blows as if they were mere love taps. She managed to block his fist from her face, and she had her legs wrapped tightly around his waist again and attempted to pin him in place. She was on top, and he was on the bottom.

He reached up and got her in a choke hold with his arm wrapped around her already bruised neck. His biceps bulging against her carotid artery. He increased the pressure on her throat, effectively shutting off blood supply to the brain and oxygen to her lungs, until she went limp beneath him.

He scrambled to his feet and looked for Kieffer. Once he had realized that his thoughts of drowning was only an illusion, the pressure inside his head had abruptly eased. He had pushed the presence out of his mind, and the pain in his brain went away entirely. But Kieffer remained a threat. The bastard was a coward, but he might have a gun. And he might try to get inside Earl's mind again. Or he might call in reinforcements.

He saw the bodies of Brakken and Edie on the floor, but no sign of Kieffer anywhere. Obviously, the man had left the way he had entered: disappeared like a puff of smoke.

Earl picked up his pistols and shoved them in his pockets. He thought about shooting Charlie in the face while she was unconscious on the floor, or better still to tear her clothes off and rape the hell out of her, but he wanted her to be aware of what he was doing to her and he didn't want to wait around for her to regain consciousness in case Kieffer came back and brought reinforcements. He grabbed his duffel and ran out the door, keeping alert for a possible ambush from the woods surrounding the property. If there were a sniper out there with night-vision optics, he didn't have a chance. One shot, and it would be all over.

But he got to the stone fence and made it over the fence without any interference from anyone. He got in his car and was almost to the Interstate before the enormity of what had just happened hit him.

Charlie, Brakken, and Kieffer had appeared out of thin air in Edie's place as if they knew where to find him. Then they started talking crazy about being gods and wanting to take over people's minds. Then he had felt somebody or something try to invade his own mind, not once but many times. He had actually felt it get inside him, violating his personal space like a rapist on a rampage. Thoughts that weren't his own had sought to control his body as well as his brain, and they had actually succeeded for a short while. He had actually felt he was drowning.

Such things were impossible. Weren't they? It was impossible to appear and disappear like some of those costumed characters in Star Trek that Scottie beamed up and down with the push of a button on a console. It was similarly impossible to know where people were and what they were doing as if you had the power to become invisible and watch them without their knowledge. Wasn't it? And it was also impossible for one mind to enter another and control its thoughts. Such things simply didn't happen in the real word. Did they?

Yet Wright had no doubt Brakken had believed these things were indeed possible, just as Brakken believed whoever controlled him and Kieffer was a real god. Wright had stopped believing in God about the same time as he stopped believing in Santa Claus, and that had been a long time ago.

Imagine! Charlie a goddess! What nonsense. What crap.

There had to be a logical explanation for everything that had happened. Perhaps he had been distracted and didn't notice when Brakken, Kieffer, and Charlie came through the door from the other room. Perhaps Charlie had tracked Earl by the SIM or GPS chip in the cell phone she had given him. Perhaps Kieffer was some kind of trained hypnotist who had mesmerized Brakken and Wright into thinking he could control their minds.

Charlie couldn't be a goddess, because he had felt her body and knew she was made of real flesh and blood like any normal human being. Granted, she was stronger than most women, and stronger even than most men. He was sure she worked out to maintain her dynamite physique, and she was no stranger to martial arts. But she was no goddess. She had bled, and she had passed out like any normal person when he had blocked the blood supply to her brain.

He wished now that he had taken the time to undress her, to examine her naked body with his eyes and his hands, just to be sure. He had felt her breasts beneath the fabric of her blouse and bra, touched her public mound through the navy-blue slacks. He was reasonably sure Charlie was all woman. Maybe she looked like a goddess, but she was still a living, breathing, human female with all of the standard equipment.

And she was as crazy as Brakken if she believed she was a goddess and her husband was a god. What Earl found hardest to believe was that Charlie said she was married to either Brakken or Kieffer, much less both of them. Roger Kieffer was more than twice her age, and he had gone to pot from sitting behind a desk at the Pentagon and then another desk on the third floor at WLSCTC. Brakken was nearly as old as Kieffer, and Brakken had never been much to look at. What could she possibly see in either of them?

Earl switched on the radio and searched for a classic rock station to soothe his nerves and ground him in reality. His face hurt. His ribs hurt. But he had survived, and that was all that mattered. As the radio scanned through the dial, Earl caught a breaking news bulletin on one of the FM stations. He went back to that NPR station and listened. Maybe they would say something about the four dead soldiers found at Fort Belvoir.

Instead, they announced that Roger Kieffer had been selected as the new Chairman of the Joint Chiefs of Staff, and that he would be given a fourth star and confirmed by the Senate in the morning. The President had also scheduled a news conference to make an important announcement immediately following the Senate confirmation. There was some speculation that the President was about to declare martial law, and that he would turn over Homeland Security to the military.

Holy shit! thought Earl Wright.

Suddenly it all made sense. What WLSCTC had been doing, all the plans and training and killing, had been leading up to this special moment when Kieffer would take over the military. Now Earl knew why Kieffer was wearing a Class A uniform. Kieffer was about to become the Chairman of the Joint Chiefs of Staff. With the assassination of the Secretary of Defense and the Secretary's deputies, Kieffer would control all branches of the military without civilian oversight. Now he knew why Charlie was attracted to Kieffer. It was all about power.

Come morning, Roger Kieffer would be the most powerful man in America, and by extension, the most powerful man in the world. Maybe he wasn't a god, but he could act like a god. And Earl had helped make it happen.

Something was inherently wrong about this whole thing. It stunk to high heaven. Roger Kieffer was a total ass and didn't deserve to be made dog catcher, much less Chair of the Joint Chiefs.

And he sure as hell didn't deserve a woman like Charlie.

Earl knew now why he hadn't killed Charlie when he had the chance to do so. Despite the fact that she had wanted to kill him, he couldn't bring himself to kill her. He thought maybe he was in love with her, and he still wanted her so badly he could taste it. He had to have her, and he would have her or die trying.

And if Charlie was married to Roger Kieffer, Earl Wright would just have to make her a widow.

He still had the XM2010 in his war bag, and he had a box and a half of match grade ammunition just waiting to be expended.

Earl turned north on the expressway and headed straight for Washington, D. C. He would be there well before daylight, and he could set up a hide near the Capitol before security got too tight.

He knew where Roger Kieffer would be in the morning. He intended to be there, too.

And may the better man win.

CHAPTER TWENTY-TWO

Anong knew America was said to be truly beautiful, but she was unprepared for the incredible splendor of Washington, D. C. at night. The city was ablaze with lights and alive with colors and sounds unlike anything Anong had witnessed before. Thousands of moving automobile headlights and brake lights, stationary spotlights on the Lincoln Memorial near the Potomac and floodlights illuminating the neighboring Vietnam Veterans Memorial, were reflected in pools of water strategically placed along a flat quadrangle that stretched from the river's edge all the way up to the lit-up Capitol Building dome atop a small hill at the far end of a long grassy plain called the National Mall. There were myriad streetlights and stoplights, neons displaying the names of hotels and restaurants, and the occasional red and blue flashing MARS lightbars of rushing squad cars or fire trucks and ambulances. The city was so alive with lights of all shapes and hues that it was obvious no one expected the darkness of death to come with the breaking dawn. But death will come, as Shakespeare's Caesar was said to have said, when it will come. Death was always waiting just around the corner, and Washington, D. C. had lots of corners.

The sun rose at 5:42 AM, Eastern Daylight Time. Minutes before, the sky in the east grew perceptibly lighter, and the few wispy clouds behind the Capitol dome morphed from grey to purple, then a brilliant bright orange. When the sun herself appeared on the horizon, the sky lit up with a full-spectrum of dazzling colors.

Sometime after seven, traffic increased exponentially. There were cars everywhere now, and long lines of vehicles—automobiles, SUVs, limousines, taxi cabs, and trucks of all makes and models—snaked across multiple bridges in both directions to fill the city and surrounding suburbs with public servants and tourists and diplomats from all parts of the world. Across the Potomac River was Arlington National Cemetery and the Pentagon, and on this side were the United States Capitol, executive office buildings, cabinet offices, and a plethora of non-profit headquarters and lobbyists of all persuasions. There were memorials and museums, the Library of Congress and the Smithsonian, restaurants and delis.

It was a weekday morning in the nation's capital, and people prepared for business as usual. In a few weeks, the city would practically shut down for the Independence Day holiday and extensive summer vacations. Already, yachts lined the rivers and the harbors at nearby Chesapeake Bay. But today was a workday, and people went to work as they always did, riding in cars, cabs, and on the Metro.

No one thought about death, because no one wanted to think about death. No one, that is, except those whose business was death. All around the city there were people who were getting ready to attend the appointment of the new Chairman of the Joint Chiefs of Staff: the acting Secretary of Defense and Secretaries of the various military services, plus the Chiefs of the military services themselves, including the National Guard, plus the Secretary of Homeland Security and members of the National Security Council and the Directors of National Intelligence. They dressed in their shiny uniforms or expensive business suits and made their way to Capitol Hill and then the Senate floor. Members of Congress—the remaining Representatives and Senators—planned to be there, too, including the Vice President of the United States. The President planned to remain at the White House, getting ready to hold an important news conference as soon as the confirmation ceremonies concluded.

Somewhere close by, Anong sensed, were Mahesvara and Uma, the Prince and Princess of Death and Destruction.

Manjusri and Vajrapani were here with Anong only in spirit form, along with the spirits of Bill Ramsey and Randy Edwards. Their physical bodies remained behind at Fort Belvoir where Lokesvara, the Ranger, Colonel McMichaels, Eddie Morsay, Deb Johnson, Bill Porter and Anong herself still sat on the floor in lotus. Manjusri and Vajrapani had accompanied Anong here in spirit form to watch for Mahesvara and Uma to physically appear in or near the Capitol Building. She had felt their presence when Mahesvara and Uma had materialized near Richmond shortly after midnight, but then they disappeared as they walked between worlds. Anong had finally tracked their energy signatures to Washington, and now she was certain they were both physically present in that domed building at the far end of the mall while Anong and her companions watched from the other end of the mall.

Vajrapani had wanted to intercept Mahesvara and Uma before they reached the Capitol Building, but such a thing was not meant to be.

Lokesvara had told all of them that Mahesvara was driven by lust, greed, desire, delusion, and pride, and those five poisons prevented Mahesvara from becoming an enlightened being. "Wherever Mahesvara goes, he spreads those poisons through his avatars. They lust for power as he lusts for power. Power feeds their egos and his. They are greedy for power, always desiring more. They gain power through fear. Our job is to make Mahesvara feel powerless, to strip Mahesvara of his ego and pride, so that he may become enlightened. Because Mahesvara cannot be permanently killed or destroyed, he must be tamed."

"How can he be tamed?" Vajrapani had asked.

"Only you can tame him. You must become more fearsome than he. You must be more ruthless, more adamant. You must be willing to kill the avatars of Mahesvara. Though Mahesvara himself cannot be killed because he has never been alive, his avatars can. You must kill them. All of them."

"I cannot," said Vajrapani. "I have killed enough. I will not kill again."

"It is Vajrapani's job to kill," said Manjusri, "when killing is required to protect the Dharma. Killing can also be an act of mercy when the karmic demerits being earned by the actions of potential victims are so great that the only way to save them from certain rebirth in hell is to kill them before they complete those acts. It is no different than what we did in that house in Thailand when we killed the fifteen men raping those innocent children. Killing, under such circumstances, is an act of compassion."

"I will kill them, Master," offered Anong. "I have not yet made a vow to refrain from killing."

"No, my child," said Lokesvara. "Killing must only be done by one with sufficient compassion and siddhi to unfailingly transfer the intended victim's spirit to a higher realm at the precise moment of death. One must be trained in the Pho-wa to accomplish the taking of the life of another sentient being without incurring karmic debt. Otherwise, killing becomes murder. You know nothing of the Pho-wa. I cannot ask you to incur such a debt."

"You do it, then," said Vajrapani. "You have both the compassion and the siddhi. You can kill the avatars of Mahesvara. I won't."

"Only you have the requisite ability and knowledge and compassion and ferocity to subdue Mahesvara. He has no respect for wisdom, and even less for compassion. He will see my intervention as a sign of weakness, not of strength."

"What do I have that you don't?"

"The Vajra, for one. In the aspect of Rudra, Mahesvara is known as the Thunderer. Like Vajrapani, he can control the destructive power of the storm. He can call down thunder and lightning and cause floods. Only the Vajra has the power to offset the power of Rudra, and only Vajrapani can wield the Vajra."

"What else?"

"There will be military men present and Mahesvara will use all of them as avatars. The Ranger understands the military mind, and he will help Vajrapani to disable them without needlessly killing them. If killing is necessary, he will know when and how to do it."

"What else?"

"Vajrapani can use the Noose to subdue Mahesvara. Only the pasha noose, when held by Vajrapani, has the power to bind Mahesvara to the Dharma. You must defeat Mahesvara by challenging him. You must order him to seek refuge in the Buddha, the Dharma, and the Sangha. When he refuses, you must fight him and defeat him, killing all his avatars. You must humiliate him in front of others, thus wounding his pride. Then you must subdue him and destroy his ego. It won't be easy. He will use every means at his disposal to defeat you, to humiliate you instead, to walk all over you. He will tempt you, but you must remain adamant. Only you can defeat Mahesvara. If you fail, heaven won't be able to help you or any of us. We'll all perish, and the world may perish along with us."

"Are you certain there is no other way?"

"I'm certain," said Lokesvara.

Now Anong and her cohorts returned to their bodies at Belvoir, and as they readied themselves for battle, the Bodhisattva Manjusri gave final battle instructions to his troops.

"There will be only five of us to stand against Mahesvara and his minions," Manjusri said. "Ksitigarbha will stand at the north, Maitreya will stand at the east, I will stand at the south, and Anong will stand at the west. Like the four gates controlling the cardinal directions of a mandala, we will guard against access and egress from the battle area while Vajrapani challenges and confronts Mahesvara and Uma, Mahesvara's consort. As each of the avatars are defeated or killed by Vajrapani, Mahesvara may transfer his consciousness to another human in the room. When Mahesvara runs out of avatars to act for him, he will be forced to face Vajrapani directly. What you will see then is the emanation body of Mahesvara, fierce and ugly beyond description. Be not afraid, or he will feed on your fear."

"Can we not help Vajrapani?" asked Ksitigarbha.

"Yes, of course. Each of will play an important part in defeating the five poisons: lust, greed, desire, delusion, and pride. Ksitigarbha will attack lust when it appears, Maitreya will attack greed, Anong will attack desire, and I will attack delusion. Vajrapani will attack pride. Each of us are armed with the tools to defeat one of the poisons. We must be steadfast, adamant, and relentless."

"What about Randy and me?" asked Bill Ramsey, speaking through Colonel McMichaels.

"Now that your spirit is grounded to new bodies," said Manjusri, "you can astral travel anywhere. Your job is to patrol the area around the capitol. Watch for Mahesvara to call in reinforcements, which he is certain to do. Report to me immediately if an outside force assembles. We want to keep outside casualties to a minimum."

"Yes, Sir!" said Ramsey.

"Mahesvara has thrown the world out of balance by means of the five poisons. He has no compassion and will show no mercy. In order to defeat him, we must become like him. We must be relentless, adamant with diamond-hard resolve. If he becomes a fearsome monster, we must be more fearsome. But we must never lose compassion. For our compassion will show him the way to the clear light. He cannot be reborn because he has never been born. But he can be transformed by enlightenment. After Vajrapani defeats him, if he is able to defeat him, I shall show Mahesvara the light. If we have successfully removed the five poisons from Mahesvara's spirit, he may become transformed. For all sentient beings, even criminals and monsters like Mahesvara, may become enlightened."

"Enough talk," said Vajrapani. "Now is the time for action. For it is our actions, not merely our words, which determine the future."

"Then let us act," said Manjusri.

* * *

Earl Wright had found the perfect hide. He was camouflaged high atop a tree in the United States Botanic Gardens Park, just across Independence Avenue from the United States Capitol, where he had a straight line-of-sight to the front steps of the Capitol Building approximately 800 meters northeast of his position. He had the XM2010 rifle with a twenty-power scope attached and three loaded magazines—one loaded into the rifle and two spares—hidden beneath the woodland ghillie. He was high enough to see over the other trees between him and the Capitol steps. He had a clear shot when he was ready to take it.

Though the Senate floor was on the far side of the building, he would simply wait patiently for Kieffer to emerge with his entourage after the confirmation. Kieffer and the Service Secretaries and Senators had promised to hold a news conference on the Capitol steps immediately after the President declared martial law over on Pennsylvania Avenue. Earl had heard the news conferences announced on the radio, and he had planned accordingly.

He had scouted the area before security became really tight, and he was ensconced in his hide well before the first fingers of dawn crawled across the horizon and Secret Service cordoned off the streets around the Capitol.

He felt he could kill for a cigarette and a cup of coffee, but he knew he had blown his last chance hours ago. Edie had filled the Bunn with coffee and water and flipped the switch. She'd told him he could smoke if he wanted, but he'd waited to light up until the coffee was ready. Big mistake. He should have had a smoke before Charlie arrived. After she got there, he didn't have time for nicotine or caffeine. He had been too busy trying to survive to think about cigarettes and coffee until now. And now was too late.

He had stopped at a truck stop on the way into the city, but he only took time to fill the gas tank, empty his bladder, and had quickly moved on. He didn't stop again until he was in the heart of the city. He parked the Ford Taurus as close to the Capitol as he could find a parking place and boldly walked the eight blocks to the Botanic Gardens on the sidewalk. Dressed in BDUs, he looked like any active duty soldier on leave carrying his duffel bag between duty assignments. Washington was used to seeing soldiers in uniform. No one gave him a second glance or questioned his presence. He climbed the tree, put on his ghillie, and took out his rifle. He loaded his three magazines with Match-grade rounds, tapped each twice to settle the powder near the primer, and locked and loaded the weapon. He was ready to rock and roll.

What he planned to do was pure suicide, and he knew it. His chances of getting away after killing Kieffer on the Capitol steps were slim and none. Why was he doing this?

Wright had always been a risk-taker, and he'd taken great risks to life and limb many times in the past and always managed to survive. But this was different. This time it was personal. This time it didn't matter if he got out alive, though he certainly intended to try. All that mattered was killing Kieffer.

Kieffer and Charlie had made a complete fool out of him. They had lied, but he had expected that. Everyone lied. They had used him for their own purposes, and he had expected that, too. But they had maneuvered and manipulated him in ways he hadn't expected and couldn't forgive. He had felt violated by Mahesvara's presence inside his head, and by the fact that Mahesvara could have Charlie anytime he wanted and Wright could not. That made him angry.

They had poisoned his soul with lust, with self-delusion, with greed. With desire. He had never wanted anything as badly as he wanted Charlie. Even now, he wanted her more than he wanted coffee or a cigarette or even to live.

And he couldn't have her.

He had seen that truth in her eyes when he had her pinned to the floor. He meant nothing to her. He was a tool to use and then discard. It was if she had sensed his weakness and had made him fall in love with her in order to exploit him, to make him do her will.

He had dreamed of making her want him the way he wanted her, and he knew now it had been a fool's dream that could never come true. She wanted someone else. And that hurt his pride.

The answer to why he was doing what he was now doing became obvious: His pride was hurt. Proud men who lust for a woman who wants another and not them do desperate things. They delude themselves into thinking that if they remove the other from the equation, they can take that other's place. Did Wright want to take Kieffer's place?

He saw Kieffer and Charlie naked, in coitus. Then he visualized kicking Kieffer out of bed, gutting him with a K-bar, pulling out Kieffer's intestines. Then he saw himself and Charlie drinking Kieffer's blood and feeding on Kieffer's flesh.

What the hell is wrong with me? Why am I thinking this way?

The sun rose higher in the sky. All around him Washingtonians went about their business oblivious to the man with the loaded rifle hiding in the tree. People saw only what they wanted to see, what they expected to see. Those who bothered to look his way saw only a tall maple tree full of green leaves, perfectly normal for the end of June. Earl Wright felt like the invisible man. He felt he could do anything and nobody would ever know.

* * *

Randy Edwards recognized what he thought was Wright's energy signature from a distance, and he called out to Bill Ramsey's spirit and asked Ramsey to confirm Wright was indeed hiding in the tree. Randy couldn't see the man himself, but the energy signature spelled Earl Wright in capital letters. Bill had more experience with making observations on the astral plane, and he quickly zoomed in and verified that it was really Wright in the tree.

"He has a sniper rifle and he's hiding under a ghillie. But it's definitely Wright."

"Who do you suppose he's gunning for?"

"Us, probably."

"Doesn't he know we're dead?"

"Not unless he was the one who shot us. But I guess it had to be him who pulled the trigger at Belvoir. Anderson and Jens are still in California or Seattle, and the rest of the guys are dead, captured, or still west of the Mississippi."

"How would Wright even know we'd be here today?"

"He couldn't. So I guess he's not here to kill you and me. He must be here as a backup for Kieffer."

"You suppose?"

"Yeah. He and Kieffer both worked for WLSCTC, didn't they? It makes sense. He's here to protect Kieffer."

"What are we going to do?"

"You keep an eye on him. I'm going inside the Capitol to tell Manjusri."

“What should I do if he tries to leave or begins to shoot?”

“What *can* you do? You need a body to interact with the real world, and your borrowed body is back at Fort Belvoir. All you can do here is observe what he does.”

“Okay. I’ll stay on him.”

“Good. I’ll be back in a flash.”

* * *

Anong materialized inside the Senate chamber at 9:04 AM. With her were Vajrapani, Manjusri, Maitreya, and Ksitigarbha. The sudden appearance of five unexpected and unusual-looking visitors interrupted the opening prayer by a guest clergyman. The clergyman so totally freaked out when he saw four of the Eight Great Bodhisattvas in the flesh in the same room with him that the prayer died in his throat. He had recognized them immediately from pictures in a textbook on comparative religions that had been required reading in seminary. Since Manjusri carried the flaming Sword of Enlightenment, he knew they weren’t here to help him lead the Senate in prayer.

The Sergeant-At-Arms and several Secret Service Agents drew their weapons and rushed forward, prepared to expel the armed intruders from the building or shoot them dead.

Ksitigarbha and Maitreya lit up like the sun, stopping the men in their tracks before they could open fire or stumble blindly into someone or something. Temporarily blinded, they didn't dare shoot without hitting a Senator or honored guest.

There were probably two hundred people in the room, including a half-dozen or so in the visitor's gallery. Some of the men were in military uniforms—Class As or dress blues—but most wore expensive business suits. Anong recognized Kieffer from Mahesvara's energy signature, and Charlie stood off to the side, dressed in a tailored navy-blue skirt, matching jacket, and a white blouse. Her throat was swollen and bruised. Her nose was bent out of shape. Her eyes filled with hate as soon as she saw Anong. The temporary spell of enchantment had worn off completely days ago, since it had been hastily constructed and never anchored to last, a big mistake. Next time, Anong knew, Uma wouldn't be as easy to enchant.

The carpet was a deep dark blue, and there were what appeared to be lines of white stars in geometric patterns dotting the floor like the stars on the blue field of the American flag. There were two sizable desks near the front of the room. One was polished wood with a single leather executive chair, and there were unfurled flags on standards to either side of the desk, one of which Anong recognized as Old Glory and the other she didn't know at all. On the wall behind and above the desk were engraved the words "E PLURIBUS UNUM," which Anong knew meant "from many one" in textbook Latin. The other desk was made of solid marble, and it was twice as large as the first desk and had four smaller leather chairs lined up behind it. In front of the marble desk were two tables with three swivel chairs behind each desk. Between the desks and the Senate gallery stood three wooden podiums.

The rest of the floor was occupied by one hundred wooden writing desks that looked a little like old-fashioned school desks with a hinged lid, except they were much larger than a school desk and made of highly-polished wood. Behind each desk was a comfortable-looking wood executive chair with padded seat and back of rich black leather. The desks were arranged in a semi-circle around the two big desks in the front of the room fanning out like the main floor seats in a theater or auditorium, two or three desks in each section of the front row, four or five in each section of the second and third rows, and five or six in each section of the fourth row. Some of the desks had Senators standing next to them, but most were empty. A few Senators had congregated near the back or the front of the room where they still remained standing after chatting with honored guests before the session was called to order.

Everyone in the room appeared blinded by the bright light. Everyone, that is, except Anong, Manjusri, Vajrapani, Ksitigarbha, and Maitreya.

And Mahesvara and Uma. The light seemed to have no effect on them at all.

Mahesvara stood up straight near the front of the room, dressed in a green Army uniform with four equally-spaced silver stars on each of the epaulettes. He had five rows of ribbons over one pocket and a black and white name badge on the other. The name badge read "Kieffer" in capital letters.

"How dare you interrupt these proceedings!" demanded Mahesvara.

"I dare because I am Vajrapani," replied the bodhisattva, stepping forward to face the avatar of Mahesvara. "I command you," he said, sounding like a sergeant giving orders to his troops, "to take refuge in the Buddha, the Dharma, and the Sangha so you might achieve enlightenment."

"Who are *you* to command *me*?" roared the general. "I'm the creator and the arranger of the triple worlds, the master of all spirits, the god of all gods. Why should I do as you, a local ghost, command?" Mahesvara turned to Manjusri. "Just who does he think he is to give orders to a god?"

"I'd do as he commands, friend," said Manjusri. "Go for the refuges while you still have the chance. Don't make Vajrapani—this cruel, mean, angry, ferocious spirit—destroy you with his flaming Vajra."

"You want to see cruel, mean, angry, and ferocious? Let me show you what fear is all about!" shouted the general, and he changed shape. Gone now were the uniform and the frail human shape of a middle-aged man. In its place stood the cruel, vicious form of Mahesvara himself, lightning and flames shooting out of the emanation straight at Vajrapani's heart.

"I'm the Lord of the triple worlds," he roared. "You do what *I* command. I don't do what you command."

"You are nothing," said Vajrapani, deflecting the lightning bolts with his Vajra. "You are lower than dung beneath my feet." Vajrapani raised the Vajra and unleashed his own lightning. The bolts from the Vajra sailed true, and they tore into the human flesh of Mahesvara's avatar and ripped what had been Roger Kieffer to pieces.

Mahesvara materialized inside another human, this time the Air Force Chief of Staff. One moment the general was blind and immobile, and the next he was filled with wrath.

"I can endure death," said Mahesvara. "But I will not do as you command."

Again the lightning flared. Both adversaries threw lightning bolts and insults, challenges and ultimatums, at each other.

Neither gave an inch.

The walls of the Senate chamber became pock-marked with huge craters where bolts of lightning missed their targets and chipped away at the venerable building instead. The blue drapes behind the flags were burning brightly now as flames leapt toward the high ceiling, and the flags themselves burst into flame along with the wooden desk in the front of the room.

Uma stepped into the fray, revealing her true self as a fierce raksasa, a demon in her own right. She was blood-red, naked, still a beautiful woman except for her face. She had fangs like a naga, a serpent, and her hair was all greasy and knotted like a tangle of snakes. She wore a necklace of human finger bones, and nothing else.

She cupped her breasts in front of Vajrapani as if to entice him. She opened her legs and showed him her sex, dripping wet with lust. “You want me,” she said. “I can tell you want me. Come, let us copulate and forget the others. We can do it right here and let them watch in envy.” Vajrapani remained adamantly steadfast. His diamond resolve was focused solely on Mahesvara.

“Do as I command,” Vajrapani ordered again. “Seek refuge in the Buddha, the Dharma, and the Sangha.”

“Why should I do as you say?” asked Mahesvara. “I am a god, and you are nothing. I am a true emanation of Shiva, the Destroyer, and I will destroy you.”

“You and what army?”

Suddenly, the other mortals in the chamber seemed to come to life. Senators, generals, clerks, Service Secretaries, Secret Service agents, and Capitol security. Mahesvara had taken possession of all of them, and his divided consciousness blinked away the bright light that had blinded them. Those with guns opened fire. “Here is my army,” roared Mahesvara.

Vajrapani parried their shots with bolts of lightning.

Anong watched in horror as each person became an emanation of Mahesvara, fierce, ugly, angry, and filled with power. Though they were still mortal, they had sprouted multiple heads, multiple arms, horns, fangs, and armored flesh like armadillos.

“I am legion,” said Mahesvara. “You cannot defeat me.”

The ungodly army lurched forward like zombies in a bad horror movie. No sooner was one felled by lightning than another took its place.

"Each mortal you kill adds to your karmic debt," said Mahesvara. "You are damned by your actions."

"You are the one who is damned," said Vajrapani. "Seek refuge before I walk all over you."

"Give up this fool notion of honor, Vajrapani. Join me, and you will never have to answer for your crimes. Oh, yes. I know all about you. I know about your vows and the terrible karmic debt you incurred when you broke them. I can see into your heart, Mister Lone Ranger Vajrapani as only a god can. I know you regret killing anyone. Join me, and I promise you won't have to kill anyone anymore. I will grant you peace and eternal rest. Give yourself to me, and I will absolve you of your sins."

"If you can see into my heart," said Vajrapani, "then you know I was born to kill." He sent a blast of lightning at Mahesvara's avatar, and the man burst into flames as Mahesvara transferred his consciousness into the body of the Vice President of the United States.

"Kill him!" Mahesvara, in the form of the Vice President, ordered the zombies. "Kill them all!"

Anong fired up her internal athenor and woke the sleeping Kundalini. She opened her third eye and sent the Sudarshana Chakra spinning toward the hoard of demons. The 108 serrated edges sliced through armored flesh and severed heads and limbs from bodies.

At the same time, Manjusri moved forward with his flaming sword, slicing away at delusion with truth. The avatars fell right and left, their forms returning to fully human as life left and Mahesvara's spirit abandoned them for others. Bodies piled up. The blue and white carpet turned red.

Mahesvara must be importing avatars from somewhere, thought Anong. Most of the original two hundred lay dead on the floor, and there were more adding to the pile of dead bodies every minute. But now there appeared even more minions than ever before lined up to attack Vajrapani and threatening to overwhelm him with their sheer numbers. Some looked half-human while others were pure monsters straight from hell, creatures that had no right to be here on earth but who had answered Mahesvara's call for reinforcements.

There seemed to be a neverending flow of emanations of Mahesvara's evil, and even Maitreya and Ksitigarbha were besieged by terrible monsters. Some had weapons—guns or swords—and others had deadly claws and fangs that were just as dangerous. Though Bodhisattvas were pure spirit, they inhabited mortal bodies that could be killed or mutilated.

Neither Ksitigarbha nor Maitreya were killers at heart, and they fought defensively. Their major weapon—the light of reason—was ineffective against lust-filled demons. It might slow them, but it wouldn't stop them.

Anong continued to hurl the Sudarshana Chakra at opponents. But she felt her power draining. Soon the serpent would need to rest, the chakras would stop spinning, and she, too, would be vulnerable.

"To your positions at the cardinal directions," shouted Manjusri. "We must seal the gates. Allow no more to enter."

Anong moved quickly to the west wall. She saw Ksitigarbha move to the south, Maitreya to the east, and Manjusri to the north.

"Allow none to pass," instructed Manjusri. "Vajrapani cannot defeat an unlimited supply of avatars. Hold your position and let your light keep the darkness out."

Mahesvara hissed. "I do not need avatars to defeat you. I will defeat you myself. All of you. Beginning with the holder of the Vajra."

"You haven't a prayer," taunted Vajrapani. "I have right on my side. Right thinking, right living, right intention, right actions. What do you have?"

"Desire," said Mahesvara. "I desire to win. I desire to destroy you. I will destroy you. All of you."

"Then I, too, shall take on desire. For I desire to defeat you in order to preserve the Dharma. I shall kill your avatars and destroy all you have worked to accomplish."

"Then I will have won by default," said Mahesvara. "For you, who have renounced desire and killing, will have become like me. Tell me, Vajrapani, will it be worth becoming like me to defeat me?"

"If that is what it takes to defeat you, then so be it."

Vajrapani's visage became fiercer than ever. He grew eight heads and eight arms and eight legs. The color of his body changed to jade green. His eyes glowed bright like the sun and the moon. He raised the Vajra and the Kris and the pasha Noose and waved them right in Mahesvara's face.

The two faced off, firing lightning bolts and shouting insults at each other.

Anong would have found the whole thing comical if the situation weren't so deadly serious. Uma, completely naked and red-skinned, jumped up and down like a cheerleader at a football game, urging her team to victory, and Anong felt herself wanting to do the same.

Once Anong and the three Bodhisattvas took their places at the four corners of the room, the flow of avatars from outside abruptly ceased. It was almost as if they had turned off the spigot. But the damage seemed already to have been done because there were hundreds of demons in the room and all had fangs and claws and murder in their hearts.

Vajrapani fought valiantly against overwhelming odds. When the remaining avatars rushed him all at once, he slew many of them with the Kris. He whirled and spun and danced and dodged. He slashed and stabbed. He was a one-man killing machine.

Within the three realms of existence, or so it was written, the formless realm had no master, whereas the realm of form was ruled by Brahma, and the realm of desire was ruled by Mahesvara. Now Mahesvara called upon Brahma for the power to control forms, and the prayer must have been heard and granted because Mahesvara's form changed almost immediately. He became a massive serpent, giant, more than twenty feet long with a triangular head and two long fangs dripping venom. It looked big enough to swallow a man whole, and its jaws became unhinged as it stared hungrily at Vajrapani and his four companions. It was not an illusion; it was real and it was deadly.

And the remaining avatars changed shape too, becoming coiled cobras that struck blindly at anything that moved.

The huge serpent, towering above everybody and everything, moved in for the kill.

Vajrapani raised the Vajra and lightning blasted holes through the carpeting and the floor beneath, having passed through the monster serpent's body with no effect. "I hate snakes," Vajrapani said. "I hate snakes with a passion." The Ranger had once been thrown into a snakepit during elite Ranger training in Florida. It was a rite of passage for members of his unit to kill all the snakes in the pit with their bare hands, then skin them, and eat them. If a man got bitten, and some did, it was considered part of life-and death survival training to treat the fallen for snakebite by using your mouth to suck out the poison through the two punctures before the man died. The Ranger wore a snake-skin necklace, made from the snakes he had killed and eaten, as a symbol of his mastery over all snakes.

The cobras scattered, and some of them were killed and others injured as lightning rained down everywhere.

But the monster that was Mahesvara was unscathed. It struck at Vajrapani and would have devoured him if Anong had not used what little remained of the Kundalini power within her to send the Sudarshana Chakra spinning between them. Mahesvara jerked back just in time to avoid being decapitated by the one-hundred and eight serrated blades of the flying wheel.

Anong fell to her knees on the floor, totally exhausted by the effort, too weak to stand. She saw cobras slithering toward her, attracted by the sudden movement of her fall. If any one of the dozen or so coming her way punctured her flesh with their fangs, she would be dead within minutes.

But Vajrapani had seen what had happened, and he had also asked Brahma for a boon. And Brahma, always wanting to play fair, had granted the boon.

Vajrapani morphed into a giant bird, an American eagle, and he flapped his four-foot-long wings and flew over the triangular head of Mahesvara straight at the approaching serpents, snatching them up in his mighty beak and severing their heads from their necks. He grabbed two or three of them at a time, clamped down with his beak, and dropped them to the floor where the two halves continued to writhe. Some of the remaining cobras attacked the still-moving scaly halves of their fallen comrades, oblivious now to the bigger prey on the other side of the room. They fed on their own kind and ignored everything else.

Mahesvara struck at the bird but missed, his giant triangular head and long neck hindered by the bulk of the long body that stretched out behind him. The eagle swept around and dove at the serpent and pecked at the top of its head.

Reminiscent of the epic battle of Garuda versus the nagas that Anong had seen depicted on the walls at Angkor, the two adversaries went round and round like the turning of the wheel of life, the wheel of samsara. At one moment, the snake was on top. The next moment, it was the bird on top. The eagle held the snake in its claws, and the snake held the bird wrapped in its coils. The snake struck with its fangs and missed. The bird pecked with its beak and missed. Neither managed to kill the other. The battle continued to rage seemingly forever.

Anong stayed on her knees. She didn't have the energy to stand, and she didn't have the energy to sit. She could barely hold her head up.

Never before had she felt so week, so powerless.

Uma noticed her weakness and started toward her. "The shoe is on the other foot now, little one," said the demoness. "I will have my revenge for what you did to me in Dubai."

Too weak to work a spell of enchantment, Anong watched Uma come closer. Any moment now, Uma would sink her fangs into Anong's neck and rip her head off. It would be payback for the noose Anong had put around Charlie's neck and nearly choked Uma to death.

But Manjusri had stepped forward, and he placed the flaming sword between them. Uma backed away from the sword of righteousness as if its very presence was abhorrent to her. She emitted a horrible hiss, the kind of sound a cat might make if someone had just stepped on its tail.

Now the eagle flew overhead, its giant wings beating the air to create terrific downdrafts, and the serpent snapped its head around to strike at it. But the eagle continued to soar in a high circle just beyond the serpent's reach, and the serpent tried to twist its long body to match the eagle's speed, tying itself in knots as it attempted to keep its eyes glued to the ever-moving bird.

Finding himself unable to keep up with the eagle, the serpent changed back into the demonic form of Mahesvara, and the demon stretched up one of his multiple limbs and grabbed the bird by its tail, snatching it from the air.

The bird changed back into Vajrapani and broke free of the demon's grasp.

"Give up!" roared Mahesvara. "You cannot win."

"Last chance," returned Vajrapani in a voice like thunder. "Seek refuge in the Three Jewels. Seek wisdom and enlightenment before it is too late."

"You cannot kill me," said Mahesvara, puffing up to his most wrathful form. "I am self-existent, the great god of gods. I create or destroy all beings. You, Vajrapani, are but a Yaksa, a reincarnated ghost. Who are you to order me to act as you? You should do as I command, not the other way around."

"You are a wicked being who causes much harm by your relentless greed. You are a stinking demon who feeds on the charred flesh of cremated corpses. You seek to destroy all that is beautiful and holy. We, the protectors of the Dharma, cannot and will not allow that to happen." Vajrapani turned to Manjusri. "Bhagwan," he said, meaning Master, "this great Mahesvara relies only on his own knowledge and power, his high position matching his pride in himself. He won't submit to the teachings of the pure Dharma of all the Tathagata. How can I let him get away with this?"

"You can't," said Manjusri, and he began to chant, his voice filled with power and beauty. "*Om Nisumbha Vajra hum phat*," he sang.

To which Vajrapani added his own "Hummmmmmm!" Then he said, "*Om padarakarsana vajra hum*," and Vajrapani raised the Vajra and the scepter emitted a clear light so brilliant and beautiful and powerful that Mahesvara could not stand against it. Both Mahesvara and Uma were thrown to the ground where they lay flat on their backs, their nakedness exposed for all to see.

Vajrapani placed his right foot on Mahesvara's face and his left foot on Uma's breasts. Then he took the pasha-noose and wrapped it about both of them.

Bound now by the Dharma, humiliated and degraded by Vajrapani's actions, Mahesvara's wrongful pride and arrogance were trampled beneath Vajrapani's feet and Mahesvara was finally able to see the light. As he became truly enlightened, Mahesvara was instantly transformed into pure spirit. Both Mahesvara and Uma disappeared from the realm of forms.

"Where did they go?" asked Anong, finally gaining enough strength to speak.

"They have entered the gate of Samadhi," said Manjusri. "They are in nirvana."

"How could one so evil achieve nirvana?" asked the girl.

"When Vajrapani trampled their egos beneath his feet, their pride was vanquished and they were able to become enlightened. When one is enlightened, all former trespasses become nonexistent. It is only through ignorance, arrogance, and pride that we remain trapped in the world of forms. When one foregoes arrogance and pride and becomes truly enlightened, one is transformed but not destroyed. Such is the way of the Dharma."

With the disappearance of Mahesvara and Uma, the avatars resumed their human forms. Many of Mahesvara's minions were still alive, and they wandered about the Senate chamber in a daze. They had no memory of what had just happened. The demons Mahesvara had called had returned to hell where they belonged.

"Our work here is done," said Manjusri. "We should leave before any become cognizant of their surroundings. I'm sure the police will arrive shortly."

"Master," said Anong. "I have a boon to ask."

"What is it?"

"I have always wanted to see America. Please, may I stay in Washington for a while and see the wonderful sights?"

"America can be a dangerous place, especially for a girl-child. I do not want to leave you here alone, and I cannot stay in America with you."

"Did I not fight alongside you? What might I face in America that is more dangerous than what I have just faced?"

"She can stay with Deb and Bill," offered Ksitigarbha. "She can have the spare bedroom now that Randy Edwards doesn't need it anymore."

"Are you sure?"

"She'll be fine. She was a big help today. We couldn't have stopped Mahesvara without her. She's a brave girl."

"Then Vajrapani and I will leave. We still have work to do." Anong was about to say goodbye, to throw her arms around her mentor and thank him, but Manjusri and Vajrapani had already disappeared.

So, too, had Ksitigarbha and Maitreya disappeared. In their places stood Deb Johnson and Bill Porter.

“Come,” said Deb, taking Anong’s hand. “We’ll go out the west stairs and walk to the metro station. You can begin sightseeing right away.”

“Oh, joy!” exclaimed Anong.

* * *

Bill Ramsey’s spirit returned almost immediately after it had left.

“Did you tell Manjusri already?” asked Randy. “What does he want us to do?”

“I didn’t bother him,” said Ramsey. “They were in the middle of a big battle and I didn’t want to distract any of them.”

“Who’s winning?”

“Too soon to tell. I got a quick look at Mahesvara, though. Man, is he ugly!”

“Ugly as sin?”

“Worse. He had a whole bunch of heads and arms and legs. And he smelled rotten like he’d been sleeping in a coffin with rotting corpses.”

“You’re kidding, right?”

“No. That’s what I really saw. That’s what his spirit was like. He was wearing the body of the Vice President, and that’s probably all that a living human would see. But I saw his spirit. And I had to get out of there. It was too much for me.”

“It was really that bad?”

"Take my word for it, it was worse."

"Wright hasn't moved. I have to give him credit. He makes one hell of an ideal sniper."

"Let's see if we can rattle his cages," said Ramsey. "C'mon. Let's breathe down his neck."

Both spirits moved in real close to Wright, up close and personal. Ramsey floated over Wright's left shoulder and Randy floated over his right shoulder. They were close enough to touch the man, but when they tried to grab him their hands passed right through Wright's flesh as if he were only a hologram.

Or they were ghosts.

"Boo!" shouted Randy.

Wright didn't react.

"Darn. I've wanted to do that since I became a ghost, but I guess it doesn't have the same effect it does in the movies."

"We exist on parallel planes," said Ramsey. "He's in one dimension and we're in another, higher dimension. We can see him, but he can't see us."

"You sure about that?"

"Positive. We don't exist in the material world."

"Then how can we inhabit the bodies of the Colonel and Eddie Morsay? How were you able to enter my body?"

"We were invited in."

"I didn't invite you."

"No. I was able to sneak in when your spirit was out of your body. Nature abhors a vacuum. When a body is left unoccupied and unprotected, a spirit can sometimes cross over and fill the void. As I understand it, this is only possible at certain times, especially after seventy-two hours have passed and the spirit hasn't gone into the light. On the forty-ninth day after I died, my spirit was allowed to cross over to the physical world. I could have been reborn as a fetus during conception, or I could easily slip into an adult who had just had an orgasm. You were in ecstasy, your spirit had temporarily left your body, and I was able to sneak in and you couldn't stop me."

"Lucky me."

"Lucky for both of us."

"What will happen to us now? You died again. I died for the first time. Aren't we supposed to go somewhere?"

"We will. When our mission is over. We still have work to do here. When our work is finally finished in the real world, we'll see the clear light and pass over to the spirit realm. Right now, we're between worlds. We're neither fully here nor there. The spirit realm is somewhere else entirely."

"Heaven?"

"Somewhere like that, I guess. Perhaps it's purgatory. Or limbo."

"What will happen to us when we enter the spirit realm?"

"I don't know."

"Scared?"

"A little. Are you?"

"Yeah. I did some bad things. I don't know if I'll get into heaven."

"Then you'll get a chance to come back, to be reborn. You'll have another chance to get it right."

"How many chances do we get?"

"I don't know. As many as it takes, I guess."

Wright moved the rifle slightly to his left, and Ramsey and Randy followed the movement to the west doors of the Capitol. One of the doors had opened, and three people had come out.

Ramsey recognized the figures of Deb Johnson, Bill Porter, and Anong. They stood on the top of the Capitol steps and looked around at the city. Deb pointed past the mall at the obelisk that was the Washington Monument, and Anong had an excited look on her face as if she were seeing the place for the first time, which Ramsey guessed was probably true.

"He's getting ready to shoot," said Randy. "We've got to do something."

Both spirits grabbed for the rifle muzzle and tried to jerk it away from the target, but to no avail. They saw a puff of smoke come out of the muzzle as the rifle jerked, and then they heard the shot.

Wright worked the bolt, settled in for another shot, and fired again.

CHAPTER TWENTY-THREE

Earl Wright felt he was being watched. He glanced around out of the corners of his eyes, using his peripheral vision as he had been trained, but he saw no one anywhere near.

He had been waiting patiently for hours for the ceremonies inside that building to conclude, and now the time was here. He was glad he hadn't had any coffee. If he'd had to pee, he wouldn't have been able to break cover and look for a bathroom. But he didn't have to pee.

He knew Kieffer and Charlie were supposed to be inside that building. Kieffer was being given his fourth star, and soon he'd come out onto the steps with a bunch of politicians and make an announcement. A dozen or so television vans were parked around the Capitol now with their telescoping antennas raised. A select group of reporters, both print and air, were gathered near the bottom of the marble steps with cameras and microphones ready. Security had gotten tight about two hours ago, and there were probably half a hundred police officers and Secret Service men milling around.

But Wright was practically invisible inside his ghillie, and he was certain no one had spotted him. He could see them clearly through his scope, but he was confident they couldn't see him.

He felt a sudden breeze, but there was no breeze. The leaves of the tree weren't moving as they would have if there had been any kind of wind. It felt almost as if someone where breathing down the back of his neck.

He moved his thumb up to switch off the safety. Then he assumed a good spot weld, and concentrated on the view through the scope.

The doors at the top of the stairs began to open. Correction, it was only one of the doors. Three people came out of the shadows into the bright sunlight. They were looking off into the distance, and one of them pointed to something beyond the far end of the mall. It was as if they were so interested in seeing the sights they hadn't noticed the huge crowd gathered at the bottom of the stairs, nor the cameras.

One of the three standing at the top of the Capitol steps was Deb Johnson.

Wright knew he'd never get another chance like this. He had intended to shoot Kieffer, but Kieffer was still inside the building. Did he want to wait and take out his intended target? Or should he take a shot at this target of opportunity?

He decided to take his shot at Deb Johnson. He swallowed a breath, held half in, and took up the slack on the trigger.

He had Deb dead in his crosshairs, a perfect shot to the center of her torso, right between the breasts. The copper and steel-jacketed 14.3 gram hollow-point boat-tail Sierra MatchKing bullet would travel at 2,850 feet per second, enter the front of her body exactly where the crosshairs had been placed, tear out her heart and lungs, and exit the back with a sploosh of blood and bone to decorate the doors and the sidewalk.

That sudden breeze hit him again just as he pulled the trigger, jerking the rifle slightly to the right but not enough to completely ruin the shot. Before the recoil had dropped the muzzle's flash suppressor back into position, he had moved his hand to the bolt lever, ejected the empty casing, chambered another round, and locked the bolt into place. Brakken had been correct about muscle memory. Wright felt as if he had been doing this all of his life and never taken a break.

He sighted through the scope again and saw that Deb was down. She lay flat on her back in a pool of blood. He debated taking a second shot at her, and decided shooting at a prone target that was already dead was a waste of ammunition.

He moved the scope to the man who was kneeling over Johnson's body and couldn't get a good head shot. He went for the guy's torso, knowing wherever he hit would do maximum damage.

Again, he felt the wind kick up, though the leaves didn't stir. He jerked the trigger and watched the man fall on top of Johnson.

He thought about the girl, and decided she was nobody important. He sent his third round into the crowd, scattering them as they ran for cover. Then he leapt from the tree, shed the ghillie, shoved the rifle in his duffel, and ran for the car.

* * *

Anong squinted in the bright sunlight, her eyes trying to focus on the tall white monolith in the distance. Deb had said the Washington Monument was on the National Mall directly in front of the Capitol, about halfway between the Capitol Building and the Lincoln Memorial. She told Anong she couldn't miss it. It was the tallest building around.

"There," said Deb, pointing. "See it?"

Anong was staring at the 500 foot high obelisk when suddenly Deb flew backwards to land hard on the top of the marble steps. Anong thought she heard Deb's head bounce. Deb lay flat on her back, blood leaking from holes in both the front and back of her uniform.

Bill reacted almost instantly, falling to his knees over Deb's body and trying vainly to stench the flow of blood. Then Bill Porter, too, flew back as if someone had kicked him in the midsection.

Now Anong heard screams from the grounds around the building as she noticed people running from the bottom of the steps toward vans parked nearby. Though she hadn't heard the shots, it finally dawned on her that someone was shooting at them with a gun. Someone had shot Deb and Bill. She was certain she would be next.

She thought about teleporting away to safety. It would be so easy to do.

But she couldn't leave Deb and Bill. She had to find a way to help them.

She was still incredibly weak from the terrible drain the Kundalini had taken on her body, using up almost all of her energy. She wished Manjusri or Vajrapani were here to help, to tell her what to do next, but they had left Anong alone to go back to Angkor. She thought about teleporting to Angkor and bringing them back. But that would take time, and Deb and Bill didn't have time. If they weren't dead already, they would be soon. They were both bleeding badly, and they'd bleed out in a matter of minutes.

If only Ksitigarbha were here, the Sacred Girl could surely heal them, for Ksitigarbha was a true healer. But Ksitigarbha couldn't materialize without Deb's help, and Deb was either dead or unconscious.

Whether Deb and Bill lived or died was now up to Anong. She knew the Kundalini could both kill and heal. She had used most of it up today in killing. Was there any Kundalini power left to heal?

She went inside and woke the sleeping serpent. It didn't want to stir, but she made it move by sheer willpower. She fired up the dan-tien and began the Tummo breathing.

Anong's hands began to glow. Using the Kundalini energy to heal instead of kill felt different, strange. Did she even remember how to do it?

She laid one hand on Bill Porter and the other on Deb Johnson. Both were so still. But both bodies still felt warm to her touch. Was that only because heat the Kundalini energy produced was pouring forth from Anong's body into their bodies? Were they already dead and cold and all this was wasted effort?

Anong felt the life energy drain out of her, slowly at first, then more rapidly. She didn't know how much longer she could keep this up. It was taking a terrible toll on her, and Anong was aware she could die herself if she gave away too much of her life force.

Blood stopped leaking from Bill. Slowly, the hole in his side began to fill in.

Deb, however, lay so deathly still. The bullet had entered her torso to the left of the heart, and there was blood all over the front of her uniform. Anong didn't dare think of what Deb's back looked like.

Suddenly, there were sucking sounds coming from the hole in Deb's chest as Deb's remaining breast heaved as if she were breathing. Maybe she was still alive and could be healed.

Anong had to keep trying.

Bill moaned. That was a good sign. He was definitely alive.

Anong became light-headed and motes swam in front of her eyes, big black spots that threatened to blot out the sun like passing clouds. She was rapidly running out of energy, and there was nothing she could do about it.

And then the serpent inside her collapsed to the pit of Anong's stomach, and the fires in her belly sputtered and went out, and she felt so very cold, so very alone, so completely helpless.

And then the clouds in front of her eyes filled her vision entirely as her eyes swam way up in her head and she felt herself falling….

* * *

Wright ran. There were dozens of others running away from the direction of Capitol Hill where shots had been fired, but Wright was way ahead of all of them. He found his car exactly where he had parked it, with a red tow sticker pasted to the rear window. He could see "No Parking" signs posted on yellow plastic cones along both sides of the street now that hadn't been set out yet when he'd left the vehicle more than six hours ago. Probably part of the increased security that was coming with the declaration of martial law.

He peeled the sticker off and wadded it up and threw it away. Then he got into the Taurus and made two right turns and was headed out of the city.

He heard lots of sirens heading his way as police responded to reports of shots fired near the Capitol. If they were really on the ball, they'd set up roadblocks in a hurry, but Wright knew that wasn't going to happen soon enough to stop him from getting across the river and out to the beltway. He pulled over as several ambulances and fire engines sped past in the opposite direction. He obeyed the speed limits and did nothing to attract attention to himself or his car.

Where should he go? He had been mulling that over in the back of his mind for hours, and he still didn't have a definite location in mind. He was most familiar with the territory that lay to the south, and he had briefly considered going back to Richmond. But he knew they would be looking for him there. If not the feds, then Kieffer and Charlie. Richmond was no longer an option.

He had no idea what lay immediately to the west of Washington, D. C. He was on I-66, headed toward I-495. He decided to stay on I-66 heading west. He decided to go as far west as he could get. In fact, it might not be a bad idea to keep going west all the way to California. He had spent a few months TDY at the National Training Center at Fort Irwin on the edge of the Mojave Desert while learning urban warfare tactics back in 2006. Irwin was in the middle of nowhere, about a hundred and fifty miles northeast of Los Angeles. He could be there in two or three days, tops. Then he would go to ground and wait for the hoo-haw to blow over.

Then he would find a way to come back and take out Kieffer.

He knew he had to stop somewhere soon and buy civilian clothes. Though he was comfortable in BDUs, he didn't want to stand out. He could keep the boots, but jeans and t-shirt would probably be less conspicuous for a cross-country drive.

He still had a few thousand dollars stashed in his warbag, contingency funds from WLSCTC to support the teams of snipers during their extended stay in the safe houses. It would get him to California easily. Then he could think about some way to pick up a few additional bucks and start a new life. There were always jobs available for someone with his unique skill sets.

He took exit 1-A and headed toward Roanoke on I-81 south. He'd pick up I-40 in Tennessee, and take it all the way out to California.

Wright stopped outside of Blacksburg for gas, and he bought jeans and a couple of t-shirts at a strip mall.

FM reception wasn't worth shit way out here in the boonies, and he switched to AM and searched past the mostly Christian radio stations until he found a country music station that had five minutes of news on the hour. The latest from their Associated Press wire feed said there were hundreds of people dead inside the Capitol Building, and several people were reported shot on the Capitol steps. Among those confirmed killed were the Vice President of the United States, the Secretary of Homeland Security, General Kieffer the newly appointed Chairman of the Joint

Chiefs of Staff, the acting Secretary of Defense, and most of the United States Senators. There was no mention of Deb Johnson by name. Obviously, there were too many casualties to name them all.

Wright wondered what had happened inside that building that killed so many. Who took out Kieffer for him? Deb Johnson? He didn't see how. She hadn't been armed when she came out of the Capitol Building. She looked exactly like a tourist, with a nerdy husband or boyfriend on one side of her and a girl that was the right age to be a daughter or niece on the other side of her, interested more in the sights of the city than wary of a possible threat. No, whoever took out Kieffer, it wasn't Deb Johnson.

And what about Charlie? Had Charlie been killed in the Capitol, too? Was she one of the unnamed casualties? God, he hoped not.

Wright still had a feeling he was being watched, a feeling he'd had since before he'd pulled the trigger on Johnson and the feeling didn't want to go away. He saw nothing unusual ahead or behind him, just the usual stream of big semis and run-of-the-mill highway traffic. He hadn't seen a camera mounted anywhere now for miles, and no aerial surveillance, not even a traffic copter. He knew there were the usual birds high in the sky—the inevitable surveillance satellites—that recorded everyone and everything, but they were always there and he couldn't do anything about them. It would take an analyst with the patience and skill of a Deb Johnson to comb through all those images and track him from the capitol to his present location. That could take days or weeks. By then he'd be long gone.

But the feeling persisted. Someone was watching him, someone he couldn't see. Earl Wright felt haunted, as if the ghosts of people he had personally killed or ordered killed were following him, looking for ways to avenge their deaths.

* * *

Anong awoke in a hospital bed. She was dressed in a light blue hospital gown and there were tubes stuck in her right arm that were connected to drips of clear liquid, and there was a pulse monitor clamped to her right index finger, and a blood pressure cuff on her left arm above the elbow.

A nurse—obviously the west's equivalent of a Bhikkuni, a Duon Ji, in this Roman Catholic Hospital—came in from the nurse's station outside Anong's room, bringing a tray of food which she placed on a table next to the bed. Then the nurse sat on the edge of Anong's bed.

"How you feelin', hon?" asked the nurse. Anong knew nuns were called "sisters" in America.

"Tired," said Anong.

"You've been sleeping for almost two whole days," said the Sister. "You must have been exhausted. You'll feel better after you eat breakfast."

"What's wrong with me?" asked Anong.

"Exhaustion and dehydration, mostly. Plus you're suffering from shock. We've had you on a saline drip for the dehydration, and we've been feeding you vitamins and glucose intravenously. At first, we thought maybe you had been shot like the others. But you have no external wounds, no physical wounds of any kind. You'll be just fine in another day or two. But you need to eat to regain your strength."

"The others…are they all right? Deb and Bill?"

"Are they your parents, hon?"

"My adopted parents," said Anong. "Debra Johnson and Bill Porter. Are they all right?"

"Bill Porter will be fine. He lost some blood, but we replaced that in time. The gunshot wound had miraculously closed on its own before he reached the emergency room, and we don't think there's any lasting internal damage. Thank God, the bullets missed his vital organs. And his immune system seems to be working overtime. He'll be good as new in a day or two."

"What about Deb?"

"Deb didn't make it, hon. She passed away on the operating table. Honestly, the surgeons don't know how she lasted as long as she did. I'm sorry. She's beyond pain and suffering. God called her home to heaven. It was God's will."

Anong felt her eyes flood with tears. "I tried to save her," she sobbed. "I thought I could do it, but I didn't have enough strength. I failed. I let Deb die."

"No one could have saved her," said the nurse. "You can't blame yourself."

"But she was Sacred Girl," weeped Anong. "What will happen to Sacred Girl now that Deb is gone?"

"All life is sacred," said the nurse, not understanding exactly what Anong had meant by her words. It was more than language that separated the two women. They were coming from philosophies so essentially different that common ground, though it existed, was impossible to find.

"I can't believe Deb died," said Anong, so lost in her grief that she paid no attention to what the nurse had just said. "I can't believe she'd leave us."

"You need to eat now, hon, before your food gets cold. You need to build up your own strength." She moved the arm of the table over the bed so the food was right in front of Anong's face and removed the plastic cover from a plate of scrambled eggs. "Eat, then sleep. When you feel up to it, we'll take you for a walk to see Bill Porter. I'm sure he'll be happy to see you."

Anong ate.

* * *

Bill Ramsey and Randy Edwards had followed Earl Wright from Washington to the sticks of West Virginia and then into Tennessee. Though Wright couldn't see them, they occupied the car with him, breathing down his neck from the back seat of the Taurus.

"I still can't believe Deb and Bill are dead," said Randy. "I can't believe we saw this bastard shoot them both and we couldn't do anything to prevent it."

"That's what it means to be dead," said Ramsey. "You can't affect events in the physical world. Better get used to it."

"At least we know exactly what happened and where Wright went after the shooting."

"We've got to let Eddie and the Colonel know, too, and the sooner the better. I'll stick with Wright, and you go back to Eddie Morsay and tell him. The Colonel can notify the FBI and they can contact the state police and maybe they can set up some kind of a roadblock and arrest Wright before he kills again."

"Wright won't surrender without a fight," said Randy. "He'll go down shooting."

"Too bad you and I can't be the ones that take him down. We have to let others do the fighting for us now because we have no bodies of our own. I'll settle for seeing Wright go down, no matter who does it."

"Maybe Eddie and the Colonel will want to get in on the action and let us tag along."

"Go ask them," said Ramsey, and Randy departed.

Wright made it all the way to Little Rock, Arkansas, before he stopped for the night at a cheap motel not far from the expressway. Ramsey watched him carry the duffel bag inside his room, unpack the sniper rifle, and disassemble it for cleaning. The guy had a virtual arsenal with him in that duffel bag, and Ramsey admired the man's thoroughness in cleaning, lubing, and checking over each weapon before going to sleep. Besides the XM2010, he had an M4 carbine, two Smith and Wesson Military and Police .40 caliber automatic pistols, a nine millimeter Beretta, and an M1911 .45 automatic. He checked each magazine carefully, making sure each was fully loaded and the spring was tight. Then he packed the weapons away, all but the M9 Beretta which he kept next to him on the bed. He went to sleep fully clothed with the Beretta close at hand.

Randy returned around three AM. "What took you so long?" asked Ramsey.

"Deb definitely died," Randy said. "But Bill's still alive. He's in the hospital. So is Anong."

"Anong was shot?"

"No. But she's exhausted. She used up almost all of her life force trying to save both Deb and Bill. She managed to save Bill. She almost died herself trying to save Deb. She's a very brave little girl."

"What did Eddie say?"

"He and the Colonel plan to track Wright on the big screen at INSCOM. I gave Eddie a description of the car, the plates, and its location on I-40 west and I watched as they picked up the car with one of the satellites and locked on. They want to watch Wright for a while and see if he'll lead them to the rest of the snipers. There are ten armed teams still at large in Denver and Seattle, and probably half as many running around LA."

"The FBI hasn't caught them yet?"

"No. Those guys are too good. They've had plenty of training in survival, evasion, and escape. But Wright probably knows where they are."

"Why not just pick up Wright and make him talk?"

"You think he'll surrender? If they try to pick him up now, they'll only lose the best lead they have when he shoots it out with the cops."

"So what do we do?"

"We stay on him like flies on excrement. We report any contacts he makes to Eddie and the Colonel. Maybe we'll get lucky and wrap up this whole mess before too long. And, yes, Eddie and the Colonel said we could ride along with them when it's time for a showdown."

"Good," said Ramsey. "I didn't get a chance to pay Dick-head back for killing me. Maybe I'll get a chance to pay Wright back for killing Deb. I sure would like that."

CHAPTER TWENTY-FOUR

Bill Porter was sitting up in bed watching television news when the nurse brought Anong to Bill's room. A CNN anchor annouced the entire nation remained shocked and in mourning three days after the death of the Vice President and others at the Nation's Capital. No one knew how so much destruction could have taken place in such a short time, and the mystery of what had happened in the Senate chambers still remained a mystery.

None of the survivors could recall any of the events that took place inside that locked room. It was almost as if their brains had been washed, or they had been possessed, or something equally sinister occurred solstice morning. A sudden flare of bright light interrupted television feeds—including C-Span and all of the national network cameras covering the United States Senate—between 9:04 AM and 10:30 AM, prompting rumors of some kind of government cover-up. CNN promised to examine the more probable theories about what had happened during a prime-time special tonight at nine.

Anong had seen other newscasts that had speculated about the devastating violence that had begun and ended so quickly on the morning of the summer solstice. Now that martial law had been declared, the President assured the American people that such events could never happen again. None of the TV anchors seemed to believe him.

Bill had been moved from the intensive care ward to a regular room one floor above where Anong was staying in a similar, though smaller, room. Bill was still hooked up to drips of plasma and pain meds. Several beeping machines monitored his vitals continuously and closely, keeping a running record of his progress. The nurse said the doctors couldn't believe he was practically healed after suffering such traumatic tissue and organ damage. They thought it was a miracle he had survived at all, much less healed so quickly. Some of the doctors wanted to write a paper about it for a medical journal.

"Yes," said Anong. "It was indeed a miracle."

"Thank you," Bill said as soon as he saw Anong, and his pale face lit up with a big smile. "I know what you did, Anong. I appreciate what you did for me and tried to do for Deb. I owe you my life. I don't know if I'll ever be able to repay you."

"I am sorry it wasn't enough to save Deb," said Anong.

"You tried," said Bill. But he didn't seem as filled with grief by Deb's passing as Anong was, and that seemed very strange for a man who had lost his fiancé. Perhaps he was still in shock. "No one could have done more," he told her.

"Now don't you stay too long and tire yourself or Mr. Porter out, hon," said the nurse. "When you're ready to go back to your room, buzz the nurse's station and I'll come get you."

When the nurse had left the room, Bill excitedly whispered, "Deb's with me, Anong."

"Deb died," said the girl.

"Yes. Her body died, but her spirit now lives inside of me," said Bill. "You kept her alive long enough for her to transfer her full consciousness into me. I will always be grateful for that. The Deb that I love is still with me. We are closer now than we have ever been. She can't stay with me forever, but we're both grateful for every minute we have together."

"Is Ksitigarbha with you, too?"

"No. Ksitigarbha is waiting in the spirit realm for someone to let her in. I already have Maitreya. Ksitigarbha can't use the same body as another Bodhisattva."

"I will let her in," said Anong. "I would be honored to share my body with the Bodhisattva Ksitigarbha."

"Sacred Girl was hoping you would say that. Go into lotus and open yourself to her. You will feel her spirit join yours."

Anong sat on the floor in lotus and began to meditate. Within moments, she felt a presence inside her, filling her with love and compassion. Sacred Girl had joined with her, and they were now one.

Whole new worlds opened up to Anong, and many things appeared clearer than ever before.

"You'll get used to it," said Bill. "You're still yourself, but there's an added dimension to the way you see the world.

You'll soon learn to separate yourself and go about your life as usual. But Ksitigarbha will be there when you call upon her."

"Is that the way it is with you and Maitreya?"

"Yes," said Bill. "I often forget that Maitreya is a part of me. When I call upon him to act, however, he takes over my body completely. Then it's as if I'm a passenger in a car. After I hand over the keys, I get to ride along. I see what he sees, he can talk to me and I can talk to him, but he's in complete control of the vehicle. I can't steer, I can't put on the brakes. When he's ready, we simply switch places, and I'm back in the driver's seat again."

"And you trust him with your car?"

"Implicitly. He's a much better driver than I am."

"If I call upon Ksitigarbha, can she heal you?"

"I'm already healing from within, thanks to you. If I become completely healed too soon, the doctors will keep me here to run tests to find out why. I don't want to be stuck here. I want to get out of the hospital and find whoever shot Deb and me."

"If you find them, will you kill them?"

"No," said Bill Porter. "But I want to stop them from killing anyone else. Maitreya can do that. But first, he needs to know who did it."

"Perhaps Eddie or the Colonel would know."

"The hospital won't let anyone but family visit, and I can't take phone calls."

"I have the strength now to teleport. I can go to Fort Belvoir and ask them."

Before Bill could stop her, Anong blinked out of existence in the hospital and blinked back into existence in Deb's office at Fort Belvoir. Eddie sat at Deb's desk and looked at satellite photos of the shooting at the Capitol.

"Hello, Eddie," said Anong.

"Anong! I was so worried about you. Are you okay? I came to the hospital to see you last night, but they wouldn't let me talk to you because I wasn't immediate family."

"I am well, thank you," said Anong. "I wish I could say the same for Deb. Her spirit is inside Bill Porter now, and Ksitigarbha's spirit is inside me. Bill is still in the hospital. He sent me to ask you who killed Deb. Do you know?"

"Earl Wright shot Deb and Bill," said Eddie. "Ramsey and Edwards saw it happen, and they are tracking Wright."

"I will tell Bill Porter," said Anong. "He is hungry for that information."

"Tell him we'll get Wright and make him pay for what he did. We have Wright's car under aerial surveillance."

"I will tell him," said Anong, and then she was gone.

When she blinked back into existence inside the hospital room, the nurse was in the room questioning Bill about Anong's whereabouts.

"I didn't see her go out," said the nurse. "I was right outside the room all the time. I tell you, she couldn't have walked past me."

"We see only what we expect to see," said Anong, and the nurse turned around to see Anong standing right behind her. "Isn't that correct?"

"Yes," said the nurse, falling prey to Anong's powers of enchantment. "We see only what we expect to see."

"And we hear only what we expect to hear. You will not hear me tell Bill Porter that it was Earl Wright that shot him. Nor will you remember I was gone from this room. Will you?"

"No," said the nurse.

"Then," said Anong, "I am ready to return to my room."

"Thank you, Anong, for all you have done for Deb and me," said Bill.

"Use the information about Wright wisely," said Anong, walking to the door with the nurse. "Now that I know where you are, I will visit with you often."

"See you soon," said Bill, as Anong and the nurse left the room.

CHAPTER TWENTY-FIVE

Deb surprised Randy and Ramsey when she suddenly appeared in the back seat of Wright's car right next to them. "Hi, boys," she said. "Thanks for keeping tabs on Wright for me."

"We heard you had died and thought you had gone into the light," said Bill Ramsey. "How come you're still here, Deb?"

"Bill Porter gave me temporary refuge in his body. I'm not bound to one place now. I can send my spirit traveling until I've completed my mission and I'm ready to go into the light. Anong told Bill and me that you were tracking my murderer. I thought I'd take a look for myself at the elusive Mister Wright. You actually saw him shoot me?"

"Yes. Wright pulled the trigger. That's him behind the wheel," said Ramsey.

"He's a pretty good shot to hit both Bill and me at nearly a thousand meters."

"I think he's the same guy who killed me at Belvoir," said Randy.

"Too bad he didn't stay in the Army," said Deb. "We need guys that can shoot like him."

"He got greedy," said Randy. "It can happen to any of us."

"I suspect he was so good, he got promoted out of his comfort zone," said Ramsey. "It happens a lot in the Army."

"That's why I'm glad I'm a warrant officer," said Deb. "*Was* a warrant officer," she corrected. "I found the perfect niche for me, and I got to stay in it my entire career. Sure, I had different duty assignments, and some of it was routine and boring. But I was able to advance within my chosen career field without being saddled with lots of command time and even more routine staff assignments. I got to do grunt work myself, and I never had to worry about finding make-work for subordinates."

"Best of all possible worlds," said Ramsey. "I put in my time as a platoon leader, then a company commander. I was a battalion S-3 and doubled as the S-2. I spent half of my time dealing with unit personnel problems and troop discipline before getting promoted into operations and intelligence. I had to be a jack of all trades, including father-confessor."

"Me," said Randy, "I was just a grunt. I never had to think for myself because someone was always telling me what to do."

"Now that's the best of all possible worlds," said Deb. "Thinking can only get you into trouble."

"It got me killed," said Randy.

Wright stopped on the west side of Albuquerque on the second night. He ate an early dinner and consumed six cups of back coffee. Then he went out to the parking lot for a smoke and made three telephone calls on a cell phone by using the speed dial function.

"The ballgame's not over," they heard him say to the person at the other end on each of the calls. "We played well in the first eight innings and we thought we were ahead of the game, but they managed to retire the sides and now it's tied up, top of the ninth, and we need a new pitcher. You can sit out the rest of the game, if you like. Or you can cover the bases and the outfield and we can still come out of this winners if you toss me the ball and let me pitch. To stay in the game, meet me at the pitcher's mound day after tomorrow."

"What was that all about?" asked Deb.

"Beats the hell out of me," said Randy.

"He used the same kind of pre-programmed phone Anderson was issued to take orders," said Ramsey. "I think Wright just contacted the three remaining teams and set up a meet." Wright finished his cigarette and lit another with a beat up old Zippo that looked like it had been with Wright through a couple of wars. He leaned against the hood of the car and looked like he was trying to make up his mind about something.

Then he got back inside the car, got back on I-40, and drove west toward Gallup. The road was mostly deserted except for eighteen wheelers hauling goods across country, Wal-Mart trucks from Arkansas, furniture trucks from the Carolinas. They passed an occasional old beat-up and dusty pick-up truck driven by local Native Americans or Mexicans hauling hay or produce, but only one or two conventional cars, mostly tourists. There wasn't much to see except a beautiful sunset beyond the mountains far to the west. Wright by-passed Gallup, then turned north on 491.

"Where the hell is he going?" asked Randy.

Suddenly, Deb knew. "WLSCTC owns property near here. They had a training facility hidden away in the hills. It's isolated in the middle of nowhere, but it has an airfield and a few small planes and helicopters. It's where they trained their security personnel in rapid response. I saw it listed as one of the assets when I began my investigation."

"That's where they trained their NCOs," said Ramsey. "Before they sent them to Pakistan to train the rest of the troops."

"Do you think the snipers knew about the place?"

"No," said Ramsey. "But the team leaders did. They said some of the NCOs called it the little league park. It's where they learned to play the game before heading to the big leagues."

* * *

When Anong and Bill Porter were released from the hospital, Eddie Morsay was waiting for them with his wife's car, a smoky-grey metallic Buick Regal, to bring them back to Fort Belvoir for a luncheon meeting at the officers club with Colonel McMichaels and some of Eddie's and Deb's co-workers. They also talked to an FBI liaison who first pressed them for details of what had happened on the Capitol steps and then brought them up-to-date on the Wright situation. Anong and Porter received temporary clearances to enter INSCOM, provided Eddie would act as an escort, and they were officially allowed to watch the latest movements on the big screen in real time.

The former WLSCTC training facility had been closed months ago after the last of the NCOs had gone to Pakistan or Botswana, but Wright had now reopened it and moved in. Wright had a laptop computer with a portable Sprint internet connection he had brought with him, and NSA had intercepted several e-mails Wright had sent from a newly-opened G-Mail account. Wright had been a very busy boy. Wright had sent discrete inquiries to several of the larger security contractors. According to one of the e-mails, he was offering the services of highly-trained teams for "special missions" at a price to be negotiated. One of the less reputable firms had already responded favorably.

Now Earl Wright appeared to be expecting visitors at practically any moment, because he had opened the gate. He kept checking his watch and watching the road for vehicles. He had donned Army digital camouflage-patterned battledress, what the Army now called Universal Camouflage Patterned Army Combat Uniform (ACU) or multi-cams, with a tactical vest and a boonie cap to shade his eyes, and he had assumed a supported prone position on the roof of one of the buildings overlooking the single entrance to the facility. He had a spotter scope set up, and what appeared to be the newest model of the Army's most accurate sniper rifle on a bipod. He had a variety of other weapons laid out for easy access. It looked like he was ready for war. Shortly after noon, a small convoy of SUVs turned off the highway and drove up the gravel road toward the WLSCTC complex. Anong counted ten vehicles.

"Those must be the guys from either Seattle or Denver," said the Colonel. "The guys from LA that are left are scattered and still hiding from the cops somewhere in the city. They couldn't muster ten full vehicles if they tried."

"Denver," said one of the techs who had backtracked the convoy. "They came down I-25, through Vegas and Santa Fe, to Albuquerque, then I-40 over to Gallup."

"Okay," said the Colonel. "We'll wait until Seattle gets there, then we'll round them all up."

"How will you do that?" Anong asked Eddie.

"We have tactical assault teams ready to move in by helicopter. We have assembled rapid deployment task forces at the White Sands Army base, augmented with seasoned combat troops from the 1st Cav at Fort Bliss, about four hundred miles south of Gallup. They can be on-site in less than an hour."

"Air assault will mean heavy casualties on both sides," said Bill Porter. "A lot of good men will die."

"We're prepared to take casualties," said Eddie. "We can't let these guys regroup. Who knows how many more might die if they freelance out to the highest bidder? This is our one chance to take all of them down, and we're going to do it. Air assault is the best option available. We know they have snipers, but we'll go in fast and furious before they know what hit them. If push comes to shove, we'll send in a Raptor with sidewinders and take out the whole base and everyone in it."

Bill didn't say anything more.

* * *

Randy, Ramsey, and Deb watched over Wright's shoulder as the SUVs came lumbering up the gravel road, raising clouds of dust like one of New Mexico's sudden dust storms. Why was Wright on the roof with a rifle? Was Wright going to take out his own men with sniper fire? Why on earth would he do such a thing?

Three armed men got out of each of the dust-covered vehicles, but a fourth man remained behind the wheel and kept the motor running. Immediately, the three men from each team dispersed to assume defensive positions, scanning the area through their rifle scopes, becoming thirty separate targets scattered over too large a distance to engage with a single weapon.

Wright addressed them through a microphone connected to loudspeakers mounted on the outside walls of some of the buildings. "Put the weapons on the ground, boys, and back away from them now." His words echoed through the entire compound, and it was impossible to tell where the speaker himself might be located.

"What's the deal?" shouted one of the men who must have been the NCO or a team leader. "You asked us to come, and we came."

"Who do you work for?" asked Wright.

"You give the orders. We work for you."

"Good. Then put down your weapons and back away. Shut down the engines, boys. Get out of the vehicles. That's an order."

Reluctantly, the men complied.

"I needed to know if you'd been turned like that traitor Edwards," said Wright when the last man was out of his vehicle. "You can pick up your weapons now. I'll meet you in the old mess hall in ten minutes. You remember where it is? For those of you who have never been here before, it's the steel-fabricated building off to your left."

Wright gathered up his own weapons and the spotter scope, and then he climbed down from the roof on an aluminum ladder set up on the side away from the main gate. Randy, Bill, and Deb followed him into the steel-fabricated building.

"I'm glad to see you all made it," said Wright. "And it's nice to know you all remembered your training."

"We're still in the dark," said the team leader who had spoken up before. "What's going on?"

"Dickhead is dead or captured, and so are most of the other teams. We're down to less than a hundred men."

"Bad news," said the team leader.

"Kieffer—he was the brains behind all this—died in DC four days ago. WLSCTC is out of business, and we're on our own."

"Jesus!" said one of the other men. "Does that mean we won't get paid?"

"Probably worse than that," said Wright. "By now, the feds have all of WLSCTC's personnel records. They'll go through everyone on the payroll. They'll know your names and social security numbers. They'll have frozen your bank accounts and put you on their most wanted list. We're all wanted criminals now, boys. Me included."

"You said the Big Boss would make sure that didn't happen. He was going to be in a position where he could fix things like that."

"Almost worked," said Wright. "But almost only counts in horseshoes and hand grenades. The Big Boss is dead, and everything has fallen apart."

"So what do we do now?"

"The only thing we can do. We carry on with what we know. WLSCTC isn't the only game in town, and I've contacted some of the other leagues. We'll hire on as freelancers to do special jobs, the same kinds of things we've been doing, but we get to call all the shots. Once we get some cash flow or corporate backing, we can buy new identities. Then we can take some big bucks with us when we retire to the Bahamas. You guys with me on this?"

"Sounds like we don't have a choice," said one of the men.

"Good," said Wright. "Any questions?"

"Yeah," said one of the guys. "When do we get some R and R?"

"I don't mind waiting for pay," said another guy. "But you promised us some women after we took out the senators and the judges. If you want us to be happy campers, you'll get us some women."

"Okay," said Wright. "I'll arrange it and let you know. Meanwhile, you guys settle in. Team leaders can open up the bunkhouses and break out the linens from the storerooms. I want one team on the roof at all times waiting for the Seattle boys and anyone who manages to come in from LA. Brace them like I did you. If they say they're working for Charlie, waste 'em."

"Who's Charlie?" asked one of the team leaders.

"Someone I should have killed while I had the chance," said Wright.

When the Seattle teams arrived, Wright repeated the same speech to them. Now they had eighty men signed on to continue killing people. Among the new arrivals were Anderson and Jens, whom Randy said he recognized. They all agreed to hire out to the highest bidder.

"I'll put out the word on the internet that we're in business again," Wright told his men.

"I'm going back to tell Bill," said Deb. "These guys have got to be stopped."

* * *

The Lone Ranger had traveled all over eastern Europe in spirit form for two days, scanning for residual energy traces that Lokesvara said would be there. Lokesvara was doing the same thing in China, Korea, and Japan.

"Nature abhors a vacuum," the old monk often said, and it was true. Though Mahesvara's evil was gone from the world, there were other evils that wanted to take his place and spread the same poisons.

Charlie's network of operatives still existed, and power-hungry men and women were positioning themselves to take control of abandoned assets. Desire did not belong to Mahesvara alone. Nor did greed.

In Germany, for example, where the spirit of Adolph Hitler had been kept alive for nearly a century after the man's death, neo-Nazis met in secret and planned the extermination of Jews. In Russia, where the spirit of Joseph Stalin endured despite the fall of the Soviet Union, criminal organizations pedaled drugs and spread the five poisons from the Baltic to the Urals. Greed was now considered a good thing. It was okay to want more than an equal share.

Two individuals, one male and one female, seemed to be coordinating these efforts from secret. Whispers on the wind said their names were Alpha and Bravo.

Alpha controlled drug trafficking from the Middle East to the heart of Europe, including Great Britain and all of Scandinavia. Bravo ran sex trafficking in India and Southeast Asia, and supplied girls from Russia to men in western industrialized countries and men in oil-rich Arabia.

They did favors for people, and they had tons of money at their disposal. They had an agenda. And they were dangerous. Freed of the constraints of Mahesvara's control, they moved to consolidate their own power. They were no longer avatars. They were now prime movers.

Their goal was to enslave the whole human race by making it easy for people to indulge their primal passions. Once addicted to feelings of ecstasy, they would be easy to manipulate and control. Because body, mind, and spirit were so intimately connected in human beings, there had always been more than one way to take possession of individual mortals, to own them body and soul.

Forget fear, Alpha and Bravo told their clients. Enjoy life to the fullest. Don't think, just feel. Feel good. Feel the ecstasy that only sex and drugs are able to deliver. Indulge now. Depend on us to provide you with everything you need. Who needs religion? Who needs to obey laws? Who needs to be tied down with rules? Why suffer feelings of fear and uncertainty when we can help you escape quickly and easily? Life may end at any time, and why miss out on feeling good while you still can? Have you tried having sex on drugs yet? If you haven't, you may be missing the high of your life.

After the overwhelming fear everyone had felt during the past few weeks—as leaders around the world had been brutally slain, many in or near their own homes; when the rules of civilized life had changed so drastically and so abruptly because surviving politicians feared for their own lives more than the lives of the people they were elected to represent; when the entire world had teetered so precariously on the brink of nuclear annihilation—people felt an uncontrollable desire to indulge in pure escapism. They felt entitled to indulge. And indulge they did.

Some indulged in sexual excesses so extreme, so perverse, that there were no names for what they did. Some escaped into alcohol or drugs, and days passed without a conscious thought entering their heads. Many did both. Some saw things they devoutly desired for themselves that belonged to others—money, television sets, automobiles, even spouses and children—and they took them by stealth or by force.

It was almost as though Mahesvara had so corrupted the human spirit during his time on earth that his conversion and transcendence had little effect. What had been set in motion remained in motion until acted upon by an equal but opposite force, some power that might change its current direction or stop it completely.

The Ranger felt he had his work cut out for him. Would cutting off the supply of drugs and unnatural sex at the source be enough? Could it prevent the deaths of those who would soon die of overdoses from drugs and sexual violence? What else might he do to help people see the light?

He began by looking everywhere for Alpha and Bravo. If they were mortal, he would eventually find them.

And then what? Kill them? Add to his already considerable karmic debt?

He decided he'd let Vajrapani cross that bridge when he came to it.

* * *

Earl Wright sent an e-mail message to Laura at WLSCTC's headquarters in Dubai. Laura had often acted as an intermediary between Brakken and Charlie, and Brakken had once told Wright to get in touch with Laura if neither he nor Kieffer were available.

Laura responded almost immediately. Though WLSCTC had been shut down in America, the parent company and its many subsidiaries continued.

Wright asked Laura to have Charlie call him on the special cell phone, but Laura responded that Charlie was not available. She would see if Alpha or Bravo would like to respond instead.

Bravo telephoned within thirty minutes. Wright couldn't believe his ears when he answered the phone.

Bravo sounded exactly like Charlie.

"Where are you?" she asked.

"Where are *you*?" he asked in return.

"Where I always am," she said. "But I asked you first. Where are you and what do you want?"

"I'm back in business," said Wright. "I have a hundred men who need women. Can you supply?"

"Of course," she said. "Can you pay for them?"

"I can trade," said Wright. "Same deal as before. Only now we're free-lancing. You take care of us, and we'll do your dirty work for you. We can negotiate prices later."

"I can use a man like you, Mister Wright," she said, and the way she said his name made Wright envision Charlie. She sounded so much like Charlie, Bravo could be her twin. "Where do you want the girls delivered?"

"Juarez," he said. "In Mexico. Just over the border from the U. S."

"You're in Mexico?"

"We will be. As soon as the last stragglers get in from Los Angeles."

"I do have girls in Ciudad Juarez," she said. "I have a house with thirty girls. Will that be sufficient? I can get more girls if you need more."

"How about fifty? Can you have fifty waiting in three hours?"

"I can have a hundred waiting in three hours," she said.

"Fifty will be enough."

"Done," she said. "Let me give you an address. It's a big house."

"We'll find it," said Wright, filing the address in his memory.

"I look forward to working with you, Mister Wright," she said. "My sister spoke highly of your talents."

"Your sister?"

"You knew her as Charlie," said the voice. "She wasn't really my sister, but we acted like sisters. We are a lot alike."

"Is she still alive? I would like to see her again."

"I haven't heard from her for nearly a week. I have to assume she is not alive. And neither is her husband."

"Too bad," said Wright, feeling both saddened and elated at the news. "She was a beautiful woman."

Wright heard laughter. "What's so funny?" he asked.

"She wasn't beautiful, Mister Wright," said the voice, still filled with laughter. "She was ugly. As ugly as sin. And so, Mister Wright, am I. Never forget that."

"I won't," said Wright as the connection was terminated and the laughter died in his ear.

CHAPTER TWENTY-SIX

"They're on the move," said one of the techs that monitored satellite feeds. "All of them. They just got into their vehicles and it looks like they're heading back to the highway."

"We waited too long," said Eddie. "We should have taken them when we had the chance. We can't do an air assault on vehicles moving down a busy public highway without creating collaterals. The collateral damage on civilians could be significant. We can't allow that."

"We can still get them," said the Colonel. "We just need to wait until they reach their destination, then isolate them."

"They're headed south," said the tech. "Back toward Gallup."

"They're going to pick up I-40 at Gallup," said the Colonel. "I'm betting they'll get on the interstate and head west, toward LA."

Deb said nothing. She had returned to Bill Porter's body, informed Bill of what Wright had told his men, and decided to remain at INSCOM and watch the activity in the compound on the big screen. She could also stay abreast of the status of the assault task force that was ready to move at a moment's notice, as soon as the Colonel gave the order.

Now that martial law had been declared and was in effect, the U. S. Armed Forces could legally act against American civilians in this country. Instead of the military augmenting civilian authorities, it was the other way around. Civilian authorities could be used to augment military operations.

And with the death of so many generals, Colonel McMichaels had been nominated for his first star and was officially a temporary Brigadier General. Of course, the members of Congress would need to approve the appointment and Congress was in total disarray at the moment. But it was going to happen. The military could use a few good men like McMichaels at the helm. Meanwhile, General McMichaels was in charge of the task force, and he had the authority to send soldiers into battle.

"They're turning onto I-40," said the tech. "But they're heading east toward Albuquerque instead of west toward LA."

"Alert the guys at White Sands and Bliss," ordered the new General. "I want choppers in the air now. We need to stop Wright and his crew before they get to a heavily populated area. We'll try to isolate them on the highway."

"At the speed they're going, they'll be in Albuquerque before we can do that," cautioned Eddie.

"Damn," said McMichaels. "Okay. We'll have to wait. I'm betting they'll skirt Albuquerque and keep going east. We can catch them before they get to Amarillo. That stretch of I-40 through west Texas is pretty barren. Tell the task force commanders that they have a green light as soon as the convoy clears Albuquerque."

But the convoy didn't continue straight east. They turned southeast on New Mexico state route 6.

"Where the hell are they going?" asked McMichaels.

"They're heading for Mexico," said Eddie. "They'll pick up I-25 south. They'll go right by White Sands. They just cut our response time in half."

"Get the choppers airborne. We've got to hit them before they reach Las Cruces. We can't let them get over the border. To hell with collaterals. Take them out now."

Eddie called the task force commanders and relayed the go information, including map coordinates. He said there were twenty vehicles in the southbound lanes of I-25. Other traffic was practically non-existent. The men in those vehicles were heavily armed, and resistance should be expected. As many of the men in those vehicles as possible should be taken alive for questioning, but it was imperative they all be stopped before they reached a populated area or crossed the border. As a last resort, the gunships were authorized to shoot up the entire convoy.

"The General says take them down, and take them down now."

Deb watched the big screen split as one half followed the convoy down I-25 and the other half picked up the four AH-64

Apache helicopters and six MH-60 Blackhawks lifting off from Holloman Air Force Base, followed by an F-22A Raptor. The sleek Lockheed-built stealth fighter carried a lot of firepower with its 20-millimeter cannon and six sidewinder missiles. It looked like a little like overkill, but overkill was sometimes a good thing. If the men in the Blackhawks couldn't stop the convoy, the Apaches and the Raptor definitely would.

"Time for us to go," Deb told Bill. "Maybe Maitreya can prevent needless bloodshed."

Bill blinked out of existence at INSCOM and blinked back in the middle of I-25, a mile ahead of the convoy.

It was time for Deb to finally meet Earl Wright in person.

* * *

Earl rode in the front seat of the lead vehicle, a red V-6 Dodge Durango Citadel. There were three men in the back seat, and Jens was driving.

"We'll need to stop for gas in Las Cruces," said Jens. "We're below half a tank."

"You're the driver," said Wright. "Pick a place with a restaurant attached. We'll chow down before we cross the border."

"They going to let us across with all the weapons we're packing?"

"We'll leave one vehicle behind with the weapons. Anyone want to volunteer to stay with the vehicle and guard the guns, or should I pick someone?"

"I'll stay," said Jens. "I'm older than the rest of the guys and don't get as horny."

"Bullshit," said one of the guys from the back seat. "You're just scared you'll pick up a disease from Mexican pussy."

"Crabs," said another guy. "I heard all them Mexican bitches got crabs."

"Knock it off," ordered Wright. "Or I'll make you stay behind instead of Jens."

"There's something in the road up ahead," said Jens. "Jesus! It looks like some guy just standing there in the middle of the road."

"Go around him," said Wright.

Without warning, the human figure changed right in front of their eyes. It seemed to grow larger and brighter.

Suddenly, Wright couldn't see. It was as if an atomic bomb had just exploded, so bright was the brilliance of the light. Jens jammed both feet down hard on the brake pedal and the Durango skidded at least twenty yards before it ran completely off the road and landed in a bed of loose sand and sagebrush where it nearly tipped over but managed to right itself because the sand gripped two of the four wheels like a vise.

Behind them, they heard multiple crashes as several of the other vehicles collided at seventy-five miles an hour. No one could see anything. It felt as if each of their retinas had been burned out by the bright light that had erupted like an atomic fireball.

Wright was nearly smothered by the still-expanding air bag that filled the entire passenger compartment.

"What the fuck!" he said as he tried to extricate himself from the air bag and the locked seat harness.

"There was a guy in the road," said Jens. "And then he just blew up."

"Like suicide bombers in the 'Stan," said one of the guys in the back seat. "I'm blind. Can you guys see?"

"No," said Wright. "The blast must have damaged our optic nerves."

"There was no blast," said Jens. "Just a burst of light. No shock wave to go along with it. Did you feel a shockwave?"

"If it wasn't a bomb," said the guy in the back seat, "then what the fuck was it?"

"That's what I want to know," said Wright. "Get your guns out boys. We're under attack."

"Won't do any good," said Jens. "I can't see to shoot. Can you?"

Suddenly, the front passenger door was wrenched open. Wright felt strong hands grab his shoulders and shirt collar and lift him bodily out of the vehicle. Whoever it was, was really big and powerful, bigger and more powerful than any person had a right to be. Earl was 5 foot ten inches, nearly six feet tall, and he weighed a solid 180. This guy had just picked him up like a rag doll and tossed him on the ground like a piece of discarded litter. Who the fuck was this giant?

"Hello, Earl," came a booming voice that nearly shattered Wright's eardrums. "I'm the spirit of Deb Johnson come to pay you back for killing me. And payback can be a bitch."

"Johnson's dead," said Wright. "Besides, you sure as hell don't sound like a woman."

"My voice changed. Didn't your voice change when you became a man?"

"That was puberty," said Wright. "And I don't believe in ghosts."

"You should," boomed the voice. "I could turn you into a ghost right now. But I'm doing you a favor, Earl. I'm saving your life. Order your men to throw down their weapons and step away from the cars. Raise your hands above your heads so the soldiers who'll be here any moment now can see you're unarmed."

"What soldiers?" asked Wright.

And then he heard the sound of a jet aircraft coming in low and fast, a sound he'd heard many times in combat when he'd call in air support for ground operations in Iraq or Afghanistan. The single jet buzzed the expressway from the east, and Earl heard the whine of its twin Pratt and Whitney turbothrust engines

Doppler out as the plane banked to the north and came around again for a second reconnaissance run.

And now Earl's ears picked up the familiar sounds of nearly a dozen choppers heading in from the same easterly direction, the distinct whirrs of Apaches and the whup-whups of slower-moving heavily-laden Blackhawks.

"You can't see them, so you can't fight them," said the voice. "And even if you could see, you wouldn't stand a chance against all that firepower. Do you want your men to be slaughtered like sheep? If the armed men in the choppers don't get you, the guns and missiles on the Raptor definitely will. You're out here in the middle of nowhere and there's no place to run and no place to hide. You have bullseyes written all over you. Your choice, Earl. Do you want your men to live or die?"

"Drop your weapons, boys," Wright shouted. "Move away from the vehicles a few paces and raise your hands."

"You, too, Earl. You're their leader. Lead by example."

Earl removed the pistols from his pockets and threw them to the sand. Then he raised both hands above his head.

"After you're taken into custody, your sight will return," said the voice.

"Who are you, really?" Wright asked. He wanted to know, needed to know. Deb Johnson was dead. He'd shot her right through the heart. It couldn't be Deb Johnson. Could it? "Who the hell are you?"

But the only answer he heard were the sounds of the first helicopters setting down on the cement tarmac of the two-lane highway, followed by other choppers landing nearby, and the sounds of dessert boots hitting the pavement as dozens of men jumped down from the choppers to rush toward him with weapons locked and loaded, and someone yelling through a bullhorn that barely carried over the deafening sound of the rotors, “Face down in the dirt, scumbags! And I mean now!”

CHAPTER TWENTY-SEVEN

"I can't believe they're giving up without a fight," said General McMichaels. "Jesus! They're just standing there with their hands in the air!"

"It looks like the accident took all the fight out of them," said Eddie. "We got them! We finally got them! All of them! And without firing a shot!"

"Did anyone see exactly what happened?" asked the General.

"I think the sun must have reflected off something very shiny on the pavement and the bright light momentarily blanked out our screens," explained one of the young techs. "It doesn't happen often, but it does happen sometimes when the sun is at just the right angle—or the wrong angle in this case—and hits the satellite lens with more lumens than even our digital cameras can filter out. It came on suddenly and ended just as suddenly. That's entirely consistent with the earth's motion relative to the sun at this time of day."

"So we're left with about twenty minutes of missing footage, just like on the Watergate tapes?" asked Eddie.

"What's the Watergate tapes?" asked the young technician, sounding like he really didn't know.

"Okay. Let's try to piece it all together without the high-tech stuff. The bright light from the sun reflecting off something shiny on the pavement blinded the drivers, causing a major pileup on I-25. At the same time, that same reflected sunlight knocked out our satellite images. But that doesn't explain why Wright and his men just gave up. Does it? They threw down their weapons and reached for the sky as if they knew we were coming to take them down. They surrendered before our men even got there. How do you explain that?"

"I can't," said Eddie. "Anyone else have an opinion? Porter? What do you think?"

"I'm afraid I missed all of the excitement," said Bill Porter. "I stepped out of the room for a moment. When I got back, it was all over."

Anong didn't say anything. She had noticed when Bill disappeared into thin air, and she had seen him reappear in this room at the same time as the satellite images came back online. He didn't simply walk out of the room and then walk back like he wanted the others to believe. She knew Maitreya had paid an impromptu visit to Wright and his men in New Mexico. She had seen Maitreya's blinding light before, and she knew how powerful that light could be, powerful enough to knock the satellites offline for twenty minutes or more.

"What will happen to Wright and the others now?" Anong asked.

"They'll be tried in a military court," said the General. "Under martial law, if they're found guilty of the assassinations, they'll be put to death. It's out of our hands."

"Good," said Anong. "They killed Deb. They deserve to die."

Both the General and Eddie became suddenly silent, as if they were lost in thought or listening to something or someone speaking inside themselves. Anong suspected that Ramsey and Edwards had returned and were explaining what they had witnessed in New Mexico, including the intervention by Maitreya.

"Well, that's it then," said the General, sounding satisfied. "We finally got them, they're all in federal custody, and we can wrap this up for now. Thank you, ladies and gentlemen, for your technical assistance. You can go back to business as usual."

"What about martial law?" asked Bill Porter as they walked back to Deb's office. "Now that the threat is over, how soon will the President rescind martial law? Will the country go back to the way it was?"

"That's up to the politicians," said the General. "It's out of our hands."

"There will always be another threat," said Eddie. "And then another and another. Threat assessment is why they pay us those big bucks. We'll never be out of a job."

"But no immediate threat. So do we still need soldiers deployed to all the major cities?" asked Bill. "Do we need armed men walking the streets of America like we once had in Afghanistan and Iraq?"

"That's a policy decision, and it's way above my pay grade," said the General.

"I guess I'm worried about someone else like Kieffer, unscrupulous and power-hungry, manipulating the military into doing his bidding. With the Bill of Rights suspended, ordinary people have no protection. The military is supposed to defend us against all enemies, foreign and domestic. But who will defend us against the military if it falls into the wrong hands?"

"*I* will," said the General with amazing conviction. "And you will, too, Mister Porter. And so will Eddie Morsay. Believe it or not, there are good men in the military, and there are some good politicians, too. And good people like you all over the country who will step up to the plate and hit home runs when called to do so. We love the game and we respect the rules. We'll cry foul until the umpires listen to us. We'll insist on a fair game and a level playing field."

"And if the umpires don't listen, what then?" asked Bill. "Will you take the ball and go home to sulk like a child or a prima donna? Will you disappoint the fans and leave the stadium entirely? What happens if it's last of the ninth, bases loaded, and the game tied or the visitors leading?"

"We'll play ball and win," said the General. "We'll play by the rules even if no one else does. And we'll still win because we believe in the game and how it's played."

"I don't understand all of this talk," said Anong. "You wish to play games? Are you not grown men? Should you not rather be studying and learning? Should you not become teachers? Or healers?"

"We should," said Bill. "Heaven knows, we need good teachers and healers. But somebody has to watch out for the bad guys. And the bad guys like to play games. They see us as chess pieces, mostly pawns, to be moved about the table at their whim. We become caught up in their games whether we like it or not. Should we just bow out and let the bad guys win?"

"They will only win if you play their game by their rules. Either don't play their silly game or make them play by the same rules you play by."

"Words of wisdom from a child," said Eddie.

"I am not a child," said Anong.

"Of course not," said Bill. "You fought like a grown woman in the Capitol, and you saved me and tried to save Deb like the true healer you are. I think Eddie was trying to paraphrase Christian scripture, Psalms 8:2: 'Out of the mouth of babes and sucklings hast thou ordained strength because of thine enemies, that thou mightiest still the enemy and the avenger.'"

"What does that mean?" asked Anong.

"I believe it means," said Bill Porter, "that if everyone listened to you, there would be no more war."

"Good luck with that," said Eddie.

* * *

Bill Ramsey was finally ready. He had finished his job. His mission was complete. After reporting to Colonel—now General—McMichaels that Wright had been captured and that Randy said he was assured that most of the remaining assassins—including Anderson and Jens—were in custody, Ramsey said goodbye to the General and the others and looked for the clear light to appear.

Ramsey and Edwards saw the clear light at the same time. Their spirits floated free of their mortal hosts, and the bright light beckoned to them and they eagerly entered the light without hesitation. That they saw the clear light and not encroaching darkness though the tunnel bode well. They had done their jobs to the best of their abilities, and now it was time to rest.

After a period of time when they relived their previous lives and learned from their mistakes, they would be reborn and given another chance to become fully enlightened. Whether they were reborn male or female mattered little. Enlightenment eventually came to all who would seek it.

Perhaps they would meet again in their new lives. Ramsey had come to think of Randy and Bob McMichaels and Eddie Morsay and the Ranger as brothers, and Deb and Anong as sisters. Lokesvara was, and always would be, a father figure. It was hard to imagine Lokesvara being reborn as a child, an infant who needed his diapers changed. The thought seemed somehow incongruous. If there were any justice in the world, then Lokesvara would be reborn with all of his faculties intact. He would be a wise old man at the age of six months.

Now Ramsey saw the spirit guides approaching from the end of the tunnel. And he saw that another spirit had joined them already, and Deb Johnson glowed with a beauty and a radiance that had only been hinted at in the flesh.

"Welcome to paradise," she said to Ramsey and Randy.

CHAPTER TWENTY-EIGHT

The Lone Ranger's work was far from done. Would his work ever be done? Probably not. He yearned to set aside his weapons and spend the rest of his days in quiet contemplation, but such was not meant to be. He was a Bodhisattva, and he had vowed to protect the Dharma and to show other beings the clear light, to lead them on their own paths to enlightenment, to end the terrible suffering caused by desire—by samsara—before he allowed himself to find peace and rest. That was his calling, and that was the vow that took precedence over all other vows. Lokesvara had been right. The Ranger had been born to kill, but to kill for a purpose, and that purpose was not only to protect his own life but to protect those who were too weak to protect themselves. Greedy men and women looked to take advantage of others, to enslave ignorant people to passions—to desire—and thus prevent them from seeking enlightenment. Desire hid the light of reason from hungry eyes. Desire devoured compassion, consumed right thinking and right actions. It was only when one desired nothing for oneself and everything for others that enlightenment was possible.

Unlike Mahesvara and Uma, Alpha and Bravo were mere mortals. They had served as avatars, motivated only by desire and extreme greed. When Mahesvara and Uma left this plane of existence for a higher one, Alpha and Bravo were left to fend for themselves.

Unfortunately, Mahesvara's evil had so tainted both of them that they not only continued peddling their poisons, but they increased their efforts ten-fold. Before, they had been working for Mahesvara. Now they were working solely for themselves.

It was pure greed. They would enslave people to their passions so that Alpha and Bravo might profit from it. They corrupted everything they touched.

Because Alpha had been much harder to uncover than Bravo, the Ranger began with Alpha.

His real name was Gustav Hahn, and he lived in Hamburg, Germany. He was 48 years old, and he had been born long after the Second World War was merely a memory. He had grown up in the shadow of the iron curtain, and when the Berlin wall fell in 1990, he was a young university student who was recruited by German drug lords to supply heroin to the many young people in Denmark, Sweden, and part of the eastern zone, including Poland. Because he majored in languages and travel was considered part of his university studies, he had the perfect cover. He rose quickly in the organization because of his knowledge of language and customs, and he established a network of dealers that pedaled poison from youth hostels in sixteen countries. He became the drug czar of the European Union in 2008.

Sometime between 2010 and 2012, he sold his soul to the devil and became an avatar of Mahesvara. In return, he had access to resources he had only dreamed about before.

Now Hahn had ties to the black market in Russia and the Middle East, and he controlled the flow of weapons as well as drugs. He was incredibly wealthy. He was on the board of directors of some of the largest banks in Europe, and few knew or cared how he had acquired his wealth.

One day, Hahn's secretary saw him leave his office and get on his private elevator, but he never got off the elevator. Other people reported seeing a tall man with a shaved head, black business suit, and highly shined shoes get off the same elevator in the lobby, but Hahn was not with him. Hahn had never been seen again by anyone.

Rumors flew through the black market underground that Hahn had been offed by a business rival. Some people even said Hahn had put pressure on the wrong people in Russia, and the Russians had ordered a hit by a professional assassin. But, like Jimmy Hoffa, Hahn had simply disappeared without a trace and what had really happened to him remained a mystery. Interpol shook up the drug trade looking for leads, and the price of drugs skyrocketed as supply lines were momentarily disrupted by all the investigations. Someone even said Hahn had planned his disappearance to jack up the price of drugs. There were those who wouldn't put such a thing past him.

Bravo was easier to find than Alpha.

Bravo's real name was unknown or long forgotten. She had been a Bosnian Croat from Foca, and she had been eleven in 1992 when Serbian paramilitary overran her town and made sexual slaves of all the women and girls, even children as young as ten. She was held in detention in a house until 1995, raped daily by a variety of men. Then she escaped and became a prostitute and worked her way into Greece, where she became the young mistress of an aging politician, recruiting other young women to service the politician's friends at parties and in private, and soon she had established a long list of regular clientele and she became wealthy.

From a poor little girl who possessed nothing but her body and her wits, she became a businesswoman who owned considerable property in Greece and Italy. She had bank accounts in Switzerland and Germany, in Dubai and in and London, England.

The more she acquired, the more she wanted. She expanded into Eastern Europe, then into Russia. When she needed more girls than she could recruit, she bought children—some of them bastard children of the men who had raped her—in Bosnia, Albania, Bulgaria, and even India. Eventually, she expanded into the Far East and bought children in Burma, Thailand, Cambodia, Laos, and Indonesia.

In 2012, she met a woman who called herself Charlie and who offered protection and political connections so Bravo could expand into the Middle East and Africa. Because she was used to giving herself to men in exchange for money and power, she had no problem giving herself to Mahesvara.

As Bravo's empire grew, so did her wealth. She allowed her friends in Dubai to make investments for her, and she bought land in France, Ireland, Argentina, Mexico, and even the United States.

The Ranger found Bravo in a palatial estate in the south of France, not far from Marseille.

She was no longer a young woman, rather someone approaching his own age. He simply appeared next to her as she lounged on the deck of an Olympic-sized swimming pool surround by topiary. She was topless, drinking Cognac from a snifter, and alone. There were servants in the house and on the grounds, but they were too far away to see or hear.

Besides, she was hidden from their eyes by the topiary.

"You're about to take a little trip," the Ranger told her. "You've been working much too hard, and it's time you took a badly-needed rest."

"Are you a travel agent?" she asked, startled by his sudden appearance. "How did you get in here? Did someone send you? Who are you?"

"Who I am doesn't matter," said the Ranger. "Who you become does. You'll have a long time to think about the consequences of your actions. When you are eventually reborn, you may choose to become a different person."

"Get out of here!" she demanded.

"I'm leaving. And so are you."

Her eyes widened as he morphed into Vajrapani. Where once the neatly-dressed fortyish man with the shaved head had stood, now stood a seven-foot tall giant holding a scepter and a rope.

"Be gone," he said, pointing the Vajra. And she was gone.

*   *   *

Anong was glad to be home. The Duon Jis remarked on how she had seemed to have grown during her visit to America, and they welcomed her back with warm smiles. She was one of them now, a real woman, and she knew she would soon let them shave her head and eyebrows as she transitioned from novice to apprentice and take her first vows. There was much she had to learn if she were to teach the world to see the light, to enter into the light instead of the darkness, and she was ready to begin.

Vajrapani had returned also to Angkor Wat, and so had Lokesvara. Soon Anong, in the form of Ksitigarbha, would accompany Lokesvara and Vajrapani as the three Bodhisattvas guided disembodied spirits from this world to the next.

Perhaps someday violence would end, and all sentient beings—all people in every part of the world—would transition peacefully from one life to another. That day, long in coming, was devoutly to be desired.

ABOUT THE AUTHOR

Photo credit: Abbye Garcia, Rock Valley College

Paul Dale Anderson has written more than 27 novels and hundreds of short stories, mostly in the thriller, mystery, horror, fantasy, and science fiction genres. Paul is the author of *Claw Hammer, Daddy's Home, Pickaxe, Icepick, Meat Cleaver, Axes to Grind, Pinking Shears, Deviants, Running Out of Time, Impossible, Abandoned, Winds, Darkness, Mysterious Ways, Light* and the critically-acclaimed Instruments of Death crime-suspense novels from Crossroad Press.

Visit Paul's web pages for more information:
www.pauldaleanderson.net, www.4windsnovels.com, and
http://www.amazon.com/Paul-Dale-Anderson/e/B00A9XFLBQ/

Paul has also written contemporary romances and westerns. Paul is an Active Member of SFWA and HWA, and he was elected

Vice President and Trustee of Horror Writers Association in 1987. He is a current member of International Thriller Writers, Author's Guild, and a former Active Member of MWA.

Paul has taught creative writing at the University of Illinois at Chicago and for Writers Digest School. He has appeared on panels at Chicon4 and Chicon7, X-Con, Windy Con, Madcon, Odyssey Con, Minncon, the World Horror Convention, and the World Fantasy Convention. Paul was a guest of honor at Horror Fest in Estes Park, Colorado, in 1989. He is currently the chair of the 2015 HWA Stoker Awards Long Fiction Jury.

Paul is also an NGH Certified Hypnotist, an NGH Certified Hypnotism Instructor, a certified Past-Life Regression Therapist, and an IBRT certified professional member of the International Association for Regression Research and Therapies.

Be sure to read these other thrilling novels in the Winds series:

Abandoned (Eldritch Press, March 2015)

Darkness (2AM Publications, June 2015)

Winds (2AM Publications, October 2015)

Time (2AM Publications, (March 2016)

CPSIA information can be obtained at www.ICGtesting.com
Printed in the USA
LVOW06s1154200915

454932LV00001B/235/P